A PERFECT ARRANGEMENT

by Jane Andrews

Chapter One

He had never seen anyone so beautiful in his life.

Marco Benedetti considered himself to be something of an expert when it came to women – in his twenty-nine years he had notched up plenty of experience with the fairer sex – but this girl took his breath away. Leggy and lithe, with long, dark hair that cascaded down her back, she epitomised his ideal woman. His gaze travelled appraisingly over high, firm breasts and a trim waist, set off to perfection by the figure-hugging black dress she was wearing; as she turned slightly, he noticed that it clung to a perfectly sculpted derrière.

"*Santo cielo!*" he murmured appreciatively, realising that he wanted her there and then, despite the fact that this was supposed to be his engagement party, the day on which he pledged himself to another woman.

His face clouded as he thought about the fiasco he had somehow allowed himself to become embroiled in. He wasn't the marrying kind – Ricardo, his older brother, was the family man, with a wife and two small daughters that framed the centre of his universe – but he, Marco, was not in the habit of falling prey to any kind of emotional attachment. He was proud of himself for conducting his personal liaisons in much the same way as his business affairs: each evening would be concluded to the mutual satisfaction of both parties, and he never promised anything he knew he couldn't deliver. It had been a passable arrangement until that fateful evening when his father had met up with his old friend, Antonio Vendrini, for the first time in twenty or more years, whilst on a business trip to England. Marco wasn't sure how much brandy the two of them had consumed over the course of the evening, but it had culminated in them both deciding that the two families should merge their businesses – and their offspring.

"You can't be serious!" he'd exclaimed when Lucas had dropped the bombshell, secretly wondering whether this might be the onset of senile dementia. "I've never even met the woman! How can I marry her?"

His father had waved aside this legitimate concern with a characteristically dismissive shrug. "It is simple, no? You are my son; she is Antonio's daughter. You already run the new London branch of *Benedetti's* and, when you marry Sapphire, you will become a shareholder in *Vendrini and Sons* also." He grinned wryly. "I think Antonio will be happy finally to have a son, no? It has caused him much sadness over the years that he has only daughters – and that neither of them has shown any inclination to become part of the family business. They are not like you, Marco: your heart belongs to *Benedetti's* – you are a good boy who has made your papa very happy."

"Then why not leave it at that?" Marco had argued practically. "Why not let me carry on as I am, running the London branch and organising my own love life?"

His father had sighed. "Because I am an old man, Marco, and your mother and I would like to see you settled with a good woman before we die. Besides," – here he allowed a huge grin to transform his face – "Antonio and I always said that his eldest daughter would marry my eldest son, or vice-versa. We both forgot that promise as time elapsed; but now we have reconnected with each other, it all makes perfect sense. Our two families and our two businesses will unite – what could be better?"

"I don't want a wife," Marco had replied shortly. "Anyway, why should I get married? Ricardo's already given you your grandchildren – it's not as if you need me to keep the family name going." He'd paused. "I don't even know what this girl looks like."

His father had produced a tattered snapshot. Marco had been surprised – no one carried around actual photographs these days, not when smartphones could store thousands of pictures that were available at the touch of a fingertip.

He'd examined the well-worn photo carefully: it showed two girls, both blonde, both wearing shapeless white kaftans. The clothing was sufficiently unflattering for him to surmise that these were fuller-figured women who were forced to disguise their ample curves on a daily basis. One of them had a rounder face than the other, he'd noted; he'd supposed they were reasonably pretty, but neither of them had aroused his interest.

"I remember their mother when she came to Italy, twenty-five years ago." Lucas's voice had sounded wistful; his eyes had taken on a dreamy look. "Antonio and I were working as waiters in the Hotel Donatello. She was on holiday with her parents and when she met Toni, they began a - what do you call it? - a holiday fling. Then, when she left to go home to England, a fortnight later, Antonio followed her. They were married a year later."

It had all sounded ridiculously twee, like the sort of romantic fantasy one would expect to hear from the lips of a silly schoolgirl and not from a hardheaded businessman in his fifties, Marco had thought crossly.

His father had continued to reminisce. "She was so beautiful: blonde, blue eyes – like both her daughters, see?" He'd jabbed the photograph. "Antonio wrote to tell me about the birth of his first daughter: they named her Sapphire because of her blue eyes, he said; but I think now she prefers the name Saffy."

This was growing worse and worse. Marco had tried again. "Papa, I know you mean well, but …"

He'd paused delicately, trying to form the words he needed to escape from this mess without breaking his father's heart. "What does Sapphire think about this?" he'd asked instead, convinced that any modern woman would find the idea of an arranged marriage a complete anathema.

"She is a good girl." His father's response had surprised him. "She will do as she is told." Noting the frustration in his son's face, Lucas had continued, "At least meet the girl, no? If you and she do not like each other, of course we will not make you wed. But if you should suit ..."

Marco had been unable to dash the hope in his father's eyes. Mumbling something to the effect of "thinking about it", he had resolved that his first meeting with Sapphire Vendrini would be his last.

* * *

Saffy poured herself another drink with trembling fingers, aware that she felt ridiculously nervous. *What's wrong with me?* she asked herself silently, realising she already knew the answer. This whole party was a shambles: as if anyone would agree to marry someone they had never met!

Moodily swirling the Pimms in her glass, she relived the moment when her father had broken the news. At first, she had thought he was joking; then, as he continued to look at her expectantly, she had realised, in horror, that he was deadly serious. "I can't marry a stranger!" she'd burst out impetuously. "You must be crazy if you think I'd ever agree to anything like that!"

She would have said more, but her stepmother, Eleanor, had swept her into the kitchen, under the pretext of needing her 'help' with something, and begged her to think the matter over.

"You know the doctor has said your father mustn't get over-excited," she'd told Saffy pleadingly. "After his last heart attack ..." She'd paused, letting Saffy complete the sentence in her own head.

Eleanor was right, of course: Dad had suffered three heart attacks in the last two years, each one progressively worse than the one before. Having lost her mother thirteen years previously – to breast cancer that had remained undetected until it was too late – Saffy couldn't afford to run the risk of saying or doing anything that might be detrimental to her father's health; so she had sighed and promised to meet this Marco person, if that would make her dad happy.

Now, however, she was having second thoughts. Always more comfortable in jeans than dresses, she felt overexposed in this clingy outfit which had been Eleanor's idea, not hers. The cut of the dress seemed designed to emphasise all the parts she normally kept hidden, almost as if inviting observers to focus on her breasts and backside. She had noticed far too many lascivious glances already; and as for that man over there, by the fireplace, who was practically undressing her with his eyes ...

With a jolt, her brain took in for the first time just how good looking the stranger was. Long, lean legs were encased in well fitting black trousers; and his suit jacket was thrown casually over the chair next to him, so that she was able to see how his expensively tailored shirt covered an impressively muscled chest and enjoyably broad shoulders. Her gaze returned to his face, to the chiselled jawline and incredibly sexy stubble – so different to the man who was her intended fiancé (she'd googled him and seen a photo of a man with a rather alarming beard), who must be at least a good ten years older than the Adonis in front of her.

As she scrutinised him, he looked up and caught her eye. His lips quirked into a grin that was half-friendly, half-predatory. Saffy shivered: whoever he was, this man spelled Danger with a capital 'D'; nevertheless, she could not tear her gaze away from him.

He was moving towards her now, crossing the room with a purposeful stride. The glass trembled in her hand. As he reached her, she took a long, slow gulp of her drink, almost as if willing the cool liquid to calm her rapidly beating heart.

"I hope you liked what you saw …" His voice was a soft caress, dangerously close to her ear.

She stared at him uncomprehendingly.

"You were looking at me and wondering what I'd be like in bed." It was a statement, not a question. She was amazed at his arrogance.

"As a matter of fact," Saffy tried to keep her voice disinterested, detached, "I was wondering where I'd seen you before."

It was true: there was something oddly familiar about this complete stranger – something familiar, but something disturbing too. Involuntarily, she tugged the hem of her dress, trying unsuccessfully to cover more of her long, bare legs.

Marco's gaze followed the movement, tracing the shape of her as perfectly toned legs disappeared into neat ankles. He nodded appreciatively: he'd always liked women in short skirts and high heels, although a woman in nothing but heels was sexier still. He wondered idly for a moment what this delectable creature would look like when he slipped the dress from her shoulders and watched it slide to the floor …

He came to with a start, realising that she was speaking again. "There are so many people here I don't know at all," she was saying, a perplexed frown wrinkling her forehead.

"Me, I know hardly anyone also," Marco responded diffidently, "but there is one person in particular I would like to know much better ..." He paused deliberately, certain that she would understand his meaning.

Saffy was aware that her pulse was racing and she suspected that her heart was beating at twice its normal speed. *What's wrong with me?* she asked herself desperately. *I'm supposed to be meeting my future fiancé, not lusting after some sex-crazed Lothario!*

The sensible reaction would be to turn her back on him and search the room for her father or Eleanor. Instead, she smiled coquettishly at this perfect stranger – and he was oh, so perfect! – and heard herself asking him if he would like to get her another drink.

* * *

Marco knew, without a shadow of a doubt, that this woman wanted him. He had seen it all too many times before: the pupils dilated with desire; the eye contact that lasted just a fraction of a second longer than it should; the unconscious licking of the lips. Mentally he cursed his timing: under normal circumstances, he would buy her a drink, then take her out onto the terrace for some fresh air, which would inevitably result in a series of lingering kisses and a hasty journey by taxi back to his warehouse conversion flat, where he would make love to her expertly and methodically until she dissolved in a pool of pure pleasure. He was good at what he did, and he knew it – prided himself that he had never had any complaints, except for when he ended the liaison. This woman, though, could turn out to be his match: he was willing to bet that she was an animal beneath the sheets – or on the floor – or against the kitchen worktops ... Her full lips suggested passion; her remarkable body promised unimaginable sexual gymnastics. He had grown hard thinking of her; but first he would have to give his would-be fiancée the slip.

Saffy watched the confident way this ladies' man sauntered across her parents' living room, wondering if she were playing with fire. Never before had she wanted anyone as much as she wanted the charmer who had so blatantly chatted her up: she wasn't sure she *liked* him – he was far too arrogant for one thing – but her breasts tingled when he was near her and she knew that if he tried to kiss her, she wouldn't stop him – no matter who saw.

Her train of thought screeched to a halt as she was struck by a sudden, brilliant idea: if this Marco person her father wanted her to marry saw her kissing someone else, surely then the engagement would be off? It seemed like the perfect solution to her problem – but what if the stranger didn't want to kiss her? No, she was being stupid: there had been a definite sexual energy between them, one that had crackled so fiercely she was surprised that no one else had noticed it.

Across the room, Marco turned his head to look once more at this unexpected bonus. He should really make the effort to find Sapphire and at least make a pretence of talking to her – that way, his father would be satisfied that he had kept his side of the bargain – but his attraction to this beautiful woman was too strong: it was almost a physical hunger, gnawing away at his insides.

As he looked longingly at her, a name registered in his ear. What was it his father had told him? Antonio's daughter was called Sapphire, but it was shortened to Saffy. Whirling round, he observed a plumply pretty girl who looked to be the right sort of age, in the process of being courted by a youth who looked all of twelve. Although she was too fleshy for Marco's taste, the young man who addressed her so earnestly was obviously smitten: he was unable to tear his eyes away from either her dancing blue eyes or her remarkably generous bosom.

There it was again: Marco was sure the love-struck swain had addressed the object of his ardour as 'Saffy'. He breathed a sigh of relief: the couple's body language hinted that they were equally enamoured with each other, meaning that this ridiculous idea of an engagement need never even be entertained. And he would tell his father, with a clear conscience, that he had tried to follow his wishes, but that Sapphire had chosen to bestow her heart elsewhere.

He grabbed the glass of Pimms and headed back towards the woman he actually wanted.

* * *

Saffy sensed her would-be admirer's presence before she noticed that he was once more at her side.

"Another Pimms - is that what you wanted?" His voice was husky with desire.

She took it from him with trembling fingers, inadvertently brushing his skin as she did so. Heat flamed between them: she was reminded of fireworks, ready to explode.

"You feel it too, don't you?"

How could anyone convey such intense longing in a few murmured words? she thought woozily, realising that she had downed her first Pimms far too rapidly and on an empty stomach, and that nervousness was making her drink this one far too quickly too.

He spoke again. "You want me as much as I want you. I can feel it, *cara*."

Slowly, he reached out his hand, traced her jawline, then tilted her head so she was looking up at him. His lips crashed down on hers in an explosion of intensity, so that for one brief moment she was only aware of the dizzying sensation he evoked within her.

Reluctantly, she pulled away from his kiss. "I can't. I'm sort of with someone else."

She couldn't kiss him again until she'd met Marco, made him aware that – no matter what their parents wanted – she wouldn't be marrying him. She couldn't be with anyone else now – not after that kiss.

To her surprise, he gave an apologetic shrug. "I too am not a free agent. This party – it is actually for me, and the girl my parents want me to marry." Seeing her horror-struck face, he went on hurriedly, "But this engagement will not happen – not now I have met you. I have not yet spoken to this girl, but I promise you, my heart was not in the match – it would have been a marriage in name only; whereas *you, cara* …"

He paused, letting his eyes linger on the delights he was sure he would be tasting very soon.

"Even if I was married already, I would have to have you," he said slowly. "I need to take you to my bed, despite your own circumstances, this 'sort of someone else' you say you are with." He extended a hand towards her. "I have forgotten my manners. I am Marco Benedetti, and you are …?"

"Sapphire Vendrini, your fiancée!"

And, with that, she slapped his face.

Chapter Two

For a moment, Marco was too stunned by Saffy's slap to do anything other than stare at her in disbelief. "No!" he protested eventually. "Sapphire is blonde – I have seen a photo."

"What photo?" She was glaring at him now, her previous desire completely dissipated.

Wordlessly, he pulled the tattered snapshot out of his pocket and handed it over. Saffy looked at the crumpled print and gave a low laugh of derision. "You stupid idiot! Sophie and I are in costume – we were both angels in our school Christmas show five years ago. Look, we've got wings and halos. I had to wear a blonde wig so we looked the same."

Marco examined the photo more closely, only now spotting the clues he'd missed before. Then the full impact of her words hit him: Sophie, not Saffy. So, the blonde girl he'd seen being wooed by an ardent suitor must be …

Her gaze followed his and she smiled involuntarily at the sight of her younger sister, only to frown a moment later with concern.

"What's she playing at?" Marco heard Saffy mutter under her breath. "If Dad or Eleanor see her …"

He couldn't understand what the fuss was about. Sophie looked like a girl who could take care of herself, and she was clearly smitten by her youthful swain. Besides, Marco had more important things to think about right now, including how long he would have to wait before taking Saffy back to his flat and giving her a damn good seeing to. He touched his face tenderly: the passion with which she'd slapped him boded well for the bedroom antics to come.

Closing the gap between them, his hands moved instinctively around her waist, pulling her towards him for another blistering kiss, but she pushed him away. "No you don't!"

"What?" He was puzzled now, so she elucidated.

"Don't you dare try to kiss me again!" Her tone seethed with indignation. "How could you try to pick up another woman at our engagement party!"

He matched her heated fury with icy disdain. "Since *you* were the 'other woman', *cara*, it hardly counts. Besides," his voice was deceptively smooth, "you yourself were kissing a man you did not know – even though you were 'sort of with someone else'!"

"That's not fair!" she breathed, the fire in her eyes betraying her passionate nature. "I was only kissing you because I wanted an excuse for Lucas's son to decide not to marry me. I hated the idea of this engagement as much as you did – but I went along with it to please my father." She paused soberly. "He's had three heart attacks recently. We're all being careful not to do anything that could trigger another one."

Marco stared at her once more, his expression a curious mixture of surprise and incredulity. "You're trying to tell me that you only kissed me to make another man jealous?"

"Not jealous – angry," she corrected him; but he was already continuing.

"I don't believe that for one minute," he said flatly. "No one could respond to a kiss the way you did unless she wanted everything else that would follow it." His eyes narrowed dangerously. "If I wanted you, I could have you, *cara* – you know that here" – he placed his hand over his heart – "and here" – now he gestured at his groin.

"You really do have a massive ego, don't you?" she shot back at him, unwilling to admit, even to herself, that he was probably right.

He raised his eyebrows in a maddeningly supercilious fashion.

"I've bedded enough women to know when someone is desperate to have me," he said arrogantly.

To her horror, she found herself mesmerised and not repulsed by his outrageous comment. He would be an expert lover, she was sure of it; but did she really want to be just another conquest, another name on a mile-long list?

"What happened to your beard?" she asked, deliberately changing the subject. Noting his incomprehension, she clarified, "I googled you, to see what you looked like – there was a photo of you in your capacity as CEO for the English branch of *Benedetti's*, but you looked ten years older at least."

Marco scowled. "My father made me keep that photo on the website. He thought people would have more respect for someone who looked older …" He paused deliberately. "… And more experienced," he finished, giving the suggestion time to sink in. "Besides," he grinned mischievously at her and the smile lit up his whole face, "my Tinder photo is much more up to date. I'm surprised you didn't see that one."

"I don't do Tinder," she said crossly, at the same time thinking she wasn't at all surprised to learn that Marco did. He was that sort of man, she decided: one who used women for his own pleasure instead of wanting a more meaningful relationship.

"That's a pity …" His voice was now once more silky smooth. "Think of the time we could have saved if I had seen you months earlier and swiped right."

"That's assuming I would have swiped right too!" she flashed back at him, guessing that this was the way people expressed their interest. She had no personal knowledge of the app, finding the idea of choosing a potential partner based merely on their looks to be both shallow and tacky.

He gave her a lazy smile. "*Cara*, you 'swiped right' when you started undressing me with your eyes half an hour ago!"

He really was an infuriatingly sexist pig, Saffy thought despairingly. Then, as she deliberately avoided his gaze, her eye fell once more on her younger sister and she remembered why she had felt concerned earlier.

"Oh, Soph ..." she muttered, half under her breath, "*what* are you playing at?"

Marco had followed the direction of her eyes. "You look troubled," he remarked, wondering if this were part of her flirtation technique – if so, it was having the desired effect: he felt piqued that Saffy's attention wasn't fully focused on him.

"Sophie isn't supposed to have boyfriends," her sister explained. "Dad's very protective – *over*-protective. I wasn't allowed to start dating until I left home to go to university, and Sophie's only just turned eighteen. She's still doing her A levels. Dad'll be furious if he sees her talking to that boy over there - or any boy, for that matter."

To anyone else, this would have seemed ridiculously archaic behaviour; but since Marco was Italian too, and since he was also an uncle to two nieces, he understood where Saffy's father was coming from. If he'd had a sister of his own, he didn't doubt that he would have made it his mission to defend her virtue, just as Antonio was protecting his younger daughter.

"She'd better be careful, then," he observed idly, "because your father's looking in her direction now."

"Kiss me!" Saffy's voice sounded urgent. As Marco reached for her, she added, "No, not here." Dragging him into the centre of the room, she seized his startled face in both her hands and kissed him fiercely.

Marco was surprised: not by the intensity of the kiss – he'd already identified her as a passionate creature – but by her sudden desperation for him. He responded to her obvious need, pushing his tongue inside her mouth, plundering, possessing.

Finally, she broke away from him. "That should do it!" she said breathlessly.

Before he had time to ask her what she meant, a hand fell on his shoulder and Marco found himself staring into the unflinching eyes of Antonio Vendrini.

* * *

"So …" The older man's voice was measured and slow: he was someone who would take no prisoners, Marco decided. "So," he repeated, "your papa and I made the right choice, no? You and Sapphire – how do you say it? – you have the hots for one another, no?"

Saffy's cheeks bloomed with a becoming shade of pink but her tone, as she answered her father, was uncharacteristically demure. "We were celebrating our engagement, Dad."

Marco's eyebrows shot up. He opened his mouth to intervene, but Saffy shot him a pleading look so he remained silent.

"This is excellent news!" Signor Vendrini's face glowed with delight. "We must make an announcement now!"

Before either of the pair could stop him, he had grabbed a fork from the nearby table and tinkled it against his wineglass, signalling to the entire room to stop and listen.

"My friends …" The words tumbled from his mouth proudly. "I wish to welcome Marco Benedetti to our family. He has just asked my daughter, Sapphire, to marry him – and she has agreed!"

There was a murmur of congratulatory noises, and then the previous hum gradually began again as, one by one, people resumed their conversations. Marco looked daggers at Sophie. "What on earth was all that about?" he hissed as her father slipped away.

Saffy bit her lip. He was annoyed by how desirable it made her look. "I'm sorry," she said contritely, "but I needed a diversionary tactic to stop him going for Sophie."

Marco looked at the empty space previously occupied by Saffy's sister. "Let me get this straight ..." His voice was dangerously quiet. "You kissed me the first time to make another man angry; and then you kissed me again so your father wouldn't notice his other daughter talking to a would-be lover?"

Saffy nodded, somewhat shamefacedly.

"And you felt no desire at all for me when you were doing so?" Marco sounded casual, but inside he was fuming. The little bitch had used him!

Saffy considered her response carefully. If she told him the truth – that kissing him had made her bones turn to water and her insides melt away – Marco would be unbearably smug. What was more, he might try to seduce her further; and she couldn't trust herself to fend off his advances if things became more interesting.

"It was okay," she said ungraciously. "I mean, I've had worse ..."

Not for the first time that day, Marco stared at her in disbelief. *Had worse?* Women usually raved about his kisses, telling him he was the best they'd ever had. For the first time in his life, he felt inadequate.

"That still doesn't explain why you told your father we were engaged," he commented eventually. "I said I wanted to sleep with you, not marry you!"

Saffy sighed. "An engagement doesn't have to end in marriage. If we say we're engaged, then both our fathers will be happy and they'll stop pestering us. We can break it off in a few months' time and tell them we just weren't compatible after all."

"And just how far would you go to keep up this deception until then?" Marco asked silkily, his hand tracing Saffy's clavicle in a most tantalising way. Before she could answer, he breathed huskily in her ear, "I'm sure your father taught you to test the goods before making a purchase …"

Why did he make her skin tingle when he touched her? Saffy thought helplessly. "You were the one who said it would be an engagement in name only," she reminded him, stalling for time.

Marco looked her squarely in the eye. "Yes, *bella mia*, before I met you, that was what I had decided – that I would marry you but still keep a mistress; but that was when I thought you were a plump, blonde English girl with child-bearing hips, not a fiery creature with a sexual appetite to match my own."

He was taunting her, she knew; nevertheless, she rose to the bait.

"So what guarantee do I have that you'd be faithful to me now you've seen what I look like?" she challenged him. "What if I became pregnant? Would you take a mistress then because I was 'plump', as you put it?"

Marco's fingers had moved from her collarbone to her shoulders, caressing the soft skin just below her neck in a way that almost made her moan with pleasure.

"When – not if – I take a mistress, I will not ask your permission," he promised her, his deceptively soft tone counterbalancing the hardness in his eyes.

Saffy recoiled as if slapped.

"It is the Italian way, *cara*." His expression was bleak. "The wife has full control of the home and children and turns her gaze aside when her husband 'works late'. She does not complain since she is well provided for. Besides, his absence gives her freedom to take lovers of her own."

"Is that what your parents' marriage is like?" she asked in horror.

Marco shrugged. "It is what all marriages are like. My brother, Ricardo, has not strayed – yet; but he has been married for only seven years. Men are not programmed for lifelong fidelity. Ricardo will succumb one day, as will his wife."

"Just as well that we aren't doing this for real, then," Saffy commented drily, "because *I* happen to believe in the sanctity of marriage."

For a moment, they glared at each other; then Marco relented. "Perhaps we should start again. Why don't we pretend that we have just met and I have asked for your phone number?" He fished an expensive looking mobile out of his pocket. "You give me your number and I will give you a call. We will go on a 'date' and let that be our chance to get to know one another properly." Seeing her hesitation, he added, "Our families will expect it. Besides," he quirked an eyebrow at her, "if we don't spend time together, how will we be able to convince anyone that we have changed our minds about wanting to get married?"

For a moment, she was silent; then, reluctantly, she nodded. "Okay. I'll give you my number. I'll even go for dinner with you – as long as you realise it's only dinner."

Marco's eyes gleamed. "Is that a challenge? Because you wouldn't be the first woman I've talked into bed."

She could well believe it. This man oozed sexual confidence from every pore.

"Well, maybe it would do you good to find a woman who can resist your charms," she told him sweetly, determined not to let him have the last word. "After all, that would be a good reason for breaking off our engagement – if we decided we weren't sexually compatible."

"Except that no one who saw me kiss you earlier would believe that for one moment," Marco said softly. His mouth hovered dangerously close to hers. "This heat between us – anyone can feel it. You know it yourself, even though you don't want to admit it."

"Okay," she told him raggedly, "I admit we've got chemistry; but, unlike you, I can control my hormones - and that's why I'm walking away now."

Turning on her heel, she stalked away from the only man she had ever wanted to sleep with.

Chapter Three

Saffy decided she couldn't stay long at the party after that. Not only was she fighting her most unwelcome attraction to Marco, but she felt slightly ashamed of how she had manoeuvred their engagement merely to detract attention from her sister.

That's not the only reason, is it? a little voice said inside her head. *You just wanted an excuse to see him again ...*

She told herself she was being silly: she was quite sure that Marco wasn't the sort of man who needed to put a ring on a woman's finger before he took her to his bed. He struck her as a practised seducer: one who would ravish a woman first and ask for her name later.

Aren't you being a little hard on him? her inner voice chided. *At least he seems to want to get to know you first ...*

Nevertheless, Marco had made it quite clear that he had only one thing on his mind when it came to Saffy. She wondered how long she would be able to resist his advances, aware that no man had ever affected her like this before.

"Saff!" Sophie's voice interrupted her reverie, making her start guiltily.

"What's wrong?" she asked, noting her sister's frantic expression.

"Not here." Sophie sounded furtive. "Why don't I drive you back to your place and we can talk there?"

"Okay." Saffy still found it odd that her little sister could not only drive but had passed her test on the first attempt, whereas *she* had taken four tests in as many years and failed each one spectacularly.

"I'll just tell Dad and Eleanor we're going," she added, realising that Sophie's offer probably stemmed from a desire to put some distance between herself and their father – who had been watching his younger daughter like a hawk ever since the toast to Saffy and Marco had finished.

* * *

As they climbed into Sophie's electric blue Fiat ten minutes later, Saffy felt, once more, a mixture of guilt and remorse. Eleanor had been so excited about the engagement, assuming that the two sisters wanted time together to talk wedding dresses and bridesmaids' outfits, that Saffy had instantly anticipated the disappointment her stepmother would feel when the engagement was broken off in a few months' time.

"So," she pulled her seatbelt across her chest and fastened it as Sophie adjusted the mirror, "what's the problem?" Although she framed it as a question, she already knew the answer.

"It's Adam," Sophie said simply as she put the car into gear and began to pull away.

"The boy I saw you talking to earlier? Hadn't you only just met each other?"

"Not exactly …" Her sister's evasion made Saffy look at her sharply. "We've been … studying together since last September – he's doing A level music too, and the boys from St Andrews have been coming to us for music lessons ever since their own Head of Music quit. I told you all that months ago, remember?"

Saffy calculated rapidly. This was March: that meant that her sister and Adam had known each other for six months, but this was the first time Sophie had mentioned him. However, this wasn't really surprising, given that their father had deliberately chosen a single-sex private school for both of them, in an attempt to keep them away from any potential male interest.

"How well do you know each other?" she began carefully.

Sophie's cheeks flamed.

"Soph!" Saffy couldn't prevent a scandalised tone from entering her voice.

"Nothing like that!" Sophie said hurriedly. "But we've spent time together in lessons and we've had coffee in our study periods – when we've been off at the same time – and stayed after school for extra music practice; and we've kissed …" She broke off, obviously wondering if she'd said too much.

"So he's the same age as you?" Adam had looked younger, Saffy thought: he was still a boy, so different to Marco, who was very obviously a man …

She realised Sophie was still speaking. "We're in love, Saff, and I can't tell Dad or Eleanor because I know they won't approve."

Saffy stared at her little sister with incredulity. *In love?* Sophie didn't know what she was talking about.

But apparently she did. As the story unfolded, Saffy learned how the two teenagers had been initially attracted to each other but both too shy to do anything about it. All that had changed at the sixth form Christmas party, a joint venture for the boys' and girls' schools, when - emboldened by a combination of mulled wine and mistletoe – Adam had kissed Sophie for the first time. They'd spent the rest of the party in one of the music practice rooms, letting one kiss follow after another until both felt they had reached Grade 8 for their technique. For the past three months, they had continued to meet in secret, taking advantage of the fact that they were the only A level music students in Year 13 and that they were expected to practise unsupervised.

Saffy wasn't sure how to respond to any of this. It was somewhat galling to learn that her baby sister had a far more exciting love life than she did herself; at the same time, her heart ached at the longing in Sophie's voice and the desperation she felt at having to keep her boyfriend a secret.

"I think you should talk to Eleanor," she said at last. "She'll probably be quite sympathetic – don't you remember her telling us once about the boyfriends she had at school when she was younger than you? She'll know where you're coming from."

They had pulled up at Saffy's residence now – a small flat directly over the tiny jeweller's that she co-owned with James, a friend from her recent undergraduate days. "Do you want to come in for a bit?" she offered, thinking it might do Sophie good to get it all off her chest, but the younger girl shook her head.

"No, I'd better be getting back. You know what Dad's like." Then, as she was about to drive away, a sudden thought struck her. "Hang on! I've been so preoccupied with Adam that I haven't even said 'Congratulations!' I thought you hated the idea of marrying Marco – you hadn't even met him until today."

Saffy hesitated. If she told Sophie that the engagement had been merely a diversionary tactic to draw attention away from her sister, she couldn't guarantee that Sophie wouldn't tell Eleanor. She was notorious for 'letting things slip' when she wasn't thinking.

"Mind you," Sophie was continuing, a wicked gleam in her eye, "I can see why you said yes – that man is gorgeous! He's a bit old for me, but still …"

Saffy's pulse quickened as she thought of Marco and the way his lips had met hers. She relived the giddy sensation of his fingertips tracing her collarbone and caressing her shoulder.

Sophie laughed. "Sapphire Vendrini! You little minx! I can tell exactly what you're thinking …" She kissed her sister affectionately on the cheek. "Let's hang out together next weekend. I'll ask Dad and Eleanor if I can stay at yours and we'll have a proper girlie evening together – it's ages since we've done that."

Saffy was still thinking about Marco as Sophie drove away.

* * *

She was thoughtful as she unlocked the outside door that opened onto the staircase leading up to her flat. Sophie obviously thought she was in love, but she was only eighteen and she had never had a boyfriend before. Saffy also had a sneaking suspicion that the clandestine nature of it all had added a certain *frisson* to the young couple's relationship: would they both be so enamoured with each other, she wondered, if they didn't see themselves as a modern-day Romeo and Juliet, kept apart by unsympathetic parents?

Sighing, she unlocked her front door and entered her tastefully restored Edwardian style living room. James and his partner, Connor, both had an eye for interior design – how clichéd for a gay couple to be experts in wall coverings and soft furnishings! – and, with their help, she had turned the filthy, abandoned storage space above the shop into a light and airy room which led to a small kitchenette at one end and a bedroom and bathroom at the other. Luckily, the cast iron fireplaces and original cornicing had been left intact, and she had removed the moth-eaten carpet to reveal original floorboards that now gleamed beneath a wax coating. A rich, ruby red Persian rug, her pride and joy, covered most of the seating end of the room, whilst the squashy sofa boasted a beautifully embroidered throw that she had picked up for next to nothing when carbooting with James and Connor. They had advised her on her tiny kitchen too, updating it with oak units and worktops that skillfully concealed her fridge freezer and washing machine. The stove was a reproduction gas cooker, in keeping with the era. She owned no dishwasher, but since she only ever cooked for herself, there was never more than a plate or two and the odd saucepan to clean anyway.

She carefully removed her shoes, leaving them neatly by the front doorway and relishing the freedom of being bare foot. Padding into the bathroom, she turned on the hot tap, thankful that she had set the timer earlier to heat the water, and poured in a generous amount of bubble bath. A heady aroma of essential oils filled the air: jasmine, laurel and rosemary mingled with the clouds of steam that emanated from the inviting looking suds.

Saffy peeled off her close-fitting dress and underwear and sank blissfully into the deep, warm water, not bothering as she usually did to pile her hair on top of her head but instead letting it trail in the water as she leaned back and immersed herself properly. James and Connor had both urged her to get rid of the bath completely and turn the space into a wet-room, but she had refused. Now, as she luxuriated in her well-earned pampering session, she thought for the umpteenth time how right she had been to follow her instincts. The bathroom was her haven and her heaven: the one place in which she could totally relax.

Not that she disliked the rest of her flat, she thought hastily. She had achieved a cosy effect in both bedroom and living room: the former housed a vintage iron bedstead, topped with a patchwork quilt, and she had found a hand stitched sampler for the wall in a local charity shop. Oak bookcases in both rooms housed an eclectic collection of contemporary novels, classic literature and the well-loved stories from her childhood, along with more practical volumes on cookery or jewellery design. The battered dining table at the far end of her living room was laid with an intricately embroidered tablecloth and a Victorian teaset that had been waiting forlornly for a buyer at a church jumble sale – since she ate most of her evening meals from a tray whilst she watched television, the table top was left untouched, allowing her china to remain in pristine condition.

*

She suddenly thought of Marco, wondering for a brief second what *his* living quarters were like. He was the sort of man to have mirrors everywhere, she thought grimly – not only would he want them wall-to-wall to facilitate his self-adulation, but he would probably have them on his ceiling too so he could admire his technique when he was servicing any of the countless women he'd boasted about. He would probably have a giant waterbed, and outlandishly tasteless velvet bedcovers in a tiger print: everything about his apartment would not only scream 'bachelor pad!' but would flash it up in neon lights. There was no way she would ever set foot in a place like that! she decided, savagely soaping her legs – so why did she still feel a spark of longing for this man she knew she detested?

* * *

It would have surprised Saffy to learn that Marco was also thinking of her. Despite feeling manoeuvred into this engagement by way of Sapphire deceiving her father, he couldn't prevent his pulse from quickening at the thought of her in his bed, wrapping those ridiculously long, but oh so sexy, legs around him. He lay back now on his Egyptian cotton sheets and surveyed his bedroom, wondering how she would react to the cream leather bed – six feet wide – and bespoke carpentry. He had spent a fortune on this room, hiring the best craftsmen he could find: he'd always thought of it as a worthwhile investment, since every woman he'd brought back here had been sufficiently impressed to want to spend the night. He didn't go in for any of that nonsense, of course: sex was a pleasurable pastime, but he wasn't foolish enough to run the risk of becoming emotionally involved with anyone – not after Nadia.

His eyes clouded as he remembered his first and only love. He had been a callow youth of twenty-three, still naïvely believing in the concept of fidelity. Nadia was a client who had been doing business with *Benedetti's* for some time: in her early thirties, she was a good ten years older than he: an attractive blonde who wore lowcut blouses and a supercilious smile. She had done all the running – suggesting 'business dinners' at which she leaned forward provocatively, tantalising him with her generous cleavage, or licked her lips in a manner that blatantly hinted at something else. When she'd asked him in for coffee at the end of their third meal, he'd already become infatuated with her, believing her desire for him to stem from something more than mere lust. He'd fallen for her – totally and irrevocably; had even thought she was 'the One'; and then an overheard snippet of conversation in the men's bathroom had burst his bubble for good when he realised that she was sleeping with several of his fellow workers as well.

From that moment onwards, he had hardened his heart, vowing never to let a woman dupe him again. He had managed to keep his emotions firmly under control – until today, that was, when he had seen Saffy across a crowded room and registered that he had finally found a woman who could be more than just a casual fling. She wanted him physically, he was sure of that; but could he make her fall in love with him? Only time would tell.

Chapter Four

Saffy slept badly that night: partly because she was still worried about her sister and Adam; but mostly because she was beginning to feel guilty about her sham engagement. It was all very well to kid herself that she was only pretending to like Marco for her father's benefit; but deep down she knew that she wouldn't have leapt into any of this had she not found herself violently attracted to the man who had been chosen as her potential bridegroom.

Even now, she wondered why Marco had gone along with it. He didn't strike her as the sort of man who had any difficulty enticing women into bed. Perhaps he was bored? she mused idly; or maybe he saw her as a challenge: he had certainly seemed put out when she had walked away from him at the party.

Speak of the devil … That was a text from Marco now, flashing up on her phone. She hadn't taken his number when she'd given him hers, but he'd started the message in his typically arrogant fashion: 'Marco here. Be ready at seven thirty tonight, *cara*. I'm taking you out for dinner. I've booked a table at *Di Paulo's.*'

He wasn't asking her, she noted in disbelief: he was telling her. How dare he assume she had nothing better to do (she didn't) and how like him to make all the arrangements without consulting her first.

Two could play at that game. She rapidly pinged back a reply. 'Tonight no good. I'm busy. Some other time maybe.'

Seconds later, her phone rang. A furious Marco was on the other end. "Just what, exactly, are you doing that makes you too 'busy' to see your fiancé?"

"Pretend fiancé," she corrected him, but he swept on.

"I take it you are not busy every night this week, no?"

"I might be free on Wednesday," she began cautiously.

Immediately, Marco pounced. "Wednesday night it is, then. I'll pick you up at seven."

"No!" She surprised herself with the forcefulness of her reply. "I'll meet you there. What time did you have in mind?"

"The table was booked for tonight at eight." Marco's tone was icy cold. "You are lucky that I am a valued customer at *Di Paulo's*, or we would not be offered another table for later this week after cancelling at such short notice."

"That's hardly my fault!" she flashed back at him. "You should have asked me first, not gone ahead and booked a table because you felt like it." Then a thought struck her. "You only met me yesterday, so this would have been a last minute booking for tonight anyway – or had you already reserved a table for you and someone else?"

"I will rebook and text you the time," Marco said shortly, ignoring her question, "but I am already beginning to think this was a mistake. I am used to dating women, *cara*, not spoilt children."

He hung up before she could think of a suitable reply.

*

She was still fuming as she showered and dressed. What had she been thinking when she gave him her number? Marco Benedetti was nothing more than a sexist pig, and now she was going to have to spend an entire evening in his company.

"Somebody's in a mood this morning!" James commented as she stalked into the shop beneath her flat. Her business partner looked at her narrowly. "Sapphire, you little hussy! You've got yourself a man!"

"No, I haven't!" Her reply was just a little too quick.

James quirked an eyebrow at her. "Darling, you only ever flounce about like that when there's a man involved – do tell all!"

"There's nothing to tell," Saffy protested, but James wasn't going to let her off that easily.

"What's his name?" he insisted. "And where did you meet him? You hardly ever go out." A sudden thought struck him. "Have you finally succumbed to the lure of Tinder?" he asked eagerly.

"You should know me better than that!" Saffy retorted.

"Desperate times call for desperate measures," James said airily, "and *you* must be desperate, my love, because I make it eight months at least since you last went out with anyone apart from Connor and me."

Sapphire fidgeted uneasily, not wanting to be reminded of the disastrous evening ten months ago, when she had been in the middle of what promised to be a very successful intimate dinner – with a man she had met in the local supermarket – only to have it interrupted by the arrival of her date's wife. In vain Saffy had protested that she hadn't known Malcolm was married – he'd removed his wedding ring for this evening as well as for their previous four meetings: the wronged wife hadn't believed a word of it and had created a totally embarrassing scene, hurling abuse at her rival and accusing her of being a marriage wrecker. It had been a sufficiently unpleasant experience to put Saffy off accepting any further invitations from apparently 'nice' men.

James regarded her sympathetically. "You're a hot, hot woman, Sapphire Vendrini," he said eventually – "I'm gay, and even I can tell – and you're far too young to be swearing off men for good just because that prick, Martin –"

"Malcolm," Saffy corrected him.

"Whatever – just because some prick 'forgot' to tell you he was married. So …" He paused for breath. "Where *did* you meet this guy, then? And what's he done to put you in a mood?"

Saffy hesitated, unsure how much of her unconventional engagement she wanted to reveal. "He's the son of my dad's best friend from years back," she said at last. "Both our dads thought it would be a good idea to get the two of us together – but Marco's just so arrogant!"

"Marco?" James's eyes gleamed. "Is he an Italian stallion, by any chance, Saff? You know how I love a Mediterranean man!"

"Connor's got green eyes and blond hair," Saffy pointed out, "and you're always telling me he's the love of your life."

"That doesn't mean I can't look, though," James said smoothly. "It's okay to wander round an art gallery as long as you don't try to take any of the paintings home with you."

Despite herself, Saffy grinned. James often made outrageous comments, but he and Connor seemed genuinely happy together. They enjoyed a colourful relationship, with lots of over the top spats – which she suspected were contrived to amuse the rest of their friends – but nevertheless had remained blissfully content with each other since their university days, when James and Saffy had been fellow students on the same design course, and Connor had been one of her closest friends in the Hall of Residence.

At the time, when even Connor himself had been unaware of his sexuality, she'd had a massive crush on him, reading far too much into the time they'd spent together and naïvely imagining that he felt the same way. She'd even confided in James that she'd met someone who might be 'the One'. James had promised to vet him for her – "My little Saffy deserves the best!" he'd told her in his endearingly camp fashion – but had ended up falling for Connor himself, agonising for the next few months over whether or not he should act on his desire or wait and let nature take its course. Saffy, meanwhile, had been totally unaware of all the subtext, failing to notice James's sudden confusion around Connor, or the fact that her best friend had stopped drooling over unattached men in the student bar. She'd even tried to fix him up with the friend of a friend – until she realised that the youth in question was a staunch Tory and directly opposed to James's leftwing tendencies.

Things had come to a head part way through their second term, when the three of them had gone to a 'Rocky Horror' screening – dressed up, naturally – and James had finally told Connor how he felt. When Connor reciprocated, Saffy had thought herself heartbroken, not to mention betrayed; now, however, she found it hard to imagine either of her best friends being involved with anyone else. She was grateful that, several years later, the three of them were still friends; and that she and James co-owned as well as co-ran 'Jo Bangles' together.

James was still fishing for more information about Marco. "Have you taken him out for a test-drive yet?" he enquired cheekily.

Saffy shot him a withering look.

"I only asked ..." James took on a wounded tone. "C'mon, Saff – let's hear all the gossip. Is he an animal in bed?" He rolled his eyes suggestively.

"Considering we've met each other once – and that was at a party at my parents' place yesterday – the answer's no," Saffy said shortly, wondering what James would say if she told him she and Marco were engaged.

"Well, he must have done something to annoy you," James commented, "because you flounced in here like a prima donna whose manager had forgotten to order a crate of champagne for her dressing room. Don't tell me he's another married man."

"Of course he isn't!" Saffy flashed back. "I'm not going down that route again! No, Marco's very definitely single – and that's part of the problem. He thinks he's God's gift to women and that all he has to do is click his fingers to get a woman to fall into bed with him. He's the most arrogant, sexist …"

She broke off suddenly as the shop door tinkled and the man she had been describing strode into view.

*

For a moment, Saffy was too stunned to continue her conversation. Marco, likewise, seemed bereft of words, instead, glaring at Saffy as if she were some sort of unpleasant smell.

James watched them gleefully, fully aware of the tension between them. These two were desperate for each other, he thought with amusement, but they were both too stubborn to admit it.

"Why don't you introduce me to your … 'friend', Saff?" he murmured eventually, lacing the appellation with just enough emphasis to make it sound mocking.

Saffy glowered at him. "James, this is Marco Benedetti," she said abruptly – "the one I was telling you about."

By way of reply, Marco stuck out a hand in James's direction. "Good to meet you, James. I am Sapphire's fiancé." The words were a definite challenge.

If James was surprised by this information, he managed to keep his feelings remarkably well hidden. "Congratulations, Marco," he said politely.

"And you are?" Marco looked at him pointedly.

"James Green – Saffy's partner."

Marco looked thunderous whilst, inside, Saffy groaned. "Business partner," she corrected hastily, mentally vowing to castigate James as soon as Marco left the shop.

"You didn't tell me you had a business partner, Sapphire." Marco's tone was as icy cold as it had been an hour previously, when they had argued over dinner plans.

"There's a lot we don't know about each other yet," she said evenly, attempting to calm the situation. "I'm sure you have plenty of attractive women working with *you*, Marco – ones you haven't bothered telling me about yet."

"Naturally." Marco sounded bored now. "*Benedetti's* would not even consider hiring any female staff who were not easy on the eye."

He was goading her, and she knew it; but she refused to stoop to his level.

"How nice for you," she said agreeably. "You must feel like a little boy in a sweet shop every day when you're at work."

Behind Marco's back, James stifled a smile.

"So, I will see you on Wednesday, then," Marco continued, as of they were still carrying on their phone conversation from earlier on. "We will have a drink at the bar first, so I expect to see you there at seven thirty."

With that, he swept out, leaving Saffy fuming and James trying not to laugh.

"What's so funny?" Saffy snapped as the door closed behind Marco.

"You, Darling – well, both of you. You'd better do the deed soon because all this pent-up sexual frustration is making you bite each other's heads off at every given opportunity."

Saffy gazed at her friend in horror. "I am *not* sexually frustrated," she managed at last.

James gave her a pitying look. "Sweetie, you were both so obviously gagging for it I half expected you to tear each other's clothes off in front of me and just get on with it!"

He couldn't be more wrong! Saffy thought crossly as she began rearranging a window display. Marco might be very good looking – and incredibly sexy to boot – but there was no way she would let herself become one of his conquests. She had far too much self-respect for one thing, plus she found him totally arrogant. But James's words had hit home, and for the rest of the day Saffy found a most unwelcome image popping into her head of Marco ravishing her on the shop counter whilst the rest of the customers looked on and applauded.

Chapter Five

Saffy spent most of Tuesday and Wednesday worrying about her dinner date with Marco. He seemed to be making more of an effort than she'd expected, sending her flowers – a large bouquet of creamy white lilies, pink tinged carnations and pale, pastel roses, which was delivered to the shop on the Tuesday morning, catching her totally unawares and making her feel guilty when she thought of all the names she'd been calling him in her head. James had been suitably impressed: "This one's a keeper!" he'd told her, his tongue firmly planted in his cheek and prompting Saffy to entertain thoughts of throttling him instead of Marco.

There had also been a few more text messages: the first one, which arrived on Monday evening, simply said, "Sorry we got off on the wrong foot. Truce?"

In a fit of petulance, she'd replied with a thumbs up emoji, determined she wasn't going to waste any real words on him; she also had a sneaking suspicion he would be irked by her lack of manners. However, when the next text arrived the following morning, she was unable to prevent herself from smiling: Marco had sent a GIF from Fawlty Towers of a perplexed looking Manuel, captioned 'But I learn'. Perhaps he wasn't as arrogant as she'd first thought if he could send himself up like that.

*

Meanwhile, James was agog to find out what she was going to wear. "But it's *Di Paulo's*, Darling!" he protested when Saffy muttered something about not bothering to change out of her work clothes. "You have to look as if you've made an effort."

"You know I don't like dressing up," she told him crossly. "Anyway, what's wrong with what I'm wearing now?"

James eyed her critically.

"Nothing's *wrong* with it," he said eventually, "but it's awfully *safe*, don't you think?

"So, what are you suggesting?" Saffy demanded. "Are you telling me I should be going out in a dress slit up to my armpits and a neckline down to my navel?"

"She wore her topless, bottomless, backless, frontless, sideless dress for months before she realised it was a belt," James recited absently. Saffy decided to ignore him.

"Seriously, though," she began again a moment later, "do you think I *should* dress up? I mean, it's not as if it's a real date – or a real engagement."

"No," James agreed, having heard the full story from his co-worker several times over by now, "you certainly haven't done things conventionally." He looked at her seriously. "In fact, there have been times in the last few days when your life has shown distinct signs of turning into some ghastly Hollywood RomCom."

Saffy opened her mouth to protest, then closed it again.

"You obviously both fancy the pants off each other," James continued, "so why not go for dinner, then shag each other senseless and get it all out of your system?"

"I don't really go in for that sort of thing," Saffy said stiffly.

James looked puzzled; then, as light dawned on him, he let out an exclamation of surprise. "What! You mean, you've never ..." He gave a long, low whistle. "I didn't think girls like you existed anymore – that puts you on a par with unicorns and dragons and other mythical creatures!"

Saffy felt her cheeks burning. "If you're going to make fun ..." she began, but James stopped her short.

"*What* are we going to do with you, my precious little Sapphire?" he murmured, putting his arms around her for a consoling hug.

Saffy wished she knew the answer.

*

In the end, she compromised on a pair of black leather trousers – "*Very* sexy!" James said approvingly – and a blue silk shirt that turned her eyes a startling shade of azure. James surveyed her critically. "It's smart casual," he decided. "You look as if you've made an effort, but not as if you've tried too hard."

"Well, I'm not trying on anything else," Saffy grumbled, having paraded in front of James for forty minutes or more whilst she went through every possible permutation in her wardrobe.

"You'll be fine, Sweetie," James said absently. "Your legs go on for miles and your eyes look like a day at the seaside. What about your hair?"

"What about it?" Saffy ran a hand through her locks distractedly.

"Up or down?" James asked her patiently.

"Down, I think. I'm not very good at putting it up …" She looked at him hopefully.

"I can do you a messy bun," James offered. "It'll look reasonably sophisticated and set off those killer cheekbones, but there'll be just enough wispy tendrils escaping to make him want to yank the pins out and watch it tumble around your face."

"Maybe not, then," Saffy said nervously. Part of her was longing for Marco to kiss her again; but another, more sensible side to her whispered that she should try to keep her distance. Being totally inexperienced in matters of sex, she had no idea how far she should let things go on a first date.

James sighed. "Relax, Saff. This is the *'Me too'* generation, remember? Marco won't jump you just because you look alluring. He'll wait for you to make the first move, and he'll take his cues from you." He looked at her and shook his head uncomprehendingly. "How on earth did you get through three years of university life without getting laid at least once?"

Saffy was silent, remembering again how much of her heart she'd invested in Connor before he'd realised he preferred men. The pain she'd felt had made her wary: from now on, she would assume that any sweet, sensitive man was probably gay; but she knew she didn't want a lager swilling rugby lout either.

"But it's not as if those are your only two options," James pointed out practically when Saffy voiced her concerns. "You must have been out with men who fall somewhere between those two extremes."

She tried hard to remember. Boys had been off-limits until she went away to university, and then Connor had occupied most of her romantic fantasies until he and James got together. Since they'd tended to spend a lot of time together as a threesome, most people had assumed she was in a relationship with one of the others; and she didn't like nightclubs or any of the other typical venues for finding a mate.

"How did you meet Malcolm?" James prompted her.

Saffy groaned. "He picked me up in the Sainsbury's café."

It was true. She had been enjoying a post-shopping cup of tea when a well-dressed man had asked if the other chair at her table was free. Over the course of their conversation, she had learned that he was a kitchen designer, who just happened to a have a convenient window right now in between clients, he told her, smiling at her in a way that crinkled his eyes and made her heart melt, and that he was recovering from a recent divorce.

She'd had no reason not to believe him: he had seemed so genuine, so sincere. When he'd asked for her number, she had hesitated for only a few seconds: he was the first genuinely nice man she had encountered. Having been on a few disastrous dates arranged for her by well-meaning friends, this seemed a better option.

They met by appointment the following week, when he took her to an art gallery and impressed her with his knowledge of both paintings and painters. (She learned later that he'd memorised the guide book in an attempt to win her over.) This was followed by dinner, a few days later, in a charming little restaurant with stunning countryside views; he was obviously angling for her to invite him back for coffee at the end of the evening, but she simply thanked him for a wonderful time, yawned and said she had an early start the next morning. She found him reasonably attractive, but she wasn't ready to take things further than friendship just yet.

Their fourth and final date had been the one at which his wife had made an unexpected appearance. They had just finished their starters – this time in a trendy wine bar-cum-bistro – and Malcolm was plying her with champagne. In vain Saffy had protested that she didn't really like champagne (the bubbles always went up her nose), Malcolm was insistent that they needed to 'celebrate finding each other'. In retrospect, she realised this was probably a standard chat-up line; at the time, she'd thought it romantic but a little over the top.

The intimate mood had shattered instantly with Janine's arrival. Knives and forks paused mid-air and heads swivelled in their direction as an extremely irate woman burst into the room, stomped over to their table and demanded to know what Saffy was doing with her husband.

Saffy had been mortified. Some of the other diners were actually filming this dreadful scene on their mobiles, whilst others were simply sitting back and enjoying the show. Apparently, Malcolm's memory lapse was something that occurred on a regular basis because, according to his wife, there had been at least five others in the past two years. What was worse, Janine had known exactly where to find him tonight since this particular establishment was where he always took women for the third date.

She came back to the present with a start, aware that James had just asked her something.

"Sorry," she apologised, "I was miles away. What did you say?"

"What do you actually want in a man, Saff?" James repeated.

Saffy took a moment to consider her answer.

"I don't know," she said slowly. "Someone intelligent, with a good sense of humour – and someone who's a good listener, and who likes the same sort of things I do: books and art and theatre ..."

She broke off, wondering why James was laughing. "What's the matter?" she queried suspiciously.

"You do realise you've just described Connor and me?" James was finding it hard to keep a straight face. "I hate to break it to you, Darling, but you'll never find a boyfriend who's a clone of your gay best friends. Anyway, you've got *us* for that ..." He grinned wickedly. "What you need is a man who'll fill the gap that Connor and I can't!"

Saffy's cheeks flamed once more.

"It's all about the sex, Sweetie," James told her airily. "And from what I've seen so far, your Marco looks like a man who'll deliver ..."

Chapter Six

Saffy was still pondering James's comment when the taxi she'd ordered pulled up outside her flat twenty minutes later. A part of her was dreading this evening: she had spent most of the day wondering what they would find to talk about. Marco was six years her senior and a high-flying businessman to boot; whereas she had a degree in Jewellery Design from UAL and spent most of her time in the shop she and James co-owned, repairing broken necklace catches or selling restored vintage rings to locals who couldn't be bothered with car boot sales.

The taxi driver whistled when she told him the destination. "Special night, is it? You won't get much change out of a hundred there, Love."

As he set off, Saffy wondered, uncomfortably, whether the amount of money Marco spent on the meal was supposed to equate to what he expected afterwards. That had been one of her reasons for refusing to let him come to collect her this evening: if he picked her up, he would have to drive her home also, and then she would feel obliged to invite him in and one thing would surely lead to another. Besides, she needed to let him know she was an independent woman, perfectly capable of ordering and paying for her own taxi, and not reliant on any man.

*

As he waited impatiently at the bar, Marco wondered why he felt nervous. He was an old hand at this sort of thing – drinks, dinner, bed – so why was he suddenly worrying that Saffy would stand him up? He was still kicking himself for not trying a more subtle approach at her parents' party the previous Sunday, but he'd wanted her so much that he'd completely lost his head and switched to default setting, trying to impress her with the arrogant charm that worked so well on other women.

Saffy wasn't like other women, though: he was beginning to realise that now. Despite her background – Antonio Vendrini was a *very* wealthy man – from what he could gather, Saffy lived a simple lifestyle, forging her own way in the world instead of relying on her father's name or money to open doors for her. He had researched her carefully over the past few days since meeting her: he knew that she lived over the shop; had no car; and didn't go out much.

She was the complete antithesis to the type of woman he normally dated: well groomed professionals with carefully applied makeup and exquisitely manicured nails. Saffy's skin was clear porcelain, a startling contrast to her long, dark hair, and her nails had been neat but unvarnished. She looked like the sort of person who would enjoy a countryside walk without bothering about windswept hair or muddy footwear – come to think of it, he doubted whether any of his previous conquests even owned walking boots: they were far more likely to take Pilates classes at an exclusive gym than to exert energy climbing a hill or even crossing a stile. For a brief moment, he indulged in a daydream of walking hand in hand with Saffy through autumnal woods, a dog frolicking at their heels, before returning home to a log fire and the smell of baking.

He came to with a start. Was *that* what he wanted? He'd never seen himself as someone who craved domestic bliss – that was Ricardo's territory, not his – but, now that he was approaching thirty, he could see the distinct advantages of settling down.

Saffy might not want that though: she was only twenty-three, six years younger than he and not long out of university. She might well have other plans – to travel, maybe; or to enjoy the single lifestyle for a few more years.

His brother's words echoed in his head. He'd complained to Ricardo when their father had first broached the subject of this ridiculous engagement, but Ric had been surprisingly positive about the idea. "You've had plenty of time to sow your wild oats, little brother," he'd grinned. "Perhaps it's time to hang up your hoe and plant a cottage garden instead."

Marco had winced at the imagery whilst at the same time realising the sagacity of this advice. If it was time for him to get married, he could certainly do a lot worse than Sapphire Vendrini, he reflected now, idly swirling the brandy in his glass.

And there she was: right on time and looking as sexy as she had at the party. This time her hair was up, piled on top of her head in a way that emphasised her slender neck and delicate jawline. He could see other men's eyes following her as she made her way over to the bar to join him. *Yes,* he wanted to say to them, *this gorgeous creature is mine! You can look all you want, but she'll be going home with **me** tonight!*

He raised his glass to her as she slid into the empty chair next to him. "What are you drinking?"

"A white wine spritzer, thanks." She hardly ever touched alcohol, but she'd found that this choice went down better in company than straight lemonade.

Marco raised his eyebrows slightly but ordered what she'd asked for. "You look good tonight, *bella mia*," he said softly as he handed her drink to her. "Your hair suits you like that."

She took the glass a little suspiciously, almost as if she hadn't been expecting him to compliment her. "You don't look too bad yourself," she said drily, her eyes taking in yet another expensive suit and immaculately tailored shirt. He hadn't bothered with a tie, preferring instead to go for a slightly dishevelled look, in keeping with his dark, curly hair and designer stubble. Despite wearing such high-end attire, he still managed to give off an air of danger, almost, she thought, as if he were a modern-day Heathcliff.

"Now that you are here," Marco was saying, "you can tell me why you refused a lift. I can assure you that I am a safe driver."

"I just like doing my own thing," Saffy said flippantly. "Besides," she gave him a challenging stare, "if I'd let you pick me up, then I'd have to wait until you were ready to go at the end of the evening. If I take a taxi, I can leave when I want to."

She wasn't planning on coming home with him tonight, then? Marco felt a keen stab of disappointment.

"Being in control is obviously important to you," he guessed. "Any particular reason why? A domineering former lover, perhaps?"

"Just my dad." Saffy's face took on a curious expression. "Even now, he still seems to think I'm a teenager. I'm sure that's one of the reasons he was carrying around that ridiculous photo you've got – because he doesn't want to think that either of his little girls has grown up."

"But you're not still living at home," Marco persisted. "At least he's given you that much freedom."

"Only because he was worried about me being alone at night on public transport," Saffy argued. "When James and I bought the shop eighteen months ago," – Marco bristled at the mention of the other man's name – "Dad insisted on looking at potential premises with us. He didn't buy the shop for me, if that's what you're thinking: he gave me a loan for my share of it, but I'm paying him back in monthly instalments. Anyway, I managed to convince him that living over the shop would be a good plan because I'd be able to keep an eye on everything; plus, I'd be able to work late if I had a commission that had to be finished in a hurry, without having to travel home in the dark afterwards."

"Commission?"

Saffy nodded. "I know the shop probably didn't look that impressive to you when you popped in the other day, but we offer a bespoke jewellery service which involves me designing one-off pieces to order." She pushed a trailing tendril of hair away from her eyes. "I did a BA in Jewellery Design at UAL – the University of the Arts in London. That's where I met James: he was on the same course as me, but he ended up switching to Business Design and Management a few weeks in. We worked together on a couple of things for my Year Two Live Project and his degree show, and he helped me a lot with my third year pop-up shop – that was what gave us the idea of going into business together."

"It sounds like he's been an important part of your life." Marco was trying hard not to feel jealous, although part of him wondered if he could ever compete with someone who had been an integral part of not just Saffy's university experience but her career now.

"He's one of my best friends," Saffy said seriously – "and he's also very much in love with another friend of mine, so don't start getting any ideas about the two of us having anything more than a working relationship."

Was he really that obvious? Marco asked himself with surprise; or was Saffy just used to her boyfriends seeing James as a rival?

He pulled himself up short: had he really just referred to himself as Saffy's boyfriend? This was terrible: he never let himself become emotionally involved with the women he took out. Desperately trying to regain his self-composure, he looked at his watch, hoping that their table would be ready soon so that he could feign interest in the menu and wine list.

His luck was in: moments later, a smartly dressed waiter beckoned him discreetly and led them in the direction of a table for two, away from the rest of the restaurant. Marco had realised, several years ago, that there was little money couldn't buy: most establishments were quite happy to rearrange their normal seating for a small fee.

As the waiter tucked Saffy into her chair and lit the candle at the centre of the tasteful floral arrangement that adorned their table, Marco began to relax. He had eaten here numerous times before and was looking forward to Saffy's reaction once she discovered how good the food was. By way of contrast, now that they were facing each other, Saffy felt suddenly shy; then reassured herself with the reminder that at least Marco had no secret wife and that this time her meal could be eaten in peace.

"Have you eaten here before?" Marco asked, watching her peruse the menu. Saffy shook her head. "The pigeon is very good," he told her next, "and the chef does something wonderful with sea bass."

"I'm vegan," she told him, waiting for his reaction.

Marco blanched. Why hadn't he thought to ask her? So many people these days were vegan, or – what was it? flexitarian? – why hadn't he thought to check before bringing her to a restaurant that specialised in meat and fish dishes? This evening was turning into a complete disaster.

"Only joking!" She was laughing at him, he thought in amazement; then, as he saw the funny side, he began to grin too. "I'm sorry," she apologised, "but if you could have seen your face ..."

He scrutinised her carefully before returning his attention to the menu. Sapphire Vendrini was full of surprises. He found himself looking forward to the next one.

*

It was almost ten o'clock. In the flickering light of the almost spent candle, Saffy's face had taken on an ethereal glow. She had a healthy appetite for someone so slender, Marco thought admiringly: she had matched him mouthful for mouthful with first pigeon, then lamb, and was now polishing off a chocolate fondant. Being used to women who pecked at their food, claiming to be watching their weight, he found Saffy's attitude most refreshing.

He wondered if *all* her appetites were as voracious.

"Coffee?" he asked her now. "Or a cognac?" There was a pause. "Unless you want to come back to my place ... for a coffee there ..."

He let the implication linger suggestively, but Saffy wasn't playing along.

"I don't drink coffee," she said abruptly. "Especially not with men I don't know very well."

Marco sighed. "Sapphire, *cara*, we have just spent two hours getting to know one another over dinner – you have heard about my entire family, including my nieces" - no harm in giving her the impression that he was a family man at heart - "and I have learned about your student days in London, your time living in – where was it? Don Gratton House – and your love of theatre."

He reached across the table for her hand, clasping her fingers in his own and sending a jolt of electricity through her. "What are you so afraid of?" he asked her softly. His deep brown eyes looked into hers, searching for answers. She gazed at his long, dark lashes, then his half open lips, remembering how it had felt when he had kissed her at the party. "What are you afraid of?" he repeated.

You, she wanted to tell him, *and me,* knowing without a shadow of doubt that were she to let Marco take her to his apartment, she would be unable to keep her desire for him under control. She would let him make love to her, and then he would discard her for someone else – that was what men like him did: some of her old schoolfriends had told her their own horror stories about men who promised everything until they'd taken what they wanted. It was all very well for James to talk about the *'Me too'* culture, she thought bitterly; but sex was still a commodity and women were far more valuable when they controlled the market.

"I've got an early start in the morning," she said lightly, trying to brush the question aside. "I don't normally go out on a school night. Anyway," she gave a short laugh, "this is only a pretend engagement, remember?"

"And what if it were not pretend?" Marco pressed her. "What if we decided to go through with it and get married after all? We are both intelligent people who find each other pleasant company – and you can't deny our physical attraction to each other. You still want me, or you wouldn't be here with me now."

"Is that the best chat up line you can think of?" Saffy responded. "I've said no to 'coffee', so you offer to marry me instead, as if that would get me into bed! I know what you think about marriage, Marco – it doesn't mean anything to you. We had this conversation several days ago, remember?"

For a moment, they glared at each other, each of them unwilling to back down.

"And what if I have changed my mind?" he asked eventually. "What if I want to give marriage a try for real? I'm almost thirty, Saffy – maybe I'm tired of being the womaniser you seem to think I am. Maybe I want to find out if fidelity is possible after all."

He sounded so sincere, so plausible, that she almost capitulated – almost, but not quite. At the back of her mind, she heard Malcolm's voice, sounding so convincing as he described the breakdown of his marriage and the pain he'd been through with his divorce. She had believed every word he'd said – and look where that had got her.

No, she couldn't trust Marco – not when, only days before, he'd talked of taking a mistress once he was married. He might be the most physically attractive man she'd ever met, but she didn't want to settle for anything less than the fairytale romance her parents had enjoyed. There would be no happy ever after with Marco: her prince would rapidly become a toad.

"I think we both know that's not what you really want," she told him as she stood up to leave. "Thanks for dinner."

He watched her walk away from him for the second time in four days.

Chapter Seven

James couldn't believe it when Saffy told him she had left the restaurant without even a goodnight kiss.

"*What* were you thinking?" he asked her despairingly. "The man had just offered to marry you for real -"

"As if he was doing *me* some sort of favour!" Saffy interrupted.

"He offered to marry you," James continued, as if she'd said nothing, "and you shot him down in flames!"

"He didn't mean it!" Saffy muttered grumpily. "He just wanted to get me to go back to his apartment."

"Saffy, Darling ..." James tried to sound patient. "Does it really matter what his motives are? You fancy him, he fancies you – so what's the problem? And even if you don't think he's marriage material, you could still play along for a while and at least get some decent jewellery and a few more expensive dinners out of him."

"That sounds very calculating," Saffy commented.

James shrugged. "So what? I'm a cold-hearted bitch – but at least I know how to turn things to my advantage. You need to toughen up, Sweetie, and stop letting your moral principles get in the way of you having a good time."

"Well, Marco won't be offering to take me out to dinner again for a while," Saffy said practically. "He probably thinks it's a waste of money to pay for food if he doesn't get laid afterwards."

"Sapphire Vendrini, put those claws away!" James shrieked in delight. "It's not like you to be so catty!"

Saffy blushed. Deep down, she knew that her comment was probably unfair; but there was something about Marco Benedetti that rubbed her up the wrong way, so that whenever she was around him – or even just talking about him – she reverted to schoolgirl behaviour.

And, as it turned out, she was wrong about Marco. Midway through the morning, another text from him arrived. "You are a most infuriating woman," it began, "and so I concede I have met my match. Are you free this Saturday evening? M" Seconds later, a post script flashed across her screen: "PS I promise I will let you choose the venue this time."

She found herself smiling at the message, despite her reservations. Perhaps Marco *was* genuinely interested in her if he was still pursuing her?

"What does Lover Boy want now?" James asked shrewdly, having heard her phone ping and put two and two together.

"Another date – on Saturday." Saffy couldn't help the huge grin, splitting her face from ear to ear. Then her face changed as she remembered Sophie. "Bother! I can't make it: I promised Soph a girls' night in."

"Why not send her round to Connor and me?" James suggested. "We can eat 'Ben and Jerry's' and watch 'Sleepless in Seattle'."

He looked quite hopeful as he said it.

"Thanks," Saffy told him, aware that James loved any excuse to watch the RomComs he professed to despise, "but Soph's in a bit of a sticky situation at the moment and I think she needs sisterly advice. I'll just have to tell Marco I'm busy."

She felt guilty now for making up an excuse the previous Monday. She didn't want Marco to think she was messing him around.

"Sorry, Marco," she texted back, hitting far too many wrong buttons in her haste and having to retype most of the message, "but I already have plans for Sat eve. Do you want to make it another time?"

His reply pinged up instantly. "I will have to console myself with one of the other beautiful women on my list, then. *Ciao, cara.*"

List - what list? Saffy thought crossly, somewhat piqued that Marco didn't seem more devastated about not seeing her. He could be joking; then again, Marco was exactly the sort of man who *would* have a list, she thought darkly, one subdivided into hair colour or breast size. No doubt he was now scanning the names and deciding whether to choose a blonde or a brunette for Saturday evening. In a moment of irritability, she typed, "I hope you both have a wonderful time" and pressed 'Send' before she could change her mind.

Marco hadn't anticipated Saffy's response: he had been convinced that she was gradually warming to him, even though she had declined his offer of coffee the previous evening. Being totally unprepared for her rejection of dinner with him meant that he was now at a loose end for Saturday evening. Almost instinctively, his hand hovered over his smartphone: there were countless women who would be only too pleased to spend the evening – if not the best part of the night – with him in Saffy's absence; but, for once, he was loath to contact any of them. Saffy had got under his skin: if she wasn't available, he didn't want a substitute.

He briefly wondered who she had plans with for Saturday. She had gone to great lengths to persuade him that she and James were only business partners, but Marco wasn't entirely convinced. Perhaps it was time he paid another visit to *Jo Bangles* …

And so it was that, the following morning, Saffy heard the shop bell announce Marco's presence for the second time that week. Didn't the man have any work of his own to do? her mind enquired.

She was annoyed to see that Marco looked particularly delectable this morning, in a sand coloured shirt teamed with a navy suit that highlighted the intensity of his eyes.

"*Mamma mia!*" James whispered in her ear as he passed. Saffy resisted the urge to kick his ankle.

"So," she kept her voice deliberately casual, "what brings you all the way over here, Marco?"

"I have a commission for you, *cara*. One that requires your unique expertise." His eyes danced flirtatiously as he approached the counter. "I would like a piece of jewellery for a … lady friend, and I thought you would be the ideal person to design it for me."

Saffy's heart stopped momentarily at the mention of a "lady friend". How dare Marco claim he wanted a 'proper marriage' and then, less than forty-eight hours later, flaunt one of his other relationships in front of her! She stared distractedly at the man before her, scarcely taking in what he was saying.

"I will, of course, be willing to pay extra since the piece needs to be ready quickly and at such short notice." She heard the words without really registering them, but James jumped in quickly to rescue her.

"Perhaps you and Saffy could sit down now and discuss details," he suggested smoothly. "I'll bring you both some coffee. How do you like it, Marco? Hot and strong?"

Saffy flashed him a warning glance.

Minutes later, she and Marco were sitting in the comfortable armchairs near the back of the shop, thumbing through a folder she had put together of all her best designs.

"What type of jewellery were you thinking of?" she asked politely, trying not to mind that her pretend fiancé was buying a present for another woman.

Marco considered the question. "A ring, I think," he said reflectively. "Something not too ostentatious but it should be meaningful. Are there particular stones that have symbolic meaning?"

"Well," Saffy began hesitantly, "diamonds are meant to represent eternal love – but you probably know that already. Rubies are love, passion and emotion; zircon stands for prosperity, honour and wisdom; and pearls are for innocence …"

Marco placed his hand on top of hers as she was about to turn over.

"And what about sapphires?" he murmured, his thumb stroking her skin in a most disturbing fashion.

"Honesty, loyalty, purity and trust!" she snapped back at him. "I can't imagine you know much about any of those!"

Marco released her hand abruptly. "It wouldn't kill you to be pleasant once in a while," he said stiffly. "Especially when I am about to pay you a ludicrous sum of money for a very small piece of jewellery."

"And it wouldn't kill *you* to stop flirting all the time," she riposted. "You're incorrigible, Marco! I bet you're the sort of man who'd be eying up the bridesmaids whilst standing at the altar, waiting to get married!"

They glared at each other again.

"Coffee!" James trilled, carrying two steaming mugs over to the table in front of them.

Marco eyed Saffy suspiciously. "I thought you didn't drink coffee …"

"Usually, only with people I know very well," she reminded him, "but I can see I'll have to make an exception in your case …" She stopped suddenly, afraid he would take her words the wrong way. "Why don't you tell me what you've decided, now you've seen my sketches," she continued, trying to change the subject.

"Very well." His tone was suddenly brisk and businesslike. "I would like a ring like this one here …" He flipped through the various pages until he had located the one he wanted, "… made in platinum, and with a sapphire this size" – he grabbed a pen and sketched what he wanted – "surrounded by diamonds."

"You do realise how expensive that will be?" Saffy asked him, a hollow feeling in her chest at the thought of this unknown woman who warranted such an extravagant present.

Marco's mouth quirked into a smile. "It will be worth every penny, *cara*. This is what you might call a long-term investment."

Saffy jotted down the details, trying to ignore the sharp pain in her gut. Lovely though her flowers had been, they couldn't compare to a bespoke piece of jewellery. Marco obviously saw *her* as a short-term investment, worth the cost of a few dinners but not a few diamonds.

"What size is she?" she wanted to know.

By way of response, Marco seized her hand. "Her fingers are of a muchness with yours – your hand may be a little plumper, but not much."

Plump? Saffy felt her anger begin to rise once more.

"If it does not fit, it can always be resized, no?"

"I suppose so," she said grudgingly, but James was already ringing up the sale.

"So, with the cost of Saffy's design – because you pay extra for a Vendrini original – and the additional fee for making it up quickly …" He paused. "*When* did you say you wanted it for?"

"Will it be ready in a week?" Marco checked something on his phone. "I have an appointment near here next Friday. Perhaps I could pick it up just before lunch?"

"We'll do our best. So, with all that *and* the cost of the materials …" James named a sum that made Saffy's eyes widen: she had never sold any of her pieces for so much money before.

"That seems reasonable." If Marco were surprised by the cost of the ring he had ordered, he hid it very well. Fishing an exclusive looking credit card out of his pocket, he punched in the requisite numbers. "It has been a pleasure doing business with you both," he said politely. "Until next week, then, Saffy."

He left the shop before she could say goodbye.

Chapter Eight

"Looks like you missed your chance then," James said lightly once the shop door closed behind Marco. "Just as well you think he's an arrogant, sexist pig, Saff, otherwise you'd be feeling really fed up that he's buying jewellery for other women."

"I don't want to talk about it." Saffy stumped over to one of the display cases and made a great show of rearranging the vintage necklaces. "Marco can see whoever he likes – he's a free agent."

"It's a pity you're in love with him, then," James commented drily. "You can't blame him for looking elsewhere if you keep pushing him away."

"Isn't that what I'm supposed to do?" she queried. "Treat him mean to keep him keen?"

"Not acting too interested is one thing," James explained, "but you've effectively erected a six-foot-high electrified fence around yourself. You've got to give him a bit of a chance, girl."

"And what if I start running after him but he doesn't want me back?" Saffy's voice shook. "I don't want to feel this way, James. He's big headed and he treats women like objects – and he thinks all he has to do is throw his money around to get what he wants ..."

"And you go weak at the knees when he looks at you," James interrupted, "and you can't stop thinking about him ..."

"That's not true," she protested feebly, aware that her best friend could see right through her excuses.

"Really? Then why have you been doodling 'Sapphire Benedetti' on this order form for the last five minutes?" James scolded, snatching up the pad in front of her. "Admit it, Saff. You like him a lot, but you're scared he'll let you down like that Malcolm character did."

"He's taking another woman out tomorrow evening," Saffy said bleakly.

"Because he doesn't know how you feel," James told her. He shot her a withering look. "You women never say what you really think – men are so much more straightforward."

He pushed Saffy's mobile into her hands. "Text him now and arrange a date for next week. This is the twenty-first century: you don't have to wait for him to make the first move."

It took almost twenty minutes before Saffy was happy with her text message. She had tried hard to strike a balance between friendly and stalker: "I want him to think I'm keen enough for another date but not keen enough to follow him home or turn up at his workplace," she explained. The message she finally sent him said simply, "Thanks for the commission. Sorry can't make this Sat - spending time with my sister. Maybe dinner one day next week? S."

She spent the rest of that day brooding over Marco – as well as worrying about her little sister. Sophie hadn't been in touch since she had driven Saffy home the previous Sunday evening, although normally the two girls texted each other several times a day. She thought uneasily of Adam and hoped that Sophie wasn't going to get hurt.

A text message at half seven that evening put her mind at rest about Sophie: "Looking forward to tomorrow. Will come over around six. Soph x" They would order takeaway pizza, she decided, and watch a couple of their favourite films. Maybe a night without men was what they both needed. She felt emotionally exhausted from her fluctuating feelings for Marco.

The next morning, Saffy concentrated on her usual weekend chores: making sure her laundry was up to date; cleaning her flat ready for Sophie's visit; stocking up on ice cream and Maltesers (Sophie's favourite).

She was looking forward to dissecting her non-starter of a relationship with her little sister – Sophie might only be eighteen, but she usually gave good advice – so felt decidedly put out when her mobile rang just after six and Sophie told her she wasn't coming after all.

"Sorry, Saff," Sophie's voice croaked over the phone. "I've got a really bad throat. I think I'm just going to stay in bed with a LemSip and a hot water bottle."

"Can't you do that here?" Saffy asked, disappointed not to be having her girlie night after all. "You can snuggle up under a duvet on the sofa while we watch a film."

"I don't think so." Sophie coughed pathetically. "We can try again next Saturday though."

She could have gone for dinner with Marco after all, Saffy thought sadly as she hung up. She tried not to think of him sitting opposite an attractive woman, telling her the same stories he'd told *her* at *Di Paulo's*. Whoever she was, *this* woman wouldn't be saying no to coffee and everything that accompanied it. Maybe next time – if there was a next time – she, Saffy, should say yes too.

In the end, she rang James and Connor, knowing that they often stayed in on Saturday evenings. She would have settled for a commiseratory phone call, but James was delighted to hear from her, telling her that Connor was making a strudel and that she simply had to come and sample it.

"We're having sushi too, darling!" he exclaimed. "It's a total mishmash of cultures – a type of Japanese-Austrian fusion; or Japanese-Austrian-Italian, if you count the Prosecco – but we don't care. And we're watching *'Die Hard'*!" He lowered his voice. "Connor's choice, obvs. I'd kick up a fuss, but Bruce Willis in a vest is certainly easy on the eye. Anyway, I made him watch *'Les Mis'* – again! – the other night, so I haven't got a leg to stand on."

Saffy let the easy conversation wash over her, thinking that life sometimes had its compensations. At least James knew all about Marco, so she wouldn't have to rehash the week's disasters like she would have done with Sophie. And Connor was surprisingly acute when it came to relationships, being far less of a drama queen than his other half.

By the time she'd had a glass or two of Prosecco, Saffy was feeling distinctly mellow. Sometimes, she decided, alcohol *was* a good idea: she'd certainly stopped obsessing over Marco, even if this was only a temporary side effect.

"What you don't seem to realise, Saffy, Angel," James slurred – he'd polished off a whole bottle whilst she was still on her first glass – "is that men are very fragile creatures. They're brought up to hide their emotions, and that's why you get all this macho posturing and alpha male behaviour. Deep down, Marco's probably just as insecure as you. He's probably scared of commitment for the same reasons you are – because he's afraid of getting hurt."

"I don't know." Saffy tried to spear another tuna maki, then gave up and resorted to using her hands. "He's seemed pretty confident every time I've seen him."

"That's just an act," James insisted. "Connor," he appealed to his partner, "you know I'm right, don't you?"

"It's hard for me to comment when I've never met the guy," Connor said absently, his mind on the strudel. He thought it probably needed another five minutes, but maybe he should check it now, just to be on the safe side.

Saffy allowed the alcohol to cloud her brain. She wasn't drunk, just pleasantly fuzzy. It was quite relaxing really. She tried to think of Marco, but he had already been swallowed into a warm haze in her mind.

It was only after the strudel and Maltesers had been consumed and Bruce Willis had mown down fifty percent of the terrorists in his building that she managed to collect her thoughts sufficiently to think of her so-called fiancé.

"Maybe I should call him," she said out loud, thinking that it might an effective way to ruin the date he was currently on. It wasn't quite in the same league as Malcolm's wife turning up, but at least it was a start.

"Not a good idea, Saff." Connor remarked, without looking up. "You don't want him to think you're desperate."

But Saffy had already fished her phone out of her bag and was scrolling through her recent call log to find Marco's number. She was just about to hit 'Call' when the phone rang, making her jump.

"Hello, Marco?" she said cautiously.

"Saffy?" It was Eleanor's voice. "Can you put Sophie on the phone, please. I'm just doing the laundry, and I need to know if her cream top is safe to tumble dry."

Saffy was instantly alert. Sophie had obviously lied to them both; but where was she now?

"Erm, she's in the loo at the moment," she improvised hastily. "I'll get her to call you back."

"I tried ringing her phone, but she hasn't answered," Eleanor continued. "Can you tell her to stop putting it on silent? I'm fed up with not being able to get hold of her."

Her stepmother needed to learn how to text! Saffy thought grimly as she fired off a quick message to Sophie. "Where are you? E trying to get hold of you. She thinks you're at mine. S x"

"Trouble at t'mill?" James looked at her enquiringly, wondering if there was any decent gossip.

Saffy shook her head. She was pretty certain that, wherever Sophie was, she was with Adam; but the fewer people who knew that, the better. Secrets had a nasty way of coming to light once more than two people had the information. Besides, she couldn't help feeling protective towards her little sister.

"It's nothing," she said shortly, "just family stuff."

When she next saw Sophie, she would throttle her.

Chapter Nine

Sophie was full of contrition when she arrived on Saffy's doorstep the following morning.

"What are you playing at?" Saffy asked her severely. "Dad and Eleanor'll kill you if they find out you've been lying to them about staying with me."

Sophie hung her head. "I'm sorry," she said in a tiny voice. "I was with Adam. His parents are away."

"And …?" Saffy's question hung in the air between them.

Her sister's silence spoke volumes.

"I love him, Saff," she said eventually. "And he loves me. We just wanted to cuddle up together, honestly."

"And is that all you did?" Saffy tried not to sound disapproving.

Sophie looked at the floor.

"Were you … careful?" Saffy asked delicately.

Again, silence.

"Soph!" This time, Saffy couldn't keep the concern out of her voice.

"It just sort of happened," Sophie whispered. "I know we took a risk, but we couldn't stop ourselves."

Saffy looked around hurriedly. It was still early morning and the street was typically empty for a Sunday; nevertheless, she knew this wasn't the sort of conversation that should happen within potential earshot of anyone else. "Come inside," she urged the younger girl. "I'll make you some breakfast."

Over tea and toast, the story emerged, piece by piece. Sophie had fully intended to spend the evening at her sister's – until learning from Adam on Friday afternoon that his parents would be going to see a show in London the following evening and had booked to stay overnight in a hotel.

"They were a bit worried about leaving Adam on his own," Sophie reported, "but then he said he'd be going to university in September anyway and so he had to get used to being independent, and they decided it was okay." She buttered her toast carefully, then reached for the marmalade. "When he asked me to come over, it was just for company really – we didn't think we'd … do it."

Sophie had acted very naïvely indeed, Saffy thought crossly – in fact, both teenagers had.

"What's Adam doing now?" she asked.

Sophie blushed. "Washing his parents' bedclothes."

"Sophie Vendrini!" Saffy sounded as scandalised as she felt. "You don't mean you did it in his parents' bed!"

"It's all right for you," Sophie grumbled. "You've got a place of your own, and a double bed …" She broke off, realising her sister was staring at her.

"Yes, and when I was your age, I was still living at home and not sneaking off for sordid sex sessions!" Saffy snapped at her. "Couldn't you have waited another few months?"

Tears welled in Sophie's large, blue eyes, making Saffy feel mean. "Please don't tell Dad or Eleanor," she begged. "If they find out, they'll probably stop me seeing Adam."

"That might not be a bad thing," Saffy retorted, then relented as her sister's eyes started to leak with emotion. "Look, I know you think you're in love, Soph …"

"I *am* in love," Sophie wept. "You don't know what it's like!"

Marco had made her bones turn to water and her insides melt away; but Saffy was still too level headed to take things any further – yet.

"When you fall in love properly," Sophie continued, "you just want to be together. You don't care what anyone else thinks."

"Well, *you* obviously do," Saffy said drily, "or you wouldn't be trying to keep it a secret."

Sophie's face took on a wounded expression.

"I just think you're both a bit young for all this," Saffy said at last. "And you've got A levels coming up as well. You should be concentrating on revision, not wasting time sighing over each other. I know you think I'm being hardhearted, but if he's the right one for you, he'll wait until after your exams are over."

"You're like a robot!" Sophie burst out in disgust. "I know you've just got engaged, but you're only marrying Marco because Dad told you to, not because you're in love with him."

"That's not fair," Saffy said softly, but Sophie wasn't listening.

"He hasn't even given you a ring! This whole thing's just a business merger as far as the families are concerned and you're going along with it like the dutiful daughter you've always been. Well, *I'm* not like you – I'm going to marry someone I'm genuinely in love with."

She stopped suddenly, afraid she'd said too much.

"I *do* find him attractive," Saffy said after what seemed an interminable pause.

Sophie snorted. "You'd have to be blind not to! You don't love him, though, do you?"

"I'm not sure ..." Saffy considered the question. She still didn't know Marco very well: they'd only had one real date so far - but she knew he liked both opera and heavy rock music; that he had two small nieces he adored; that he loved long countryside walks; and that his favourite English writer was a rather obscure novelist, CP Snow, who had published most of his work between the 1940s and 1980s.

"I thought he was a sexist pig when I met him," she confessed, "but now I've spent time talking to him, I think I may have misjudged him."

James's words echoed in her memory: *'You've got to give him a bit of a chance, girl.'*

"I think I'm scared of letting myself get too close," she said now, surprising herself. "I've been let down in the past, by men I thought really liked me. You know the saying: 'Once bitten, twice shy'?"

"So why have you never told me about any of this?" Sophie demanded, picking up the teapot to see if there was anything left. "I'm your sister, but I don't have a clue what's going on in your life. You never open up about anything."

It was true, Saffy reflected, after Sophie had left. Her little sister had always worn her heart on her sleeve, crying buckets over Disney films when they were little and becoming passionate about whichever cause was currently closest to her heart. She had campaigned tirelessly against the opening of a new Krispy Kreme on the site that used to house the children's playpark and wept bitterly when the redevelopment went ahead.

By way of contrast, Saffy had always been far more cautious with her emotions. She wondered now whether it had anything to do with their mother dying when she did, when Saffy had been ten and Sophie five. Her mother had asked her to 'be strong' and look after her father and sister; and, from that moment on, Saffy had hidden her grief away, along with the rest of her emotions, trying hard to follow her mother's wish. Maybe it had made her old before her time, because when she was Sophie's age, she had been totally preoccupied with studying hard so she could go to university like her father wanted, and the social events of sixth form life had passed her by unnoticed.

Was it true, like James had commented just the other day, that she had 'erected a six-foot-high electrified fence around herself'? Did she subconsciously emit 'keep away' signals?

She resolved, there and then, that from now on she would try to be more like her baby sister.

Chapter Ten

Still mindful of both Sophie's and James's comments, Saffy made a particular effort to be pleasant to Marco when he rang her that afternoon.

"How was your evening?" she asked politely, wishing yet again that Sophie had cancelled earlier so that she could have gone out with Marco after all.

"Fine, thank you." He didn't seem to have missed her at all, Saffy thought dejectedly. "The company was excellent – although not quite up to Wednesday's standard ..."

Her heart lifted at these words; and it would have gone into orbit altogether had she realised that Marco's companion for Saturday evening had been the bottle of Scotch he had downed whilst eating takeaway curry and watching *Sky Sport*.

"How was your sister?" he asked now, matching her civility with his own.

Saffy was now faced with a quandary. If she admitted that she hadn't seen Sophie after all, then Marco would assume she had invented an excuse merely to avoid spending time with him. Besides, the fewer people who knew that Sophie hadn't been with her the previous evening, the better. She couldn't run the risk of gossip getting back to her father and Eleanor.

"Okay," she said cautiously. "She's got a lot on her mind at the moment, though – her A levels start in May."

"It probably did her good to do something completely different last night, then," Marco replied, unaware of the irony of his statement.

"Maybe." Saffy tried not to give anything away. "I don't think she should make a habit of it, though," she added, almost to herself.

"So, *bella mia* ..." Marco now got around to the real purpose of his phone call. "I was wondering if, this week, you would be free again for dinner. After all, we need to keep up pretences."

So, he didn't want a real engagement after all. Saffy tried hard to swallow her disappointment.

"I was thinking, perhaps tomorrow night?" Marco sounded professionally detached, almost as if this were a business arrangement – which, of course, it was, she reminded herself. "Do you have a preference for the cuisine?"

"I like Turkish food," she said slowly. "There's a little place not too far from here: the *Village Mangal* – it's a restaurant and takeaway, but the food is amazing."

"I will book a table." Marco took charge. "I assume you will want to make your own way there again?" he asked next.

Saffy hesitated. She had been to this restaurant several times before, with James and Connor, but one of them had always driven. She would have to take a taxi and hope that the driver knew where he was going.

"So, tomorrow evening, at around eight o'clock," Marco murmured. "I look forward to it, *cara* – especially if the food is as good as you say."

He rang off before she could tell him that she was looking forward to it too.

*

Marco had only just put down his mobile when his doorbell rang. An attractive redhead was standing outside the front door, wearing a worried expression and a very short skirt.

Her face brightened when she saw Marco. "It looks like I chose the right neighbour to ask for help. I'm Siân, from number 10."

Ordinarily, Marco would have responded to such an obviously flirtatious comment with a chat up line of his own; but Saffy's image popped up in his mind instantaneously. For some strange reason, he didn't want to disappoint her. Her scathing comment was still tattooed on his brain: *'I know what you think about marriage, Marco – it doesn't mean anything to you.'* He had to prove to her that he wasn't the philanderer she thought – not now he'd met her anyway.

The redhead was still talking, her voice a husky drawl. "I've only just moved in a couple of days ago, and I'm on my own – my boyfriend shacked up with someone else and I decided I wanted a fresh start somewhere new – so, you see, I don't have anyone to help me out with things like that."

Things like what?

"I don't know if you're any good with your hands?"

Yes, she was definitely flirting, he thought, observing how she opened her eyes wide, making far more eye contact with him than was strictly necessary.

"What do you need me to do?" he asked, stalling for time.

"If you could just look at the washing machine and try to figure out what's wrong with it …"

Sighing, Marco pushed his feet into a pair of shoes and grabbed his keycard. "I'll have a look, but I can't promise anything."

It took him only a few minutes to figure out the problem. The removal men Siân had hired had plumbed in her washing machine but omitted to remove the lid covering the waste pipe, so that when she had tried to use the machine, the water had drained all over her floor instead of disappearing where it was supposed to.

"Thank you *so* much …" Siân was uncomfortably close to him when he turned round. The heady smell of her perfume at such proximity made him feel a little light headed.

"I really think I should offer you a drink to say thanks," she continued, shooting him a dazzling smile. "I've got a bottle of champagne in the fridge that someone gave me as a housewarming present – or would you prefer a beer?"

Marco swallowed nervously. His default setting urged him to share the bottle of champagne with her, preferably in the bedroom, where they would be more comfortable; but he knew he wouldn't be able to look Saffy in the eye if he did anything like that. She was so honest, so straight; whereas Siân … Siân was like him, or, rather, like the man he had been until a week ago: a free spirit who would be quite happy to become a 'friend with benefits' but would exact no promises and expect no emotional involvement.

"It's very kind of you," he said slowly, "but I was just about to go out."

Her eyes took in his well-worn jeans and faded tee shirt.

"To visit my nieces," he added hastily. They lived in Italy, along with the rest of his family, but Siân didn't know that.

He spent the rest of the day and evening hiding in his bedroom, just in case she should come back.

Chapter Eleven

When she arrived at work the following morning, James was delighted to discover that Saffy was going out with Marco again and warned her not to be so uptight this time.

"And I'm not just saying that because he's the best customer we've ever had," he began, then broke off as he realised this might not be a tactful thing to say.

Saffy, who had been feeling reasonably positive about the trip to the *Village Mangal*, was instantly plunged into gloom as she recalled that Marco had bought a very expensive ring for someone who wasn't her.

"Maybe he has a sister," James suggested tentatively.

Saffy shook her head. "He's only got a brother. Ricardo's married, but I can't imagine Marco spending that amount on a present for his sister-in-law."

"Unless he's secretly sleeping with her," James joked tactlessly. Saffy pretended not to hear.

For the rest of the day, she worked on Marco's commission, sequestering herself in the small workroom at the back of the shop. It was a while since she had been called upon to put her practical skills to the test and she was soon lost in the intricacy of carefully bending a piece of platinum into a band that would fit on her own finger. Once she had soldered the gap where the two ends of the bar of metal met, using flux paste to prevent the platinum from becoming oxidised at the high temperature she was working with, she placed the ring in a weak acidic solution to erode and remove any excess flux. This was the easy part: she had made a number of plain wedding bands in this way over the past eighteen months, although normally from gold.

Next, she looked through the selection of precious stones that were stored in a safe at the back of the room. There were two exquisitely cut diamonds that would look perfect on either side of the slightly larger sapphire. There were bigger stones in the safe; but she had learned early on that value derived from finish, not from size. These gems were perfect for the delicate look that Marco had chosen.

She would set the stones the following day, she decided, glancing at the old-fashioned station clock on the wall in front of her (James loved period detail) and realising that she needed time to get ready for her evening out.

Back in the front of the shop, she let James know that she was done for the day. "I know it's slightly early," she aplogised, "but I want to wash my hair and you know it takes ages to dry."

"We're going for the long-haired siren look tonight, then?" James asked slily. He gave Saffy a deliberate wink. "Make sure you wear something knockout – that way you might get some jewellery out of Marco yourself!"

James's sense of humour was in very poor taste recently, Saffy decided as she stripped off her work clothes and stood under the steaming showerhead. As she lathered her hair, she thought about Marco, trying to work out whether he was genuinely interested in her or whether he only saw her as a potential conquest.

For a moment, she allowed herself to indulge in a brief fantasy of the two of them being properly engaged and planning a wedding together. Marco would wear a dove grey suit, she thought dreamily, and she would float down the aisle in a close fitting, white silk dress, with flowers in her hair and …

What was she doing? Marco would never *really* want to marry her; and she wouldn't marry him either, not if he was serious about keeping a mistress. They would have looked good together, though, she thought sadly, washing away her dreams along with the moisturising conditioner. But, then again, she couldn't fall in love based solely on what she wanted her wedding photos to look like …

She closed her eyes, trying to let the hot water blot out the emptiness inside her.

Marco was slightly annoyed to find there was no parking for the venue Saffy had chosen. Upon making enquries, he was told that there was a multi-storey car park just a few minutes' walk away. By the time he'd left his Jag there, not without reservations, and walked back to the restaurant, Saffy had arrived too and was waiting, rather nervously, just inside the entrance.

As he caught sight of her, Marco was struck by a sudden sense of *déjà vu*: she looked as stunning as she had on the day he had met her. Not only was her hair down once more – she'd had it tied back in a ponytail both times he'd visited the shop – but she was wearing a dress: a very sexy dress that dipped low at the back, exposing an expanse of porcelain skin.

"*Buonasera, cara.*" He bent to kiss her cheek in greeting, but she turned her head so that his lips met hers – whether by design or by accident, he wasn't sure.

Saffy closed her eyes as Marco's mouth covered hers, drinking in the cocktail of aftershave and pheromones. As the kiss deepened, she was aware of her spine tingling and her heart throbbing. Moaning a little, she pressed herself closer to him, but he was already pulling away, looking rather surprised by her enthusiasm.

"I think the waiter wants us to follow him," he said, a little pointedly.

The little Turkish man in front of them was actually the restaurant's owner, but Saffy didn't like to point that out. He led them to a tiny table for two, near the back of the room and next to the takeaway counter. Marco looked at it with distaste.

"Haven't you anything more private?"

"This *is* a private table," Saffy hissed at him. Nudging him as discreetly as she was able, she gestured in the direction of the other tables: not one of them seated fewer than six people.

"Anyway," she added as an afterthought, once their waiter had departed to fetch the breadbasket, "we're here for the food, not the ambience."

"Evidently."

Marco looked at the Formica-topped tables despairingly. Why, oh why, had he let Saffy choose the venue? This must be her way of getting back at him for some crime he hadn't realised he'd committed.

But when the food came, he had to admit that she was right. The complimentary bread was warm and doughy and arrived with garlicky humus, cool mint yoghurt and a spicy tomato dip. For their starters, they chose vine leaves stuffed with rice and pine nuts and flavoured with lemon, and *sigara böreği*, tiny pastry triangles filled with feta and spinach; then Marco ordered a lamb casserole whilst Saffy took a vegetarian kebab, which consisted of grilled aubergines, mushrooms, peppers and onions, on a spicy tomato sauce, served on a bed of rice. "I love meat," she explained when Marco raised his eyebrows at her choice, "but the flavours in this are fantastic. Have a taste."

The mouthful he took told him exactly why she rated the food here so highly.

As they ate, Marco began to delve a little more deeply into Saffy's personal details. "Are you and your sister close?" he asked. "There must be - what? five or six years' difference in your ages?"

"We're fairly close," Saffy said, a little guardedly. "Sophie was only five when our mother died. I was the main person looking after her until Dad met Eleanor – and that wasn't until years later."

"Does she spend a lot of Saturday evenings with you?" Marco wanted to know next. As she tried to work out why he was asking her this, he qualified it with an embarrassed, "I'm only asking because I wanted to know if you might be free to go away with me for the weekend some time."

"Let's not run before we can walk," Saffy told him; although inside she was exulting at the thought that this looked like becoming something serious.

By way of response, Marco leaned forward and clasped her hands. "Saffy, I know we've only known each other a week, and we haven't even slept together yet, but I can't help thinking that our parents may have inadvertently made the right choice in pushing us together. What do you say to us doing this properly? I don't mean marriage," he added hurriedly – "not yet, anyway; but maybe we should give things a try between the two of us and see how it works out. I'm getting too old for one-night stands: I want to settle down properly and see what it's like to have a relationship."

For a moment, Saffy wasn't sure whether to feel flattered or offended. On the one hand, Marco was as good as admitting that she would be suitable girlfriend material; on the other, he wasn't promising forever: it seemed more a case of trying her on for size, like a new pair of shoes, and wearing her for a week of two to make sure she didn't give him blisters.

"What if things don't work out?" she queried cautiously.

Marco shrugged. "We're both adults. If it doesn't work out, then it doesn't work out; but if we never try, we'll never know."

"And if it does work out?" she asked softly, almost holding her breath as she waited for his reply.

He looked intently into her eyes, still caressing her fingers with his own. "If out *does* work out, *cara*, then it will be the merger of a lifetime for both our families."

*

Neither of them wanted pudding after eating so well. "What about a Turkish coffee?" Saffy suggested, but Marco shook his head.

"Don't think I'm a coffee snob, but I prefer my own coffee at home." He grinned suddenly. "I have a state-of-the-art coffee machine *and* I grind my own beans. The kit cost a fortune, but it was worth it. The company even provides what they call a 'White Glove Service', where they send someone round to teach you how to use both machines once they've been delivered." He paused. "I can't cook; but my coffee's amazing."

"Sounds like I should give it a try, then," Saffy said, half-jokingly.

Marco looked at her. "No time like the present. Why don't I take you home and we can drop off *en route* at my place so you can sample the goods?"

"I really hope that wasn't a euphemism for something else," Saffy said severely as she pushed her chair away from the table and stood up, "or I'll be taking a taxi home on my own, Marco Benedetti!" Gazing at his crestfallen face, she relented. "Okay, I'll come back for a coffee – but I need to be home by midnight."

She left him to settle the bill whilst she went to the Ladies' Room; but, try as she might, she couldn't keep a small smile of satisfaction from her face.

Chapter Twelve

All the financial arrangements had been dealt with by the time Saffy returned. "Are you sure you're okay to drive?" she asked worriedly, remembering that Marco had been drinking beer with his meal.

Marco shook his head. "I had one Peroni, *cara*, that is all. I know I should have had Turkish beer in keeping with the food, but Italian beer is so much better. Anyway," he took her hand, "if I am to have you home by midnight, we had better not waste any more time."

Hand in hand, they strolled to the car park where, to Marco's relief, his Jag remained untouched.

"That's a bit clichéd, isn't it?" Saffy asked, when she saw Marco's car.

"Not at all." Marco seemed unruffled by her comment. "When I was a boy," he explained, "I used to read my father's car magazines and dream about all the exotic foreign cars I would buy when I was older." She had a brief image of him as a curly haired eight-year-old. "My first car was a Ferrari Spider – she was beautiful and very fast, but I still wanted a foreign car. When I came over to England three years ago as CEO of the new English branch of *Benedetti's*, I told my father I would need an English car - a right hand drive – if I was to be safe on the roads; and I also told him that Jaguar was the safest brand; and so my dream was finally realised."

"And are they the safest cars?" Saffy questioned curiously.

"Who cares? I got my Jag!" Marco opened the passenger door for her. "With extremely comfortable leather seats," he added proudly.

Saffy hid a smile. In some ways, Marco was still a little boy at heart. She found it most endearing.

Don't let yourself get too close! she warned herself as she slid herself into position and wrestled with the seatbelt. But it was already too late for that if she was going back to Marco's place now. She had a feeling that she wouldn't put up too much of a fight if he wanted her to stay past midnight.

As the car purred along the country roads, Saffy found herself studying Marco once more. Now that he had kissed her again, albeit briefly, she found herself longing for more of him, couldn't help wondering what his hands would feel like as they slipped her dress from her shoulders and caressed her body.

"A penny for your thoughts, *cara*."

"I was just thinking how good the food was tonight," she lied, not wanting to give him the satisfaction of knowing that she had been fantasising about him.

Marco nodded gravely whilst still keeping his eyes on the road.

"You have good taste, *cuore mio*! How did you know about that place?"

"I've been there before," she hedged, "with friends."

"Friends – or boyfriends?" The moonlight cast shadows on his face, making it hard for her to read his expression.

"Just friends." She deemed it prudent not to mention James by name.

"Then your friends have good taste also."

They were on an A road now, having left the built-up areas behind them. Marco gently increased the speed: Saffy saw the needle creep up to seventy, but the car was so smooth that she hadn't registered how fast they were going.

"Not long now."

Within minutes, they were approaching a huge, old fashioned building with heavy, iron gates. Marco tapped something on his key fob and the gates swung open, floodlights coming on simultaneously.

"It's all part of the security system," Marco explained. "These apartments have their own security guard too."

It seemed a million miles away from Saffy's little flat above the shop.

Marco followed the gravel driveway round the back of the building to a much smaller, modern looking edifice. "Each apartment has parking for two cars," he explained. "It's one of the big selling points of this place – that and the communal gym."

Smoothly, he pulled into a parking slot labelled '12A' and switched off the engine. "Come on – I'll show you around."

Leading her back to the imposing front doors of the main building, Marco fished out a keycard and held it in front of a metal grille. The doors swung open silently to reveal a sumptuous hallway-cum-lobby – almost like the Reception area of a grand London hotel, Saffy thought wonderingly – with squashy upholstered sofas and an impressive counter, behind which sat a uniformed figure.

"Evening, Joe." Marco nodded to the security guard.

"Good evening, Signor Benedetti." The guard acknowledged Saffy. "Evening, Miss."

Marco led the way through the lobby to an arresting Victorian style lift: the kind like an ornate cage. "How are you with enclosed spaces?" he asked her.

"Absolutely fine," Saffy replied promptly. She thought the lift was probably a similar size to her bathroom, but she didn't like to say so.

Within minutes, they had reached the third floor. Marco fished out his security card once more. Saffy felt this was like living in a hotel. It was all very plush and hi-tech, but she thought she preferred her cosy little flat.

The apartment, once she stepped inside, was a huge surprise. It was mostly open plan, with an enormous living room, three or four times the size of her own, boasting an entire row of floor to ceiling windows along one side. On the opposite wall, a large framed print of Kandinsky's *'Circles'* rubbed shoulders with a Bridget Riley and another piece of modern, abstract art that she couldn't identify. The paintings seemed tiny compared to the vast expanse of wall. A very avant-garde fireplace held what looked like a bundle of artificial twigs; Marco pressed a control pad which looked as if it belonged in a sci-fi film and the fireplace shimmered with light.

Everything seemed very modern, from the tiny spotlights that studded the ceiling to the hi-tech kitchen at one end of the living room. Marco's coffee machine had pride of place: a monstrosity that took up an entire work counter. There was a gigantic American style fridge-freezer in stainless steel and a shiny mini-range cooker which looked as if it had never been used. Peering inside the top oven, she saw that she was right: the instruction manual was still sitting inside it.

"Don't you do *any* cooking?" she asked him.

Marco shrugged helplessly. "There's a little café round the corner, about five minutes' walk away. I go there for brunch at the weekends, and they do a Sunday roast too. Most of the time, I either eat out or order takeaway. Anyway," his face suddenly brightened, "you didn't come here to eat so I've got nothing to worry about."

He walked over to the coffee machine and flicked a few switches. "How do you like it? I prefer a proper Italian espresso, but this baby can do other things too."

"Have you got any milk?" Saffy asked doubtfully. She normally chose a skinny latte in *Costa*.

Marco opened the fridge door. A rather sad looking piece of cheese and some tired tomatoes stared back at him pathetically. There was a two pint container of semi skimmed milk in the door. He took the lid off and sniffed it carefully. "I think this is okay – what do you think?"

Saffy winced at the sour smell. "This went off over a week ago," she told him, pointing to the Best Before date. Marco looked sheepish.

"Do you want me to see if any of the neighbours have got some milk?" he offered.

Saffy looked at her watch. "It's just gone ten, Marco. It's a bit late for anything like that."

"I'm sorry." Marco's expression had reverted to his little boy look. His eyes were full of apology.

"It's okay," she told him. "I'll just have a glass of water. Coffee would only keep me awake now anyway."

"Yes," Marco's tone was mischievous, "I seem to recall I promised to have you in bed before midnight …"

The room suddenly stilled. Saffy was aware of the beat of her own heart, of Marco moving towards her and taking her face in his hands. As his lips moved towards hers for the second time that evening, she abandoned herself to the moment and let herself drown in the feelings he evoked.

Some moments later, they pulled apart.

"Did you know," Marco's tone sounded conversational, but his pupils had dilated and his breathing seemed to be as rapid as hers, "that when two people kiss, they exchange DNA in their saliva? That's why you feel a bond with someone after you've become intimate. It's a scientific fact."

"Do you want to exchange more DNA?" Saffy murmured back. Marco's eyebrows shot up.

"Perhaps we should move this over to the sofa," he said at last. Saffy acquiesced, letting him propel her in the direction of an unfeasibly large behemoth of squishiness. Blissfully, she sank back into the cushions, letting Marco's mouth cover hers once more. As his hand began to glide over her shoulder and beneath her dress, she wondered, woozily, how far she would let him go this time.

*

A moment later, Marco shifted uncomfortably. Large though the sofa was, it didn't compare to the comfort of his bed – but would Saffy think he was trying to take things too quickly if he suggested a change of venue? She seemed far less experienced than most of the women he brought back here.

While he deliberated his next course of action, Saffy opened her eyes. "Can I use your bathroom?" she asked shyly, suddenly aware that she probably reeked of garlic after all that humus. Marco must have some mouthwash, she reasoned; and, while she was at it, she should check that her mascara hadn't run.

Marco reluctantly disentangled himself from her and stood up gingerly. "I'll show you where it is."

Opening the door at the far end of the room, he led her into what looked suspiciously like a master bedroom. Saffy panicked momentarily.

"The bathroom's *en-suite*," he explained, navigating her past a ridiculously wide bed with a cream leather headboard. "You need to walk through the dressing room," – *Marco had a dressing room?* Saffy thought with incredulity – "and the light switch is just to the left of the door."

He disappeared out of the bedroom, presumably to give her some privacy. She found herself pleasantly surprised by his sensitivity.

Taking advantage of the fact that she had been left alone, Saffy decided to take her time and look round properly. Both the bedroom and dressing room were far more tasteful than she would have expected. The bedroom, which must have been at least twenty feet wide, had built in bookcases, stuffed full of books in both English and Italian, either side of the outrageously opulent bed, which, she was glad to note, was furnished simply with a plain white duvet cover, set off by a black satin comforter and black and white cushions. There were built in drawers and wardrobes too, although why someone who lived alone needed so much cupboard space was a mystery to Saffy – especially when the dressing room boasted another double row of triple door wardrobes. There was an L-shaped set of drawers and small cupboards at one end of the dressing room, although it looked as if Marco used that as a home office because instead of the surfaces being covered with make-up and jewellery – which is how *she* would have utilised the space – there was an expensive looking laptop, flanked by a printer and several box files.

The bathroom, though, when she opened the door, made up for everything else by being gloriously tacky. A large jacuzzi bath sat atop several steps, adorned with gold taps in the shape of dolphins. Similar taps decorated the twin basins and the bidet. The floor and vanity unit tops were marble – they would be unbearably chilly in winter, she thought, shivering as she ran a finger over the smooth surface; and everything was in an unbecoming shade of *eau de nil*. As a final nod to the Hollywood glamour of yesteryear, the mirrors above both basins were surrounded by spotlights. All in all, it was a triumph of misguided style over substance.

How could anyone have such inexplicably bad taste? Saffy wondered as she hunted for mouthwash and inadvertently found a party-sized box of condoms. (The latter made her panic again; but then she consoled herself with the thought that, unlike her sister's boyfriend, at least Marco was responsible.)

*

Spraying herself liberally with the lemon air freshener she found in the cupboard under one of the basins (she hadn't thought to pop deodorant or perfume into her handbag before leaving her own flat), Saffy made her way back into the living room, where Marco was sipping a cup of espresso as he waited for her.

"Nice bathroom," she said cheekily.

Marco groaned.

"In my defence," he said a moment later, with as much dignity as he could muster, "the bathroom is the one room I haven't touched yet. This flat belonged to a footballer and his girlfriend before I moved in, and it took me ages to remove the 'bling' they had everywhere."

Saffy raised an eyebrow.

"Chandeliers in every room," Marco whispered. "A tiger print sofa and leopard print dining chairs! The kitchen cupboards were decorated in gold leaf, with crystal doorknobs, and they even had a little gold cherub as a light fitting, hovering over the marble breakfast bar with two miniature chandeliers in his hands!"

Saffy couldn't prevent herself from laughing at the horror in Marco's eyes as he relived the awful décor.

"Are you sure you don't want to leave the bathroom as it is, then?" she asked mischievously. "You have to admit it's a talking point ..."

"As soon as I have time, I am hiring a decent company to get rid of that travesty of a bathroom and replace it with something I can actually find relaxing," Marco promised her. He put his mug down abruptly. "But we are wasting time discussing my remodelling plans. I think we were doing something far more interesting before you disappeared ..."

Enfolding her in his arms once more, he began to kiss first her mouth, then her ear, then the side of her neck. Saffy felt herself dissolve into little spasms of pleasure: if Marco carried on like this, she would be unable to stop him doing anything he liked to her.

When he scooped her up a moment or two later and began to carry her into the bedroom, Saffy knew that this man was her destiny. He had effectively destroyed every one of her defences so that all she could think about was how much she wanted him – whether it was forever or only for this one night. He was just laying her carefully on the bed when the doorbell rang.

Damn it! Saffy thought with exasperation.

Chapter Thirteen

"Ignore it." Marco's voice sounded muffled as he busied himself once more with Saffy's neck. The ringing persisted.

Swearing softly, Marco sat up. "I'm sorry, *cara*. Whoever it is, I will send them away quickly and then we can resume where we left off."

She nodded, but the mood was already broken. As Marco made his way back towards the living room, Saffy asked herself whether this might not be for the best. She had been so carried away by desire that she had been on the verge of sleeping with Marco – and on only their second date!

Perhaps it was time she left. She stood up, feeling the softness of a quality bedroom carpet beneath her bare feet.

Quietly tiptoeing back to the living room to retrieve her shoes, she caught an unmistakably female voice as Marco opened his front door: "Not too late, am I?"

"Siân!" Marco sounded surprised to see her, whoever she was, but he could just be a better actor than Saffy had thought. "What are you doing here?"

Saffy froze, trying not to alert Marco to her presence. He still had his back to her and he was currently blocking the doorway, making it impossible for her to see what this Siân creature looked like. Was she a current girlfriend? Saffy wondered.

"You rushed off before we had time for a drink yesterday," Siân's tone oozed flirtation, "so I thought I'd bring a bottle over here now. I had a feeling you'd still be up."

"I …" Marco sounded awkward. "It's not a good time right now," he apologised.

"Don't worry, Marco – I'm leaving!"

Marco spun round at the sound of Saffy's voice, aware of what this must look like. "Saffy, this is one of my neighbours," he said feebly. "Siân, this is Saffy – my fiancée."

Siân pushed her way into the apartment and sized up her rival. Saffy did likewise, noting the other girl's flaming red hair, cropped to an elfin pixie-cut that suited her delicate bone structure and wide, green eyes. She was wearing far too much make up, Saffy thought distastefully, and far too few clothes! Siân's skirt skimmed her thighs, barely covering her bottom, and her sweater seemed to have shrunk in the wash since it revealed most of her midriff. A girl who turned up at a man's flat at that time of night, dressed like that and bearing alcohol, obviously had only one thing on her mind. Saffy wondered, uneasily, whether this were a regular occurrence and whether Siân ever spent the night in her own home.

"Congratulations, Marco." Siân's words sounded more like a challenge than a compliment. "You haven't mentioned a fiancée before," she added as an afterthought.

Marco gritted his teeth. Since he had spent no more than ten minutes or so in Siân's company the previous day – and most of that had involved him trying to work out what was wrong with her washing machine – obviously he hadn't said anything about Saffy; so why was Siân now trying to make it seem as if he'd been doing something underhand?

"I'm sure you two have a lot of catching up to do." Saffy's tone was icy cold as she fished her mobile out of her handbag and ordered an Uber. And to think that she had almost let Marco seduce her! "I'll wait downstairs for my taxi," she concluded.

"No!" Marco let out a strangled reply. "Siân can come back any time …" His voice tailed off as he realised he was only making things worse.

"Thank you for dinner," Saffy said politely but frostily, declining to kiss Marco again. "Nice to meet you, Siân."

She rushed out of the apartment before either of them could see the tears forming in her eyes.

*

Once Saffy had gone, Marco turned on Siân in disbelief. "What did you do that for?"

"Do what?"

She was watching him like a cat with a bird, ready to deliver a killing blow at any moment.

"You let Saffy think that there was something going on between us."

"Isn't there?" Siân came a little closer, thrusting out her chest in a provocative manner. "You're not the sort of man who likes being tied down, Marco – not unless it's part of something fun in the bedroom! Anyone can tell just looking round this place that you don't go in for cosy, homecooked dinners or nights snuggling up in front of the telly. Let's face it – what you've got here is a classy seduction pad, not a long-term nest!"

"I have to go!" Marco pushed Siân out of the way, grabbing his car keys and his mobile. His key card for the front door and the lobby was still in his trouser pocket. "I need to see if Saffy's waiting downstairs."

"Do you want me to come back later and tuck you into bed?" Siân called after him mockingly as he sprinted to the lift. She looked at the bottle of wine clutched in her hand – it would have to keep for later …

*

Saffy was still sitting in the foyer when Marco arrived. She gave a start when she saw him, hoping it wasn't obvious that she'd been crying.

Marco was too relieved to see her to notice that her eyes were slightly red-rimmed. "It's not what you think," he began, without preamble.

"What's not what I think?" Saffy was stalling for time.

"You know … Siân. I only met her for the first time yesterday, honest."

"Well, you seem to have made friends pretty quickly!" Saffy snapped. "Or does she make a habit of calling on all the neighbours late at night in little more than her underwear?"

"You're jealous …" Marco said in surprise. Saffy must like him more than she was letting on if she was making such a fuss about another woman.

"Of course I'm jealous!" she yelled back at him. "You were in the middle of kissing me when another woman turned up on your doorstep, obviously hoping for a bit of action herself! How else would you expect me to feel?"

"Saffy, *cara*," Marco tried to defuse the situation, "I didn't invite her round, if that's what you're thinking – and I certainly haven't kissed her – or done anything else to her," he added hurriedly. "Why do you think I introduced you as my fiancée? It was so she would know I am taken."

Saffy looked up at him, her lip quivering. "You swear you haven't slept with her?"

"I swear," he promised, dropping a kiss on the top of her head. "We have exchanged a few sentences, but that is all – no DNA or other bodily fluids."

She looked at him sharply.

Marco sighed. "Saffy, why would I want anyone else now that I have met you? Siân is a very sexy woman, but she is not Sapphire Vendrini. I want you and you only, *bella mia*. You have to trust me."

"But those things you said at my parents' party …" she reminded him.

He sighed again. "I was showing off. I went to that party to please my own parents, thinking that I would meet some boring English rose that I would never have to see again – and then I saw *you*, and without knowing who you were, I knew that I had to get to know you." He groaned comically. "You have ruined me, Saffy: I used to be a ladies' man, and now all I can think of is you!"

He bent down and kissed her very slowly on the lips. "Either come back upstairs with me, or let me drive you home."

"It's too late," she said softly as the security cameras focused on a car driving through the gates. "My Uber's here."

Rising to her feet, she was surprised when he clasped her in a fierce hug. "Come back again, little one," he murmured in her ear. "My bed will seem empty without you."

"That's your fault for choosing such a massive bed, then," she scolded him, a twinkle in her eye. "It's nearly eleven, Marco. I really do need to go. Thanks for a wonderful evening."

It hadn't ended quite as he'd planned, Marco mused as he watched Saffy climb into her taxi, but at least she was still speaking to him.

Chapter Fourteen

It wasn't until Wednesday morning that Saffy realised she couldn't find her favourite bracelet. It wasn't worth much, but it had sentimental value, being one of the first items of jewellery she had made, several years before going off to university to learn how to do it professionally.

The last time she had worn it was when she went over to James' and Connor's the previous Saturday; she hoped it hadn't fallen off in the cab on her way home.

Her phone beeped whilst she was having breakfast. She knew, without looking, that it would be another text from Marco. He had begun texting her first thing every morning, as soon as he woke up (he was a later riser than she), and the two of them would exchange texts every couple of hours throughout the day, work permitting. She hadn't seen him since she left his building on Monday evening, but he had asked her to trust him where Siân was concerned and so she had tried not to think about the scantily clad redhead trying to get her claws into Marco.

"*Buongiorno*, Saffy, *luce dei miei occhi!*" the text read.

Saffy grinned involuntarily. *Buongiorno* was one of the few Italian phrases she knew, despite her heritage. Her mother had insisted on both her daughters growing up speaking English at home, having heard horror stories from other parents who had tried raising their children bilingually only to find that they struggled with both languages. She had told Antonio that the girls could learn Italian at school – but the private school that both had attended from the age of three – and where Sophie was now, incidentally, finishing off her A levels – had only offered French at Key Stages 1 and 2 with additional Spanish or Russian later on.

Since their father was able to get by more than adequately in his no longer broken English – and one would hope so, too, after twenty-five years in England! - Saffy had made little effort to learn more than a few basic phrases in Italian which she could trot out if any of her father's family visited. *È bella rivederia zia Francesca* and *Come stai?* had stood her in good stead thus far, even if her father's elderly aunt Francesca, who spoke no English at all, usually went off into a completely unintelligible stream of excited Italian so that Saffy was forced to nod politely without having a clue what she was agreeing to.

She was thankful now that she'd installed the 'reverso' app onto her phone so that she could translate Marco's messages. *'Bella mia'* was 'my beautiful one' – her father used that a lot when addressing Eleanor – and *'cara'* meant 'dear one' or 'darling'. She held her finger down to copy Marco's latest offering and discovered that this morning she was 'the light of his eyes'. It sounded ridiculously over the top, but she was still smiling when she arrived at work half an hour later.

*

"You're in a good mood this morning!" James commented as she entered the shop. "Finally getting some, are we?"

Saffy blushed.

"I haven't seen Marco since Monday evening," she reminded him.

"You mean when that trollop tried to gatecrash your brief encounter," James sniggered, having had the full story from Saffy. "Tell me, did Marco actually have an encounter with your briefs, Saff, or didn't he get that far?"

"Do you have to drag everything down into the gutter?" Saffy asked him despairingly.

James considered her question. "Well, I don't *have* to," he said at last, "but it's so much more fun when I do!"

"I don't suppose I left my bracelet at your place on Saturday, did I?" Saffy asked next, trying to change the subject. "You know, the one with all the polished stones?"

James was suddenly serious. "You haven't lost it, have you? That bracelet's a work of art!"

"I know I was wearing it when we were eating sushi," Saffy replied, wrinkling her nose as she tried to remember, "and I *think* it was still on my wrist when Bruce Willis killed Alan Rickman, but I can't be sure."

"I'll get Connor to help me look for it," James promised. "By the way, speaking of jewellery, how's Lover Boy's commission coming on? You've only got two and a half days left."

"I think I'm on track," Saffy said reflectively. "Yesterday, I did the halo setting and the three gem settings; today I should be aligning the cups and soldering everything together. If I manage to smooth it off today, I can mount the stones tomorrow."

"You always did love this side of things, didn't you?" James didn't often reminisce, but, when he did, he often sounded wistful. "Do you think I should have stuck it out, Saff, instead of jacking it in after three weeks and doing business instead?"

"You said your fingers were too big for all the fiddly work," Saffy reminded him gently. "Anyway, I'm glad you *did* switch to business: one of us needs to know how to balance the books and keep the accountant happy!"

"When are you seeing Marco again?" James was prone to switch conversational topics suddenly, leaping from one to another and back again like a frog on a lilypond.

"He said he was working late the rest of this week. They've got a big order to get out apparently."

Saffy tried to sound casual, but James could tell she was worried.

"Not all men are Malcolms, you know, Saff," he told her, watching her hand shake as she tidied a tray of rings that didn't need rearranging.

"I know. I'm probably just being silly." Saffy looked despondently at the space on her finger where a ring would have been had it been a *real* engagement and sighed. Marco was texting her every day and had sent more flowers yesterday: she knew she should feel grateful for that. Nevertheless, she could not entirely ignore the growing feeling of disquietude that gnawed away at her as she sat in the workroom, making a ring for a woman that Marco valued more highly than her.

*

In his own way, Marco was feeling as frustrated as Saffy. After the success of Monday evening – well, it had been successful right up until the part where Siân had arrived, he thought ferociously – he would have liked nothing better than to have taken Saffy out again the following evening, and the next, when hopefully they would have managed to consummate their relationship with more success.

Relationship. He tried the word on for size, finding that it no longer scared him the way it used to. He could be himself with Saffy, he decided. Usually, he played up the Italian Lothario image, almost caricaturing himself as an arrogant, overconfident ladies' man – he found it generally had the desired effect on women. Years of practice had honed his seduction technique as well as his performance: he found he could run through the motions now almost without thinking what he was doing: more and more frequently, he found himself switching to autopilot, pressing all the right buttons in the requisite order, so that he was able to get a woman from nought to sixty in almost no time at all.

Saffy was different, though. He found himself wanting to savour every moment with her, to learn what *she* wanted and not just employ his standard bag of tricks. The way she responded to him drove him wild: she made him feel as if he was the only man who had ever made her come alive.

He tried to concentrate on the board meeting that was going on around him, but it was no use: forming his face into what he hoped was a serious expression, Marco abandoned himself to a *very* satisfactory fantasy about his pretend fiancée.

*

The ring was finally complete. Saffy gave it one last polish, wondering yet again whose hand it would grace. Slipping it onto her own wedding finger, she admired how the two perfectly cut diamonds twinkled next to the polished sapphire, her namesake. Whoever the recipient was, she was a very lucky lady.

"Nice work!" James said approvingly when she carried it into the shop to show him. It was almost six and dusk was just beginning to overwhelm the twilight; even so, the ring sparkled as if sunlight had hit it. "I think that's your best one yet!"

"Do you really think it's okay?" Saffy asked anxiously. For some bizarre reason, even though the ring was for a possible love-rival, she wanted Marco to be impressed with her craftsmanship.

"Put it this way," James murmured, "if someone offered *me* a ring like that, I'd say yes to anything – regardless of whether they were male or female!"

His reply did nothing to lift Saffy's spirits. *What have I done?* she thought in horror. *I've just made Marco irresistible to another woman!*

She wondered whether it was too late to cancel the commission …

Chapter Fifteen

Marco arrived promptly the next day, just before twelve. He eyed the ring critically.

"You have done well," he commented at last. "I think the lady in question will not be disappointed." He hesitated. "Do you have a box for it?"

Wordlessly, Saffy fetched one of the customised ring boxes that bore *Jo Bangles'* name on the lid and carefully placed her work of art inside it.

"I hope she appreciates it," she said, a little stiffly.

Marco looked at her. "Are you free this evening?"

Since Saffy's plans currently involved watering her plants and cleaning her kitchen worktops, she replied in the affirmative.

"Good." Marco was wasting no words. "I would have taken you out now, to express my appreciation for the excellent job you have done, but, alas, I have a business lunch. I will return at seven and we will go for food then – unless you would rather eat later?"

He was learning, Saffy thought grudgingly. "No," she told him, "seven's fine. I'll see you then."

"Well!" James uttered, once Marco had left, "you must be doing something right!"

"What do you mean?" Saffy was puzzled.

"Darling, he couldn't take his eyes off you the whole time he was here. Don't tell me you weren't aware of it!"

She'd been so intent on showing him the ring and hoping he wouldn't like it, that she'd been totally oblivious to anything else.

"So what?" she responded crossly. "He's just spent thousands of pounds on a ring for someone else!"

"You've got to let it go," James advised her. "What if the ring's a goodbye present for a woman he's just dumped?"

Saffy looked at him witheringly.

"Marco strikes me as the sort of man who probably gives all his exes a diamond handshake," James continued blithely.

"You're not helping," Saffy warned.

She was out of sorts for the rest of the day, only cheering up slightly when James suggested she should order all of the most expensive things on the menu, regardless of whether or not she liked them, just to show Marco she wasn't a pushover.

*

Seven o'clock arrived and, with it, Marco. He looked tired, explaining that he was feeling frazzled after an intense week of negotiations with several prestigious companies who were potential new clients. "I am looking forward to an evening of normal conversation," he sighed. "Since I saw you for dinner on Monday, I have spent every night extolling the virtues of our bespoke computer systems to one firm after another."

"What makes your systems so special?" Saffy asked as they walked out to Marco's car, realising as she did so that if she was letting him drive her to the restaurant, she would have to let him bring her home afterwards. Well, she would cross that bridge when she came to it.

"It's partly the quality of the components," Marco began, opening the car door for her and leaning over to help her with her seat belt, "but mostly the aftercare service we provide: we're available 24/7 if anything goes wrong and, unlike lots of companies, we don't do it all over the phone: we send specialist technicians round to fix any errors on site."

"How did your lady friend like her present?" Saffy changed the subject abruptly. All this talk of computers was making her head spin.

"I haven't had the chance to give it her yet," Marco punched something into the SatNav and pulled away smoothly, "but I think she'll be pleasantly surprised."

It wasn't long before they were pulling up at a familiar looking bistro. Saffy's heart sank: this was where Malcolm's wife had turned up and set her straight.

"I haven't been here before," Marco was saying as he gallantly held her door open for her and waited for her to alight, "but several people I work with have recommended it."

A sick feeling arose at the back of Saffy's throat. What if some of those people had been present when Janine gatecrashed the meal? It was all highly embarrassing.

Marco seemed unaware of her discomfort. Taking her by the hand, he led her inside. Saffy was relieved that the waiter didn't seem to recognise her.

Sinking into her seat, she scanned the room quickly, making sure that Malcolm wasn't there with another of his floozies. (Not that she had been a floozy herself!) All seemed safe. As the waiter lit their candle, Saffy started to relax.

They dined on homemade pate with a wonderful rustic bread, followed by duck with cherries and the best fondant potatoes Saffy had ever tasted. Although the food was excellent, they took ages to eat it, punctuating their meal with humorous anecdotes and snippets of trivia. It was wonderful to be at this stage, Saffy thought dreamily, and to have so much to discover about each other.

Wiping the side of his mouth with his napkin, Marco looked at her. "Do you have room for dessert?"

Saffy shook her head reluctantly. "I'm absolutely stuffed! That food was amazing!" And how wonderful to get through all of it without an irate wife turning up!

"Coffee, then?" Marco didn't seem to want to leave.

"I thought you only liked your own coffee from your special machine," she teased him.

Marco grinned back. "There's a first time for everything. Maybe I just don't want this evening to end."

How could such a corny line make her feel so ecstatic?

"I'll take a hot chocolate then," she told him, having spotted it on the menu earlier.

Marco pulled a face but ordered it anyway.

The waiter returned a few moments later, bearing a large demi-tasse of hot chocolate and something covered with a while cloth which he placed in front of Saffy.

"What's this?" she asked in surprise.

"House speciality," Marco said smoothly. "I thought you might like it."

Saffy removed the cloth to reveal a Jo Bangles box sitting on a dessert plate.

"Go on, open it!" He seemed as excited as a little boy on Christmas morning.

Saffy slowly opened the box and gazed at the ring – *her* ring – winking away at her. "That's the commission I made for you," she said stupidly.

Marco plucked the ring from the box and slipped it over Saffy's finger. "This isn't necessarily an engagement ring," he said hurriedly. "It will help further the pretence for our parents, and it will also show other women – like Siân – that I am no longer a free agent." As her eyes grew wider, he continued softly, "And if this *does* work out between us, then you will have the satisfaction of knowing that I cared enough to buy the very best: the perfect ring to symbolise what I hope will be the perfect relationship."

"This ring was for me all along?" She was still having difficulty believing it.

"Saffy, *cara*, there hasn't been anyone else since I met you. I hoped you would realise that by now."

"Thank you," she whispered, gazing up at him with shining eyes. "It's beautiful."

"It was made by a very talented designer!" Marco winked at her. "Now, drink up your chocolate before it goes cold."

*

Saffy was silent on the drive home. She still couldn't believe that Marco had spent the best part of ten thousand pounds on a ring for her after knowing her for less than a fortnight.

A sudden thought struck her. Would he now expect her to sleep with him, just because he'd given her an expensive present? What did one do under such circumstances?

They were home already. Marco turned off the engine and looked at her expectantly. "Are you inviting me in for coffee?"

"Maybe next time." She was staring straight ahead, not wanting to meet his eyes. "If I let you in now, Marco, and – *something happens* – I wouldn't want you to think it was just because you've given me jewellery." She swallowed hard. "And it would make *me* feel like you'd bought me."

"I see." Marco's face was impassive. "A good night kiss before you go?" he suggested.

She turned towards him and his mouth crashed down on hers as it had done so many times in the past fortnight. Drowning in desire, she clung to him. In the light of the streetlamp overhead, his eyes glittered like the diamonds in her ring. Gasping for breath, she pulled away.

"Are you *quite* sure you don't want me to come in with you?"

His hand traced the back of her neck, calming, soothing.

"Better not." She looked up and made eye contact once more. "Thanks for a wonderful evening – and for my ring."

One last kiss and then she was out of the door and fumbling for her key. He watched until she had disappeared out of sight, but it was a good ten minutes or more before he was able to drive away.

Chapter Sixteen

As he drove away, Marco found himself respecting Saffy's decision. He was impressed that she was honest enough not to want to confuse gratitude with desire – many women in the past had slept with him for a lot less than a diamond ring - although he would have been quite happy had she let him accompany her upstairs after all.

No, Saffy was worth waiting for, he thought now as he navigated the winding country roads back to his own home. He had a good feeling about this: she was straightforward: what you saw was what you got. It made a refreshing change from the type of woman he normally dated: everyone these days seemed to be playing some sort of game.

Speaking of games, Siân was lingering in the foyer when he arrived.

"Marco!" Her voice sounded surprised, but he wasn't convinced. "No fiancée tonight?" she pressed him.

"I've just taken Saffy home," Marco muttered. "We're both very tired."

"It's a shame you couldn't snuggle up together, then." Siân's eyes looked wide and innocent but Marco didn't trust her. "I could bring that wine round now, since you're on your own," she continued.

"Not tonight, Siân." Marco decided to be brutal. "I love Saffy," he told her.

Siân let out a low, husky laugh. "I love cheese – but it doesn't stop me enjoying other food as well ..."

She was still laughing as he turned and headed for the lift.

*

Within the safety of his own apartment, the enormity of Marco's words finally sank in. Had he really told Siân he loved Saffy? It was true, he realised: the way he felt about her was more than just intense physical attraction: he loved spending time with her, wanted to know all about her. Was his frozen heart finally thawing? Had Saffy managed to melt the icy wall he'd built around himself ever since Nadia had almost destroyed him?

Glancing at his watch, he saw that it was not too late to send Saffy a text. "*Bouna notte*, little one," he typed. "Hope you sleep well. M x"

Seconds later, a reply pinged back. "You too, S x"

Maybe their fathers had made the right decision after all, Marco decided as he crawled into his wide, empty bed, because, at this moment in time, he thought Sapphire Vendrini was the best thing that had ever happened to him.

*

Marco usually rose early on a Saturday to hit the gym before the other residents did. This morning, though, he decided on a lie-in, getting up only to switch on his coffee machine. Carrying the hot, bitter liquid back to bed, he crawled back under the duvet and imagined how life would be if Saffy were there with him. He should definitely stock up on milk and other essentials, just in case he managed to persuade her to come back here again; although, judging by the way she had responded to him – last night *and* last Monday – she wouldn't need much convincing …

When the doorbell rang, some twenty minutes later. He ignored it. It was probably only Siân, with some new pretext to get him into bed. He grinned at the sudden change in his circumstances: several weeks ago, he would have laughed if anyone had told him he'd be turning down no-strings-attached sex with an alluring temptress.

He must be popular this morning because, a little later, his mobile rang. A breathless Saffy gabbled incoherently at him. "Thank goodness you're in. I was afraid you'd be out."

"Saffy," he explained patiently, "you have called my mobile. It doesn't matter where I am."

"I've just had a phone call from Eleanor," she continued. "She and Dad have invited us for Sunday lunch tomorrow – I think it's meant to be our first official event as an engaged couple …" Her voice tailed off: she was obviously worried that he would feel pressured into something he didn't want to do.

As a matter of fact, Marco had a sudden longing for a family Sunday. He had been in the UK for three years now but he still missed his mother's home cooking, his father's jokes and his brother's little girls – not to mention the lazy weekends they all used to spend together.

"Marco?" Saffy hoped she hadn't scared him off.

"That sounds wonderful," he said heartily. There was a pause. "And what about today?" he asked her next.

"*What* about today?" Saffy sounded puzzled.

"Are you free to do something with me?" he asked her softly.

"I wish I was." She sounded genuinely regretful. "I've promised to go shopping with Sophie, and then we're going to see a film."

"So I will have to wait. Should I book you now for next Saturday, or is that day already filled too?"

"No, you can have me to yourself next Saturday." He could almost hear the smile in her voice.

"*Ciao, bella.*"

"See you tomorrow, Marco."

He was looking forward to it already.

*

Sophie stared at her sister in horror. "I can't keep those in my bag! What if Eleanor saw them?"

Saffy's frustration grew. "It's a packet of condoms, Soph – not a gimp outfit! And I'd feel much happier about you seeing Adam if I thought you were being careful."

"Can't you look after them for me?" Sophie asked hopefully.

"That's hardly practical," Saffy pointed out. "Do you really want to make a detour to my flat every time you're in the mood? Why can't you keep them in your car, or hide them in your makeup bag or something?"

"We won't get the chance to do it again for ages anyway," Sophie grumbled. "Adam's parents hardly ever go out and I'm supposed to be staying in on school nights until I've finished all my exams. It'd be much easier if I knew someone with her own flat …" she ended pointedly.

"You are *not* using my flat as a secret love nest," Saffy said severely.

"Well, you're the one putting condoms in the basket," Sophie swiftly retorted. "Bit of a mixed message there, don't you think?"

Saffy felt exasperated. It had been Sophie's idea in the first place to pop into Boots – she wanted to trawl the make-up counters for anything on sale – but they were already at loggerheads.

"Let's have a coffee," she suggested. "There's a *Costa* a few doors away."

"Only if you're paying," Sophie said promptly. "And if you buy me a muffin."

It wasn't until they were sitting at a table and Saffy was raising her coffee mug that Sophie noticed the ring.

"Good grief, Saff!" she exclaimed in surprise. "That's gorgeous! Did Marco give it you?"

Saffy gave her a diluted version of how Marco had commissioned her to make the ring without telling her who it was for.

"That's so romantic!" Sophie's eyes were shining. "He got you to design your own engagement ring! If Adam ever proposes to me, I want you to make a ring just like that one for him to give me."

Privately, Saffy thought it unlikely that the young couple would last much longer than the rest of their time in the sixth form, but she deemed it prudent not to say so.

They were about halfway through their coffee when Sophie let out a sudden squeal of surprise. "Adam! What are *you* doing here?"

The young man Saffy remembered from the party stood there shyly, looking somewhat embarrassed. "I was just out shopping," he said finally. "I saw you through the window as I was walking past."

Since they were sitting well towards the back of the room, this sounded most unlikely. The two of them must have planned this beforehand, Saffy thought grimly. When she got Sophie on her own, she would throttle her!

Her conscience pricked her as she remembered thinking the same thing just a week ago, during the awkward telephone conversation she'd had when she was at James' and Connor's. She hated lying to anyone, especially her step-mother, who took her maternal duties very seriously. It had been bad enough letting her father and Eleanor think that she and Marco were getting married because they were genuinely in love, when all she had really been trying to do was to stop Sophie getting into trouble.

The problem was, Saffy had always looked out for Sophie. Many were the times over the years when she had ended up taking the blame for Sophie's various crimes: to this day, Eleanor still thought Saffy had broken the cut glass bowl that had been a favourite wedding present, when the truth was that Sophie had been learning to juggle and had a bit of a mishap.

"I know," Sophie said now as if the idea had just occurred to her, "why don't you join us for the rest of the day? We can go and look at sheet music together in *'Perfect Pitch'*. And Saff and I were going to see a film too – you know, that one you said you wanted to see."

And now *she* would have to play gooseberry to the pair of them for the rest of the day! Saffy thought crossly. Sophie really was the limit!

*

By the time Sophie dropped Saffy back at her flat, towards early evening, their relationship was decidedly strained. The two lovebirds had spent their entire time together being nauseatingly couple-y, culminating in a rather public snog-fest in the luxury seats at the back of the cinema. Saffy was annoyed, to say the least. She and Sophie normally enjoyed their days out together, but the addition of Adam had completely changed the dynamic, making Saffy feel superfluous to requirements. She should have done something with Marco after all.

Her pulse quickened as she thought about a particular something that Marco did very well indeed. Maybe she shouldn't be too hard on Sophie, she mused: after all, if the positions had been reversed and they had bumped into Marco and not Adam, she felt sure that she would have behaved just as disgracefully in the cinema as Sophie had with her own boyfriend.

"Thanks for everything, Saff," Sophie said earnestly as her sister climbed out of the car. She blushed as she continued, "I know you've worked out that we didn't exactly bump into Adam by chance, but I couldn't see any other way of getting to spend a Saturday with him. You know what Dad and Eleanor are like."

"I appreciate you wanting to spend time together," – Saffy chose her words carefully – "but it would have been nice if you'd asked instead of just engineering it all."

"At least you know we didn't get up to anything we shouldn't," Sophie joked. It was true: Saffy had resolutely made Sophie take Adam home first, before dropping her off. She wondered now if all her weekends for the foreseeable future would be spent chaperoning her little sister.

"I'll see you tomorrow," she said now as she located her door key and prepared to wrestle with the rather unco-operative Yale lock.

"Saff ..." Sophie was suddenly serious once more.

"What is it?"

"You won't tell Dad and Eleanor about Adam, will you?"

"No," Saffy sighed, "I won't say anything. But as soon as your A levels are over," she added, "I really think you should sit down and be honest with them both."

Chapter Seventeen

Marco was surprised by how nervous he felt as he prepared to meet Saffy's relatives the following day. It wouldn't be the first time he saw them, of course: he had met Antonio Vendrini and his wife briefly, at the party; but that was totally different to spending an entire afternoon with them, with only Saffy and her sister for protection. It suddenly mattered that he made a good impression.

He dressed carefully, as was his habit, taking special care to come across as someone hardworking yet sober – good son-in-law material, he thought wryly. The navy suit he finally settled on was one of *Enrico Monti's* finest and he teamed it with a crisp cotton shirt in blue and white stripes and a burgundy silk tie. His hand shook slightly as he tied a Hanover Knot – this was ridiculous: it wasn't a job interview, for goodness' sake!

It certainly felt like one though, during the first fifteen uncomfortable minutes when he and Saffy were sitting in her parents' conservatory, sipping aperitifs and admiring Eleanor's Japanese garden.

"So, Marco …" Antonio's voice still held a trace of an Italian accent, much like Marco's, although the younger man had been in the country far less time than his prospective father-in-law. "Your papa tells me you are making a good job of running *Benedetti's* in London," he continued. "Tell me, what do you see as your main strengths as a businessman?"

Immediately, Marco launched into his stock response: good instincts, determination, the drive to succeed.

"Yes, yes," Antonio sounded impatient, "all that is a given, no? But what if you were not working for your father but for someone else? Would you still put your heart and soul into it if you were working for … *Vendrini's*, for example? Or would you find a way to merge the two companies?"

Marco had done his homework. He knew that Antonio Vendrini had started off delivering pizzas for a well-known chain when he had first come over from Italy at the age of twenty-six. Realising that people would always prefer to have things delivered to their door rather than go out and collect them in person, he had set up a delivery company of his own: *'Vendrini's – no job too small!'* the slogan had run. In the days before the internet had truly taken off, he had built up a client list of elderly ladies or harassed mothers, who had been happy to pay a small fee for having their groceries collected by someone else. He had delivered restaurant food too; then, when someone had asked whether he could transport furniture, had added the words *'or too large'* to his mission statement.

Six months later, he had recruited three more drivers, bought a removal van and a second Ford Transit, and was the official courier for a number of companies in the local Business Park. Two years after that, he had a whole fleet of vehicles, an entire team of drivers and an official office next door to one of his major clients. There had been several interested parties offering to buy him out over the years, but Antonio had always declined. The business was his first baby: he couldn't bear to give her away to another man.

"I would start by making *Vendrini's* the sole courier for *Benedetti's UK*," he said slowly. "We currently use *Fast Lane* – the Italian side takes care of international shipping; but I know *Vendrini's* prides itself on the personal touch. If we had a last-minute order, for example, I am sure that *Vendrini's* could deliver on time, no matter how late in the day it was."

He paused and looked at Saffy's father expectantly, exuding a confidence he only half felt. It had taken him the best part of the three years he had been running the UK side of the company to learn what their customers prioritised, and speedy, efficient delivery was high on the list. It would be a gamble to change couriers now, but he trusted *Vendrini's*.

Antonio was listening intently. "You are right," he mused. "We are a name associated with reliability, as are you. You would add something to your website, no? 'All our systems are delivered by *Vendrini and Sons*, the UK's favourite courier service.' And we would have your name on our site too: 'In partnership with *Benedetti's*: the leading supplier of internet systems.' Or whatever other words that you deem fit."

Turning to Saffy, he gave her a wide grin. "See what your fiancé has done, *piccina mia*! We have not even sat down at the table and already he has negotiated a business deal!"

Placing an arm around his future son-in-law's shoulder, Antonio began to steer Marco out of the room. "You will join me in my study and we will discuss this in more detail." They left the room before Saffy had time to object.

*

The meal itself was turning out to be far more enjoyable than Saffy had expected. Her father and Marco seemed to have bonded over more than just business: Antonio was now extolling the virtues of his golf club and urging Marco to become a member.

"You will need something to do when Saffy and her sister are spending an entire Saturday shopping," he declared enthusiastically, "and what better way to relax than a few rounds of golf and an enjoyable couple of hours in the bar afterwards?"

Meanwhile, at the other end of the table, Eleanor was trying to get Saffy to talk wedding venues. "I had a lovely spa break at a country house hotel not far from here," she was saying. "They do wedding packages and there's a tiny church in the grounds which would be ideal for the ceremony."

"It's a bit soon to be thinking about anything like that," Saffy said hurriedly.

"But it really isn't!" Eleanor protested. "These things usually have a two year waiting list. You should at least go and look at it and see whether you think it's suitable."

As Marco looked up from his chicken, she appealed to him. "Marco, I was just telling Saffy that the two of you should check out Latimer House for your wedding. It's a beautiful place with stunning views. I think you'd like it."

"I haven't heard of this place before," Marco muttered. "What do you think, *cara*?" he asked, addressing Saffy directly.

"I've already told Eleanor we're not thinking about details yet." Saffy tried to sound casual, but there was a wasps' nest of agitation inside her. Things had been going so well with Marco: she hoped Eleanor's comment wasn't going to make him panic.

But, strangely enough, Marco seemed keen on the idea. "We were planning a day out together next Saturday," he told Eleanor. "Perhaps this would be a good place for us to visit."

"We should all go!" Eleanor's face lit up at the idea. "The two of you can see what you think of the facilities; we can have a meal in the restaurant; and then you and Antonio can have a game of golf whilst the girls and I use the spa."

"Is there a golf course?" Antonio asked at the same time Sophie burst out, "What? You want me to come too?"

Golfing was available at several nearby clubs, all within a few miles of the estate, Eleanor told them knowledgeably – one of her friends was a seasoned golf widow and often booked a weekend in the spa whilst her husband was making use of the courses in Chesham or Chalfont St Giles. As for Sophie, Eleanor looked at her with concern, surely she deserved a break from all her studying? It would do her good to forget about A levels for a day and spend time with her family.

Sophie, however, was adamant that she wasn't going, pleading an extended essay that needed to be finished within the next ten days. In the end, Eleanor agreed that Sophie could stay at home on her own – which, in real terms, probably meant that she would sneak off to spend the day with Adam instead, Saffy thought.

After this, the conversation turned to Marco's family in Italy, with Eleanor wanting to know all about his little nieces. "In a way, it's a shame they're in Milan," she sighed. "When you and Saffy start having children of your own, their cousins will be too far away for them to play with."

Saffy almost choked on her food: it had been bad enough that Eleanor was making them look at wedding venues – before she and Marco had even decided whether they liked each other enough to have a relationship; but mentioning babies was just the sort of thing to make any man decide to cut his losses and run for the hills.

Marco looked startled at Eleanor's comment but rose to the occasion admirably. "Of course, I would like nothing better than to make lots of beautiful babies with my equally beautiful Sapphire," – Saffy blushed uncontrollably at these words – "but that is something for the future, no?"

As the conversation resumed, he took the opportunity to murmur, "But we could start practising straight away, if you like," in Saffy's ear.

It was certainly a tempting prospect.

It wasn't until much later that Saffy and Marco finally managed to escape to the garden for a bit of 'alone time'. By now, Saffy's head was in a whirl: far from being put off by her family, Marco seemed to have embraced them: he had even tolerated her father's terrible jokes.

"I'm sorry Eleanor's been so full on," she said abruptly, once they were put of earshot of the house.

Marco looked puzzled.

"You know – all the wedding talk." She paused. "We don't have to go to that country house next weekend – I'll tell her we have other plans."

"And what if I want to go?" Marco asked softly. "I would very much like to take you there," he added a moment later, investing the words with a double meaning. "Do you think they have four poster beds?"

Saffy swallowed nervously. "I don't know if I'm ready for that, yet, Marco."

His response was to cup her face in his hands and kiss her slowly and languorously on the mouth. "You will definitely be ready," he promised her. "I will see to that." His fingers entwined themselves in her hair. "I've waited far too long already," he breathed, in a voice drenched with desire. "I have to have you, *cara* – and I have to have you soon."

She was helpless to resist as his hands began to slide over her shoulders and down her back …

"Saffy!" Eleanor's voice carried across the lawn, breaking the spell woven by Marco's kisses.

Reluctantly, Saffy disentangled herself, feeling slightly embarrassed to have been caught canoodling by her stepmother.

"I've just had a wonderful idea," Eleanor began, without preamble. "Have you ever been to Ivinghoe Beacon, Marco?"

Marco shook his head.

"It's about fifteen miles away from here," Eleanor continued, her eyes sparkling. "It's run by the National Trust, so there's a visitor centre and a tearoom. It would make another wonderful day out." She paused for breath.

"But we're all going to see Latimer House next Saturday," Saffy reminded her, secretly thinking of Marco's proposition.

"So, what's to stop us spending Sunday together as well?" Eleanor demanded. "You can both come back here with us for the evening, after we've been to Latimer house, and Saffy can sleep in her old bedroom and you can have one of the guest rooms, Marco."

Saffy glanced quickly at Marco, who did not look at all impressed by the idea of separate rooms.

"Why don't we just do Latimer House next weekend and leave the walk for another time," she suggested; but, to her surprise, Marco seemed to be on Eleanor's side.

"That sounds like an excellent plan," he said smoothly, adding as a quick post script in Saffy's ear, "and I will enjoy the challenge of sneaking into your bedroom late at night, when everyone else is asleep!"

Saffy didn't think there was much hope of that: she and Sophie had grown up with attic bedrooms and a shared bathroom in between, the premise being that they could make as much noise as they liked at the top of the house without disturbing their father and Eleanor. The rooms were charmingly quirky, built under the eaves with slanting ceilings and original wooden beams, but the restricted ceiling height meant that each room was equipped with just one narrow single bed and she was sure that this would complicate any chance of a romantic encounter.

Eventually, Eleanor left them to their own devices, returning to the house to make tea and coffee.

"Where were we?" Marco murmured, reaching for her once more.

Saffy tried to lose herself in the moment, but she was unable to recapture the passion she'd felt earlier, her mind too unsettled by Eleanor's plans for them both. Everything seemed to be moving far too quickly. She was surprised that Marco didn't think so too.

"Doesn't it bother you?" she asked now, pulling away from him.

He looked puzzled.

"My family taking over," she explained. "They're just wading in and deciding everything for us – or, at least, Eleanor is."

Marco sighed. "Saffy, you were the one who decided we should pretend to be engaged. Can you blame them for being excited?"

"No, but …" She bit her lip absentmindedly, trying to find the right words. "I don't want them to scare you away," she said at last. "You and me getting to know each other is one thing, but it's above and beyond the call of duty to expect you to spend your weekends with my family."

"You forget that my own family is over eight hundred miles away," he reminded her. "It has been very lonely for me since I moved to the UK, Saffy."

"What, even with all your Tinder conquests?" she retorted, unable to keep the acerbic sting from her voice.

"That was before I knew you," he said simply. "Surely you did not expect me to live like a monk since being here?"

*

Of course she hadn't, and that was part of the problem, Saffy reflected later that evening, once she was safely back in her little flat: Marco had boasted, when he met her, of the numerous women he had bedded; how could she, Saffy, compete with any of these faceless creatures who were probably as skilled at lovemaking as she was at making jewellery? Marco obviously expected her to know what she was doing: it would be highly embarrassing to have to admit to him that she was completely inexperienced.

He had offered to drive her home from her parents' house at the end of the afternoon, but she had declined, claiming that she needed to talk to Sophie. She *had* wanted to warn her sister not to misbehave the following Saturday, when the rest of the family was out for the day; but her real reason for turning down Marco's offer of a lift was because she was scared of letting him into her home. She still couldn't trust herself to resist his advances.

Would it really be so bad if something happened? she asked herself now. *At least that way you'd get it over with, and then maybe you could relax a bit more.*

But surely sex shouldn't be something one did just to get it out of the way, her conscience argued. Wasn't being in love with someone important too?

She was still weighing up the pros and cons when she finally fell asleep.

Chapter Eighteen

Marco had another full-on week of business meetings and dinners with clients, so it was not until the following Saturday that he and Saffy would be meeting up again.

"I am so sorry, *cara*," he told her when he rang her on the Monday, "but it is impossible for me to reschedule any of these appointments."

Saffy was surprised by how disappointed she felt.

Saturday dawned, bright and clear. It would have been a perfect morning for carbooting with James and Connor, who had invited her to keep them company on a trip to Denham, but instead she was being forced to go and look at a venue for a wedding that would probably never happen, Saffy thought crossly. What was worse was that she would then have to spend an entire afternoon at the spa with Eleanor: much as she liked her stepmother, the prospect of spending hours with her in a sauna filled her with dread.

It didn't take her long to pack for the weekend: she had dressed up a little for the trip to The Latimer, teaming a brown suede mini-skirt with a black top and knee-high boots: the effect was casual yet chic. Since they would be walking on the Sunday, she had packed her jeans and walking boots, along with a light raincoat, just in case. She would leave her hair down for now, she decided, and tie it back in a loose ponytail for the walk.

A part of her was still surprised that Marco had signed up for all of this. She would have expected someone like him to fill his weekend with far more glamorous pursuits than going round country houses.

Speaking of which, there he was now, ringing her doorbell like a man possessed. She hurried down the flight of stairs that led to her front door.

"Buongiorno, little one," he greeted her as she opened the door. "I trust you are ready?"

By way of response, she pointed to the travelling bag in her hand.

"I have already programmed my Sat Nav," Marco continued. "We are to meet at ten and it is just past nine – that leaves us a little time if you want to show me your home …"

"I've shown you mine, now you show me yours?" she quipped, attempting to dampen the increasing attraction she felt for him.

"You know it's going to happen, Saffy. If not now, then soon." His words were a simple statement of fact.

Wordlessly, he removed the bag from her hand and took hold of her. Desire crackled between them, but Saffy was resolute.

"I think we need to leave now," she told him breathlessly, wondering if he could hear the hammering of her heart. "I don't want to rush things, Marco. When it happens, I want us to take our time."

"You are right," he said abruptly, releasing her once more. "But don't make me wait too long, *cara*, or I will be unable to hold back for long enough to do us both justice."

She had plenty of time to wonder what he meant as she set her burglar alarm and locked her front door.

*

Eleanor had been right when she said that Latimer House had breathtaking views, Saffy thought grudgingly as she and Marco traipsed dutifully after her stepmother, taking in the stunning panoramas of the Buckinghamshire countryside. The house itself dated from 1838, replacing the original Elizabethan building which had been gutted by a fire some years previously – according to the pamphlets that were dotted around the hotel's reception area. It was obviously used as a business conference centre as well as being a hotel and spa, but some of the rooms retained their character.

"This is lovely," Saffy breathed as they entered a long, airy room with wooden panellling and a log fire. Huge floor to ceiling windows looked out over rolling hills, whilst fields stretched as far as the eye could see. Splashes of colour in the beautifully kept flower beds just outside the windows softened the velvety lawn, and a lazily meandering stream marked the boundary between the house and a neighbouring farm.

"If you had a summer wedding, you could have photos taken out here," Eleanor broke in eagerly, ushering them through open French doors and into the balmy April air. "You could have some taken in front of the house, and some facing the other way, with the scenery as background."

Marco addressed Saffy. "What do you think, *cara*? A summer wedding would give us over a year to plan." Before she could reply, he turned back to Eleanor. "Were you thinking of here for the ceremony too? Because I was thinking of something a little more traditional."

Too stunned to contribute to the conversation herself, Saffy could only listen in horror as Eleanor began to outline her ideas for her stepdaughter's wedding. Apparently, there was a small church in the grounds of the estate – "Catholic, I hope," Marco interjected at this point. Catching Saffy's eye, he added, "If I am going to get married, then I want to do it properly." – although the hotel was licensed to hold civil ceremonies and civil partnerships.

"And they can cater for up to two hundred," Eleanor went on.

Saffy wondered absently whether there would be room for extra invisible people at what was still technically an imaginary wedding.

"What about the bedrooms?" Marco asked next, winking at his fiancée as he said it.

Eleanor consulted her notes. "They have a hundred and three rooms for overnight wedding guests," she reported.

"Maybe you and I should inspect the honeymoon suite," Marco murmured in Saffy's ear, surreptitiously stroking her bottom as he said it.

Luckily, they were interrupted at that moment by Antonio, who had been tied up in reception, making a business call. Declaring wedding talk to be "women's work", he swept them all back inside to sample the bar's facilities and, within seconds, had embroiled Marco in the saga of a troublesome client who was three months overdue with paying his invoices.

Saffy let the background hum of their conversation wash over her, trying to work out what was going on. Marco appeared to have settled seamlessly into her family – in fact, he seemed more at ease with them than she did herself. Surely he wasn't making all this effort merely to get her into bed? Did that mean he genuinely liked her, then? she wondered, aware that she still didn't trust him, but equally cognisant that her disaster with Malcolm had probably made her suspicious of any man who claimed to have feelings for her.

It wasn't until a few hours later, after lunch and before her father and Marco vanished for their game of golf, that she was able to drag her 'fiancé' aside and demand to know what he was playing at.

"All I am doing is getting to know your father a little better." Marco looked genuinely surprised at her question. "We are going to be business partners – you know that."

Was that all she meant to him, then? Was she merely a commodity to be bartered as some part of a more important transaction? Saffy stared at Marco, trying desperately to see what was in his heart.

"It just doesn't seem right," she muttered. "Pretending we're getting married, I mean."

"Who says we're pretending?" Marco asked her practically. "So far, we are enjoying each other's company - and there is every indication that we're going to have incredible sex in the not too distant future. Most people would say that sounds like a pretty good foundation for a marriage."

"And our fathers' business merger has nothing to do with it?" she challenged him. "Would you still want me if I wasn't a Vendrini?"

"Saffy ..." He was suddenly serious, staring into her troubled eyes with intensity. "I wanted you from the moment I first saw you," he said artlessly. "Before I knew who you were ... Before I had the chance to let common sense intervene." His fingertips lightly traced her jawbone. "I was determined not to go ahead with this ridiculous idea of marrying someone I hadn't even met," he told her, "and then I saw *you*, at the party, and I knew you were the only woman I could ever contemplate having a serious relationship with – and that was when I thought Sapphire Vendrini was a plump, blonde girl that I would have to get rid of so I could have a chance with you instead."

Bending his face to hers, he kissed her languorously on the mouth, making her pulse race and a dizzy sensation sweep through her entire body.

"*You* are the only woman for me now, *cara*," he promised her. "I admit that we are still getting to know each other, but I would not say that marriage is impossible ... or unlikely."

She would have said something in reply, but a noise behind her announced her father's presence: he was ready to whisk Marco away from her.

She watched them leave, the dazed expression on her face mirroring the confusion in her heart.

*

For the rest of the afternoon, Saffy's mind was in a whirl. She was still struggling to reconcile Marco's apparent declaration of – what? love? lust? – with the bitterness he had demonstrated only a few weeks ago when he had claimed that all married people cheated on each other. As she slid into the warm water of the hotel's pool and began the first of the forty lengths she usually aimed for on the infrequent occasions when she went swimming, she contemplated his actions over the three weeks she had actually known him, trying to work out whether his recent words to her had been sincere.

It would help if she were clearer about her own feelings, she decided, turning neatly as she reached the far side of the ridiculously small pool. She was physically attracted to Marco – there was no doubt about that – and he had shown himself to be surprisingly thoughtful with the flowers, the phone calls and text messages, and the ring; but what exactly did that prove? For all she knew, he did the same thing with any woman he wanted to sleep with: flowers, jewellery, honeyed words – maybe this was all part of his standard seduction technique.

"Saffy!" Eleanor caught up with her, panting for breath. "I'm going in the sauna now – do you want to come too?"

Saffy shook her head, aware that, if she and Eleanor were sitting side by side, her stepmother would want to talk about wedding plans again. "I'd like to get some more lengths in," she told her. "I might come and find you later."

Slicing through the water with her customary crawl, she kept her eyes open, willing the sting of the chlorine to bring her to her senses. Marco was desperate to bed her, she knew that much; but would he still be interested in her once he had taken what he wanted? And did she want to give herself to him if there was a possibility that he would cast her aside afterwards? Having held onto her virginity for so long, she didn't want to waste it on someone who might not appreciate it.

Is that what you're going to do for the rest of your life, then? a little voice whispered inside her. *Are you going to keep on putting off sex because you can't be sure that it's going to be forever?*

Thoughts bombarded her brain, in synchronicity with the water splashing round her face. Her little sister had taken the plunge whereas she, Saffy, was still only poking her toe in the shallow end. Maybe, she mused, as lap swallowed lap, she just needed to dive in and get it over and done with. Perhaps she should let Marco come to her room tonight after all …

Chapter Nineteen

Having decided to let Marco have his way with her, Saffy could not hide her profound disappointment when he took her aside later on, after returning from his rounds of golf with her father, and told her that he wouldn't be able to spend the rest of the weekend with her after all.

"I am sorry, *cara*, but I have just had an email from a client in Edinburgh and I will have to drive there straight away to try to sort out a problem with the system we sold him." Noting the expression on her face, he continued, "We will do the walk your stepmother spoke of next weekend. And we will go out for dinner together this week – I promise."

"Your Marco is a good boy," Antonio said reflectively as he watched the younger man retreating to the car park. "I know he would rather be with you, but he is putting his papa and the business first. He is trustworthy, no?"

"Just as long as he doesn't make a habit of it," Eleanor interjected - rather surprisingly, Saffy thought. "I know he runs the UK branch of *Benedetti's*, Saf – but couldn't he have got someone else to go to Scotland instead? This was supposed to be time he was spending with you."

Antonio opened his mouth to protest, but Eleanor waved him aside. "Don't let him set the pattern now, or you'll never get out of it. I love your dad, but his unorthodox business hours drive me crazy at times. He was taking business calls the second we arrived here today!"

"You cannot run a company and refuse to deal with clients when they need you!" her husband argued.

Eleanor shook her head. "Sometimes, you need to say no." Her voice was suddenly gentle. "You know what the doctor said about your heart, Toni: too much work and not enough rest isn't good for anyone."

"Are we talking about me or Marco now?" Antonio demanded petulantly.

"Both." Eleanor's tone was firm. "You're going to have to start putting your foot down, Saffy, love – just like I have to do with your dad. It's for the good of his health, and the health of your relationship. Now, who wants a coffee before we go?"

*

"So …" James didn't even wait until Saffy had entered the shop properly on Monday morning before pumping her for details about her weekend.

"So what?" Saffy asked innocently, knowing exactly what her friend wanted to know.

"How was the Big Weekend? Come on, I want to hear all the juicy details." He was worse than Sophie, Saffy thought with amusement, remembering how her sister had been equally prurient on Saturday evening, wanting to ascertain whether Saffy had 'done it yet'.

"There's not a lot to tell." She tried not to let any of her real feelings show. "We went and saw this country house hotel with my parents, then Marco got a call from work and had to leave early to drive up to Scotland."

James's face fell. "What, so you didn't …?"

"Not this time, no," Saffy teased him.

James pounced on her words. "But you're planning to – I can tell! Sapphire Vendrini, you little trollop! When's the big seduction?"

"As if I'd tell *you*!" Saffy retorted, pretending to be affronted.

"I was only going to offer you some tips!" James pouted, matching her playful mood with his own. Momentarily serious, he continued, "This is a huge step for you, darling. What's brought on the change of heart?"

Saffy paused for a while before making her reply. "I like him a lot," she said eventually, choosing her words carefully to avoid tempting Fate. In her past experience, it was usually once she confessed to thinking she might be in love with someone that it all went wrong.

James looked at her narrowly. "You like *me* too – but that doesn't make you want to leap on top of me and tear my clothes off!"

"What would be the point?" Saffy asked practically. "I'm not your type, am I?"

"But if I wasn't gay," James protested, "would you 'like' me enough to want to have your wicked way with me?"

She was silent for a moment, considering her response. James was good-looking – if you liked broad shoulders, tousled blond hair and classically perfect features – but she felt no desire for him whatsoever; nor had she at university, before she knew which team he played for.

As she tried to formulate a tactful response, James burst out laughing. "Saffy, I love you to bits and I really shouldn't wind you up like that – it's okay that you don't fancy me, honest. Besides," he shot her a wicked look, "your Marco's probably gagging for it as much as you are if you've made him wait so long. You'll have to put him out of his misery quickly or the poor boy will explode!"

Saffy felt her cheeks redden at her friend's saucy comments. "Can we change the subject now?" she said primly, feeling more than a little uncomfortable. It was one thing to hint that she might be thinking of taking her relationship with Marco to the next level; another entirely to have James wanting to know the date, time and location – which she was sure would be his next question if she didn't shut him up fast.

"I only asked …" James put on a wounded air, but Saffy wasn't fooled. She knew her friend wasn't at all sorry for having embarrassed her: it was one of his hobbies.

*

For the rest of the morning, Saffy threw herself into her work, taking advantage of the absence of customers to hide herself away in the back workroom and work on some sketches for a range of jewellery she was hoping to make up over the next few months. She and James had talked at length about how she could use her expertise to boost business. He'd suggested a series of newspaper ads in the local freebies, using photographs of her handmade pieces with the tagline 'Exclusive to *Jo Bangles*'.

After the busyness of the weekend – she'd still spent Saturday evening and Sunday with her family, despite Marco's absence, aware that, if things were progressing between the two of them, she might soon find much of her formerly free time accounted for – it was blissful to relax with her sketchpad. Silence reigned, punctuated only by the beeping of Saffy's phone whenever a text message arrived from Marco. He was still in Edinburgh, he told her, but hoped to be back by Tuesday or Wednesday. She didn't mention any of this to James, who would have only made inappropriate allusions to the size of Marco's caber if Saffy had referred to anything Scotland-related.

At quarter to one, James popped his head round the door. "I'm just popping to the baguette shop – can I get you anything?"

Saffy was in two minds whether to accept his offer: the artisan bakery next door made beautiful sandwiches, but she always felt put off by the blackboard outside the shop. Whoever was responsible for writing the daily menu had no concept of layout, squashing all the specials together so that would-be customers were promised 'Bacon Lattes' and 'Pulled Pork Brownies'. Although she knew these delights didn't really exist, just seeing the words juxtaposed always made her feel a little queasy.

"I'll grab something later," she told him, intent on her work.

"Make sure you do," was James' parting shot. "You're skinny enough as it is, young lady, without skipping meals."

*

Of course, she totally forgot to eat, so engrossed in her idea for a range of bracelets with the same design in each colour of the rainbow that six o'clock arrived in what seemed like indecent haste. She could have sworn it was only half an hour since James had mentioned lunch.

"Make sure Marco takes you somewhere nice tonight and feeds you up a bit," James instructed her as he came to say goodbye. He kissed her cheek. "I'll see you tomorrow, Angel. Don't do anything I would!"

Saffy waited until she heard his car pull away before she locked the workroom and scurried out of the shop. By now she was too hungry to cook, but the chip shop was only five minutes away. She would treat herself to scampi, chips and coleslaw in front of the TV. Fine dining with Marco was lovely – but sometimes slobbing out was what hit the spot.

*

Marco rang just as she was finishing the last mouthful. "I've missed you, *cara*, but I will be home soon and then perhaps we can complete our unfinished business?"

Saffy wasn't sure she liked the matter in hand being referred to as 'business': it made it all seem somewhat clinical. Nevertheless, she had resolved to take the plunge, so she might as well get the first time over and done with.

"What about Saturday?" she asked him now. "If you come over to my place, I'll cook for you."

"It would be safer than eating in my apartment," he agreed. "You have seen how I live, Saffy. My lifestyle isn't compatible with domestic arrangements – not yet, anyway." There was a pause. "I'm assuming I'm invited for breakfast too," he continued.

Saffy panicked momentarily, aware that Marco had quite rightly interpreted her invitation as one to stay the night. How was one supposed to reply in such circumstances? she wondered. Was she supposed to pretend that it was just dinner; or should she attempt a more worldly-wise façade and pretend she did this sort of thing all the time?

"Let's just see how things turn out," she stammered eventually, wishing that James were on hand to give her some advice.

"*Molto bene*, we will spend the evening together then, and perhaps the night too. And Saffy –"

"What?" she asked, a little warily.

"I like your family very much, but this weekend, I want you all to myself. If your stepmother has planned another walk, you will have to tell her to wait for another time."

*

Saffy didn't sleep well that night, her mind overwhelmed by the apprehension she felt. Sophie had seemed incredulous upon learning that her big sister was still a bashful virgin and had urged her to "get on with it" as soon as possible. "Everyone's nervous the first time," she had told her, inadvertently giving away too much of her own love life when she'd added, "but once you get past that, it's much easier. You'll be at it like rabbits in no time at all!"

Saffy hoped now that Sophie and Adam weren't "at it like rabbits" when they were supposed to be revising for their A levels. She didn't doubt that the young couple thought they were in love, but there was plenty of time to think about that sort of thing once the exams were safely out of the way.

A text the following morning told her that Marco would be back on Wednesday. "I will book a table for dinner," he told her. "It is too long since I have kissed you, *cara*."

She spent most of Tuesday fretting over what to wear – as well as wondering whether he would invite her in for coffee again. Now that she had decided to let Marco deflower her, a part of her wondered whether she should let it happen before Saturday evening – that way, she would be able to relax and enjoy herself properly after their romantic homecooked meal.

In the end, she let slip to James that Saturday was the allocated night – not merely to stop his incessant questions, but because she wanted to gain a male perspective on the plans she had made so far.

James was delighted to offer the benefits of his considerable experience - "Although I'm as virginal as you when it comes to the opposite sex, Sweetheart." – pointing out that most of the things that Saffy had deemed essential were totally unnecessary.

"I know you girls like candles and romantic music to get you in the mood," he sighed, "but as far as Marco's concerned, the second you take your top off, he'll be ready for action."

"But I don't want him to see me naked!" Saffy objected in horror, still clinging to the idea of everything happening in the dark and under the bedclothes.

James eyed her strangely. "Just how do you envisage having sex if you keep all your clothes on?"

A becoming shade of pink suffused Saffy's cheeks. She had a favourite fantasy in which she and Marco started kissing, before he slid her dress off her shoulders and onto the floor, then scooped her up in his arms and carried her into the bedroom. He would still be in his shirt and trousers, whereas she would be wearing flattering yet sexy underwear – something soft and silky, she hazarded. She normally fast forwarded over the nitty gritty of when and how they lost the rest of their clothes – or what happened when they did - and skipped to the part where they were lying in each other's arms after the event, with Marco whispering endearments and telling her that it was the most incredible night of his life.

"I think you're overthinking it," James said at last. "Just relax and let things happen at their own pace, Saff. Marco will know what he's doing, even if you don't."

This wasn't exactly the most comforting thought: Saffy felt irrationally jealous of all the women who had come before her, as well as worrying that she wouldn't live up to their polished performances. How wonderful to be Sophie, who'd had no previous partners to compete with and a boyfriend as clueless as she was herself!

She spent the rest of Tuesday and Wednesday working on her bracelet collection. Some of the colours were easy: rubies, citrine, emeralds and amethysts were the obvious choice for red, yellow, green and violet; but she needed to make a definite distinction between blue and indigo – would lapis lazuli and a much darker sapphire work? she wondered - and source the right shade of amber for the 'orange' hue.

She was so engrossed in her work, that she managed to miss a call from Marco on Wednesday afternoon, having forgotten that she had left her phone on silent from the previous evening when she went to bed. His voice message told her he was back at the London office but very tired. "Not too tired for dinner, *cara* – but definitely too tired for anything else."

She wasn't sure whether to feel relieved or disappointed.

Chapter Twenty

As her doorbell rang that evening, Saffy felt suddenly shy. Even though she knew this was 'just' dinner, she couldn't help reminding herself that in a few days' time she and Marco would be lovers. She opened the door to him, wondering what his body looked like beneath his immaculately ironed shirt and tailored trousers.

Marco was almost obscured by an enormous bouquet of jewel-bright flowers: crimson roses, parrot tulips in variegated yellow and red, purple irises and white and yellow narcissi combined in a riotous blaze of colour that reminded her of the bracelets she'd been working on. She would place the flowers in her workroom, she decided, seeing them as an omen that Marco had subconsciously tuned in to her own mind.

"Thanks for the flowers," she said breathlessly. "They're beautiful."

Marco looked sheepish. "I meant to order you some more lilies, but I had so many things on my mind that I forgot. These are just cheap ones from the supermarket, but I couldn't resist the bright colours." He looked at his watch. "Will they wait until later for you to put them in water? I have a table booked for eight, and it's quarter to now."

Since she had been ready for the last hour and fifteen minutes, all Saffy had to do was grab her coat and set the burglar alarm. Within minutes, they were both in Marco's car, purring along the winding road that led to Beaconsfield.

"I booked us in at the *Brasserie Blanc*," Marco said, breaking the silence. "I can recommend the seafood soup and the cheese soufflé."

Saffy tried not to think about the other women Marco had taken there.

"How was Edinburgh?" she asked, changing the subject.

Marco pulled a face. "I spent three days visiting four clients – I realised that once I was up there, it made sense to meet with the other companies we'd installed systems for – that way, I won't have to go back again for a while. Although …" He looked across at her. "There's a charming little hotel not far from the Scottish border. I found it by chance a year ago when I was looking for somewhere to stay. It looks like a miniature castle, with turrets, but it only has five bedrooms. I think it's privately owned. The dining room has huge French windows onto the grounds and you can see deer and rabbits while you're eating your breakfast."

"It sounds lovely," Saffy said earnestly.

"It is." He paused again. "It might be somewhere to think about … For a romantic break."

In the silence that followed, Saffy thought that Marco must surely be able to hear the rapid beating of her heart. Their relationship was definitely progressing to another level – but was she ready for it?

By the time they arrived in Beaconsfield, the tension between them had thickened into a blanket, wrapping itself around both of them, as if urging them to be together. As Marco's fingers closed around hers to lead her to the restaurant, Saffy felt the familiar spark of longing and knew that he sensed it too.

"This waiting is only making me want you more," Marco murmured in her ear, placing a hand proprietorially on the small of her back while they followed the *maître d'* to their table.

"We could skip dinner," she whispered back at him, amazed at her own boldness.

Marco grinned ruefully. "Saffy, I have driven over four hundred miles today just to get back from Scotland, and then another thirty miles to come and see you. I am totally exhausted – wait until Saturday, when my batteries will have recharged and I will have the stamina to spend all night making love to you."

Once they were seated, he added, "But it is good to know that you want this as much as I do. You have spent so long putting me off that I was beginning to think I had imagined the heat between us."

Luckily, the arrival of the menus meant that Saffy didn't have to reply to this.

"So," Saffy said some time later, when her stomach was nicely full of soufflé and salmon, "you need to tell me your secret, Marco."

He looked startled. "What secret, *cara*? There is no other woman, if that is what you are worried about."

Saffy laughed. "I find that hard to believe!"

Marco was confused. He genuinely hadn't looked at another woman since meeting Saffy; but, apparently, that wasn't what she meant.

"You told me yourself that you're not domesticated," she reminded him gently, "but your shirts are always perfectly ironed and your apartment was so tidy it looked as if no one lived there. I think you've got a cleaning lady on the side!"

"I pay extra for the optional maid service," Marco confessed. "Most of the residents are busy professionals: it makes sense to let someone else take care of that side of things."

"It's a big apartment to keep clean," Saffy said idly.

"It's really two apartments knocked into one," Marco admitted. "The couple before me wanted huge rooms for all their entertaining. Siân's apartment is half the size."

He regretted the words as soon as they left his mouth.

"She asked me to look at her washing machine just after she moved in," he said hurriedly, aware that it sounded like a feeble excuse. "I only saw her kitchen, Saffy."

"She's very attractive." Saffy's voice was tight.

"She's not my type." Marco paused, desperate for Saffy to believe him. "What do I have to do to convince you that I'm a changed man? I want *you*, Saffy – not Siân; not any of the beautiful women I see at work every day – just you."

He took a sip of mineral water before continuing, "I have spent two weekends in a row with your family, Saffy – doesn't that tell you how serious I am?"

"Maybe," she conceded grudgingly, "but I still don't like that Siân girl, Marco – I don't trust her at all."

"Then trust *me* instead," Marco said gently. "I've invested too much in this relationship to mess it up by cheating on you, if that's what you're worried about."

She had no option but to do as he'd said.

*

She felt slightly more confident by the time Marco dropped her off at her flat forty minutes later. This time, there seemed to be an air of inevitability, so that their kisses were less a final payment and more a deposit for the purchase that would take place in a few days' time. She hoped he wouldn't be disappointed once they'd sealed the deal.

It was quarter past ten, but she wasn't sleepy yet, so she picked a couple of cookery books off one of her shelves and curled up with them under her duvet, trying to decide on the perfect menu. She would start with something light – seafood salad, perhaps, or a smoked mackerel mousse – and finish with her mother's recipe for chocolate brownies, served with fresh raspberries and vanilla ice cream; but what to choose for her main course?

Marco had expressed interest in walking to Ivinghoe Beacon this weekend and, although Saffy had done the walk the previous Sunday with Eleanor - Sophie having claimed to have too much revision to do to take time off for anything as frivolous as exercise - she thought this sounded an excellent idea. After some discussion, they had fixed on Saturday, Marco's reasoning being that they would walk up an appetite for her cooking – although she suspected that, if things went to plan later on, neither one of them would feel like getting out of bed on the Sunday.

Something she could bung in the slow cooker, then, leaving it to do all the hard work while she was working up a sweat climbing a steep hill. She would make Moroccan lamb: it was one of the few dishes that actually seemed to work better when cooked slowly and it was probably the most successful meal in her rather limited repertoire. (James and Connor had done most of the cooking when the three of them had been at university.)

Marco had promised to arrive by ten so that they had time to look round the visitor centre and eat lunch before embarking on the arduous climb to the beacon. That meant she had Thursday and Friday to shop for lamb, apricots and all the other ingredients she needed, as well as buying some decent underwear (surely that should be *indecent* underwear? she smiled to herself), having her legs, underarms and bikini line waxed, and finding time for a hairstyle and manicure. It seemed like a lot to do in two days, considering she had to fit in work as well.

She had been hoping that James would be sufficiently sympathetic to let her take Friday afternoon off, but when she asked him on the Thursday, he seemed resilient to the idea, even going so far as telling her that she had to spend all day in the shop on Friday because they had a valued customer coming in.

"It's not that I don't know how important this is for you," he told her airily, "but the only thing you really need to bother about is buying some decent wine to put you both in the mood. Your hair's fine as it is, and you can paint your own nails." Noticing the expression on her face, he added, "And you certainly don't need to wax – have you seen how hairy continental women are?"

It was almost, she thought in desperation, as if James were trying to sabotage her love life just when it seemed about to get going.

*

Friday dawned, bright and clear, the sun unseasonably warm for April. Saffy glanced at the postcard blue sky, hoping that the weather would remain fine for Saturday. It seemed silly not to take advantage of living in such picturesque surroundings, particularly when Marco seemed to like walking as much as she did.

James was uncharacteristically on edge that morning, checking his phone every ten minutes or so and jumping whenever the shop door jangled. Saffy hoped he hadn't had another row with Connor: the two of them got on well, but James had a habit of winding Connor up to the point where he sometimes found himself knocking on Saffy's door late at night, begging to sleep on her sofa. This was the last thing she needed right now, when the only overnight guest she wanted was Marco.

After half an hour or more of James fidgeting about, Saffy could stand it no longer. Her bracelet designs were complete and she was itching to make up at least one prototype before finishing for the weekend. "If you need me, I'll be in the back," she told her colleague. Within minutes, she was lost in the intricacies of soldering links of gold into a delicate chain.

It was hours later when James popped his head round the door. "Customer for you," he said nonchalantly.

"Can't you handle it?" Saffy asked, without turning round.

"Apparently not." The ghost of a smile lurked in her friend's eyes. She wondered what he was up to.

Feeling somewhat irked to be torn away from her work, Saffy followed James into the front of the shop. A familiar figure was standing by the till.

"Marco!" Saffy said in surprise. He hadn't mentioned meeting up when he'd texted her earlier.

"*Buongiorno, cara.*" Marco kissed his fiancée chastely on the cheek. "I was wondering if you would like to join me for lunch."

"Is there a problem with tomorrow?" Saffy asked worriedly.

He laughed. "There is no problem, *cara* – but the sky is blue, the weather is warm, and there is jazz in the park down the road." He pointed to two Waitrose carrier bags. "I have made a picnic."

"How very English of you!" James murmured.

Marco shot him a frosty look. "In the three years I have been in your country, I have had plenty of time to learn my way around the delicatessen counter," he said drily.

Saffy was relieved to hear this, having had disturbing flashbacks to the out of date milk in Marco's fridge.

"Is that okay with you?" she queried, seeking her colleague's approval.

James raised his eyebrows. "You haven't had a proper lunchbreak all week. At least you won't forget to eat if Loverboy's keeping an eye on you."

"I'll be back about two thirty then," Saffy told him, hastily grabbing her jacket and picking up one of the bags. "Come on, Marco."

*

Once they were out of earshot, Marco threw her an angry look. "I don't like your boss, Saffy. He's far too familiar with you – and with me."

He was still smarting at being called Loverboy, she hazarded.

"He's not really my boss," she said after a pause. "We're equal partners - he just handles more of the business side of things because he's better at it than me."

"You're sure there has never been anything between you?" Why was he sounding so jealous?

"I'm not his type," she said shortly. "Just leave it, Marco. James and I are friends, but that's all there is to it. Let's not get into an argument over it."

"You are right." Marco gave in with bad grace. "Perhaps I am over-reacting, but I can't help feeling jealous when another man looks at you."

"I can promise you he's never thought of me like that," Saffy said, wondering how Marco would react if she told him James was gay. She decided not to say anything: it wasn't her secret to tell. Instead, she touched his arm lightly. "How much further? I'm starving!"

It wasn't long before the park was in sight. The balmy weather had attracted numerous office workers, teenagers on their school lunch break and harassed looking mothers with prams or pushchairs, and these dotted the grass on folding chairs in front of the makeshift stage that had been set up for the jazz band. Flower beds were ablaze with bright yellow daffodils, orange gerbera and scarlet peonies; whilst the soft cooing of wood pigeons suggested that they too were ready for food.

Marco steered Saffy towards a couple of chairs slightly away from the crowd. "Sit down," he instructed her, busying himself with unpacking one of the bags.

Saffy sank into the comfort of the canvas seat, taking in the relaxed atmosphere around her. Ties were being loosened and jackets removed as the warmth of the sun began to take effect. Even the mothers seemed calmer, fondly watching their toddlers stagger after pigeons with little success; not seeming to mind when tiny fingers spilt drinks or dropped sandwiches.

When she glanced at Marco again, he had laid out an impressive array of food on a plastic tablecloth on the grass. A readymade salad of rocket, spinach and other leaves was flanked by a tub of pâté, a French stick, assorted plastic containers bearing delicatessen stickers and a wrapped Brie. A bottle of wine, a corkscrew and two hastily assembled plastic wineglasses completed the repast. Saffy felt enchanted.

"For someone who claims not to be domesticated, you've done a pretty good job with the food," she commented. "I'm impressed with the tablecloth – and the wineglasses."

"I saw them in the supermarket when I was queueing to pay," Marco confessed, "so I thought, 'Why not?' and I bought them." Deftly inserting the corkscrew, he opened the wine and poured a little into one of the glasses. "This should be okay, even if it is a relatively cheap wine." Swirling it around in his glass, he sniffed deeply, then took a sip. "Not bad," he decided.

"I don't know anything about wine, so I can't comment," Saffy told him. "I wouldn't mind some of that bread and pâté, though – and whatever's in those little pots. Have we got plates?"

Marco put his hand to his forehead despairingly. "How could I buy glasses and a corkscrew but forget plates? *Che stupido!*"

"We can improvise," Saffy said soothingly. Delving into her bag, she produced a packet of tissues. "We'll use these as serviettes to catch the crumbs, and we can eat the salad straight out of the container."

Luckily, the salad bowl was one of those types with a plastic fork in the lid, and several of the little pots were found to contain such delights as sun dried tomatoes, peppers and artichokes – all of which could be happily eaten with the fingers. There were white anchovies too, and three types of olives. Saffy gazed at it all appreciatively. "I love Mediterranean food, don't you?" she asked Marco.

"If you had grown up in Italy, as I did, you would just call it food," Marco joked, winking at her, his previous annoyance already dispelled.

"The bread's French," Saffy said severely. "Where's the knife for the pâté?"

Once more, Marco looked aghast.

"You're not as domesticated as I thought, are you?" Saffy scolded him. Foraging in her bag once more, she pulled out her purse and withdrew a credit card. "It's one for emergencies," she explained as she saw Marco gazing at her in disbelief. "It's never been used, so it should be quite clean."

Breaking a piece off the French stick, she deftly split it down the middle with her fingers, then proceeded to spread it liberally with pâté, using her credit card as a knife.

"You are a resourceful woman, Sapphire Vendrini." Was that admiration in his voice? Handing her a glass, he raised his own, adding, "*Salute!*" before he clinked it against hers.

Saffy bit into her crusty bread with relish, first placing her glass on the tablecloth. "I'm not a big wine fan," she confessed, seeing Marco's quizzical look.

Marco pretended to be affronted. "How can you be Italian if you don't like wine?"

"Half-Italian," she corrected him. "My mother was English, remember?"

"And that is why your English accent is so perfect," Marco declared. "Me, I have been learning English since I was ten, but I still sound like an Italian and not a native speaker."

Privately, Saffy thought that Marco's accent was extremely sexy – but she wasn't going to give him a swollen head by admitting it!

"Do you speak any other languages?" she asked, plunging her fingers into the pot of olives and helping herself to one stuffed with garlic.

Marco watched as she took first an artichoke, then a strip of yellow pepper, both dripping with olive oil, and popped them into her mouth, licking her fingers unselfconsciously as she did so. He was surprised by the eroticism of such a simple gesture.

Saffy was looking at him expectantly. Marco suddenly remembered her question.

"I speak French and Spanish too," he offered, "but my English is much better."

"Why is that?" Saffy pressed.

Marco shrugged. "I suppose my father made both of us focus more on English because it was necessary for the business. We do a lot of trade with the States, and that is conducted mainly in English."

"But you read English novels as well, don't you?" Saffy asked. "I saw your bookcases."

Marco chewed a piece of bread reflectively before replying. "I had to study English Literature at school as part of my *esame di maturità* at the *liceo*. I realised I liked Graham Greene and Charles Dickens, even though some of Dickens' language was challenging. What about you? Do you read in Italian?"

Saffy pulled a face. "I can hardly speak it, let alone read it! I did French at school, and Dad's always spoken English to us. Mum didn't speak Italian, so he had to learn pretty fast."

"So, I will have to teach you everything I know, then?"

His suggestion caressed her like the warm April air. She lowered her eyes, too embarrassed to reply.

Marco laughed. "You are very beautiful when you blush, *cara*. It is most endearing."

As Saffy continued to gaze at her feet, she became aware of a couple of pigeons searching for crumbs.

"Did you know that pigeons make brilliant parents?" she asked suddenly, turning to Marco in an attempt to change the subject. "We had a pair of them who adopted us at university."

"Us?" Marco queried.

"Me, James and another friend of ours," Saffy explained, not noticing the cloud that had passed over her fiancé's face. "First they built a nest on our balcony, then the female laid her eggs and they both took turns sitting on them until they hatched. We used to spend hours watching them."

"So, you and James lived together when you were at university?" Marco pursued, his voice tight. He wasn't liking this information one bit.

"We shared a house in our final year – I thought I'd told you before." Saffy was so caught up in the memory of scattering seed and watching fluffy bundles of feathers gradually transform into fully fledged birds that she failed to register Marco's changed mood. "Anyway, they used to sit on the nest in four hour shifts: one of them would go off and forage for food while the other kept the eggs warm; and then, when the chicks hatched, they still took it in turns. It was a brilliant example of co-parenting."

"Was he your boyfriend?"

"What?" Saffy was momentarily caught off-guard.

"Was James your boyfriend?" Marco repeated, his tone saturated with jealousy.

"No!" Saffy uttered in surprise, startled by Marco's apparent anger. "I'm not his type, Marco – and he's not mine," she added meaningfully.

Time paused for a few seconds and then Marco relaxed, reaching out and stroking her cheek.

"I'm sorry," he said, after a moment. "I just hate to think of you being with another man."

"It's your Latin temperament," she told him, with a note of resignation. "My father's just the same."

A few minutes of awkward silence ensued before the sounds of jazz began to drift over the park. Listening with only half an ear, Saffy allowed herself to be wrapped in the warm, mellow tones. Languorously, she relaxed into the melody, leaning into Marco's arms as she did so and letting his arms steal around her in time with the music. The slow, soulful song of a saxophone slowly wound its way to a close as an air of contentment settled over the two of them. It was the sort of afternoon where no one wants to go back to work.

Eventually, Saffy sighed. "It's been wonderful, Marco, but I really do have to get back to the shop."

"You are sure?" His eyes searched hers. "You know I cannot see you tonight, *cara*."

"You didn't say ..." she began, then stopped, feeling confused.

Marco was looking as puzzled as she felt. "But when I spoke to James yesterday, I asked him to give you the message that I have to see a client this evening. I told him to tell you to expect to see me for lunch instead."

So *that* was why James had refused to let her take time off for shopping or to get her hair done, Saffy realised. He'd known all along that Marco would be paying her a visit.

"I tried ringing your phone several times," Marco continued, "but each time there was no answer, so I rang the shop instead. Did James not tell you?"

She really must start checking that her phone was on when she was working, Saffy thought guiltily. It wasn't the first time she'd missed one of Marco's calls.

"At least we still have a whole day together tomorrow," she reminded him.

Marco's eyes gleamed. "And the night as well ..."

Saffy lowered her gaze, unable to prevent a warm glow from filling her cheeks.

"Thanks for a lovely lunch," she said softly, as she brushed the crumbs from her lap.

He extended a hand towards her. "Let me walk you back to the shop. I have time before my next meeting."

They wandered lazily back along the road, fingers intertwined, warmed as much by each other's presence as by the sun overhead. As they reached *Jo Bangles*, Marco released her hand with reluctance. "Until tomorrow morning, *cara*."

She raised her face to his and he kissed her slowly and sensuously on the mouth. Saffy felt a tingle of expectancy, hinting at the following evening's anticipated pleasure. By the time Marco pulled away, her whole body was quivering with desire.

"What have you done to me, Sapphire Vendrini?" Marco was obviously as affected as she was. "I should be driving to see my client now, but all I can think about is taking you in my arms and carrying you up the stairs to your bedroom."

"Tomorrow night," she promised him. "I won't let anything stop us this time, Marco."

She should have realised then that her words were tempting Fate.

Chapter Twenty-One

James had been totally unrepentant about not passing on Marco's message from the previous day – "I wanted it to be a delightful surprise, Darling!" – but he had finally agreed that she could have the rest of the afternoon off to prepare for Project Seduction, as he insisted on calling it.

"You could have had the time off anyway," he'd told her infuriatingly, "but I knew Marco wanted to take you out for lunch, so I had to keep you in the shop."

He could have done that without the need for subterfuge, Saffy thought crossly, as she hastily tidied her workroom, but then subtlety had never been James's style. She was still nervous every time he saw Marco, knowing that her friend was liable to make some sort of outrageous comment that Marco wouldn't appreciate at all.

She would hit the High Street first, she decided. The secondary shopping street, where *Jo Bangles* was situated, housed an eclectic collection of specialised shops – '*Guns and Wellingtons*', a pottery painting business, a dance shop specialising in tutus and tap shoes, and an establishment that sold local school uniforms - along with the baguette shop, a *Tesco Metro*, two Indian takeaways and several estate agents; whereas on the High Street she could find *Waitrose* (much nicer for the groceries she needed to buy), her preferred hair and beauty salon, and a shop whose windows were full of enticingly seductive underwear. She had walked past the latter countless times but never had the courage to enter.

Today was different, though. She was a woman on a mission - and it was time she treated herself to some new underwear anyway, she argued, as her fingers skimmed the racks, appreciating the silky touch of camisoles and French knickers as she hunted for her size.

In the end, she spent far more than she'd intended, choosing a rather demure camisole set in powder blue and an extremely racy bra and thong combination in black lace. She had no doubt which of these Marco would prefer, but the more substantial set would hide a multitude of sins – her main reservation about Marco seeing her in her underwear was that he would notice the flabby bits she was sure she possessed. Perhaps it would be better to rely on camouflage the first time?

Leaving the shop rather self-consciously – and wishing that the name of the shop wasn't emblazoned so blatantly across her carrier bag – Saffy headed for the beauty salon. There were no hair appointments available until the following day, she was told, but she was able to have a manicure and polish right away. She almost asked about waxing too, but chickened out at the last moment, deciding she would buy a new razor and tackle her underarms herself – along with anything else that needed attention.

By the time she staggered home with her new underwear and several *Waitrose* bags containing lamb, prawns, apricots, Moroccan spice in a handy tin, honey, butternut squash, tinned tomatoes, dark chocolate, raspberries and luxury vanilla ice-cream, Saffy felt exhausted. No wonder men usually chose to take women out for dinner if so much effort was involved in cooking a meal. She was also thankful that Marco had offered to bring the wine since she was totally clueless when it came to matching food with alcohol.

Since she'd eaten so well at lunch time, she didn't bother cooking for herself that evening. Instead, she microwaved a plastic pot of Thai vegetables and rice that she'd spotted when she was looking for couscous – it seemed like an upmarket version of a Pot Noodle, but she didn't care: it was hot and filling, and that was all she needed right now.

*

Saturday arrived with a rosy dawn. Saffy studied the sky anxiously, hoping this wasn't the harbinger of bad weather. She desperately wanted to walk to Ivinghoe Beacon with Marco – partly because the views at the top were so glorious, but also because she was hoping that strenuous exercise in the day might slow him down in the bedroom later. She was still nervous about it, not wanting him to compare her unfavourably to the experienced women who had preceded her.

She was ready by the time Marco arrived. He looked approvingly at her long legs, clad in tight, faded jeans, then stared questioningly at her raincoat. "You won't need that – it's going to be fine all day."

"It's better to be prepared," she instructed him. "You wear several layers, so you can take them off one at a time, as and when you need to."

"How many of the layers are you planning on taking off during the course of our walk?" Marco asked, a glint in his eye.

"The trail's always full of hikers," Saffy said briskly, "so if you were thinking of getting up to anything, the answer's no."

"A pity," Marco murmured under his breath. "There is always a certain *frisson* when one thinks about being caught ..."

Saffy looked at him sharply – *that* was the sort of comment she would have expected James to make!

"We'd better get going," she said shortly, picking up her rucksack and heading for the door. Then, noticing Marco's feet for the first time, she stopped. "Where are your other shoes?" she wanted to know.

"My what?" Marco was wearing well-worn hiking boots that suggested he was a seasoned walker, but Saffy decided he hadn't thought things through.

"The shoes to change into after the walk," she explained gently. "You don't want muddy boots all over your car, do you? And I don't want them walking in here afterwards either," she added.

Marco groaned. "Do we have time to go back to my place for spare shoes?"

"Probably not," she told him. "The walk will take a couple of hours at least, and we want to look round the visitor centre first and have lunch."

"Then I will have to put a plastic bag on the floor of my car and walk around your flat barefoot," Marco shrugged with acceptance. "Are we ready?"

They were – although Saffy insisted on popping into the kitchen to check she really had switched the slow cooker on and not merely imagined it.

SatNav made short work of the journey, so that thirty minutes later they were driving through the gates to the Ashridge Estate and along the winding road that led to the carpark for the woodland trails. Marco looked about him appreciatively. "You have now shown me two beautiful places, Sapphire. I will have to return the favour and take you to see *my* favourite spots."

"I'd like that," Saffy murmured, thinking that this was beginning to feel every day more like a real relationship. "Maybe we could do that next week?"

"If you like ..." Marco tried to sound nonchalant. "But you will have to make sure your passport is up to date: I want to show you the Tuscan countryside, where my brother lives with his wife and children. After all, I have spent time with your family – it is only fair that I allow you to spend time with mine."

"Seriously?" Saffy's eyes shone. She hadn't visited Italy for over ten years – Sophie was susceptible to travel sickness, as well as having an irrational fear of flying, so that consequently their family holidays had become very much UK-based – but the idea of going back there with Marco instantly took on a romantic tinge. She could picture him now, sitting on a *terrazza* as the sun gently sank into the horizon behind him. He would be wearing a white linen shirt to contrast with his dark hair and eyes, whilst she would be dressed in something long and floaty, perhaps with flowers in her hair. There would be a jug of wine and a bowl of olives on the table in front of them and ...

"Saffy?" Marco looked at her curiously. "What were you thinking about? Your mind is not here."

She blushed, unable to admit that she had been picturing them holidaying together.

"I was asking you which way I turn," Marco repeated. "There are several car parks, *cara* – which one do we want?"

She was busy then for the next few minutes, making sure that she gave adequate directions. Within another couple of minutes, they had pulled into a parking space within view of the wooded walks the estate was famous for.

Marco switched off the engine and turned to her with a smile. "Are you ready?"

"Just a sec." Saffy dived under her seat for her walking boots and thick socks. Whilst she was tying her laces, she became aware of Marco's fingers gently stroking the nape of her neck and she tingled with sheer pleasure.

"Don't stop!" she said without thinking.

As she raised her head, Marco's mouth found hers. Passion flared between them, overwhelming them both with desire. Marco's kisses became more intense, his hand sliding beneath her jumper, searching for her breast. Instantly, Saffy pulled away. "It's a car park, Marco!"

"So?"

"So we'll get done for indecent exposure if we're not careful!" she snapped back, adjusting her clothing and sitting up.

Marco looked completely unrepentant. "You cannot blame me, *cara*, if I find you irresistible," he said smoothly, but Saffy was already opening the car door.

"I think we both need a cup of tea," she called over her shoulder, clambering out of the car and striding off in the direction of the visitor centre.

Marco had to wait another moment or two until his ardour had cooled sufficiently to let him leave the vehicle.

*

A couple of hours later, Marco gazed at the beautiful sight in front of him and sighed with contentment. Saffy's bottom, in those close-fitting faded jeans, really was the most perfect thing he had ever seen.

"Are you okay?" Saffy slowed to a halt and looked back at him with concern.

Marco reassured her. "I am fine – I'm just enjoying the view." His words may have sounded innocent, but it was just as well Saffy couldn't see the images that were currently running through his mind as he took in her glowing face and windswept hair and pictured how she would look after an energetic night of love-making.

They were approaching a stile. Ever the gentleman, Marco assisted Saffy over it, helpfully making sure that her rear was adequately supported by his hands. Much as he loved walking, he was, by now, desperate to get Saffy into bed – did they really need to bother with a meal together after this, he wondered, or could they just skip that step and get on with what they both so obviously wanted?

"How much further?" he asked her

"Tired already?" she teased him. "I thought you were a man with plenty of stamina, Marco!"

"I am," he assured her, "and I will prove it to you very soon, *cara*."

His deep brown eyes fixed on her meaningfully. As she had in the past, she blushed and lowered her gaze – almost, he thought, as if she were embarrassed by the suggestion of sex.

"How far until we reach this beacon of yours?" he repeated.

"About another mile – it's all uphill though." Clasping his hand in hers, Saffy urged him forwards. "Come on, Marco – I can't wait to show you the view from the top."

Thinking about the view underneath *her* top, Marco let Saffy lead him forwards, his eyes taking in the rolling chalk downlands and lush meadows that surrounded them on either side as they began the final stage of their walk.

It had been worth it after all, Marco thought, some time later, as he and Saffy stood on top of the hill, gazing down on the picture-perfect landscape below them. Although he felt invigorated from the climb, his need for Saffy was still just as intense as it had been earlier on. Maybe they should just go back to his place instead and enjoy the comfort of his six foot bed?

No – too many other women had rolled around in his master bedroom: the first time with Saffy needed to be special: somewhere with no memories for either of them. Should he book a hotel room then?

"How many men have you had in your flat?" he asked her abruptly. Saffy looked puzzled. "How many lovers?" Marco pressed, aware that he must sound ridiculously jealous, but racked with a sudden insecurity about the evening.

"None," Saffy said simply. "I've never invited anyone back – apart from you."

Marco stared at her incredulously. "Not even one"

"My last boyfriend turned out to be a married man," Saffy said drily. "Luckily, I found out about his wife before things got to that stage."

"But there must have been others ..."

For a moment, Saffy was silent. "I was in love with someone at university," she said eventually, "but it didn't work out. When I graduated, nearly two years ago, I went back home for a while and then James suggested the two of us opening a jewellery shop together, and I said yes, as long as it had a living space for me – I was going crazy being back at home and being treated as if I was still Sophie's age. I loved living with James and Connor at university, but I didn't want to share a flat again – I wanted my own place."

"And there was no one else in between university and this married man?"

"No one serious," Saffy corrected him. Three coffees with nice but uninteresting men, friends of friends; the odd dinner here and there; and Malcolm. It made for a pretty boring list, so she compromised by saying, "A lady doesn't kiss and tell, Marco – I'm sure you know that."

"So, I will be the first to christen your bed, then?" The gleam had returned to Marco's eye. Saffy started to feel nervous again.

"Isn't the view spectacular?" she said in desperation, gesturing at the panorama spread out before them.

Before Marco could reply, an ominous rumble was heard in the distance and the sky suddenly paled to a shadow of its former shade. Within seconds, large drops of rain had begun to fall from the hitherto clear sky. Saffy fumbled in her rucksack for her raincoat. "At least we got to the top before it started raining," she said breathlessly.

But it would be three miles of walking in the rain to get back to the car park, Marco thought savagely, and he would definitely have to go home and get changed before he could return to Saffy's flat.

His night of passion seemed to be slipping further and further from his grasp.

Chapter Twenty-Two

Saffy regarded Marco with those bewitching blue eyes of hers. "Are you sure you don't want to come in for a coffee first, to warm you up?"

Marco shook his head. "The sooner I leave, the sooner I will be coming back, *cara*. I will need to shower and change."

They were both soaked to the skin after the unexpected cloudburst, despite Saffy's raincoat.

"It gives me a bit longer to get food ready then," Saffy remarked, looking up at him from under her long, dark lashes.

"Remind me again what we are having and I will bring the right wine. I have a built-in wine cabinet in my kitchen which keeps whites chilled and reds at room temperature." Marco was so obviously proud of this toy that Saffy couldn't restrain herself from laughing at him.

"It's lamb," she told him. "I hope you like spicy food, though, because it's Moroccan-style."

"We ate Turkish food together," Marco reminded her, "and my mouth was not offended by spices then. Besides," he gave a sudden, disarming grin, "I can't cook, but I can order Indian takeaway food – and that is *much* hotter than anything you could offer me."

Saffy sneezed then and Marco felt guilty. "You are standing here talking to me when you should be inside, keeping warm."

"I'm going to run a bath as soon as you've gone," Saffy confessed.

"Then perhaps I should stay and scrub your back," Marco murmured, his mind immediately filled with very enticing images of Saffy wearing a few bubbles and not much else.

At this, she blushed most becomingly. "Maybe another time – once we've ... got to know each other properly," she ended delicately.

And so Marco had to be content with driving back to his own apartment and showering solo in his ridiculously opulent bathroom.

Once he had gone, Saffy turned the taps on and let the bath begin to fill whilst she inspected her slow cooker. Everything seemed to be behaving as it should: the meat was tender, the sauce had thickened and the flavours were perfectly balanced. As long as she didn't burn her brownies or drop the prawns, it should all be okay.

Sinking back into coconut scented bubbles – she often used her shower crème as bubble bath – Saffy contemplated her imminent deflowering with some amount of trepidation. Would it hurt? she wondered. And would people be able to tell afterwards? Sophie hadn't looked any different – but then she'd never looked particularly virginal in the first place with her generous bosom and naturally bee-stung lips.

Saffy was still worried about her little sister. Exams weren't far-off now, but Sophie was still, from what she could gather, spending far too much time with Adam and not enough with her clarinet.

As she shampooed her hair a few minutes later, she found she still couldn't get Sophie out of her mind. She, Saffy, had always been so sensible, whereas Sophie's nickname for years had been Little Miss Impulsive. Was that simply an accident of birth? Would Sophie have been calmer if she'd been born first, instead of Saffy? And would she herself have given in to her own wild side more often had it not been for the fact that, as the older sister, she had to set an example?

Sighing, Saffy reached for the conditioner, totally unaware that, within a few hours, Sophie would disrupt both their lives.

*

By the time Marco returned, bearing red roses and a bottle of expensive looking wine, Saffy was clean and dry, the dark sheen of her her soft silky hair a stark contrast to the dove grey dress she was wearing. Marco looked her up and down approvingly. "*Bella mia*! You look very desirable!"

Saffy's dress clung to her curves, accentuating her figure. Although she had planned to wear her powder blue camisole set, she had realised that it just didn't work with this dress; but the underwired bra pushed her breasts up provocatively, making her feel far sexier than she usually did.

Marco had changed into a clean pair of jeans and a casual shirt in a shade of khaki that somehow made his eyes an even deeper brown. Just looking at him, Saffy felt herself teetering on a cliff edge of desire, ready at any moment to start falling far deeper than she ever had before.

As his hands reached out and pulled her to him, Saffy gave in to the longing that had been building inside her ever since she had first seen Marco – was it really only four or five weeks ago? She responded to his kisses greedily, letting her fingers entwine in his hair, pressing herself against him so that she could feel the tautness of his muscles as her breasts squished themselves against his chest. His hands slid down her back, cupping her buttocks with a desperation akin to her own. "What are you doing to me, Saffy?" His voice was almost a murmur of despair.

If he had continued kissing her, she would have melted into him completely, allowing him to do anything he wanted. Instead, he pushed her away reluctantly.

"There is nothing I would like better than to skip dinner and move straight onto dessert, but we have both had a strenuous walk today, *cara*, and we need to eat. Besides," his eyes glinted dangerously, "if I am going to make love to you all night long – and I very much intend to do that – then we will require a lot of energy."

She knew he was right: she was already feeling light-headed from lack of food – or was it from lust, she wondered? – and it seemed a pity to waste everything she had prepared.

"Why don't you go and sit down at the table?" she suggested, gesturing towards the elegantly set table, which had been relaid for the occasion with pretty side plates, two crystal wine glasses borrowed from James and Connor, and antique silverware that she had picked up at a boot sale and lovingly polished until she had restored it to its former lustre.

"Perhaps I could use your bathroom first?" Marco looked suddenly shy. "I would like to wash my hands before I eat," he added as an afterthought.

Saffy led him to the requisite door, realising as she did so that he must be sadly disappointed with her living space: the entire flat would have fitted easily into his living room.

Marco was, in fact, thinking just the opposite: Saffy's flat was small, but it felt like a home. Everything seemed welcoming, from the warmth of the polished floorboards to the candles burning softly in pots of coloured glass on her bathroom windowsill. He could see himself living here, he decided now, as he ran his hands under the hot tap before drying them on a fluffy lilac towel. This place was full of light and colour, yet there was a cosiness about it too. The slightly ajar door must lead to her bedroom – he was tempted to peep inside but restrained himself: it wouldn't be long until she was leading him in there for what promised to be the most exciting night of his life.

By the time he reached the table, Saffy was already there. She had placed his bottle of wine next to some glasses, along with a jug of water. "I don't drink much," she confessed, "but don't let that stop you enjoying it."

Since he could see that their starter consisted of seafood, Marco waved the wine aside. "It can wait for the meat. I will have water too." He poured a generous measure into two tumblers and passed one to Saffy, noting as he did the unusually wrought candlestick which held two tulip shaped candles in rich ruby and orange.

"I don't normally bother when it's just me ..." Saffy wondered if she was babbling. "With candles on the table, I mean. I wanted to make an effort tonight, though."

Marco hardly tasted his starter, too busy watching the way the candlelight lent Saffy's face an ethereal glow to pay much attention to what he was eating. Her eyes sparkled like her namesake and she smelled of the coconut shower creme he had noticed in the small, tidy bathroom earlier; for some reason, he found this far more enticing than the heady, musky perfumes his previous women had worn.

As he reached the last prawn, he couldn't resist teasing her a little. "I know why you have chosen this, *bella*: you know prawns are a good source of zinc, no? They help make lots of healthy sperm!"

Saffy's cheeks flamed as brightly as the candles. "I'll just check on the main course," she said demurely, picking up Marco's empty bowl along with her own.

In the kitchen, she splashed cold water on her cheeks, trying to tame the heat she felt. Her hands shook a little as she picked up the dish of couscous and carried it through. Marco gave her a slow, sultry look, the ghost of a smile hovering round his lips. He seemed to like embarrassing her, but she knew it was borne out of affection and not malice. Holding his gaze, she smiled back, trying to convey just how much he meant to her.

Returning for the tagine, she anxiously ran through a mental checklist: the brownies were cooling; the raspberries and ice cream were in the fridge; and she already knew that her lamb was perfectly cooked. Somehow, though, she knew that none of this mattered: people might say that the way to a man's heart was through his stomach, but she had a feeling that she could have served Marco a Happy Meal and he would have still wanted to sleep with her.

*

Marco couldn't believe the taste sensation in his mouth. If all of Saffy's cooking was like this, then he was a very lucky man.

"This is magnificent," he told her now, helping himself to another spoonful of meat and two more of sauce.

"It's one of the only things I can cook." She sounded apologetic, but he wasn't sure why. "I used to make this at university ..." She stopped suddenly, aware that Marco wouldn't want to know that it was one of James's recipes. "I can make lots of different cakes," she continued, after a pause. "That was one of the things I used to do with my mum, before she died. Dad used to go off playing golf on Saturdays, so the three of us would bake together. Sophie was too little to be much use - we used to give her a wooden spoon and let her stir our mixture before it went in the oven – but I loved it. I think if I hadn't opened a jewellery shop, I would have run my own micro-bakery instead."

"Your names are very alike," Marco commented idly.

Saffy grimaced. "I hated it when we were at school. Being called 'Saffy and Sophie' made us sound like a double act – or a really naff programme off kids' TV."

"Naff?" enquired Marco.

"You know – something really lame or uncool. Anyway, I was only 'Saffy' because Sophie couldn't say 'Sapphire' when she was little, and then it sort of stuck," Saffy explained.

"The name 'Sapphire' suits you," Marco said soberly. "You are very beautiful and very precious, *carissima*. And when you are happy, you sparkle like your namesake."

The room fell silent. Saffy tried desperately to think of something to say in return, but found she was tongue-tied.

"I'd better go and get the dessert," she stammered at last. "Have some more wine, Marco."

"You are sure you will not have some yourself?" he asked her, draining his own glass before he reached for the bottle. "It is a good year."

"Just half a glass," she acquiesced, thinking that maybe she needed a little Dutch courage after all now that dessert was the only thing between them and the bedroom.

Grabbing the plates, she escaped to the sanctuary of the kitchen, opening the fridge door and standing in the cool air that emanated from it until she felt able to return to the table.

Marco was pleasantly surprised by dessert. He didn't usually have a sweet tooth, but the slight bitterness of the chocolate, offset by the tart raspberries and the distinct taste of vanilla pods in the ice-cream, formed a combination that was hard to resist.

Saffy sipped her wine nervously, hardly aware of what she was drinking, her mind preoccupied with whether or not she had impressed Marco. Despite knowing he wanted her regardless of her culinary prowess, it suddenly seemed vital that he liked her brownies. She knew this was irrational but she couldn't help seeing it as an omen of some sort.

*

"So, young lady ..."

The bowls were empty, their wineglasses only half full. Marco arose from the table and took hold of Saffy's hand. "I think we will be more comfortable on your sofa."

As if in a dream, she followed him, her heart beating at twice its usual speed as she began to contemplate whether they might not make it as far as the bedroom. Sinking down onto the sofa, she let him push her back into a prone position so that she was totally at his mercy. His mouth covered hers; his hand began to slide under her dress and onto her bare thigh; and then the doorbell rang.

*

"Ignore it," Marco murmured, his breath hot against her ear. His hand crept tantalisingly further up her thigh.

The bell rang again, an insistent, impatient sound that obviously wasn't taking no for an answer.

Marco swore.

Seconds later, Saffy's phone started ringing. Although it was in the bedroom, where she normally plugged it in to charge it, the ringtone was as obtrusive as the doorbell had been. Marco sat up angrily. "Why now, of all nights?" he wanted to know.

Her phone had stopped ringing, but Saffy could hear the ping of a text being delivered. Seconds later, the ringtone started again.

Adjusting her clothing, Saffy scrambled to her feet. "I'll switch it off."

She stumbled into her bedroom, still half-woozy from the intensity of Marco's kisses, and grabbed at her phone, pressing the call reject button to silence the clamour for attention.

Just as she was about to switch it off, she glanced at the screen. All her calls were from Sophie, and a text message was flashing in front of her eyes. "Saf, let me in. It's urgent."

Pulling the bedroom door shut, Saffy hit call back. "What are you doing, Sophie?" she hissed, not wasting any time on pleasantries. "I can't let you in – Marco's here."

"I know it's meant to be your big night," Sophie's voice sounded strained, "and I wouldn't be interrupting if it wasn't an emergency. You've got to help me, Saf."

Saffy hesitated. The last thing she wanted was to let Sophie into the flat whilst Marco was there – it would kill the mood instantly. "I'll come outside to see you," she said grudgingly. "Get back in your car – we can talk there."

"Don't mention anything to Marco," Sophie's voice was urgent. She hung up before Saffy could protest.

*

Saffy was still staring at her phone when Marco popped his head around the door a moment later. "Is everything dealt with?"

"Not quite," she told him ruefully. "I need to pop out for a few minutes – but I'll be straight back, I promise. And then we can carry on with what we were doing." She shot him a meaningful look.

Marco's eyes took in the iron bedstead and patchwork quilt. "I will wait here for you, *cara*," he told her softly, arranging his long limbs on top of her bed. "Hurry back."

She bent and kissed him, wishing that she didn't have to walk away from him for even a few minutes. "I want this as much as you do," she said unevenly.

By way of response, he placed her hand on his trousers, letting her feel how hard he was. Their eyes met.

"I'll be back soon," she whispered, scooping her door key and mobile into her handbag and hurrying out before she could change her mind.

Sophie's car was parked in the little layby in front of the row of shops that contained *Jo Bangles*. Saffy opened the door and climbed inside. "This had better be important, Soph," she began angrily, "because that was the worst possible time for you to ..."

She broke off as she regarded her sister's tear-stained face. "What's wrong?" she asked urgently. "Is it Dad? Has he had another heart-attack?"

"It's worse than that." The words dragged unwillingly from Sophie's lips. "Saffy, I'm pregnant."

Chapter Twenty-Three

Saffy stared at Sophie in disbelief. "You can't be," she said at last.

Sophie's eyes welled with tears. "I'm two weeks late."

"Could it be exam stress?" Saffy suggested.

Sophie shook her head. "I *know* I'm pregnant. I feel sick all the time and my boobs are on fire."

"Have you done a test?" Saffy tried next.

Again, Sophie shook her head. "I daren't do one at home, in case Eleanor finds it, or Dad. And I can't do it at school either."

"So you want to do one here," Saffy guessed.

Sophie nodded. "And I was wondering ..." Her voice faltered. "... If you could buy the test for me," she finished in a rush. "I can't buy it myself, in case someone we know sees me."

Saffy thought this was highly unlikely since Sophie had a car and could easily drop into a chemist or supermarket miles from home. Nevertheless, she could tell that her little sister was scared and needed to know there was someone she could rely on.

"Why don't we pop down to the big Tesco now?" she said gently. "There's no point panicking until you know for sure that you *are* pregnant – it could easily just be a false alarm."

Within minutes, the two of them were carefully belted and heading for the all-night supermarket. Saffy checked the dashboard clock anxiously, wondering how long Marco would wait for her. Inwardly, she cursed Sophie – *why* couldn't she have waited until Sunday to spring this on her?

But then your lazy Sunday with Marco would have been ruined, she reminded herself. *At least this way you can still have the whole of Sunday together, even if you don't get tonight.*

No, that wasn't an option. No matter what happened with Sophie, Saffy was going to spend the night with her fiancé. Even though she had been dreading and anticipating in equal measure the event itself, she had looked forward to the idea of cuddling up with him and sleeping all night in his arms – even if it did seem rather clinical to go back to her flat now and climb into bed with him, rather than it being the natural progression of everything they had been sharing before Sophie's interruption.

Just then, her mobile buzzed. "Is the problem resolved?" Marco wanted to know; followed by, "Don't keep me waiting too long, cara!"

Deftly she texted back, "I want you too – but there's a bit of a crisis right now. Sorry."

Her hand hovered momentarily over the 'send' button – would he understand?

Obviously not, because her phone rang a few seconds later. "Saffy, what is going on?" Marco demanded abruptly. "This is supposed to be a special night for us, remember?"

Saffy glanced across at her sister's woe-begone face, feeling utterly and completely torn.

"I want to be with you, Marco," she said in a low voice. Sophie pretended not to hear anything, making a show of checking her mirrors, even though she didn't need to. "I do want to be with you," Saffy continued urgently, "but something unexpected's come up - I can't say anything more at the moment."

Marco let out a deep sigh. "So, are you putting me on hold for half an hour? Longer?"

"I'll get back to you in thirty minutes," Saffy promised him, aware that these shenanigans were completely killing the mood for both of them.

"I will keep the bed warm, *carissima*." His honeyed tones told her that she hadn't put him off – yet.

Not that she was likely to feel in the mood herself any time soon if she was off to buy Sophie a pregnancy test, she thought bitterly. How would she ever be able to relax and enjoy sex now if all she could think of was a potential unplanned pregnancy?

Marco was still speaking. "I must love you, *tesoro*, to wait for you like this."

He had used the L-word. Saffy's heart stopped beating for a second. "Did you just say you loved me?" she said at last.

Marco seemed temporarily confused. "I am sure I said 'like'."

But she knew what he had said. Her heart sang as she terminated the call.

*

Sophie had pulled into the almost empty car park. "We'll still be able to get one at this time, won't we?" she asked anxiously.

Since she had never had cause to buy a pregnancy test before – at any time of the day or night – Saffy shrugged. "I don't know. If we can't, you'll have to wait until tomorrow."

The anguished look in her sister's eyes made her hope that their mission would be successful.

Sophie stared at the array of boxes in horror. "I had no idea they were so expensive!"

"You're looking at an ovulation kit," Saffy told her, stifling a smile. "They're for people *trying* to get pregnant – not people who hope they're not." Extending her hand towards a test that promised 'Accurate reading in early pregnancy' along with a fairly idiot-proof photo of two tests, one bearing the word 'Pregnant' and the other 'Not pregnant', she added, "There are two in that one."

"I only need *one*," Sophie muttered.

"I think you should do it twice," Saffy insisted. "If it's negative the first time, but you haven't started in a couple of days, you should do it again, just to make sure."

A part of her was still convinced that Sophie was panicking over nothing. Her sister always took a melodramatic approach to life: if she had a slight sniffle, she always persuaded herself it was flu; and she had once claimed she had food poisoning just because she'd had a mild stomach upset.

Placing the small cardboard box in her basket, Saffy turned to Sophie. "Let's get some chocolate too - you know it helps with PMT."

Sophie was quiet on the way back to the flat. Meanwhile, Saffy tried to calculate how long she could decently wait before sending Sophie home. Marco had been very patient so far, but she couldn't expect him to hang around indefinitely until the pregnancy scare had been proved false.

As Sophie pulled into the parking space she had recently vacated, Saffy turned to her once more. "Marco's waiting for me in the bedroom. I'll have to tell him what's going on."

"No!" The word erupted from Sophie in a wail of anguish. "You can't say anything. What if he tells Dad, or Eleanor?"

"There's probably nothing to tell," Saffy argued. "You haven't even done the test yet."

"But if he knows I'm here, he'll ask questions," Sophie protested. "He must know you wouldn't walk out on him in the middle of sex unless it was an emergency."

"We hadn't actually got that far," Saffy corrected her.

"Well, he's bound to put two and two together – a teenage girl in tears usually only means one thing!" Sophie exclaimed dramatically. "Please, Saf. Once we know whether it's yes or no, I'll go – I promise. I just don't want to find out on my own."

Sighing, Saffy took her mobile out of her bag and began texting Marco. "Really sorry, but it's taking longer than I thought." She paused. How could she get him out of her flat without making it look as if she was getting rid of him? "Would you mind nipping out for some milk while I'm gone?" she continued. "There's an all-night Tesco about 5-10 minutes' drive away. I should be home by the time you're back."

She felt guilty sending a text rather than calling Marco, but she hated lying at the best of times and she knew she would struggle to sound convincing if she spoke to him.

Moments later, her phone rang. "You are not serious?" Marco sounded incredulous. "I am waiting to make love to you, and you are sending me out to buy milk?"

"For the morning," she improvised. "That way we can spend the whole day in bed together without having to leave the flat."

"For you, *bella* ..." He sounded resigned. "I take it this place sells petrol? Then I will fill up my car too – anything to make time without you pass more quickly."

Before she could thank him, she heard an exasperated sigh. "But I have no key. How will I return?"

"I'll let you in," Saffy said hurriedly. "I'll be back by then."

There was a spare key in one of the kitchen drawers, but she couldn't risk Marco returning mid-test and discovering what Sophie was up to.

*

Moments later, she heard her front door slam and looked up to see Marco leaving her flat. Luckily, he had parked his car across the road from her building, so he had no cause to glance in her direction. Once he was safely out of sight, she tapped her sister on the shoulder. "Come on – we'll have to be quick if you're still serious about Marco not seeing you."

As they made their way up the stairs, she suddenly thought of something. "What happened to the condoms I bought you?" she accused.

"We *were* using them." Sophie sounded indignant. "And then the box ran out, so Adam went and bought some more. But the first time ..." Her voice tailed off.

But you would have to be very, *very* unlucky to get pregnant the first time, Saffy thought. It was far more likely that Sophie had worried so much about the possibility of being pregnant that she had inadvertently halted her cycle – that happened sometimes.

Ushering Sophie into her flat, she pulled the pregnancy test out of her bag, failing to notice the receipt fluttering to the floor as she did so. Opening the box, she pulled out one of the sticks and handed it to Sophie. "I think you just wee on it and then wait," she told her. "Hang on, there are some instructions here."

Apparently, Sophie had to hold the indicator, with the blue cap off, in the stream of her urine for five seconds only – "Or you can wee in a cup and hold the stick in there for twenty seconds," Saffy offered. "It says you have to lay it flat afterwards and then wait three minutes for your result – there's an hourglass counter for that bit."

"Let's get it over with, then," Sophie said dolefully, taking the stick from her sister and disappearing into the bathroom. A moment later, she was out again. "I've done it, but I can't sit and watch it – it's far too stressful."

"Chocolate?" Saffy asked; but, for once, Sophie wasn't in the mood.

"I feel sick," she announced.

"That's just nerves," Saffy said soothingly. Looking suddenly pale, Sophie rushed back into the bathroom. The retching sound that followed told Saffy that her sister had just thrown up.

"Sophie?" Saffy knocked on the door, feeling worried. Pushing it open, she saw Sophie kneeling by the toilet with her head over the bowl. She had indeed been violently sick.

"Let's get you into bed," Saffy said gently. "You can't drive home in that condition. I'll ring Eleanor and tell her you're stopping with me."

Sophie nodded silently.

"I'll just get you a bowl," Saffy continued. Turning to leave the room, she caught sight of the pregnancy test. The word 'Pregnant' was very much in evidence.

*

Marco was feeling slightly annoyed as he paid for the four pint carton of semi-skimmed milk along with his petrol. He couldn't understand why Saffy kept on blowing hot and cold. Earlier on, she had seemed just as desperate as he was to rip each other's clothes off and get down to some serious sexual activity; and then the phone had rung, right after the incessant ringing of the doorbell, and she had disappeared with only a garbled explanation of some sort of 'crisis'. If he didn't know better, he would think that she was seeing someone else behind his back.

No, he reminded himself swiftly, Saffy wasn't Nadia. If she had disappeared like that, then there would be a very good reason for it. And did it really matter that she had nipped out for – he checked his watch – almost an hour, if he was going back to her now to show her exactly how he felt about her?

Back at the flat, Saffy gently tucked Sophie into bed, making sure that her sick bowl was close to hand. She would have to sleep on the sofa herself, but it couldn't be helped.

Then her face fell as she thought of Marco. She couldn't possibly spend the night with him now, not when Sophie needed her. They would have to postpone things until the following weekend.

A ring of her doorbell told her that he was already here. She couldn't tell him about Sophie –if she didn't mention that her sister was pregnant, Marco would want to know why Sophie wasn't being looked after at home; and she couldn't tell him the truth, not before Sophie had had the chance to talk to their parents.

Hating herself for deceiving him, Saffy quickly pulled her dressing gown over her dress and tried to look ill. Carefully opening the door so that she was half hidden from her fiancé, she looked at him pathetically. "You'd better not come in – I'm not feeling very well."

"Then I should stay and look after you," Marco exclaimed with concern.

"Better not." Saffy backed away from him. "I've just thrown up spectacularly," she added, banking on the fact that he was unlikely to want to deal with vomit.

"Do you know what's caused it?" Marco was looking less sure about staying now.

"No. Sorry, I think I'm going to be sick again." Saffy dashed for the bathroom – not because she felt ill but because she had suddenly remembered that Sophie's positive test result was still sitting on the edge of her washbasin. Locking the door behind her, she scooped it up and hid it in the waste bin, beneath a pile of used tissues, cotton wool balls and the rest of the rubbish she hadn't yet disposed of.

Meanwhile, Marco was pacing the living room, feeling somewhat concerned. What was that on the floor? He picked up the crumpled receipt, stared at it, then blinked. According to this, Saffy had bought herself a pregnancy test less than an hour ago. Was *that* why she was being sick?

Her handbag was on the floor, by the table. With trembling fingers, Marco opened it up and looked inside. A box proclaiming 'ClearBlue' looked up at him.

She was pregnant. He hadn't slept with her yet, but she was pregnant with someone else's child. The thought of it made him feel ill.

But just buying a test kit didn't mean she was necessarily pregnant, he argued with himself a moment later. Some women liked to keep one to hand, just in case. Maybe she was hoping that the two of them would have a baby together one day?

He was clutching at straws, and he knew it; nevertheless, he knew he had to be sure. Should he ask her? But then she would know he had looked in her bag. She might not like that – particularly if it turned out to be a false alarm after all.

She was being a long time in the bathroom. He looked at the box again: it said 'Two tests'. Praying that she wouldn't catch him, Marco opened the lid: only one test stick remained.

The thought occurred to him that she must be doing the test now, presumably to ascertain whether she was carrying someone else's child before she slept with him, Marco. Was she planning to pass this baby off as his then? His mind whirled. It was all too much to take in.

The bathroom door opened and Saffy appeared once more. He felt relieved that he had replaced her bag in time.

"Can we try this again next weekend?" she asked, not looking directly at him. She was hiding something: he was sure of it.

"Absolutely," he lied, thinking with regret how so much had changed in just a few short moments. She was still beautiful, still desirable, but she no longer tugged at his heart the way she had done up until now. He had been so sure that she was different, but it turned out she was just another version of Nadia all along.

He turned to go, then thought better of it. "Can I use your bathroom?" he asked for the second time that evening.

She nodded silently.

Once inside, Marco did what he had to do then turned on the tap, leaving it running whilst he quickly searched the room. He found the test stick with the 'Pregnant' result hidden at the bottom of the waste bin. That was that, then. Someone else had already claimed her. He switched his emotions off as efficiently as the computer systems he installed for a living, knowing that she would now never be his.

Washing his hands once more, he sighed. He had been a fool to think that Sapphire Vendrini was what she seemed. Still, at worst he was only ten thousand pounds out of pocket for the ring he had given her. And that was a small price to pay compared to the millions he could have lost in an expensive divorce some years further down the line.

Opening the door, he looked for the last time at the woman who could have been his life. She was watching him, almost nervously, as if she were impatient for him to leave.

"Are you sure you don't want me stay and look after you?" he asked, but she shook her head.

"Better not – I don't want you going down with it too."

Why couldn't she tell him the truth? he thought despairingly. Why not admit she wanted him, but she was pregnant by someone she was seeing before the two of them met?

"Goodbye then, Saffy."

He wondered, as he left her flat, whether she had registered the meaning behind his parting words.

Chapter Twenty-Four

Once Marco had left, Saffy returned to the bedroom to check on Sophie. Her sister was asleep already, her pale skin lending her a pathetic look. Next to her, the large plastic mixing bowl that Saffy had thought prudent to provide was still empty, so at least she hadn't thrown up again. Saffy would have to sleep on the sofa, though, just in case. Trying to make as little noise as possible, she gently lifted the two spare pillows off the bed and carried them through to the living room, before returning to look for a blanket.

As she watched the steady rise and fall of the younger girl's breathing, Saffy began to make a mental checklist of everything that would have to be done. Their father and Eleanor would have to be told, no matter how vehemently Sophie protested: if nothing else, they were bound to notice her getting fatter; and she wouldn't be able to hide a newborn baby.

That was assuming she went through with the pregnancy - Saffy hadn't really considered any other option, but that was because they'd both had a Catholic education. Thinking about it now, she wasn't entirely convinced that their schooling wasn't in some way partly to blame for Sophie's current condition: sex education at St Winifred's had consisted of "Don't do it before you're married", which wasn't really the most helpful advice in this day and age.

Sophie would have to make some difficult decisions. Right now, though, it was important that Eleanor knew where her step-daughter was, so she didn't worry. Saffy checked her mobile: half ten. Should she ring or text? Eleanor was one of those infuriating people who always kept her mobile switched off unless she was actually using it - she claimed it "saved the battery" – so perhaps the land line would be better?

Punching the buttons with a certain amount of exasperation – she still couldn't believe that Sophie had ruined what should have been a perfect night for her and Marco – Saffy waited for twenty or so rings before giving up. Her dad and Eleanor were obviously out. She sent a brief text instead, explaining that she and Sophie were having a 'girly bonding session' and that her sister would return home the following day – hopefully Eleanor would check for messages once she realised Sophie wasn't home. Her fingers hovered over the keyboard as she wondered whether she should also text Marco to apologise for kicking him out. No, better not: she'd told him she was ill, so she would have to keep up the pretence.

Miserably, she wondered whether Marco was as disappointed as she was.

*

Marco wasn't quite sure how he'd driven home. Too agitated to think straight, he'd hardly noticed the route he'd taken. He still couldn't believe that such a perfect day and perfect evening had ended in such a disastrous fashion.

Yet again, he pondered why Saffy hadn't told him she suspected she was pregnant. Had she sensed it for a while, the whole time they'd been seeing each other? Was that why she'd put off sleeping with him? More importantly, was she still seeing this man, whoever he was? Had she been leading a double life, juggling two men at the same time?

Pulling into the parking garage, Marco put his Jag into 'Park' and switched off the engine. He sat hunched over his steering wheel, holding his head in his hands. So many unanswered questions were making his brain hurt.

And then a sudden thought struck him: if he slept with Saffy now, would she try to claim the baby was his? What was it she'd said, just before he left? *"We'll do it next weekend."* Did she really think she could get away with something like that?

She didn't realise he knew the truth. She could call him all she liked, but he wasn't going near her now – not after what she'd done to him. He closed his eyes and he was twenty-three again, back in the men's bathroom, reliving the moment when he'd discovered that Nadia was cheating on him. He'd vowed there and then that no woman would do that to him ever again. No, from this moment onwards, Sapphire Vendrini was history.

But their fathers were friends. And the family businesses were merging. He would have to see Saffy again, whether or not he wanted to.

But wouldn't that be a perfect way to end your fake engagement? he argued with himself. *No one would expect you to marry a woman who was carrying someone else's child.*

And how could he live with the shame of everyone knowing he'd been cuckolded? he asked himself next. (Was it still being cuckolded if you weren't married? Was there another English word for it?) People would think that he hadn't been enough of a man for her, that Saffy had cheated on him because she hadn't been satisfied in bed.

*

Somehow he managed to extricate himself from the car and make his way into the building. He walked past the security guard in a dream, barely acknowledging his greeting, and stumbled into the lift. Reaching his floor, he was about to enter his flat when the hopelessness of it all overwhelmed him and he found himself desperate to talk to someone – anyone – rather than sit on his own, drinking to drown his despair.

Turning to the door opposite his own, Marco pressed long and hard on the doorbell. After a few seconds, Siân appeared. She seemed to be wearing a long jumper and little else. "What's wrong?" she asked, as she saw his face.

"Saffy's sleeping with another man," he said bleakly. He didn't mention the baby: no one must ever know Saffy was pregnant with a child that wasn't his: he couldn't live with the shame.

"More fool her, then." Siân wasn't going to waste any sympathy on someone who'd turned her down several times already.

"How could she do it?" Marco whispered. His face looked gaunt; his eyes were haunted.

Siân beckoned him inside, aware she could turn this to her advantage. "You need a drink," she told him, pouring generous measures of brandy into two glasses. She handed one to Marco and took a long sip from the other herself.

"I trusted her." Marco was still rambling on about his pathetic fiancée. Siân decided to up her game.

"I'm sure you did. No one expects someone they're going to marry to cheat on them." She paused. "Of course, you could get your own back," she said slowly, watching his face to see how he responded to her suggestion.

Marco's expression remained the same. Perhaps he hadn't heard her.

"You could give her a taste of her own medicine," Siân pursued. "Show her she's not the only one capable of pulling someone else."

Putting her glass down, she closed the gap between them. "You know there's always been something there, some spark with you and me," she murmured.

As if in a daze, Marco let her take his hand and lead him into her bedroom.

*

This encounter with Siân was, oh so different to anything he'd had with Saffy. Within seconds of entering her room, she was pulling off her jumper to reveal an athletically toned form, clad in only a skimpy pair of black briefs. Grabbing hold of him, she began to kiss him, pressing her almost naked body against him and running her hand down to his zip.

Startled, he pulled away. He wanted to punish Saffy for what she'd done to him, but not like this. Things with Siân were progressing far too quickly. He felt like he couldn't breathe.

"You know you want it." Siân moved towards him again and Marco was struck by a sudden moment of clarity. Even in his womanising days, he had always got to know someone a little first, before taking her to his bed, but Siân wasn't interested in any of that: *You know you want it*, she'd said – *it*, not *me*. Marco was just a challenge: she only wanted him now so she could score points over Saffy.

Seconds later, Marco did something he'd never imagined was possible: he walked away from a nearly naked woman who was practically begging him to have sex with her.

*

He regretted it later, of course. Lying awake in his bed, which seemed emptier than ever now that he knew Saffy would never lie in it, he began to wish he hadn't turned Siân down so hastily. Weeks of pent-up sexual frustration were taking their toll: he should have said yes to an empty encounter after all.

Servicing himself was a poor substitute, but he could take his revenge on Saffy by thinking about Siân – or any of the other numerous women who'd passed through his bedroom. Yet try as he might, he couldn't get Saffy's image out of his head, so that it was her face and no one else's when he eventually came.

*

Saffy spent an uncomfortable night on the sofa, spending hours worrying over Sophie before she finally fell asleep.

She waited until eight before tapping on the bedroom door. "How do you feel?" She'd brought Sophie a cup of tea, but her sister looked too fragile to drink it.

"Pregnant." Sophie glanced at Saffy. "The test was positive, wasn't it?"

Saffy nodded. "I'm so sorry …"

For a few moments, neither of them spoke; then Saffy decided to get the ball rolling. "What are you going to say to Dad and Eleanor?" she asked. "Do you want me to come with you?"

Sophie looked at her as if she was mad. "What are you on about? I can't tell them – they'll stop me seeing Adam."

"You can't *not* tell them!" Saffy was scandalised.

"If I don't have the baby, then they don't need to know I was ever pregnant." Sophie's mouth was set in a thin line of defiance.

"Is that what you want?" Saffy prodded gently.

A tear rolled down Sophie's cheek. "What else can I do?" she asked brokenly. "My exams start in a few weeks' time, and then I'm meant to be going off to university in September."

"What did Adam say when you told him?"

"He doesn't know," Sophie confessed. "I thought I'd wait until I was sure – because I kept hoping I was wrong – and now I don't want to tell him because I don't want him to feel scared and finish with me."

"Call him now," Saffy instructed. "You need to give him a chance to man up and face his responsibilities. You shouldn't have to go through this on your own, Soph."

Sophie blanched. "I can't tell him I'm pregnant over the phone!"

"Well … get him to come round here, then. He can tell his mum and dad you're studying together or something." Saffy was hoping that Adam would be able to make Sophie see sense about telling their parents.

*

Half an hour later, the sound of the doorbell announced Adam's arrival. He seemed slightly surprised to see Saffy when she opened the door to him.

"Sophie's got something to tell you." Saffy pointed him in the direction of the bedroom. "I'll leave you to get on with it while I put the kettle on."

Popping teabags into three empty mugs, Saffy couldn't help thinking about Marco. She was surprised he hadn't called or messaged to see how she was – did that mean he was angry with her for aborting their evening of passion?

As she waited for the kettle to boil, she couldn't help feeling a pang of regret for the way things had turned out. Everything last night had seemed so … *right* – until Sophie's phone call. She wondered if they would ever be able to recreate the perfect evening they'd lost.

By the time she carried the tea through, Sophie had given Adam the news. He looked as shocked as she did. "What are we going to do?" he kept repeating. At least he was saying 'we' and not 'you', Saffy thought.

"I think the two of you should see a counsellor," she suggested gently. "So you can talk through your options."

Adam stared at her. "What do you mean, options?"

"Whether you go through with the pregnancy or not," Saffy explained.

Adam looked incredulous. "Of course we're going through with it! It's my baby!"

"*Our* baby," Sophie corrected him, but Adam wasn't listening.

"You're not telling me you think Sophie should get rid of it? That's murder!"

"Well, what do you suggest then?" Saffy snapped back. "You're both still teenagers – you've got your whole future ahead of you."

"We'll work something out." Adam's eyes were feverish. "We'll get married, or live together - or something." His face clouded. "Mum and Dad'll disown me if they find out. We'll have to keep the baby a secret until they've got used to the idea of me being with Sophie. They know I've got a girlfriend, but they don't know how serious it is."

Saffy sighed. Far from talking sense into Sophie, Adam was just complicating the issue. There were now two sets of parents who didn't know they had a grandchild on the way.

"Why don't you just tell them the truth?" she suggested.

Adam and Sophie both began talking at once, each one protesting that this wasn't an option – not at this stage, anyway.

"You've got to keep it a secret," Sophie pleaded. "Just until the exams are over."

Adam nodded. "Once I've finished my A levels, I'll start looking for somewhere to live. We've both accepted offers from Surrey and they have family flats in their accommodation guide."

"And how's Sophie going to do a degree and bring up a baby at the same time?" Saffy wanted to know, watching their faces fall. "Look, it's all very well making romantic plans about the future, but you've got to be practical too. The first thing we need to do is get Sophie seen by a doctor – *and* tell Dad and Eleanor what's going on."

"If you tell them, I'll never speak to you again!" Sophie declared dramatically. "You have to let me handle this my way, Saff."

Adam placed an arm around her comfortingly. "She won't say anything, will you, Saffy?"

"Okay," Saffy agreed grudgingly, "I'll keep quiet for now – but once you've both finished your A levels, you're going to have to come clean. You can't get through this on your own, you know."

*

Marco was mystifyingly silent all day. Saffy was surprised by how hurt she felt: she would have expected at least one call to check she was okay. When she still hadn't heard from him by 8pm, she sent a brief text: *'Feeling much better now. Are you free for dinner tomorrow night?'* She checked her phone every ten minutes, but by the time she went to bed, he still hadn't replied.

*

Marco didn't feel like getting out of bed at all on Sunday. Usually, he went to the gym; but he'd allocated this Sunday to spending a lazy day in bed with Saffy – not too lazy, he corrected himself, remembering that they'd originally planned to let Sunday continue where Saturday night had left off – and now that he was on his own instead, he couldn't summon up the energy to do anything else.

In the end, he disentangled himself from his duvet and padded into the kitchen for a bottle of something to ease his pain. He knew he had a rather pleasing Châteauneuf du Pape in his wine cabinet, so he took it back to bed, where he knocked it back in no time at all, attempting to anaesthetise himself – but it didn't work.

By the time his doorbell rang at 2.30, there were three empty wine bottles littering the floor of his room and Marco was feeling comfortably numb – so much so that he couldn't be bothered to answer the door. Instead, he leaned back into his feather pillows and let the sound wash over him, his mind slipping in and out of a very pleasant daydream about Saffy.

The bell rang again. This time, he was struck by *déjà-vu*: last night, Saffy's bell had rung again and again, followed by her phone. She had been kissing him, on the verge of letting him finally make love to her – and then she had answered the phone and it had all gone downhill from there.

Had the call been from her lover, the father of her child? Marco was suddenly racked once more with jealousy. Who was this other man? Was it her co-worker? Saffy had sworn that the two of them were just friends, but was the Englishman secretly more than that? Marco had seen the way that James flirted with Saffy and he didn't like it one bit.

That might be Saffy at his door now, wearing a smile as false as her apology was sure to be. He hated her for deceiving him; nevertheless, he knew that, were he to let her in, he wouldn't be able to resist taking her to his bed and showing her what she would be missing for the rest of her life.

No, letting her in was a bad idea: she'd got under his skin already. If he were to have any hope of forgetting her, he had to go 'cold turkey' now – he'd looked up the phrase the night before when he'd been unable to sleep and fretting over how to break his addiction to Saffy, although why anyone should compare a plate of cold meat to letting go of a dependency was beyond him.

Eventually, whoever it was became tired of waiting and went away. Marco buried his head under the covers and tried to think about all the other women he'd slept with, but it was no use: he realised then that he wouldn't be able to forget Saffy until he'd broken her heart the way she'd broken his.

Chapter Twenty-Five

"Well?" James was agog for news. Saffy hated disappointing him.

"It didn't happen," she said shortly. "Something came up."

"Surely you mean it didn't happen because something *didn't* come up?" James sniggered; then, catching sight of Saffy's face, he became serious. "What went wrong, Darling?" he asked with concern.

"Family stuff," Saffy told him. "Let's just say that I had a phone call at an extremely inopportune moment."

"But that shouldn't ruin an entire weekend ..." James sounded mystified and Saffy couldn't blame him.

"I don't think Marco was happy about it," she volunteered. "He hasn't been in touch since."

"But he was crazy about you!" James objected. "Anyone could see that."

Saffy shrugged. "Perhaps I've turned him down once too often – he might think I'm just a tease."

"*No one* could ever accuse you of that!" James declared, enfolding her in a hug.

Saffy settled into the comfort of a safe embrace, thinking that every girl should have a gay best friend at times like these. A moment later, James let out an exclamation: "I know what will cheer you up! I've found your bracelet."

"Really?" Saffy was relieved to know that the item had been recovered.

"It's in my jacket pocket," James began, bending down behind the counter to retrieve it. The shop door jangled as he continued, "I found it under the sofa. It must have slipped off your wrist when you came round for dinner the other week." Straightening up, he found himself staring at an angry-eyed Marco.

*

"So, does my fiancée make a habit of visiting you in your home?" Marco asked softly.

The two men glared at each other. James was the first to drop his gaze. Passing the bracelet to Saffy, he disappeared into the back of the shop, muttering something about putting the kettle on.

"When did you have dinner with your boss?" Marco demanded abruptly, once James was gone. "And why didn't you tell me about it?"

Saffy stared at him in disbelief. "Are you jealous?"

"Yes!" Marco shouted, his eyes flashing. "I am jealous, Sapphire! You turn me out of your flat, but you go to another man's house for dinner. What is going on?"

"James and I are just friends," Saffy insisted.

"But you lived together at university," Marco persisted.

"We shared a flat," Saffy corrected him. "And there was another student living there too. There were three bedrooms." Not that James and Connor had needed separate rooms, but she wasn't going to start gossiping about their sleeping arrangements. Besides, she thought angrily, it was none of Marco's business what she had done several years ago – *she* wasn't interrogating *him* about his past lovers!

Trying to heal the situation, she placed a placatory hand on his arm. "I was worried about you – I didn't hear from you at all yesterday."

"I didn't feel well," Marco muttered. He looked at her narrowly. "I think maybe I had the same virus as you," he suggested slily, watching to see if she blushed. She did.

Just then, James returned, bearing two cups of coffee. Silently he handed one to each of them before vanishing into the backroom once more.

"Are you feeling better now?" Saffy asked, taking a sip from her coffee. "I thought maybe we could go for dinner somewhere?"

"Another time." Marco suddenly looked bored. "I have a date already planned for this evening – a charming woman I dated several months ago." He paused deliberately, waiting for her reaction. Saffy paled.

"You're taking another woman out for dinner?" she stuttered.

"But of course." Marco sounded surprised. "You and I did not promise to be exclusive - naturally we will see other people from time to time. I thought that was understood?"

Saffy recoiled as if slapped. How could Marco do this to her after everything he had said over the past few weeks? After all the time they had spent together? It didn't make sense.

"Will it just be dinner?" she asked in a small voice.

Marco regarded her coolly. "That's none of your business," he told her quietly. "You have been spending time with your male acquaintances – why should I not do the same with the women I know?"

He was breaking her heart, Saffy thought desperately, but she couldn't let him know it.

"Then give me a call sometime in the next week or two when you're free," she said as casually as she could. "Now, if you'll excuse me, I have to get back to work."

Walking past a startled James, who had obviously been skulking in the shadows, eavesdropping, she took herself off into her workroom and let the tears fall.

*

Later on, she had recovered sufficiently to ring the doctor's surgery where they were both registered and make an appointment for Sophie. The earliest she could be seen was Wednesday – but since the situation wasn't likely to change over the next few days, Saffy accepted a time of 10.30am, realising as she did so that she would need confirmation of this if Sophie were to take time off school to see the doctor.

Struck by sudden inspiration, she asked for a text message reminder to be sent to her the following day, giving her own mobile number instead of Sophie's, aware that Eleanor was prone to picking up her step-daughter's phone if it beeped. For someone who hardly ever switched on her own phone, she was decidedly nosy when it came to other people's texts – so much so that Saffy was amazed that Sophie and Adam had managed to keep their relationship a secret for so long.

*

Marco gazed at the woman opposite him, trying to remember what he had found so alluring the first time round. Melissa was attractive enough on the outside: a clichéd Barbie doll with big breasts and bleached hair extensions, and – if he remembered rightly – a fondness for handcuffs and black leather in the bedroom; but she was as shallow as a children's paddling pool and marginally less exciting. He was already dreading taking her back to his apartment at the end of the evening, aware that no matter how gratifying the sex would be, he would have to listen to several hours of inane chatter over dinner first.

Taking Melissa out for dinner had seemed like the perfect way to get back at Saffy, but he was exasperated by her already and they had only been talking for five minutes.

Excusing himself, he nipped out to the bathroom, where he carefully punched in the number for one of his engineers. He knew Phil was working late tonight – they had an order to get out in the morning and all the routers needed to be checked. As soon as his employee answered the call, Marco went straight to the point: "Can you ring me back from one of the company phones in a couple of minutes? I need an excuse to get out of having dinner with someone."

Returning to the table, he placed his mobile carefully beside his wine glass. Noticing Melisssa's quirked eyebrow, he grinned ruefully. "We've been having a crisis at work: I need to be on stand-by."

As if on cue, his phone started ringing, the caller ID showing up as 'Work'. Marco arranged his face into an apologetic look. "I'm sorry, but I will have to take this."

A few moments later and it was all over: Marco muttered a few clichéd words about the pressures of being in charge and the necessity to satisfy clients, placed enough money on the table to cover the drinks they'd had and a taxi home for Melissa, and left, promising that they would "do this again soon." Driving back to his apartment, he wondered how long it would be before he was able to forget Saffy and enjoy uncomplicated sex with a woman who meant nothing to him.

A sudden realisation struck him and he pulled over into a layby: he couldn't achieve closure with Saffy until he'd slept with her: until then, she would always be an unanswered question in his mind. That was the solution, then: he would make love to her and then walk away for good, telling his father that they hadn't been compatible after all. But what if she tried to claim it was his baby? He would need evidence that the child couldn't be his – could he maybe record the two of them, tell her how much he was looking forward to this first time together and capture the conversation for posterity?

What was he thinking? He gazed aghast at his reflection in the driving mirror and a stranger looked back at him: a man so desperate that he was acting like a character in one of those James Bond films his father liked so much, weaving intrigue and deception into the threads of his life. He couldn't let himself be caught up in this woman's mind-games – let her lie and cheat as much as she liked: he refused to stoop to her level.

No, he had to tell Saffy he knew about the baby, see what she said then. He should have mentioned it this morning, instead of taunting her with the mention of another woman.

He looked at his watch – it was still early: should he go to see her now? But she might be with her other lover …

What did he care if she was? He crashed his fist down fiercely on the dashboard, then wished he hadn't. His hand would be severely bruised later. No, he and Sapphire Vendrini were finished, even if she didn't know it yet. He would walk away from her as soon as he had exacted payment for the ring he had given her – and, for a price like that, the sex had better be mind-blowingly incredible, he thought bitterly.

Putting his car into gear, he pulled away and headed for home, unable to face Saffy until his heart and his hand stopped aching.

Chapter Twenty-Six

Saffy had spent a miserable evening, crying herself to sleep as she wondered what she had done wrong to make Marco sleep with another woman. She was still red-eyed at work the following morning and James was instantly alert.

"What's wrong, Darling?" he asked anxiously; followed by, "My money's on Marco – what's he done to make you so miserable?"

"Marco's seeing someone else." The words dragged unwillingly from her lips. "He said we weren't exclusive – that was after he told me he had a date with another woman last night."

She paused, expecting outraged sympathy from James – he was her best friend, after all – but he was strangely quiet.

"I think he's playing you," James said, after a while. "Try to see it his way, Angel: he's been desperate to sleep with you since he met you, and every time he thinks he's getting close, you pull away. There's no bigger turn on for a man than thinking he's wanted, but all you're doing is sending out signals that he doesn't do it for you. He's just trying to make you jealous, so you stop pushing him away and try to grab him before someone else does."

"That seems rather complicated," Saffy said doubtfully.

"It's sexual politics," James said airily. "Didn't you ever read Kate Millet's book? Connor had a copy of it when we all lived together."

"So, you're saying I just need to leap on Marco as soon as possible and things will be back to normal?" It all seemed far too easy.

"Not back to normal, Sweetie ..." James leered suggestively. "Play your cards right and you'll be able to do anything you want with him ..."

Saffy wondered, fleetingly, just how far women's rights had progressed in the last couple of centuries if James's solution to her problem was to barter herself to get what she wanted …

*

The text message from the doctor's surgery arrived half an hour later. She would forward it to Sophie once she was safely at school on Wednesday morning, away from Eleanor's prying eyes. First, though, she had to let James know that she would be popping out for an hour or so the following day.

Asking for time off for a doctor's appointment could only mean one thing as far as James was concerned. "If I were you, I'd have an IUD fitted," he advised. "The Pill plays havoc with the hormones, Sweetie – and my sister ballooned up with the one she was on."

"I'm not going for contraceptive advice," Saffy said stiffly.

It was clear that James didn't believe her, but she would worry about that later.

*

After several days of no text messages from Marco, it was a relief when one finally arrived that afternoon. It said simply, "We need to talk. I will call round to see you this evening."

Saffy's heart sank when she read it: 'we need to talk' was usually code for 'it's all over'. How had things managed to change so quickly? Just three days ago, Marco had acted as if he adored her; now he couldn't wait to be rid of her.

Nevertheless, she made an effort with the way she looked, just in case James was right and Marco was trying to elicit some sort of response from her. By the time he rang her doorbell at eight o'clock, she felt sick with anxiety; but the tight-fitting Bodycon dress and sultry eye makeup went a long way towards disguising her true feelings.

Marco's heart lurched when he saw her. Despite his intention to finish things once and for all between them, he couldn't help the spasm of desire that shot through him. First things first, though.

"You look very delectable, Saffy," he told her mechanically, not kissing her as he usually did but instead sweeping straight past her to sit on the sofa.

"So do you," she breathed, her eyes feasting on his dark hair and eyes, his designer stubble, the arrogant twist of his mouth.

The room stilled momentarily. At this point, there was nothing Marco wanted to do more than to take Saffy in his arms and lose himself in her entirely; but he steeled himself to resist.

"Come and sit down," he said at last. "We have important things to discuss."

She approached him a little nervously. "Can I get you a glass of wine? I've got a bottle of Shiraz."

She'd asked James for advice earlier, knowing only that Marco preferred red wine to white but having no idea what constituted a suitable choice. Her friend's initial advice from the previous week still rang in her ears: *'the only thing you really need to bother about is buying some decent wine to put you both in the mood.'*

Marco regarded her carefully. He could tell she was nervous – was she trying to ply him with alcohol so she could seduce him? It was time to tell her he knew what she was up to.

"I know about the baby, Saffy," he said bluntly.

She paled instantly. "How?" she whispered in horror, her eyes wide with shock.

"I found your pregnancy test in the bin, just before I left on Saturday." Marco's tone was flat, emotionless. He couldn't let her know how much it had hurt.

"It's not what you think …" She was about to explain that it was Sophie, not her, who was pregnant, but Marco was already continuing.

"How long have you been sleeping with someone else, seeing him behind my back?"

"I haven't!" she burst out, stung by the accusation. "You're the only man in my life, Marco – you must know that."

"Then where did this baby come from?" he asked practically. "I am not an idiot, Saffy – even if you think you can treat me like one!"

Saffy hesitated, on the verge of telling him the truth, then stopped. This was Sophie's secret, not hers, and she had promised she wouldn't say anything.

"I haven't been with anyone else since I met you," she said at last. "I'm not into cheating – I promise."

Seconds stretched into minutes as Marco contemplated her words. "You swear this is true?" he said eventually. "You are not two-timing me?"

Wordlessly, she shook her head.

"And the father of the baby?" Marco asked delicately. "Does he know about it? Does he want to marry you?"

"He's not in love with me," Saffy said quickly – technically, that was true – "and I don't love him either."

"So where does that leave *us*?" Marco's words hung between them, forming an almost palpable wall of mistrust. *What did he want her to say?*

"That depends on what you want …" Saffy spoke slowly, a part of her affronted that Marco should think her capable of cheating whilst her more rational side argued that she couldn't blame him for finding the test and jumping to conclusions.

Marco felt torn: he couldn't marry her now, not when she was carrying someone else's child; but, for the same reason, he couldn't sleep with her and then abandon her either. And there was still the business merger between *Benedetti's* and *Vendrini's* to consider.

"We will let things continue as they are, for the time being," he announced. "Your pregnancy is not showing yet …" He broke off as a sudden thought occurred to him. "You have not said whether you intend to have this baby or not," he said slowly. "If you and the father are not in love, then you could have a termination."

"Let's talk about that side of things some other time," Saffy said abruptly, tired of this whole charade. "Thanks for coming round, Marco, but I need to sleep. We'll catch up in a day or two."

She ushered him out of the door before he had a chance to protest.

*

When she awoke the following morning, Saffy resolved that she would have to be much tougher with Sophie. She couldn't let Marco go on thinking that she, Saffy, was pregnant when it was Sophie instead.

Sophie arrived just after 8am – she and Saffy had agreed that perhaps it would be better if Sophie didn't go into school that morning after all: Saffy could ring the school office to explain that Sophie would be late in, due to a doctor's appointment.

"How are you feeling this morning?" Saffy asked.

"Rubbish," was the honest reply. "I feel sick all the time – not just in the mornings – but I haven't actually thrown up since Saturday evening. Just as well – I don't want Eleanor to start fussing over me."

"It's only because she cares," Saffy said automatically, followed by, "You should tell her, Soph. The longer you leave it, the harder it'll be."

"Not yet." Sophie shook her head. "I told you, Saff – I don't want anyone finding out until after A levels. It's not just Dad and Eleanor – imagine what the school would say if they knew I was pregnant!"

Saffy supposed she was right: it wasn't the best publicity for a Catholic school to have an unmarried mother-to-be in the sixth form.

"Do you want a cup of tea?" she asked next, thinking that she could do with one herself.

Sophie pulled a face. "I've gone right off it. Have you got anything else?"

While Saffy fussed about, looking for herbal teabags, Sophie started to remove her blazer and tie.

"What are you doing?" Saffy wanted to know.

Sophie looked guilty. "Just trying to look less like a schoolgirl. I could pass for an office worker in this blouse and skirt.

Privately, Saffy thought her sister was making a fuss about nothing, but she held her tongue.

The tea had been drunk and one of Saffy's silk scarves appropriated to add a touch of colour to Sophie's otherwise monochrome outfit before Saffy was able to tell her sister about Marco's visit the night before. "*That*'s why you have to come clean," she said severely. "I really like Marco, Soph – I don't want him thinking I'm pregnant by someone else."

"You could have told him it was his," Sophie grumbled.

"He would have found that hard to believe, considering things haven't gone that far yet," Saffy snapped back. "You interrupted our night of passion, remember?"

"But what's he going to say now when you turn round and tell him you're not pregnant after all, then?" Sophie argued. "You'll either have to fake a miscarriage or tell him that you were lying all along."

"I never said I was pregnant," Saffy muttered, thinking what a ridiculous mess this was. "He just saw your test and jumped to conclusions."

"Well, he must like you if he's stuck around even after thinking you've let someone else knock you up," Sophie commented cheekily. Then, looking at her watch, she let out a shriek. "It's gone ten, Saff! Come on, we can't be late for my appointment."

*

It was just as well that Saffy had managed to ring St Winifred's to say that Sophie would be absent until the afternoon because not only was the doctor she was seeing running late with his appointments, but she was told she would have to see the midwife too. That involved waiting another twenty minutes until the lady in question was available.

Once Sophie had been prodded about and had given some blood samples, the midwife consulted the computer screen in front of her. "We need to do a home visit too – it's standard practice at this stage, so we can check your home will be suitable for a baby. Is it still the same address?"

Sophie looked at her sister nervously.

"Actually," Saffy heard herself saying, "Sophie's moving to Guildford in the summer. She and her boyfriend are moving in together there. So there's not much point you doing a home visit at the current address."

The midwife tapped away at her keyboard. "If you're moving to Guildford, then you're looking at the Royal Surrey County Hospital. East Surrey's good, but it's further away from Guildford. If you go on the NHS website, you can do a comparative study – we're supposed to make you aware of all your options so you can make an informed choice."

"Maybe a bit nearer the time," Saffy said hurriedly. "That's something for you and Adam to think about once you've moved."

"Is that likely to be within the next couple of months?" the midwife asked. "You'll need a twelve weeks' scan sometime in June – if you're still here, you can have that done at Stoke Mandeville and they'll transfer your notes across."

"It's really happening, isn't it?" Sophie asked in a small voice as she and Saffy left the midwife's room a few minutes later.

"Which is why you have to tell Dad and Eleanor," Saffy reminded her. "You can't do this on your own, Soph: you have to let them help you."

"Okay," Sophie tried to be brave. "I'll tell them soon – just let me have a few more days to get used to the idea."

She would probably have told them, had not Antonio Vendrini suffered another heart attack which put him in hospital for the foreseeable future.

Chapter Twenty-Seven

The first thing Saffy knew about her father's heart attack was when Sophie rang her in floods of tears later that evening.

"Sophie! What's wrong? Is it the baby?" Saffy could barely make out what her sister was saying through the huge, gulping sobs.

"Saff, it's Dad. He's had another heart attack - a bad one this time." Sophie was almost hysterical with grief.

Saffy's heart clenched. "How bad?" she wanted to know.

"Really bad. We were all having dinner when he suddenly clutched at his chest and just toppled off his chair." Sophie stifled a sob. "Eleanor tried to give him mouth to mouth – you know she did that St John's Ambulance course after the last time – and then got me to call 999. He's on his way to hospital now, in an ambulance. Eleanor's gone with him. I wanted to go too, but she said I had to let you know and that we should make our own way to the hospital. She said I could pick you up, but I'm too upset to drive."

"I'll order a taxi," Saffy said automatically. "It's all right, Soph – I'll be with you soon. I'll come and get you and we can go together. Which hospital is it? Stoke Mandeville?"

How ironic that, only a few hours earlier, the midwife had mentioned the same place but for very different reasons.

"No, he's been taken to the Urgent Treatment Centre at Wycombe – that's where people go when it's really serious," Sophie wept. "He's not going to die, is he, Saff?"

"Let's just concentrate on getting there," Saffy said firmly, unable to give her sister false hope at this stage. "He's in the best possible place, Soph."

*

She terminated the call and logged into her Uber app, but before she could book a taxi, her phone started ringing. Saffy glanced at the caller ID: Marco. He would have to wait – this was far too important. Pressing 'Reject', she ignored his call and concentrated on trying to find a cab.

Marco gazed at his phone in disbelief. Why wasn't Saffy answering? After everything she had said last night, he had been prepared to give her another chance to explain – after all, their conversation had ended before anything had been properly decided. If she got rid of the baby, then maybe, just maybe, the two of them still stood a chance; but there was no way he was sticking around playing stepfather to someone else's bastard!

Angrily, he hit redial. This time, Saffy answered. "Marco, I can't talk now." She sounded agitated. Was she with the father of her baby?

"Then it is over between us," Marco said bleakly. "If you cannot be bothered to discuss our situation -"

"My dad's had a heart attack," Saffy broke in. "I'm just trying to sort out a taxi for Sophie and me. I'm sorry, Marco, but I haven't got time to think about anything else at the moment." She sounded close to tears.

Marco swore softly. "I am sorry …"

"Save it for later," Saffy told him, hanging up and returning to Uber. Her fingers trembled as she booked the cab, wondering if her father would still be alive when she and Sophie reached the hospital. There was a car seven minutes away. As she sat and waited, she burst into tears.

*

A contrite text arrived from Marco a few minutes later. *'I am sorry, cara,'* he repeated. *'I did not understand. Can I take you to the hospital?'*

'The Uber's already on its way,' she texted back, *'but thanks for offering.'*

'*Where is he?*' he asked next.

'*Wycombe,*' she replied; then, as her app updated, '*The taxi's here. Speak later.*'

Grabbing her handbag, she left her flat.

*

Once he had read Saffy's last text, Marco felt terrible. No matter what had gone wrong between them – and whether or not she kept this baby she was carrying – this situation with her father was horrendous. He knew that Antonio had already suffered several heart attacks before now – Saffy had told him so when they first met – and that his wife was constantly trying to get him to slow down.

How far away was Wycombe Hospital? He googled it quickly, realising that it was quite close. Punching it into his map app, he studied the screen intently. He had liked Saffy's father when he had met him, and he didn't like to think of the three women being left helpless whilst the family patriarch was confined to a hospital bed. Pausing only to pick up his car keys and his wallet, he headed for the lift.

*

Desperately trying to hold herself together, Saffy gave the cab driver the postcode for her family home. "We're picking up my sister to take her to the hospital," she explained when the driver commented he'd been booked to do a journey to Wycombe. In less than ten minutes, they were pulling up outside her father's house, an anxious Sophie already waiting on the doorstep.

The two girls were quiet on the journey to the hospital. Saffy hoped that Sophie wasn't going to be sick in the car – she looked as pale as she had the previous Saturday when she'd thrown up so spectacularly in the bathroom. Luckily, the roads were fairly deserted, so within twenty minutes they had arrived.

As the driver slowed to a halt near the main entrance, Saffy gave her sister's hand a squeeze. "He'll be okay," she promised, hoping that she was telling the truth.

Sophie gave her a watery smile.

Asking for her father's whereabouts at the Reception desk, Saffy found herself directed to an open plan waiting room. The walls were covered with posters about looking after your heart and how to spot the signs of a stroke, and a handwritten notice informed anyone who was interested that a cardiac support group called 'Brave Hearts' met once a month Because of the lateness of the hour, the room was almost empty, apart from one or two people sitting on plastic chairs. Eleanor was one of them. A magazine lay open on her lap, but she seemed unable to read it. Noticing her two step-daughters, she got up from a chair to give them both a hug.

"How is he?" Saffy asked anxiously.

Eleanor's face looked pinched as she answered. "The ambulancemen managed to get him breathing again, but he's under observation for at least the next twenty-four hours. He's in the CSRU at the moment, waiting to be assessed, and then they'll either move him onto the cardiac ward, transfer him elsewhere or send him home."

"So he's not in any immediate danger?" Sophie broke in, looking relieved.

"Not exactly – he's still being assessed. But at least if he has another attack while he's in here, they've got all the necessary equipment to deal with it straight away."

"Can we see him?" Sophie wanted to know.

Eleanor shook her head. "Visiting hours ended at 8pm – not that it would have made much difference to us while your dad's under observation. I just thought we should all be here, in case …" Her voice faltered.

Saffy closed her eyes, not wanting to think about death. Irrationally, she wished that Marco was here right now: he would have taken control effortlessly, making them all feel better.

But Marco had stopped loving her – if he had ever done so in the first place. She would have to be the one to hold the family together instead. Touching Eleanor's arm gently, she told her, "I'm going to get a cup of tea. Why don't I get you one too?"

*

Marco was relieved to find that there was plenty of space in the hospital car park but annoyed to learn he still had to pay, despite the lateness of the hour. Scanning the list of charges, he realised he could park for up to twenty-four hours for only nine pounds, then felt guilty a moment later as he remembered that Saffy's father was seriously ill – why was he bothering about the cost of a ticket at a time like this?

Inside the hospital, the lights were slightly dimmed as a concession to the time. Marco found the Reception desk and waited for the sole nurse on duty to acknowledge his presence.

"You have a patient who was admitted this evening after a heart attack," he began cautiously. "Antonio Vendrini."

The nurse consulted the notes in front of her. "Are you a relative?"

Marco didn't hesitate. "Yes," he said simply. "He's my father-in-law."

Chapter Twenty-Eight

Heading towards the waiting room, Marco found Saffy coming the other way.

"Your father – how is he?" he asked anxiously.

Saffy looked stunned to see him. "What are you doing here?" she whispered.

Marco shrugged. "Where else would I be? I would be a terrible fiancé if I did not come to the hospital for something like this."

"Except we're not really engaged," she reminded him.

By way of response, Marco took hold of her shoulders, turning her towards him so that he was looking directly into her eyes. "Promise me that what you said last night was true."

"Which part of it?" Sophie said warily.

"That you have not cheated on me. That this child you are carrying was conceived before we met."

"I haven't cheated on you." Saffy wondered how to get around the rest of the question. Damn Sophie! She needed to get her act together quickly and admit what was really going on.

"And you are thinking of having it?"

Her heart almost broke at the uncertainty in his voice. She needed to reassure him and protect Sophie at the same time. "I don't want to have anyone's baby except yours," she said truthfully.

"Then you are getting rid of it?" His eyes bored into hers, searching for answers.

"Do we have to talk about this now?" Saffy neatly deflected the question, uncomfortable at all the half-truths she was being forced to tell. "My dad's just had a heart attack, Marco. I can't think about anything else right now."

"*Mi dispiace, cara.* I was not thinking. It is just that I need to know where you and I stand." He released her suddenly. "You have no idea how miserable I have been without you, *tesor.* I wanted to hate you, and then I hated myself for wanting you."

Trembling a little, Saffy stepped towards him. "Just hold me," she whispered, aching to feel his arms around her once more.

In the middle of the corridor, they clung to each other and were still there a moment later when Sophie came to find out what had happened to the tea.

*

At half ten, a nurse appeared and gestured to Eleanor to follow her. Saffy and Sophie looked at each other fearfully. What now?

But it was all okay. Antonio was not only awake but was asking for his wife. He seemed to be his normal self, apart from feeling very tired.

Eleanor returned five minutes later, the relief visible on her face. "I've told him he has to stop working so hard," she told her step-daughters, "or else the next time round, he might not be so lucky." Delving in her bag for a tissue, she blew her nose loudly. "The doctor said the two of you could go in for a minute now, before your dad goes to sleep. I think it would do you good to see him."

Sophie didn't need telling twice. Following the nurse who had been patiently waiting, she almost sprinted down the corridor, Saffy trailing after her.

Antonio was sitting up slightly in bed, propped up by a support pillow. Saffy noticed the wires leading to the mobile heart monitor on the floor next to him and wondered what the various jags and spikes signified.

"Daddy!" Sophie would have flung her arms around him, but the nurse signalled for her to keep her distance. "You mustn't over-excite him," she warned.

"My little girls." Antonio smiled ruefully at his daughters. "Eleanor tells me I frightened you all."

"You're okay now, aren't you?" Sophie's eyes pleaded for an affirmative.

"Your dad needs lots of rest for the next few days," the nurse said briskly. "It's standard practice to stay in hospital for three to five days after an attack, and then, if everything seems okay, we'll let him go home." She looked severely at Antonio. "The last time you were here, you were prescribed ACE inhibitors, but your wife says you stopped taking them."

"I felt better without them," Antonio grumbled.

"Well, tonight's escapade seems to be telling a different story, doesn't it? From now on, your whole family has to support you in this – your daughters as well as your wife. You need to take your medication every day - you'll be on statins for a while as well as the other tablets you should have been taking - and try to slow down a little as well." Turning to Saffy and Sophie, she added, "Your mum'll find it easier if you all pull together with this."

"Step-mum," Sophie muttered, under her breath.

"We'll do our best," Saffy promised, mindful that slowing down was the last thing her father wanted to do – especially when he had only recently turned fifty.

As they turned to go, Antonio called her back. "Saffy …"

"What is it?" She hurried to his side.

"Eleanor told me that Marco was here."

"He's in the waiting room," Saffy explained. "I don't think it's a good time for the two of you to talk business now, though."

Antonio shook his head. "He is a good boy, Saffy. He will take care of you." He yawned suddenly. "Tell him to come with you tomorrow – I would like to speak to you both."

"Bye, Dad." Saffy leaned over and kissed him on the top of his head. "Get a good rest - we'll be back in the morning."

She left the room, musing over what her father might possibly want to talk to them both about.

*

When Saffy returned to the waiting room, her stepmother and Marco were deep in conversation.

"Saffy," Marco began carefully, "I am going to take you and Sophie home. You are both tired, and your *matrigna* thinks you should go home together so that neither one of you is on your own."

"I'm staying here," Eleanor broke in. "I'd rather be near your dad, Saffy. The nurse told me that the first 24-48 hours after a heart attack is the time when he's likely to be most unstable. I want him to know I'm close by, just in case …"

Saffy put her arms around the older woman. This was hard for the whole family, but it must be doubly so for Eleanor with a husband who seemed determined to ignore all the advice the hospital had previously given him.

"We'll all keep nagging him until he does what he's told," she told her now. "With three women on his case, he doesn't stand a chance!"

"Thanks, Love." Eleanor smiled gratefully. "Keep an eye on Sophie, won't you?" she added, lowering her voice. "She looks so pale at the moment, and she's hardly eating a thing. I'm worried she's got exam stress."

"I'll look after her," Saffy promised, determining that the sooner Sophie told Eleanor what was really bothering her, the better. "Try to get some sleep if you can. You must be exhausted too."

Everyone was silent on the drive home. Marco was desperate to talk to Saffy about her decision to get rid of this other man's baby – he didn't want someone else's bastard; but he'd had a strict Catholic upbringing and was struggling to reconcile his inherent beliefs with the reality of an unplanned for child. They needed to talk properly; but how could they do that when her little sister was sitting next to her on the back seat?

"I am taking you to your parents' house, yes?" he asked at last, needing to say something – anything – to counteract the absence of sound.

"Do you mind making a quick detour to my flat?" Saffy sounded apologetic. "I'll need to grab some clean clothes and my toothbrush."

"I could always stop at your gaff instead," Sophie commented.

"I've only got one bed," Saffy reminded her, "and you haven't got any of the stuff you'd need with you. Anyway, my place is nearer – it makes sense to go there first and then onto you."

"I have not heard this word 'gaff' before," Marco commented, always eager to improve his English.

"That's because it's slang," Sophie grinned, "and your English is always so impeccable, Marco – and *very* sexy, by the way, when it's spoken with that slight Italian accent!"

Saffy smiled inwardly, aware that Marco was embarrassed to hear such comments from a schoolgirl. He might exude self-confidence, but beneath his assured exterior lurked a man who was just as insecure as she was.

They had reached Saffy's flat. Marco pulled on the handbrake and turned off the engine. "Can I help you carry anything?" He was angling for the chance to be alone with her, if only for a few moments. Saffy decided to take pity on him.

"I could do with a hand, actually. Sophie'll be all right on her own for a few minutes, won't you, Soph?"

It was an order, not a question. Sophie grunted in response and settled back against the leather upholstery.

As Saffy unlocked the door to the street and led her way upstairs, Marco was struck by the difference in the way he felt now. Just over twenty-four hours ago, he had arrived at Saffy's flat, full of anger and vengeance, wanting only to punish her for what she had done. Now that she had told him of her plans for the future, he found himself longing for her again: she had chosen him over an unwanted baby; and this faceless father was a ghost from her past, not a present rival.

"Excuse the mess," she began, opening the front door, but Marco was beyond caring what her flat looked like. Scooping her up into his arms, he carried her through the living room and into the bedroom, where he deposited her upon her unmade bed and began to kiss her as if both their lives depended on it.

For a moment, Saffy was too surprised to protest. Then, as Marco's kisses began to take effect, she found herself drowning once more in the overwhelming sensations he provoked. As his tongue probed and teased, her hands knotted themselves in his hair, pulling him closer until the burning heat between them threatened to consume them.

"Saffy!" Her name was a plea for help.

"Marco!" Her low moan parallelled his own, her obvious need for him driving him wild with desire. This time, nothing would stop them – and then, just as it had the previous Saturday, the doorbell rang.

The sound brought Saffy back to her senses. *What was she doing?* Her father was in hospital and she had been on the verge of giving herself to Marco, as if nothing else mattered. Wrenching herself out of his arms, she staggered to the door.

"About time too!" Sophie sounded indignant. "I'm bursting for the loo!" Then, catching sight of her sister's flushed face and dilated pupils, she added cheekily, "I haven't interrupted anything, have I?"

By now, Marco had appeared in the bedroom doorway, breathing slightly heavily but otherwise looking perfectly composed. "I'm not sure what else you want to take," he said unnecessarily. "Perhaps you should give me a hand."

"Oh, snog yourselves silly while I'm in the lav," Sophie told them airily, "but once I'm out, we're going!"

*

It was midnight. Marco had finally driven back to his own apartment, after accepting a cup of sub-standard black coffee made with Kenco. He'd drunk it politely, not mentioning his all-singing, all-dancing coffee machine at all.

Saffy had made up the king-sized bed in one of the guest rooms so that she and Sophie could lie and talk: neither of them wanted to be alone.

"He could have stayed, you know," Sophie said after a while. "I wouldn't have minded."

It was too dark for her to see the blush that spread over Sophie's cheeks.

"I don't think I'd want the first time to be here," Saffy said reflectively. "Too many associations with Dad and Eleanor. And I wouldn't relax knowing you were under the same roof."

"Mmm," Sophie agreed naughtily. "I'd have to sleep with my head under the pillow to block out the sound of you shrieking Marco's name or the headboard banging away."

"Soph!" Saffy didn't know whether to be angry or amused.

"You know you can't keep your hands off each other," Sophie continued. "At first I thought you were just going along with it to make Dad happy, but it's more than that, isn't it? I can tell." She paused. "Why on earth haven't you done it yet?"

"Because a certain little sister keeps interrupting us," Saffy told her. "You really do have lousy timing, you know."

"The baby's making me need to wee a lot," Sophie said unrepentantly.

"Speaking of the baby ..." Saffy paused.

"No!" Sophie was adamant. "I can't tell Dad and Eleanor now – not after what's just happened. You heard the nurse say he's got to be kept calm."

"Well, at least let me tell Marco then," Saffy argued. "You don't know how stressful it's been with him thinking I'm pregnant and knowing it's not his."

"I don't want anyone else knowing at the moment," Sophie said flatly. "You, me, Adam – that's three people already. It's not as if you have to spend nine months pretending that you're having a baby, is it? About 1 in 4 pregnancies don't work out – I looked it up. You can just say something went wrong and you're not pregnant anymore."

"But I don't want him thinking I was even a little bit pregnant," Saffy insisted. "You're not being fair, Soph. Think how Adam would feel if it was the other way round and he thought you were pregnant with someone else's baby."

"Well, you'd better think of something quickly," Sophie snapped, "because I'm not telling anyone I'm pregnant until I absolutely have to!"

Saffy lay awake in the dark for a long time, trying to work out some sort of practical solution to the problem. A part of her felt that Sophie was being incredibly selfish – would it *really* make much difference if Marco were in on the secret too? And then she thought of her dad and Eleanor and how shocked and disappointed they would be, and knew that, had she been in Sophie's position, she wouldn't have wanted to say anything either.

Chapter Twenty-Nine

The next morning, Saffy rang Sophie's school to apprise them of the situation with her father and ask if Sophie could take a couple of days off. "I know it's close to A levels," she told the secretary who answered, "but we need to be on standby for the next few days. Can she do exam revision at home?"

In the end, the Head of Sixth Form agreed that Sophie could take the rest of the week off as long as she collected some work from her various teachers. They would go in to see Dad this afternoon, Saffy decided, and collect the schoolwork on the way.

Sophie was surprisingly distraught at missing two days of school. "How am I going to see Adam now?" she wailed, bursting into tears. "I won't even be able to see him at the weekend – not if Dad's coming home and we all have to stay with him."

"Oh, for goodness sake, Sophie! Stop thinking about yourself and grow up!" Saffy had reached the end of her tether. "You and Adam can have as much time together as you want once you're at university. It's not going to kill you if you don't see him every day."

"You're so hard!" Sophie said with feeling. "No one would ever think you'd been my age once!"

*

James also had to be rung. Briefly, Saffy explained what had happened, adding that she needed to visit her father in hospital that day and the next, but that everything should be back to normal, workwise, by the following Monday.

James was instantly full of concern. "My poor darling! Would you like Connor and me to come round and cheer you both up tonight?"

"It's okay," Saffy said hastily, cognisant that James's idea of 'cheering up' involved large quantities of alcohol – not a good idea for any of them but especially not Sophie. "We might be staying at the hospital quite late," she added, by way of excuse.

Finally, Saffy decided to call Marco, but before she could tap his name, her caller ID told her that he had beaten her to it. "How is your father today?" he asked her.

"Okay, I think: Eleanor said he'd had a good night. Sophie and I are going in later. They're doing a few tests this morning." Saffy paused. "Last night, my dad said he'd like to see you," she told him in a rush. "Do you want to come over to the hospital with Sophie and me?"

"What time?" Marco sounded as if he were leafing through some papers. "I have a meeting I cannot get out of at two, but I can come to the hospital after that."

"We'll see you there, then – we have to go via Sophie's school to collect some homework for her. It'll be too late on our way back."

"Later then, *carissima. Ciao.*"

*

It was almost four when Marco arrived at the hospital. Saffy and Sophie had been taking it in turns to keep Eleanor company in their father's room – there were only two visitors allowed at one time - and Saffy was currently mooching about the waiting room, marking time while she waited for her fiancé.

Was Marco her fiancé? On Monday and Tuesday, she had been certain that he had grown tired of her – and the misconception about the baby hadn't helped; but yesterday he had been not only attentive but almost infatuated, his desire for her returned to its former ardour.

223

"You look tired, little one," he commented, noticing the dark shadows under her eyes.

"I've got a lot on my mind," she said truthfully.

"Are you eating properly? You must keep your strength up, especially now ..." His voice tailed off.

"About the baby ..." she tried, thinking that - Sophie or no Sophie - she had to tell him the truth.

He placed a finger to her lips.

"I do not want to waste time talking about a mistake in your past, *tesoro mio*. You do not love this man and he does not love you, whereas I ..." He looked at her hungrily. "I suppose it would not be proper to kiss you in a hospital?"

"Probably not," she murmured, nevertheless moving closer to him. For a brief moment, time was suspended, holding them in equilibrium, his longing balanced by hers. In slow motion, she reached for him, drawn to him irresistibly.

"Saffy ..." With perfect timing, Sophie ruined yet another perfect moment. It was almost, Saffy thought angrily, as if her sister could sense when something interesting was about to happen and chose purposely to destroy it.

"I just came to see if Marco was here yet." Sophie seemed blasé about interrupting the two of them. "Dad was asking for you both."

Taking Marco by the hand, Saffy led him towards her father's room. "We're here, Dad," she said, pushing the door open.

Antonio looked up at the young Italian in front of him, waving to Eleanor to leave. He and Marco liked each other: they were on the same wavelength when it came to business; shared a similar golf handicap; and it was obvious that Lucas's son adored Saffy. That drunken evening had reaped unexpected benefits: already he felt as if Marco was the son he'd never had.

"You look just like your father used to," he said, smiling at the memory. "The summer I met Saffy's mother was when we were both working as waiters in a grand hotel – your father had all the female guests chasing him, their hearts fluttering over his big, brown eyes – but I won the only woman who truly mattered."

Saffy decided it was a good job Eleanor wasn't there to hear the last bit.

"The moment I saw Louise, I knew she was the girl I wanted to marry," Antonio continued, a faraway look in his eyes. "I set up *Vendrini's* to prove to her parents that I could take care of her, that I could earn enough money for a wife and children. It took a year until I was confident enough to go to her father and say, 'See – I can look after your daughter' and we were married a month after that." Struggling to sit up straighter, he fixed the younger man with a confident stare. "But you, Marco, you have no need to prove yourself. You are a man of means, heading your father's company here in the UK and about to help join *Vendrini's* and *Benedetti's* together – so is there any reason why you and my daughter should not get married straight away?"

* * *

"You can't be serious!" Saffy gazed at her father in disbelief.

"How soon is 'straight away'?" Marco asked, his question taking her totally by surprise.

Antonio shrugged. "I have had four heart attacks now in just over two years. I am only fifty-one, but it is likely I will not see sixty."

"Don't say things like that," Saffy protested, almost in tears at the thought.

"I am being realistic, *cucciala*," Antonio said gently. "Maybe I have ten more years, maybe twenty – or perhaps only two. But I would like to see you married before I die, Sapphire *mia* – and I would like to see the wonderful grandchildren that you and Marco are going to make for me."

Saffy and Marco exchanged glances.

"So, are we talking this time next year, or earlier than that?" Marco pursued. "In six months' time? In three?" He sounded extremely business-like, as if he were negotiating the company merger and not a marriage.

"My last heart attack was four months ago," Antonio told him. "Fortunately, it was very mild – not as dramatic as this one; but being here now has made me realise that I must be prepared for it to happen again." He turned imploring eyes on Saffy. "It would make me so happy to see you married, *piccola*."

"This is April," Marco muttered under his breath, as if talking to himself. "My family will have to come over and there is no chance now of booking the wonderful house we saw the other week, but if we could hold the reception at your home …"

Saffy stared open mouthed at Marco. *What was he doing?*

"I will see what I can do," Marco promised Antonio, tapping away on his mobile phone furiously. "If we can find a church and a priest, we can turn this around in six to eight weeks."

Antonio stretched out a hand towards his future son-in-law. "I knew I had chosen well," he said simply. "You will be a good husband to my little Saffy, no?"

"Yes," Marco agreed, looking at Saffy, "I think I will."

Chapter Thirty

Once they had left Antonio's room, Saffy looked at Marco accusingly. "What do you think you're playing at?"

"I am not 'playing' at anything," Marco told her. "*You* are the one who told your father we were engaged – less than an hour after we had first met, if I remember rightly – and since then you and I have talked about getting married."

"But not this soon," Saffy said desperately. "We still hardly know each other, Marco."

"We know each other enough." Marco's deep brown eyes bored into her startled blue ones. "I admit I was angry when I found you were pregnant, but an unborn child is easy to get rid of – it is not as if you already had a child from a previous relationship and were expecting me to play stepfather."

Saffy's heart twisted at the casual mention of 'getting rid of' a baby – it was just as well she wasn't really pregnant, or such a callous statement would have reduced her to tears.

"Is that all marriage means to you?" she asked him bitterly. "Am I just a baby-making machine, one you want to fill with little Marcos?"

"No …" Marco reached out a hand and stroked the hair from her face. "You are my father's best friend's daughter and one day you will inherit *Vendrini's* – one has to be pragmatic about these things, *cara*. But you are also a very beautiful woman – and you can cook."

Saffy almost choked with rage at such a chauvinistic attitude. "So, you expect me to be an angel in the kitchen, a whore in the bedroom and a Vendrini in the boardroom?" she challenged, purposely misquoting Jerry Hall's famous statement.

"Saffy, you and I both know there will be fireworks in the bedroom – I would marry you on the strength of that alone! But you must agree that your family name helps … I am trying to be honest with you, *bella*."

"But why the rush?" she muttered, trying to ignore the way her heart beat faster whenever he was near her.

"Apart from the fact that your father wants to see you married before he has another attack?" Marco asked drily. He sighed heavily. "Sapphire Vendrini, you are the most infuriating woman I have ever known. I know you want me as much as I want you; we get on well together; our families are behind this union – so why waste time waiting?"

"But there isn't time to plan a wedding in six weeks!" she protested stubbornly.

"I have googled it." Marco waved his phone at her. "We must give twenty-eight days' notice with a designated register office, and we must state where this is taking place, so we find a church and a priest and then we apply for the license."

Saffy swallowed nervously. This was all moving far too fast.

"What about the reception?" she said at last. "I know you mentioned having it at my family home, but that would be too much stress for my dad and Eleanor. Besides," she added, "what would I wear? It takes ages for most women to find the perfect wedding dress."

"You could turn up at the church in your jeans and I would still think you the most beautiful woman there," Marco said artlessly. "Saffy, I know you think these things are important, but the wedding is just one day – our marriage will last the rest of our lives."

Pulling her closer to him, he looked around furtively. The corridor in which they stood was empty: he decided to take his chances.

"Sapphire Vendrini, will you marry me?"

Before she could answer, his lips covered hers. Desire shot through them both, leaving Saffy weak-kneed and trembling. *If only it could all be like this*, she thought helplessly as he ravaged her mouth.

"Marco," she began, pulling away. "I need to tell you the truth about the baby …"

"No more talk of babies," he murmured in her ear, "unless it is the baby you are having with me. Your little indiscretion is behind you now – as far as I am concerned, it no longer exists."

She knew she should explain, but his kisses were driving everything else from her mind. Drunk with desire, she let him pull her towards a door marked 'Cleaner's Cupboard' …

*

At the back of her mind, Saffy knew that they should be returning to Eleanor, to let her know that she could go back to her husband, but she was aflame with passion, unable to stop herself from responding to Marco's obvious need. His body pressed against hers, the taut hardness of him complemented by her soft curves.

"I have waited so long for this," his voice whispered, and Saffy realised that she had been waiting too, living for the moment when he would finally take her.

It was not the most romantic of seduction spots: the unshaded bulb overhead gave off a glare so harsh that Marco switched it off immediately. Saffy felt relieved that, this first time, he wouldn't be able to see her imperfections. Moving back slightly, she stumbled over a mop and bucket, narrowly missing an industrial sized container of bleach. For a moment, her heart quailed: did she really want to lose her virginity in such insalubrious surroundings?

But nothing, it appeared, could dampen Marco's ardour. Pulling her closer, he began to kiss her neck, whilst his fingers fumbled with the buttons on her shirt. His mouth began to move slowly down, leaving a trail of kisses down to first one breast, then the next, nuzzling each nipple through the sheer lace of her bra until Saffy thought she would faint from pleasure.

As his hand slid down to her jeans, he started to stroke her inner thighs, brushing the soft denim so lightly that she almost grabbed his hand in frustration to show him where she really wanted to be touched.

Marco's hand reached for hers, gently placing it over his own crotch. "Feel how much I want you, *tesoro*," he breathed, his eyes liquid with longing. Very slowly, Saffy began to undo his top button …

No doubt they would have consummated their relationship there and then, had it not been for the noisy entrance of the cleaner, making them jump apart guiltily. Marco was the first to pull himself together: whisking a twenty pound note out of his back pocket, he murmured something in a low voice to the angry Polish woman who was threatening to report them to her supervisor. Meanwhile, Saffy buttoned her shirt with trembling fingers, wondering what on earth had possessed her to act like that. She wanted Marco – but to attempt sex in a cupboard was surely the extreme end of tackiness!

A memory stirred within her: Marco's voice insisting that there was *'always a certain frisson when one thinks about being caught ...'* Was *that* why he'd tried to seduce her just now? Did he need the stimulation of potential discovery?

No, he had wanted her plenty of times before now: in his bedroom, in her living room ... She supposed she should be flattered that he had been unable to wait until they had left the hospital, although wasn't that reducing her to an object?

Turning to Marco, she gave an apologetic grin. "At least it wasn't Sophie this time," she said.

*

Not that Marco actually knew how many times her sister had thwarted their romantic encounters, she reflected later, as she and Sophie drove back home. She had invited Marco to come back with them for food when they left the hospital at eight, but he had declined. "It is not that I do not want to be with you, *cuore mio*," he told her, "but I think you and your sister need some time together, no? Besides," his voice lowered to a husky whisper, "I would not be able to restrain myself from taking you upstairs and finishing what we started earlier – and since your sister would be under the same roof, we can almost guarantee that she would interrupt us again at a crucial moment!"

"I wouldn't put it past her to gatecrash our honeymoon and spoil our wedding night!" Saffy agreed with feeling.

"So," Marco's hand cupped Saffy's left buttock proprietorially, "we will tell no one where we are spending our wedding night – or our honeymoon. I have waited too long for you, Saffy – from now on, I want there to be lots of joyous sex between us as we celebrate our engagement and our wedding!"

It was a very Italian turn of phrase, Saffy thought dreamily as she let Sophie's one-sided conversation drift over her head. (It was something about Adam – again – but Saffy didn't care.) 'Joyous sex' – it sounded wonderful, although maybe slightly like a rather dodgy film.

With a start she came to, realising that Sophie was talking about the upcoming wedding. "So, if you can wait until my last exam's over," she was saying, "you can have the wedding after June 17th – no, make that after the 19th: I want to go to the Leavers' Ball."

Saffy stared at her sister in disbelief. "I am *not* planning my wedding around when you want to go to a party," she stressed. "We're only getting married so quickly because of Dad - you know that."

"Yes, but everyone else will think you're getting married in a rush for another reason," Sophie said annoyingly.

"Which is ironic, isn't it?" said Saffy between clenched teeth, "since you're the one who's up the duff, not me."

"Have you told Marco yet?" Sophie asked next, changing the subject only slightly.

"What, that he's going to be an uncle?" Saffy shook her head. "I've tried talking to him about the baby, but he won't listen - he thinks I'm getting rid of it, and so now he refuses to talk about it because he doesn't think it's a problem anymore."

"He must love you, then, if he's still prepared to marry you after he thinks you cheated on him," Sophie said unwisely.

Saffy bit her lip. She hated Marco thinking badly of her; but at least she'd managed to convince him that she hadn't been unfaithful.

"He thinks the baby was conceived before we met each other," she said at last. "He doesn't mind me having a past – as long as it really *is* the past and he knows I'm not going to stray."

"I don't think that's the problem, is it?" Sophie challenged her. "I happen to think Marco's bloody gorgeous, but even so, I'd be wary about marrying someone like that, Saff. Is he really going to stop being a womaniser just because you've got his ring on your finger?"

"He says he wants to settle down," Saffy said in a small voice; but, at the back of her mind, the memory of Siân turning up at Marco's door with a bottle of wine made her more than a little uneasy. He had said he loved her, Saffy; but how many other women had he said that to before?

*

Marco rang her the following day. "I have a church and a priest. I have rung the register office too – the one in Beaconsfield – and we have an appointment next Wednesday."

It was really happening, then. Saffy felt suddenly overwhelmed. "I suppose I'd better look for a dress," she said at last. Perhaps she and Sophie could have a quick trip round John Lewis before they went to the hospital?

Sophie liked the idea of helping Saffy choose a dress but suggested that her sister look online first. "You can get some ideas while I work on my English essay," she said practically. "We'll be much quicker if you already have an idea of what you want."

The problem was that Saffy didn't have a clue: she wasn't even sure whether she wanted long or short, traditional or modern. Clicking on her size – thank goodness there were only twenty-six to choose from – she gazed in bewilderment at the selection before her. Thankfully, there were no 'meringues' - but some of the dresses looked more like nightgowns than anything else. She didn't know what she wanted, only that she hadn't found it yet.

"Any luck?" Sophie came and peered over Saffy's shoulder at the photos she was flicking through on her phone.

"Not really." Saffy gestured at the pictures in front of her. "There's nothing that's *me* – if you know what I mean."

"Why don't you sketch what you want then?" Sophie handed her sister a pencil and notepad.

Saffy hesitantly began to form her ideas into something resembling the kind of dress she wanted. A corset-style top, she decided – the kind that laced all the way up the back, so that Marco could undo it very slowly as he started to make love to her …

"What are you grinning for?" Sophie asked suspiciously.

Saffy hurriedly paused her daydream and concentrated on the job in hand,

A few minutes later, she handed Sophie her sketch. "That's what I think I want – what do you think?"

Sophie scrutinised the rough line drawing with a critical eye. The sleeveless corset top ended in a point above a long, tight skirt that flared out in a fishtail at ankle level. "I've seen something like that before," she said slowly. "Hang on – give me your phone."

Typing something into Google, she gave a crow of triumph. "Is *that* what you've been looking for?"

The dress on the screen was certainly very like the one Saffy had drawn. "Where did you find this?" she questioned wonderingly.

"I googled prom dresses," Sophie explained. "I thought your sketch looked familiar and then I realised why: I was looking at a dress like that the other day."

Saffy stared at the dress, imagining Marco's reaction if she turned up wearing something like this.

"You've got about fifteen different colours to choose from," Sophie began clicking on the different possibilities. "That aquamarine's gorgeous, and so's the lilac."

"If it's my wedding dress, it'll have to be white," Saffy said absently, already picturing herself floating down the aisle towards Marco. "Or maybe ivory …"

"No, you should definitely go for red," Sophie broke in, "since Marco thinks you're a scarlet woman already!"

Saffy didn't know whether to laugh or cry.

Chapter Thirty-One

By Saturday morning, Antonio had been declared fit enough to leave hospital – but he was under strict instructions to take his medication and get plenty of rest. Marco had been unable to visit him in hospital on the Friday, so was coming round to see him at home once he was settled in.

"I know I should be telling your father not to talk shop with Marco," Eleanor said privately to Saffy, "but the combination of the business merger and the wedding is all he can think of at the moment. Besides, the more he can hand over to Marco, the less he has to do himself – and that means more time to rest."

"Has Marco told him we're seeing the priest this afternoon?" Saffy was rather nervous about the proposed meeting: although she'd been educated at a Catholic school, she wasn't a regular churchgoer and hoped this wouldn't count against her. Mind you, Marco had been quite adamant that they needed a church wedding, but his sexual history – had he confessed it to the priest – would have probably disqualified him from ever setting foot in a church again!

No, that wasn't fair, she chided herself. Marco had a healthy sexual appetite, but he had only bedded so many women because he hadn't found the right one before her. It was still a daunting prospect, though, to realise that your husband had enough exes to fill the church – had any of them been invited, which, obviously, they weren't.

Driving to St Aidan's later on, Marco dropped an unexpected bombshell. "We have to do a marriage preparation course if we want to get married at this church," he said.

"What?" Saffy thought she must have misheard.

"The priest said it's normally nine weeks – it's one ninety minutes lesson a week – but they can fast track it 'when required'. I told him we need to get married quickly, because of your father's health, and he agreed that we can do the online version in our own time – as long as we complete it before the wedding."

What exactly did 'marriage preparation' involve? Saffy pondered as they meandered down narrow, leafy lanes. She thought uneasily of their recent fumble in the cupboard, hoping she wouldn't be required to confess all her past demeanours to the priest – it was years since she had performed that ritual.

"Why is getting married in church so important to you?" she asked suddenly.

Marco swivelled his eyes in her direction.

"It is tradition," he told her. "My family is Catholic, as am I – although I am hardly – what do you call it? devout. But you were brought up as a Catholic too – your *matrigna* said you had a convent education."

"I went to a Catholic girls' school," Saffy corrected him. "Sophie's still there at the moment, finishing her A levels." She paused. "I'm not sure I agree with Catholicism, Marco – I mean, I believe in God, but I think the church puts too much emphasis on guilt. I used to feel uncomfortable every time the priest came to take our assembly."

"But our children will be baptised as Catholics, naturally." Marco made it sound like a non-negotiable deal.

"I'm not sure …" Saffy tried to be honest without offending her fiancé. "It's such a patriarchal institution – even in this day and age. I'd like to think that my son – if I had one – would know how to treat women properly and not think he had the right to control her."

"Is that what you think I am doing with you?" Marco pulled into the church car park and switched off the engine.

"I ... no ... I mean ..." Saffy floundered, not wanting to put her foot in it. She *had* thought Marco misogynistic and patronising at first; but it had only taken a few occasions of her standing up to him to let him know she wasn't the meek, submissive creature he'd been expecting. She said as much now.

Marco sighed. "Saffy, I never thought you were submissive – it was your fiery spirit that attracted me to you in the first place. When you slapped my face at your father's party, I knew then that you were the woman for me. Every fight we have had since then has confirmed it. Our life together will have plenty of drama, but that is good, no? We are both passionate people, you and I: we are well matched."

"Let's make sure the priest can see that, then," Saffy said softly. She was still dreading being told that they weren't suited to each other and that Marco should find another bride.

"He cannot stop me marrying you." Marco had obviously read her thoughts. "A Catholic wedding is important to me, Saffy – but I would marry you anywhere, just to know you are mine."

As they walked hand in hand into the church, Saffy wondered whether Marco was aware that he viewed her as a possession.

*

The interview was over. Father Nick had looked impossibly young to be a priest but had allayed some of Saffy's fears concerning the wedding. They were able to choose a wedding service without Mass – much better, Saffy thought, since neither of them were regular church-goers – and they could choose their own readings from the Old or New Testaments, or both. She was also relieved to discover that she didn't have to promise to obey Marco.

Her cheeks flamed then as she relived the most embarrassing part of the interview: the priest had brought up the subject of sex, informing them that the church encouraged abstinence before marriage but that he was aware that many couples these days didn't bother to wait.

"Although around 85% of the engaged people who take the online marriage preparation course then see the value in saving things for the wedding night," he'd added, looking meaningfully at Marco.

Marco had said nothing at the time, but now, in the car park, he turned to Saffy. "Perhaps Father Nick was right, *carissima*. We have only another six weeks or so to wait, and then we can celebrate our wedding night properly with the most spectacular sex either one of us has ever had."

Saffy stood rooted to the spot in shock. Who was this man in front of her? Marco had been trying to get her into bed from the moment he first saw her – but now he suddenly seemed prepared to put all that on hold. Had he gone off her?

Marco smiled at her confusion. "Do not worry, little one," he murmured, throwing caution to the wind and pulling her into his arms where anyone might see. "I have waited too long already. I think God will understand if we adapt the marriage preparation course to include practising making one another happy!"

"But let's not practise in a cupboard next time," she broke in, thankful that he still wanted her after all.

They drove back to her parents' house, the anticipation of their upcoming nuptials only intensifying the longing they both felt.

Chapter Thirty-Two

Despite Marco's assertions that they would 'practise making one another happy', it was actually hard to find time to be alone together now that a wedding was in the offing. So much had to be organised, including flowers for the church and the bridesmaid (Sophie), a venue for the reception, morning suits for Marco, his best man (Ricardo) and the ushers (still to be decided), a wedding cake and cars.

Due to the lack of time before the big day, it would be a small ceremony: Marco's immediate family would fly over from Italy, but the extended family for both – including Saffy's elderly aunts – would see them later in the year when the newly-weds would have an extended holiday in Tuscany and visit as many Italian relatives as possible.

Marco had booked what he referred to as a 'real honeymoon for them both but refused to say where it was. "We will not leave until several days after the wedding, *tesoro*," he told her. "I have booked the honeymoon suite at the hotel for three nights to give us time to enjoy each other properly!"

Saffy wasn't sure. Somehow, Marco had managed to book a local 4* hotel for the reception, due to a recent cancellation, and a number of the hotel's thirty-five bedrooms would be occupied by wedding guests – she was half expecting Sophie to find their room and interrupt them again.

"It will be okay," Marco told her, stroking her hand as she clicked onto the hotel's website. "See, it is an old coaching inn from the 1400s and our room has a four-poster bed."

"It does lovely food too," Eleanor interrupted, looking up from her own laptop. She, Saffy and Marco were seated at the dining table, frantically trying to sort out as much as they could – another lost opportunity for herself and Marco to be intimate, Saffy thought glumly.

"I have the sample menus here," Marco agreed. "I thought Menu 2 looked the more appetising – what do you think, *cuore mia*?"

Saffy stared at the words, hardly registering what she was reading. It still seemed unreal.

"Yes," she said eventually, "I think there's something there for everyone."

"Do you know roughly how many people we can expect?" Eleanor asked next. "I know you've only just emailed the details, but a quick yes or no would help."

Saffy counted on her fingers: "You, Dad and Sophie – plus we should let Sophie invite a friend so she doesn't feel too lonely …" (That would be a way to include Adam, she thought.) Marco's parents, his brother and his family …"

"That's ten so far," Eleanor mused. "Are you inviting James and his partner?"

Marco bristled.

"I haven't told James yet," Saffy broke in hurriedly. "I was waiting until I go back to work tomorrow."

"He'd make a good usher," Eleanor prattled on, oblivious to Marco's discomfort. "He's so striking with his fair hair and hazel eyes."

Marco rose to his feet. "I need some fresh air," he said shortly.

Saffy wondered whether she should follow him into the garden.

"Marco's a bit funny about James," she said cautiously, once she was sure her fiancé was out of earshot.

"Just because he's gay?" Eleanor was surprised. "That's a shame, because he and Connor would have looked so well together, showing people to their seats. They're so blond and you and Marco are so dark."

"I wouldn't mention it," Saffy told her, resolving privately to work on Marco. "But maybe Ricardo's little girls could be bridesmaids," she added.

"Or flower girls." Eleanor's eyes were shining. "How old did you say they were? Four and six? That would be adorable!"

"And maybe Sophie could sing." Saffy was now getting into her stride. Her sister possessed a beautiful contralto and loved performing in public.

"So, it's really just a cake …" Eleanor murmured. "One of my friends works for the little bakery in Chalfont St Peter and they do lovely wedding cakes. I'll see what she can do as a favour to me."

"Thanks for doing all of this," Saffy said suddenly. "I know it's a lot of work."

Eleanor sighed. "If things had been different, it would have been your mum planning all of this with you and not me. I know you'll miss her on the day."

"But at least I've got you …" Saffy wasn't normally demonstrative, but she reached over and gave her step-mum a hug. "You've been really good for Dad, and you've made a brilliant job of bringing up Sophie and me."

Tears filled Eleanor's eyes. "Thanks, Love. It means a lot."

Then Marco came back in and the family bonding session was over.

*

"Are you sure, Sweetie?" James looked at her doubtfully. "It all seems a bit sudden."

Saffy had just broken the news to him and he seemed less ecstatic than she'd expected him to be.

"It's to keep my dad happy more than anything else," she volunteered.

"Yes, but even so …" James paused dramatically. "You're not pregnant, are you?" he asked hopefully.

"That would be a physical impossibility," Saffy explained, "since we still haven't got further than kissing."

"What?" James was genuinely surprised. "Even after all this time? That's pretty impressive, Darling, if he's willing to marry you without sampling the goods first!"

"Don't think it's for want of trying," Saffy told him. "it's just that every time things get interesting, we always seem to get interrupted."

Briefly, she filled him in on the cupboard fiasco. James hooted with laughter.

"Well, he certainly seems to bring out the animal in you, Saff! I would never have envisaged you as the sort of girl who sneaks off for a quickie – and in a hospital of all places!"

"It wasn't like that," Saffy protested.

"No? Well it certainly sounds like it! Are you going to be able to keep your hands off each other until the big day; or are you planning on doing it on the work counter here, after I've gone home for the night?" James queried.

"Stop it!" Saffy said uncomfortably. "You always make things sound so tacky, James!"

James pouted. "You know I love you really. By the way, I assume I'm invited to this shindig of yours?"

"Of course!" Saffy replied promptly, wondering at the same time how she would break the news to Marco. "You're my best friend. Actually," she hesitated, "I was thinking about asking you and Connor to be ushers."

"Does that include telling Marco to 'ush when he starts accusing me of trying to eye up his fiancée?" James enquired drily. "I'm afraid your Italian stallion doesn't like me, Saffy, and I can't think why – I've been positively charming every time he's met me."

"I think he just gets a bit jealous sometimes," Saffy said diplomatically.

"He does know I'm gay?" James fixed her with a challenging stare.

Saffy shifted uncomfortably. "Not exactly …"

"Sapphire Vendrini!" James exclaimed in delight. "Don't tell me you took my advice about sexual politics after all! You're using me to make Lover Boy jealous!"

"Not deliberately," Saffy hedged, well aware that she *should* have told Marco before now that James wasn't attracted to women but that it had certainly increased his own interest in her to think he had a rival. "I've told him we've never been an item and that I have no intention of ever sleeping with you," she offered.

"I know I said you should 'treat him mean to keep him keen', but you've done that on a whole new level," James said admiringly.

Saffy just hoped it wouldn't come back to bite her in the butt.

*

Since Antonio and Lucas were both keen to get all the paperwork for the merger out of the way as soon as possible, Marco was too busy to take Saffy out for dinner – or anything else – that week. Instead, they compromised by agreeing on a lunch date in Beaconsfield, after their appointment at the register office.

Saffy had assumed that registering their intention to marry would be a simple process – just filling in their names and the date and venue on the requisite forms. However, it proved to be much more complicated than that: both of them had to have an individual interview with one of the registrars to prove that they actually wanted to marry each other and weren't being forced into it.

As Saffy sat nervously in front of the man who was interviewing her, she found herself thinking of the nineties' film *'Green Card'* and wondered whether she too would be asked which side of the bed Marco slept on and whether he would be required to name her preferred brand of face cream.

*

Finally, it was all over. Marco looked up at her as she left the interview room and rejoined him in the waiting area. "I assume everything is in order?"

Saffy nodded nervously, aware that each day now was bringing her closer to becoming a Benedetti. No wonder people normally took a year or two to plan a wedding – she could do with that amount of time herself to get used to the idea of being a wife.

"We haven't talked about where we're going to live," she said suddenly, as they made their way towards the *Brasserie Blanc*.

"Where would you like to live?" Marco asked.

Saffy hesitated. "Your apartment's bigger," she said at last, "but I think my flat feels more like home."

Marco nodded. "I think so too. My place is impressive, but it is very much a bachelor pad. I think I will be able to relax better if we live in your flat."

"What, and leave that bathroom behind?" she teased him.

Marco groaned. "Don't remind me! The sooner I say goodbye to those gold dolphins, the better!"

Reaching the restaurant, Marco paused. "This still doesn't seem real, does it?" he muttered. "Six weeks ago, I did not know you – now, here I am, on the verge of getting married to you – and I have never felt happier."

"Really?" she breathed, unable to contain her delight at his words. Marco was excited about marrying her and it looked as if he had forgiven her for the positive pregnancy test. Perhaps everything would go right from now on.

Chapter Thirty-Three

Marco was working so hard that he hardly had time to sleep, let alone catch up with Saffy. At least they had managed to turn their trip to the register office into some sort of date, he mused as he sat at his computer, simultaneously trying to broker a deal for a client whilst editing the draft documents for the merger and sort out wedding cars.

What would Saffy wear? he wondered. He hoped it would be something white and traditional: he liked the idea of taking a virginal-looking Saffy to the honeymoon suite and making love to her whilst she was still in her dress.

But would she wear white, given the circumstances? Marco frowned. Despite being ninety per cent positive that Saffy had been telling the truth when she claimed not to have cheated on him, the annoying ten per cent that wasn't sure emerged from his certainty like the tip of an iceberg – and just as lethal. He wanted to believe her when she said she hadn't been with anyone since meeting him, but she was so beautiful, so sexy that she was bound to attract men wherever she went. That was one of the reasons why he'd agreed to marry her so quickly: he needed to know where she was at all times, for his own peace of mind.

What was he thinking? He was suddenly acting as if he were a fifteenth century husband, needing to keep his wife under lock and key! He would be putting her into a chastity belt next!

No, he had to trust Saffy – in fact, he was pretty sure that trust was one of the themes of their pre-wedding course – not that they'd had time to look at it together yet. They would have to get a move on, he realised, since they needed to give the certificate of completion to the priest before the ceremony, to prove they were taking the marriage seriously. And hadn't Father Nick said something about a 'sponsor couple' who would work with them as they went through the course?

Opening yet another window on his computer, he hastily typed in 'Engaged Online' and scrolled through the options. He couldn't check the content without starting the first lesson: he would have to ask Saffy when she was available. As he reached for his phone to text her, he found himself imagining the two of them spending the evening together, working their way through one or two course components, then taking each other by the hand and repairing to her bedroom. What was that line in the wedding service? Something about worshipping her with his body. Well, he was prepared to practise that bit all night if necessary!

Perhaps he should call their sponsors first, though – he didn't want anything to prevent him and Saffy from completing the course and getting married in five weeks' time.

*

Helen and Richard beamed at Marco and Saffy. "It's so exciting for us to be doing this. We only got married ourselves eighteen months ago."

They were all sitting in Saffy's flat, the remains of pasta and garlic bread still visible on the dining table. Friday had been the only night Helen and Richard had free this week, and since Saffy and Marco needed to get through at least two sessions of the online course per week, they had agreed on a seven thirty start so they could be done by ten thirty.

That still left plenty of time for other things in the bedroom, Saffy thought dreamily. She had cooked for Marco again – a much simpler meal this time, with shop bought garlic bread and tagliatelle with mushrooms and garlic: the whole meal had taken only ten minutes from start to finish, but it tasted wonderful – because she wanted him to know she wasn't a one-trick pony in the food department.

"So, one of the things we'll be looking at tonight," Helen began brightly, "is 'Marriage as a Mission'. We'll be watching some short videos and answering some discussion questions. Richard and I found that this really helped us focus on why we wanted to get married and what we both expected from our relationship with each other."

Sex, Saffy and Marco both thought simultaneously, *and lots of it!*

Richard patted Helen's hand. "But before we start, I'm just going to read this simple prayer."

It was amazing how quickly three hours had gone by – and how neither Saffy nor Marco felt the least bit of desire for each other after so much information from Richard and Helen on both abstinence and the rhythm method. Whilst Richard had heartily espoused the efficacy of cold showers and long walks to dampen sexual ardour, Helen had shown just as much enthusiasm over the daily examination of vaginal mucus to ascertain whether or not one was likely to be fertile.

"It's been a wonderful evening!" Richard declared warmly, rising to go. "Helen and I have felt really honoured to share this course with you tonight, haven't we, Helen?"

Helen nodded, misty-eyed. "It's taken me right back to when it was the two of us," she agreed. Turning to Marco, she added, "Where are you parked? We'll walk you to your car."

Since Marco had been planning to spend the night with Saffy – surely *this* time they wouldn't be interrupted? – he was unsure how to answer. And then he noticed the shadows under Saffy's eyes and remembered that it was still only less than a week since her father had been sent home from hospital, and realised that he was being selfish. He and Saffy had the rest of their lives together: he should let her sleep while she most needed it.

"I'm in the next road over," he heard himself say. Saffy shot him a look, but he pretended not to see it.

Letting her guests out, Saffy waited until Richard and Helen were safely out of earshot before yanking Marco back. "Why are you leaving?" she wanted to know.

Marco hesitated, torn between desire for Saffy and the need to show Richard and Helen that they were taking the course seriously. In the end, reason won. "We're both tired," he told her, "and I don't want to give Richard and Helen the wrong impression. They've just talked to us about the value of abstinence: I don't want them telling the priest that we were acting like animals as soon as they left."

"The only animal I'll be acting like tonight is a dormouse," Saffy yawned. "I feel like I could sleep for twenty-four hours."

"Then I will come back tomorrow when we are both refreshed," Marco told her. "These things should not be rushed, *carissima*. I pride myself on a good quality service!"

"Some time tomorrow, then." Saffy kissed him goodnight slowly, thinking that perhaps he was right. She was far too tired at the moment to appreciate Marco's love-making, so why not wait until a more opportune time?

Later on, she would wish that she had made him stay after all.

*

It must have been twenty minutes after she'd crawled into bed when Saffy was wakened by a ringing on her doorbell. Instantly she thought of Sophie – what had her sister done now? – followed by the thought that it was far more likely to be Marco, who must have decided that he didn't want to be on his own tonight after all.

Pulling on her dressing gown, she fumbled her way through the flat to her front door. Opening it wide, she was greeted by a dishevelled looking James. "Can I crash on your sofa, Sweetie? Connor's chucked me out again."

*

"What did you do this time?" Saffy asked severely as she let James in and went to get blankets and a pillow from her bedroom.

James took on an injured air. "Nothing! We were in *The Slapper*," - James's pet name for *The Boot and Slipper*, a local hostelry – "and I was just being friendly with one of the barmen -"

"You mean you were flirting," Saffy said disapprovingly.

"Okay, I was flirting," James said unrepentantly, "but it didn't mean a thing, Saff. Connor should know that by now."

"What did you say?" Saffy was intrigued. Connor was usually so placid; then again, James did seem to make a habit of trying to wind him up.

"Well, it's not so much what I *said* as what I *did*," James explained. "We were having steak, and so I thought it would be funny if I said I liked a bit of rump and pinched the barman's bottom as he was passing."

"You didn't!" Saffy was shocked. "You can't do things like that these days, James - he could have had you for sexual assault!"

"The guy's as bent as I am!" James sounded amused. "He was flattered, Saff – that's what made Connor so cross. He would have been quite happy if I'd been punched in the face!"

"I don't care. You've got to start treating Connor with more respect," Saffy scolded. "I know *you* wouldn't mind if he was flirting with someone else, but not everyone has your cavalier attitude. You've got to be a bit more sensitive."

"What, like you letting Marco think I'm banging you behind his back?" James grinned. "Pot – kettle, Sweetie."

"It's not like that," Saffy muttered.

"No? Well, you've certainly played it to your advantage," James said infuriatingly. "Anyway, I'm going to bed now. I had to walk all the way from Amersham and I'm worn out. Make sure you wake me up in the morning – I'll have to get a bus over to Chesham and try to convince Connor I've seen the error of my ways."

*

"You're going to have to stop doing this, you know," Saffy told him severely as she let James out of her flat the following morning. "Grown-ups know how to discuss things properly without turning it into a melodrama and one of you storming off."

James rolled his eyes at her. "I didn't storm off, Angel. Connor left the pub without me and I didn't have my door key. I wasn't expecting us to have a tiff or I would have made sure I had my key too."

"Well, don't do anything to make him so cross with you, then," Saffy advised.

James sighed. He enjoyed the passionate outbursts almost as much as the making up again afterwards, but he knew Saffy was right.

"I'll try," he promised, kissing her lightly on the cheek as she stood in the open doorway to make sure he was really going.

*

From his car, Marco watched the two of them with a grim face. It was obvious they'd just spent the night together – Saffy was wrapped in her dressing gown, so presumably she was still naked underneath.

He looked at the cardboard box on the seat beside him. Twenty minutes ago, bringing Saffy coffee and croissants had seemed a suitably romantic gesture towards the woman he was going to marry: he had pictured her letting him into her flat and him following her back into her room, climbing under the duvet with her and making love to her for the rest of the day. But now …

Words failed him at the thought of her duplicity. Never before had he felt such anger, not even with Nadia.

The little bitch had been lying to him all along.

Chapter Thirty-Four

As he watched James make his way towards the bus stop, Marco wondered if he should do something. Several hundred years ago, he would have been able to challenge James to a duel; but what options were open to him now? He couldn't marry Saffy after this fresh betrayal; but then what about the merger, and his father-in-law's health?

He should never have walked away from her the previous evening, he realised now. Saffy had obviously been primed for sex and, once he had rejected her, she had substituted the next available male. *How could she do that to him?* They had just sat through three hours of marriage preparation together.

Just what was it about James that made him so irresistible? he wondered bleakly. Why, when Saffy had turned *him* down countless times, was she so eager to open her legs for a man she claimed she didn't love? Was she a sex addict? He knew some people were: there were stories online of film and TV stars who'd had to undergo counselling for this sort of behaviour.

He couldn't see Saffy now. He needed time to calm down after what he'd seen. Putting his car into gear, he pulled away slowly, his entire body saturated with the misery he felt.

*

Several hours in the gym did nothing to work off Marco's frustration. He couldn't believe how angry he was. It seemed the more he thought about Saffy, the more furious he became. Maybe he should just cut his losses now and get out while his heart was still intact? Deep down, he knew that wasn't an option: Sapphire Vendrini had worked her way under his skin and into his soul: he was powerless to walk away from her.

So where did that leave him, then? Did he really want to marry a woman who had cheated on him already? With bitterness, he recollected his words at the engagement party, when he'd talked in such a blasé fashion about marital infidelity. How ironic that Saffy, the one who'd seemed shocked by his words, had been the one to stray first. His fist hit the punchbag in front of him in anger. He tried to imagine slamming it into Saffy's face but couldn't. He still wanted her, despite everything, but he had to be realistic. He would never be able to trust her again – not after this.

Grabbing his towel, he walked away from the gym and tried to wash his heartache away under a hot shower.

*

It was much later in the day when a text arrived from Saffy. "Sorry we didn't get to spend last night together. Do you want to try again this evening?"

Part of him marvelled at the nerve of the woman; whilst another, more vulnerable, side of him questioned why she wanted to see him at all when she already had a willing lover waiting in the wings.

*

Arriving at Saffy's door just before seven, Marco decided to play it cool. She had obviously gone to some trouble to create a perfect seduction scene: the room was muted, lit only by the softly glowing candles on the table and mantlepiece; a bottle of Cabernet Sauvignon was breathing on the table; and the aroma of fried onions filled the air.

"We're having steak," she said breathlessly, disappearing into the kitchen once she'd let him in. "I hope the wine's okay – the internet said that was the right one for red meat."

As she stood with her back to him, intent on the food in the pan before her, Marco decided to take a chance. Tiptoeing into the bedroom, he noiselessly started to slide open the top drawer in her bedside chest, hoping to find the evidence he needed.

No sign of condoms or sex toys, but what was this? There was an envelope buried beneath Saffy's underwear: why had she hidden it?

Saffy had actually gone to great lengths to make sure that the letter from the hospital was in a safe place. Since Eleanor was still in the habit of putting Sophie's clothes away for her – and rooting through her bag to make sure she hadn't missed any important letters from school – Saffy had decided to keep hold of the communication confirming Sophie's scan appointment. She had also thanked God – or Providence: she wasn't sure which – that she had had the foresight to give her own address and not Sophie's, mindful that, given her father's recent health scare, Eleanor would be likely to open any letter from the hospital without checking who it was addressed to.

Turning the steaks after exactly three minutes, she hoped that her hair didn't stink of onions. If this was going to be their first night together, she wanted it to be perfect; but her cuisinal repertoire was rather limited, which was why she had been forced to cook steak. Still, steak was romantic, wasn't it? And surely all that red meat would give them both stamina?

The steaks were done. Saffy placed them both on a previously warmed plate, just like the internet had told her to, and wondered where Marco was. "Food's ready!" she shouted into the void of her living room.

By the time she returned to the table, bearing two plates of food, Marco was in position at the table. Saffy nervously placed steak, sautéed potatoes and broccoli in front of him. "I hope you're hungry."

Marco tried valiantly to eat the food, but he was too agitated to taste anything.

"I'm sorry," he said at last, putting down his knife and fork, "but I can't do this."

"What's wrong? Did I overdo it?" Saffy was mortified that her cooking was so bad.

"It's not the food that's the problem," Marco said slowly.

Saffy's heart clenched.

"I know about James," her fiancé continued viciously.

She stared at him incredulously. "Know *what* about James?"

"Do not take me for an idiot!" Marco's fist thumped the table in anger. He sprang up from the table, almost knocking the wine over in his haste. "When I agreed to marry you, Saffy," he continued, "I was not buying a time-share!"

"I don't understand ..." she began nervously.

"I saw him leaving your flat, early this morning, after you had just spent the night together," Marco told her through gritted teeth.

"He may have spent the night in my flat, but he certainly didn't spend it with me!" Saffy replied, with spirited defiance. "He turned up on my doorstep, looking for a place to crash out after he'd had a row with his partner – he's done that several times before."

Marco was silent for a moment, unsure of whether or not to believe her.

Saffy sighed. "He spent the night on the sofa, Marco." She tried to catch his eye, willing him to recognise that she was telling the truth.

Marco couldn't envisage how any red-blooded male could be so close to Saffy without sampling her delights. He was on the verge of saying so when he stopped. "He kissed you when he left," he reminded her.

Another sigh. "It was a friendly kiss on the cheek," Saffy said patiently. When he still looked unconvinced, she began to feel annoyed. "Oh, for goodness' sake, Marco! If I *was* having an affair with James, I'd be hardly likely to advertise it by having a snogging session on my doorstep, in full view of the entire street!"

For a moment, they glared at each other, a stalemate of hostility.

"Why do you keep on doing this to me, Saffy?" Marco asked bleakly.

"Doing what?" How dare he suggest that this was all her fault!

"All this ..." Marco gestured expressively. "How can I trust you when you keep so many secrets?"

Saffy thought, guiltily, of Sophie's baby.

"If it were really so innocent with you and James," he continued, "then why did you not tell me earlier? Can you blame me for being suspicious when you have hidden things from me at every turn?"

"And what about you?" she asked softly. "Have *you* got any secrets you haven't told me, Marco?"

A brief image of Siân in her underwear flitted across Marco's mind. He'd been angry with Saffy – angry and hurt – but he'd walked away from the redhead's offer of sex. Should he tell Saffy; or would she see it as a sign of weakness on his part? He couldn't let her know how much it tore him apart to think of her with another man: she had to think that he was as detached as she was, or she would end up having the upper hand in their marriage.

"This is a marriage in name only, Sapphire," he told her, using her full name so she would understand the enormity of the situation. "Our fathers' companies will be joined together, and your father will have what he always wanted: a son to carry on the business once he is gone. To all intents and purposes, you and I will be a happy couple – what happens behind closed doors will be a story that only you and I truly know. But let me tell you this," he continued, hardening his voice despite the pain in his heart – "every time you take a lover, I will take one in return. If we are discreet, then no one will know. And if you find yourself with child – again – then I will give your bastard my name, to keep up pretences – but he or she will never inherit any part of *Benedetti's*. My *own* children will carry on in my stead, not yours."

"Your own children?" she repeated, not understanding.

"You will have your lovers' children and I will have mine." He made it all sound so matter of fact.

Saffy stared at him in horror. "That isn't a marriage," she whispered at last.

"I think you will find that it is." Marco was not looking at her. "Traditionally, marriages in the Middle Ages were business transactions – they were political unions, not love matches. Husbands had plenty of children out of wedlock; so did wives – they just kept quiet about who the real father of their children was."

"No!" Saffy sounded vehement. "I'm not marrying you if that's what you want! It would destroy me!"

"And if you don't marry me, it will destroy your father," Marco told her. "Or do you want me to go to him and tell him I'm breaking off the engagement and cancelling the wedding because his daughter's a whore and pregnant with another man's child?"

"You bastard!" Saffy couldn't believe what she was hearing. How could Marco use her father's health to manipulate her like this?

"*I* am not the bastard in this scenario, Saffy. You are still pregnant, no?" he challenged her. "You haven't got rid of that baby you claimed you didn't want, have you? There is a letter from the hospital in your drawer in the bedroom, confirming your twelve weeks' scan."

"You looked in my drawers?" Saffy was suddenly outraged. "That's an invasion of privacy, Marco! You had no right!"

"As your fiancé, I had every right!" Marco's eyes flashed anger.

Saffy knew that she should correct his mistake, tell him that the S Vendrini on the letter was Sophie, not her; but by now she was so infuriated that she just wanted to hurt him.

"Yes," she spat out defiantly, "I'm still pregnant! And it was the best sex I've ever had!"

Chapter Thirty-Five

After Marco had stormed out, only minutes after Saffy's outburst, she put her head in her hands, aghast at what she had done. *Why* hadn't she told Marco the truth? she asked herself silently.

It was because you were angry, her heart replied. But, even so …

What was it that made her react like this to a man she wanted and hated at the same time? And why on earth was she letting him think she was pregnant?

He shouldn't have been spying on you, she reminded herself. Marco should have trusted her; but instead he had jumped to conclusions from the start of their relationship, suspecting her of being involved with James, of all people! Wasn't it obvious that her friend was as camp as a week at Glastonbury?

For a moment, she wondered desperately if there was any way of calling off the wedding. Surely her father would want her to be happy?

But then she would have to explain *why* she didn't want to marry Marco – and the whole tangled tale of Sophie's pregnancy would come out – and *that* alone might be enough to trigger another heart attack.

He'll have to find out about Sophie some time, she told herself practically.

Yes, she argued back, *but not like this. Not while she's still a schoolgirl and before he and Eleanor have even met Adam.*

Earlier that day, Sophie had decided to invite Adam to the wedding and introduce him to her father and Eleanor then, when wine was flowing and everyone was likely to be in a good mood. Saffy was pretty sure that her father was supposed to be avoiding alcohol at the moment, but maybe the wedding atmosphere itself would help?

"Damn you, Marco!" she uttered now, still furious with him but, maddeningly, unable to stop thinking about his dark eyes or the way his hands had touched her in the past. He had ruined her for any other man, she thought savagely. He was arrogant and pig-headed, and he had no concept at all of fidelity - but she still wanted him just as much as she always had done.

The question was, did he still want her?

*

Marco's need for Saffy was so strong that he did the only thing he could think of: driving straight home, he made for Siân's door and knocked on it loudly. He didn't actually *want* sex with his neighbour, he told himself - but he was angry and frustrated, and he needed release. When she didn't answer, he knocked again – louder this time.

There was a slight scuffling sound and then Siân appeared, wearing a towel and not much else.

"What do you want?" She sounded hostile. It wasn't the response he'd been expecting.

"I think you know what I want." He wasn't wasting words.

Siân's eyes widened, then her face took on a bored expression. "It's not a good time - I've got someone here already."

That explained the towel, then: he'd caught her *in flagrante delicto*. He turned to leave.

"I'm free later," she called after him; but the mood was broken, his desire to punish Saffy already abating.

What would be the point? he asked himself silently as he opened his own door. If he slept with Siân, he knew that he would only be punishing himself.

*

He slept badly that night – even with the aid of the bottle of Scotch that he found at the back of a cupboard. Was this what Saffy had reduced him to? he thought despairingly. He'd never needed to use alcohol as a crutch before.

Saffy's parting shot still rang in his ears: "It was the best sex I've ever had!" Before, he would have laughed that off, confident that 'the best' wouldn't measure up to the Benedetti magic; now, however, he found himself wondering if that was why Saffy had strayed: had she sensed him to be an inadequate lover? He'd always thought himself pretty good at what he did; but maybe he'd been fooling himself all these years. And women could fake orgasms, couldn't they? Did that mean he wasn't really as polished as he thought?

It would have been so easy to put it to the test: to call up one of his exes and invite her over for a quick test drive; but he had lost his nerve – what if he laid out all his best moves and it didn't do the trick? Besides – and he hated admitting this to himself – there was only one woman he wanted right now, and that was the one woman he couldn't have.

*

The next few days passed in a blur for both Saffy and Marco. Neither of them could summon up the impetus to carry on planning the wedding, but luckily Eleanor was quite happy to take over, explaining that it helped take her mind off worrying about Antonio.

"It's a shame you're both so busy with work right now," she remarked artlessly as Saffy spent yet another evening at her family home – ostensibly to choose readings for the service but in reality to avoid being in the flat if Marco came round. She was still fuming at his effrontery in poking about in her drawers, trying to catch her out. That sort of distrust was certainly no basis for a marriage!

"The traditional reading's the bit from Saint Paul's letter to the Corinthians about love," Eleanor added next. "You know the one: 'Love hopes all things, believes all things, endures all things. Love never ends.' Or you might find a more modern translation of it on the internet."

Saffy googled it – more for something to do than because she actually wanted to use it as a reading. What was this version? 'If you love someone, you will be loyal to him no matter what the cost. You will always believe in him, always expect the best of him, and always stand your ground in defending him.' She wondered whether the priest would still let her have it as a reading if she substituted the word 'him' with 'her' …

*

Marco, meanwhile, was drinking heavily. Not used to knocking back more than the odd glass of wine with dinner, and maybe a brandy afterwards, he was now getting through a couple of bottles a night, hoping they would help him sleep, then waking up with a stinking hangover the next morning.

From time to time, he thought about calling off the wedding, but by now his addiction to Saffy was so strong that the idea of never seeing her again terrified him. He couldn't decide which was worse: to break off the engagement or to go through with the marriage. He'd told Saffy that he would give his name to the bastard she was carrying – he had to: he couldn't stand the shame of anyone knowing it wasn't his child – but he was already regretting the decision. Why hadn't he been more forceful about her getting rid of it?

And then his conscience pricked him as he thought about the sanctity of life and the Pope's assertion that a foetus was a baby from the point of conception. He'd never had cause to think about what he believed before – he was a Catholic, but only because he had been born a Catholic, in the same way that he was an Italian because he had been born in Italy, to Italian parents.

And if he *had* forced her to have an abortion, would he have driven her away completely? He didn't want another man's child growing up in his household, but if that was the only way for him to have Saffy, that was the price he had to pay.

But would she be his even after marriage? His alcohol-induced paranoia planted seeds of doubt in his mind. Short of taking her to work with him every day, he would have no way of knowing what she was getting up to while he was gone. She could have a different lover for every day of the week and he would be none the wiser!

His brain was beginning to hurt with the multiple scenarios he was imagining. He opened another bottle and tried to let the wine carry him into oblivion.

*

It was towards the end of the week when Marco received a text message from Richard and Helen: 'Looking forward to our next session tomorrow night. See you at 7.30!'

He and Saffy couldn't possibly have a marriage preparation class the following evening – they hadn't spoken to each other all week – but if they didn't do the course, they wouldn't be able to get married; and if they didn't get married, the merger might fall through too. Marco felt overwhelmed by it all.

But wouldn't that be the perfect solution to your dilemma? his mind probed. *That way, you could avoid getting married without having to give a reason why.*

But his family had already booked their plane tickets, and Ricardo's little girls were excited about their new dresses. Besides, perhaps things would be different with Saffy once they were married: maybe she would stop looking elsewhere if she knew that she would have her husband in her bed every night?

In the end, he forwarded the text to Saffy, leaving it up to her to cancel if she thought they couldn't pull it off.

*

Marco arrived at Saffy's in a bad mood the following evening. Part of this was due to withdrawal symptoms – he'd not drunk anything since the night before in an attempt to sober up for the marriage class – and the rest was due to extreme sexual tension.

He should throw caution to the wind and spend the night with Saffy, whether she wanted him to or not, he thought as he rang her doorbell.

Saffy opened the door with a dazzling smile. "Darling!" Richard and Helen must be here already then.

Sessions 3 and 4 were just as excruciating as the first two. There were more videos to watch and more 'discussions' in which Marco and Saffy were encouraged to talk about their feelings for each other. "So, Saffy, what is it you love best about Marco?" Helen asked as an opener.

Saffy pretended to think carefully. "What I love most about my fiancé," she said sweetly, "is the way that he trusts me absolutely and would never, ever think I could do anything wrong."

Richard and Helen looked suitably impressed. Marco felt like swearing.

"Your turn, Marco," Richard said jovially.

"I love Saffy's honesty," Marco said without a pause, matching his voice to the same fake tone as hers. "I know that she would never lie to me and she will always tell me the truth, no matter how difficult that might be."

Saffy glared at him while Helen and Richard were busy gazing into each other's eyes and falling in love all over again.

Three hours later and it was all over. They had covered finances and in-laws and Saffy and Marco were both exhausted with the effort of pretending to be nice to each other all night.

"Nearly half-way there now," Helen said merrily as she and Richard made their way to the front door. Marco lagged behind.

"Go on without me," he called to Richard and Helen. "I just need to use the bathroom."

Saffy stood back, clearing the way for Marco to walk past her, but instead he grabbed her arm. "You and I are going to the bedroom. I think we have some unfinished business."

*

"Let me go!" Saffy struggled to escape but Marco was too strong for her. Dragging her into the bedroom, he threw her roughly onto the bed then leaned his weight on top of her, pinning her down.

"What are you going to do?" Saffy tried hard not to let him see she was frightened.

"I'm going to show you what a real man is like," Marco muttered, holding her in place by her wrists with one hand while the other started undoing his belt.

"You wouldn't dare!" To her horror, Saffy found that she was actually aroused by the thought of Marco having his way with her. He wouldn't really hurt her, she knew that; but shouldn't she feel disgusted at the idea of him forcing her into the bedroom like this?

It appeared Marco had second thoughts as well. "I can't do this," he said abruptly, suddenly releasing her and standing up. Saffy was left with a profound sense of disappointment.

"I still want you, Saffy." Marco wasn't looking at her, "but I want you to want me too. And I won't take you in anger – that's never a good idea."

Saffy was quiet for a moment, thinking that maybe she'd misjudged him.

"I still haven't forgiven you for deceiving me," Marco continued, ruining any good he'd just done. "You lied to me Saffy, and that's something I can't forget in a hurry."

"You've betrayed me as well," she said in a small voice. "Rooting around in my drawers ... Reading letters addressed to me ..."

"It's hardly the same." Marco sounded dismissive.

"It's exactly the same!" she told him heatedly. "What you've done has made it impossible for me to trust you – can't you see that?"

"Sleeping with someone else is not on the same level as looking in a drawer," Marco said icily.

"So, you'd be happy if I went through your personal belongings, then?" she flashed back at him.

"I have nothing to hide." Marco was back in detached mode.

"*Really?* But you had a scantily clad girl turning up at your flat with a bottle of wine, expecting to find you on your own," Saffy jeered. "Don't tell me you and Siân haven't done the deed, Marco – she was gagging for it when I was there!"

"Whatever may or may not have happened between Siân and me is my business, not yours," Marco said sharply. He regretted kissing the girl, but Saffy had no right to be angry with him for that – and if she thought Marco had taken her to bed, so much the better. She deserved to suffer after what she'd put him through! he thought savagely.

"Why are we still going ahead with this charade of a marriage?" Saffy asked abruptly. "We don't even like each other at the moment, Marco."

"And whose fault is that?" he demanded. "*I* have not changed in the way I feel – *you* have!"

So he had never loved her then? Saffy felt deflated.

"I think you'd better leave now," she said quietly. "I've got a lot to do tomorrow, sorting out wedding stuff – unless you think we should just give up now?"

"I promised your father that I would take care of you," Marco said stiffly, "and I will honour that promise. Benedettis keep their word."

"I know." Saffy gave a sad smile. "It's your company slogan, Marco." She had only ever been part of a business transaction. Marco had agreed to marry her, and he was going to deliver on that promise.

She wondered, briefly, whether he ever let his heart make decisions for him.

Chapter Thirty-Six

For the next couple of weeks, Saffy tried not to think about Marco – which was difficult when their wedding was getting closer every day. She had ordered her dress off the internet, along with a cornflower blue number for Sophie, and had emailed details of the website and Sophie's dress to Marco's sister-in-law so she could choose dresses for the younger bridesmaids.

A levels were in full swing now for Sophie. Saffy hoped her sister would be okay: she was still feeling sick in the evenings but seemed to have regained her appetite. Adam was being very supportive, Sophie informed her: he was bringing her in little treats every day so that she could snack whenever she felt hungry and he'd also bought a book of baby names which he was reading to her in study periods.

"Isn't that letting the cat out of the bag to the rest of the sixth form?" Saffy wanted to know.

Sophie looked at her pityingly. "We go to *Costa* for our study periods. No one else we know ever goes there." They were playing with fire, Saffy thought, but at least it was only a matter of weeks now before the end of A levels and the wedding – and then she, Saffy, could stop keeping everything a secret on Sophie's behalf.

*

Marco was getting jittery about the wedding. He, Ricardo and the two fathers had all ordered grey frock coats from Moss Bros, but he was worried that something would go wrong – especially since his father and Ric had been unable to try on their outfits yet. Should he post the suits to Italy? But what if the parcel got lost? He could courier it, but it seemed a lot of effort when there was already so much to do.

Saffy had emailed him the Bible reading she wanted. He felt rather uncomfortable reading it – especially the bit that claimed love "does not hold grudges and will hardly even notice when others do it wrong" – was that a dig at him?

He reciprocated by choosing a passage of his own from the Song of Solomon in the Old Testament: "My darling bride is like a private garden, a spring that no one else can have, a fountain of my own ..." If she could send coded messages in part of the wedding service, so could he!

In his darker moments, he fantasised about getting his revenge on Saffy by ruining the service. When the priest asked whether there was any reason why the two of them should not be married, Marco stood up and yelled, "Yes! Because she's a whore with another man's baby in her belly!" then sat down again. He knew he would never really do this – not just because it would destroy both their families, but because Saffy would never forgive him if he did. Besides, he still hadn't mentioned the baby to anyone else. They would all assume it was his, of course, and that he was marrying Saffy because he'd made her pregnant – but that was preferable to the truth. If anyone ever suspected that the child wasn't his, he would be totally dishonoured.

Richard and Helen had now completed eight out of the nine course modules with them. He was looking forward to the last one: spending an entire evening with Saffy and those two was beginning to take its toll. Helen and Richard were nice people but terribly earnest. They kept asking whether he and Saffy were going to become 'regular worshippers' at St Aiden's and seemed genuinely disappointed every time he said no.

The last module would take place a week before the wedding. Richard had suggested leaving it until the night before, 'to make maximum impact on the big day', but Helen had gently pointed out that it normally took three days to receive the certificate and that Father Nick would need to see that before the service. Marco was relieved – not least because he had already planned his stag do for the night before the wedding. He knew it was cutting it a bit fine, but Ricardo wasn't flying in until Friday morning and he wasn't prepared to celebrate without his brother.

Several of the boys from *Benedetti's* were involved in the stag do too. Phil had suggested a strip club, but Marco had refused. He knew he wouldn't be able to look at a naked girl without thinking of Saffy and becoming maudlin. In the end, he'd given Phil Ricardo's details and the two had communicated via email to sort out the evening between them. Marco was trusting his brother to keep things fairly tame, since he knew Ricardo's wife wouldn't be happy if they were out till all hours.

Saffy hadn't thought about a hen night until Eleanor asked her what she had planned. "I know it's normally the bridesmaid's job to sort out the details," she began, "but Sophie's still got one or two exams left so she's a bit busy at the moment."

Saffy supposed she and Sophie could go out to dinner together. Since it was such a small wedding, she hadn't invited any friends to the reception apart from James and Connor – and she still hadn't told Marco that they were invited.

"Sweetie!" James exclaimed when Saffy mentioned this at work. "Why don't Connor and I come out with you and help you celebrate your Hen night in style?"

"Shouldn't you be at the Stag do instead?" Saffy queried.

"Well, why not combine the two into a Hag Night?" James quipped. He loved making puns.

"If I'm going out with you and Connor, it'll be more like a Fag Hag Night," Saffy riposted back.

James laughed. "*Touché*! I'm going to miss your rapier sharp wit when you leave work to have babies, Saffy!"

"I'm not pregnant yet!" Saffy said in alarm.

"No, but it's bound to happen quickly. I can tell just by looking at Marco that his loins are packed with good baby making ingredients!" James declared. "Speaking of which …" he lowered his voice conspiratorially, "have you two actually done it yet?"

"We've been a bit preoccupied with wedding preparations," Saffy said quickly.

"Rubbish!" James wasn't fooled for one moment. "He's not still cross with you because he thinks we're shagging, is he?"

"That's partly it," Saffy admitted, "and I'm annoyed with him for thinking I'd cheat on him; so, all in all, it's a bit of a vicious circle."

"Well, you'd better sort it out before your wedding night," James told her, "because the last thing you want is to start your marriage with a fight."

Chapter Thirty-Seven

James was right, of course. Saffy knew that she was as much to blame as Marco for this sorry fiasco their relationship had become. She resolved to stop goading him and try instead to remember what it was about him that had attracted her in the first place.

She would have been surprised to learn that Marco was also soul-searching. Still wanting to marry Saffy – despite the baby; despite her infidelity – he debated whether he had somehow pushed her into the arms of another man when he'd brazenly declared at their first meeting that he would take lovers once they were married. He'd half-meant it at the time – the memory of Nadia still smarted – but then, as he'd come to know Saffy over the weeks that followed, he'd realised she was more than enough woman for him and that he could finally visualise settling down with one person for the foreseeable future.

Was that still a possibility now? he wondered. Did he want a wife he couldn't trust? Perhaps if he laid down some ground rules, agreed to a clean slate so that anything that had happened before their marriage no longer counted … But there was still the baby to consider. He didn't relish the thought of playing step-father to someone else's brat.

But he had to have her. Saffy had become an obsession now: he needed to know what it would be like to touch every part of her, watch her dissolve in pure pleasure as he showed her what she'd been missing up until now.

Unless … He paused, his insecurity taking hold once more. What if he didn't measure up to her previous lovers? He'd always thought he was something of an expert; but what if Saffy wasn't as impressed as the others had been?

What's the worst-case scenario? he asked himself silently. *You marry her; you discover you're not sexually compatible; you get divorced.*

Divorce wasn't an option, though, if *Benedetti's* and *Vendrini's* were on the edge of a merger. No, if it came to it, theirs would be a marriage in name only after all: he with his lovers and she with hers.

The thought of it made his blood run cold.

*

Saffy hadn't even managed a second cup of tea the next morning when her breakfast routine was interrupted by an over-anxious Eleanor on the phone.

"We don't have an Order of Service, Saffy. You'll have to make one up and take it to the printer's today – you know the one I mean: that little shop near you that does flyers and business cards and so on."

"What?" Saffy felt alarmed. "Why do we need an Order of Service? Hardly anyone's coming." It was on the tip of her tongue to say that Marco might not attend either, but she didn't think Eleanor would appreciate the news.

"You need something for your Wedding Scrapbook," Eleanor said impatiently. *Wedding Scrapbook?* **What** *Wedding Scrapbook?* "And I know you haven't invited a lot of guests, but the people who *do* come will want to know what's going on."

Since this was something Saffy would very much like to know herself, there wasn't much she could say in reply.

"Can't you do it?" she asked eventually.

Her step-mother tutted with exasperation. "I'm already doing the flowers and the cake. Besides, you need to do *something*, Saffy. Anyone would think you didn't want to marry Marco."

*

That was the problem, Saffy thought, as she put down the receiver. A part of her wanted desperately to be Marco's wife – if nothing else, merely for the security of knowing where he was and not worrying that someone else was warming his bed when she wasn't around. He was still the most sexually attractive man she had ever known: just the thought of him kissing her made her melt in a thousand different places. He'd tied her emotions and hormones up into one enormous package which still hadn't been delivered, so that she was constantly thinking about him and what she wanted him to do to her. *I'm like an animal on heat!* she thought disgustedly.

And yet, despite her acute physical longing for him, Saffy still had reservations. Although she'd seen the softer side of Marco – the proud uncle whose face lit up when he talked about his nieces; the considerate fiancé who'd rushed to her side at the hospital – he was still sometimes arrogant and often irrationally jealous. How could he possibly think that she had cheated on him? she fumed, conveniently forgetting that she had deliberately misled him to protect Sophie.

Would things be different once they were married, when he was tucked up in her antique bedstead with her every night? A sudden thought hit her then: she had been assuming that Marco would move in with her, but what if he were expecting her to live in his apartment instead? Not only would it be too far away from *Jo Bangles*, but those huge, chilly rooms were the exact opposite of her own cosy little flat.

Impulsively, she picked up her phone and fired off a quick text: "Where are we going to live once we're married?"

She wasn't expecting an immediate reply – especially when she and Marco were hardly on speaking terms at present – but moments later, her phone rang and a distantly polite Marco was on the other end.

"We will be living in my apartment," he began without preamble. "There is more space there, for one thing, and there are certain other benefits too, like the security guard and the gym …"

"And Siân?" she interrupted, before she could stop herself.

"You are in no position to criticise *me*, Saffy, given your own track record," Marco reminded her coldly.

For a moment, they were both too angry to continue the conversation. Then, "That won't work," Saffy said decisively. "I don't like your place, Marco – it's too impersonal."

"But your little flat is too small for the two of us and a baby," Marco snapped back. "It is not my fault you are pregnant, Saffy – and very few men in my position would have agreed to marry you."

"Well, why not call it all off now, and then you won't have to go through with it!" she raged at him, terminating the call before he could make a response.

She waited for the next ten minutes for him to ring her back, but her phone was silent for the rest of the day.

*

In the end, James helped her sort out the Order of Service, typing everything up beautifully so that there was no need to go to the printer's at all. "W H Smith sell blank Order of Service covers," he told her airily, "so all we need to do is print off thirty or so inserts."

"I don't think we'll need that many," Saffy said sourly, "because at the moment it looks as if neither the bride or groom will be going!"

"You haven't argued again?" James looked at her severely. "There's no point the two of you fighting all the time unless you're having great make-up sex afterwards – and, by the look on your face, I *know* that's not happening." He put his arms around her gently. "You've got to start making an effort, Sweetie, or you might lose him for good."

"I do try …" Saffy felt tears forming in her eyes, "but he just winds me up so much, James. You have no idea what it's like."

"*Au contraire*, Angel." James fished a tissue from his pocket and handed it to her. "Connor and I have some real spats, as you know – but deep down, we both know we love each other, and that's why we always work things out."

"That only happens when you're both in love," Saffy said in a small voice. "I think Marco's only ever seen me as part of a business deal – I'm an investment for his father's company, that's all."

"I wouldn't be too sure about that," James commented idly. "He wouldn't be so jealous of me if he didn't feel something for you."

Saffy sniffed dismally. "Maybe …"

"Why don't you put his mind at rest and tell him I'm not into girls," James suggested. "It might help …" As she looked at him wonderingly, he continued, "I've been out and proud for five years now, Darling. It's not as if telling him I'm gay is going to ruin my life. And it could improve yours …"

"Well …" Saffy hesitated. Of course she wanted to be truthful with Marco, but would he still want her once he knew James wasn't interested after all?

"Forget sexual politics," James advised, reading her mind. "Sometimes you just have to say what you feel."

"I seem to have been doing far too much of that lately." Saffy was beginning to feel guilty over the number of rows she'd started.

"Just tell him you love him," James said softly, "and don't tell me you're not in love because I know you, Sapphire Vendrini, and you haven't stopped thinking about him since the day you met."

She lifted her troubled blue eyes towards her best friend, knowing that this time she had to take his advice.

*

Friday was rapidly approaching: Sophie had an A level Drama paper; Saffy and Marco had their last Marriage Preparation class; and there was only one more week to go before the wedding.

"You'll have to show Marco the Order of Service and see what he thinks," James told Saffy as she began tidying her workroom that afternoon. "You still haven't seen him this week, have you?"

Saffy bit her lip. Marco hadn't been in touch at all since their acrimonious conversation a few days previously. She had rung his phone several times, but he hadn't answered. In the end, she had sent a text message, asking him to arrive early for their class so they could "have a talk" before Helen and Richard turned up. She was hoping that he'd comply, but she wouldn't have been surprised if he decided not to come at all.

Her fears were allayed slightly when the doorbell rang at six thirty to reveal a somewhat dishevelled Marco on her doorstep. Her first thought was that he had been drinking. He looked terrible: his bloodshot eyes were ringed with grey, suggesting he'd had little or no sleep recently, and his usual designer stubble was an unkempt beard of at least three- or four-days' growth. Despite this, he was still devastatingly attractive: she could feel her insides doing strange things as she gazed at him.

"You look rough," she offered, ushering him into the living room and noting that he removed his shoes without being reminded. "Have you been partying too hard?"

Marco looked at her wearily. "I've just flown in from Italy. I should have returned last night, but the flight was cancelled and I spent all night sitting in the passenger lounge, waiting to find a seat on another one. I haven't slept in thirty-six hours."

"I thought you went Business Class," Saffy muttered. "Don't they have a special lounge for you, full of home comforts?"

"It was a spur of the moment thing," Marco told her, yawning slightly. "I flew out on Wednesday, for a meeting with my father and the other directors – we were going to Skype, but I thought if I went in person, I could take the wedding suits for my father and brother to try on." He paused. "I'm sorry. You're not interested in any of this. After all, we both know it's not a real marriage."

It was as if he were waiting for her to contradict him, but she said nothing, too hurt by his attitude to let him know how much she'd missed him or how much she wanted to repair their relationship.

"Real or not, it's still going ahead in a week's time, isn't it?" she challenged him. "That's why we're here now, waiting for Helen and Richard to sign us off on this course so we can get the certificate to make the priest happy."

"And what about making each other happy?" Marco asked soberly. "Isn't that what this course is really meant to be about, not just saying the right things in front of other people?"

Startled, she looked into his eyes and saw a vulnerability that hadn't been there before. He held her gaze, unwavering; eventually, she looked away, unable to meet his stare without giving part of herself away.

"This isn't right, all this fighting," Marco said at last. "We've both said and done things we're not proud of, Saffy, but we need to put those things aside now and concentrate on moving forwards. Do you agree?"

She nodded dumbly. This sounded like an apology of sorts. Perhaps it was the best Marco could do.

"I am prepared to forgive your past," he continued magnanimously, "but you must promise never to see James again."

"What?" She stared at him aghast. "That's crazy! You know we work together."

"Then find somewhere else. Or let me buy him out." Marco's resolve was unflinching. "But you can't carry on working under the same roof once we are married: I wouldn't have a moment's peace knowing that he was looking at you all day."

"He's gay!" Saffy shouted desperately. "There's never been anything between us, and there never will be."

For a moment, Marco seemed taken aback, then his face hardened. "And why should I believe a story like that?"

"Because it's true!" She was aware that she sounded hysterical, but she didn't care. "He's got a boyfriend. They live together."

"And yet you have not mentioned this until now …" Marco's tone was dangerously light.

"Because I didn't think you'd be stupid enough not to notice it yourself!" Frustration made Saffy uncautious. "I want *you*, Marco – I have since the day I met you." She stretched out her hand, trying to touch his cheek, desperate for him to press his lips against her own, but he pulled away from her.

"You will have to think of a better lie than that, Saffy," he told her coldly. "I've seen him holding you, kissing you."

"As a friend," she pleaded, "not a lover. You *have* to believe me, Marco."

"No, I don't." Marco's face was bleak. "*You* have to prove that you are not screwing around behind my back. I have only your word that the baby you carry was made before we started seeing each other, and you have told me nothing of the father. How do I know your affair will not resume once your child is born – if, indeed, you ever stopped seeing each other in the first place?"

"So why are you marrying me, then?" Saffy could not keep the bitterness from her question.

He turned away from her.

"I am marrying you because it is what our fathers want," he said in a strangled voice. "And because you are a beautiful woman who will be an asset to both companies – if you can charm all our male clients as effortlessly as you did me, then they will be in a much better mood to discuss business."

"You're pimping me out?" She could scarcely contain her disgust. "I'm not your property, Marco – and I'm not a company prostitute either."

He was about to tell her that wasn't what he meant when the doorbell rang once more.

"I'll get it," Saffy said through gritted teeth. "We need to get this over and done with as soon as possible."

Richard and Helen were particularly nauseating this evening. The last session, Richard explained, focused on the wedding itself and the vows the couple were going to make.

"Although lots of people today write their own vows," Helen chimed in eagerly. "We did, didn't we, Dear?"

Saffy was on the verge of asking whether the couple's appalling matching jumpers were the result of a promise to dress alike at all times.

"Well, let's start by looking at the traditional service," Richard offered, "and then think about how Saffy and Marco might want to adapt it. I understand you have an Order of Service now?"

Saffy had dutifully dropped off one of James's creations at the Church the previous evening when Sophie had wanted to drive there to test the acoustics. Now she handed one silently to Richard, realising as she did so that Marco still hadn't seen it.

"What are you entering to?" Helen asked, craning over her husband's shoulder to read it. "Pachelbel's Cannon – lovely. And what's this song from 'West Side Story' after the vows?"

"My sister's singing for us," Saffy said hurriedly. "She's got an amazing voice."

"You didn't mention that, *carissima*," Marco's endearment seemed a little forced.

"Only because you've been so busy with work, *Dear*." If Saffy over-emphasised her last word, Richard and Helen didn't notice.

"Shall we go through the vows now?" Helen asked eagerly. "We've printed them off for you so you can practice saying them to each other this evening and see which version you prefer. This is the traditional one at the top of the page."

Saffy ran her eyes over the words. "I, _____, take you, _____, for my lawful wife/husband, to have and to hold from this day forward, for better, for worse, for richer, for poorer, in sickness and health, until death do us part."

"I thought there was a line about 'forsaking all others'," Marco commented, peering over the top of Saffy's head. She felt sure that was a dig at her.

"Oh, there is," Richard reassured him, "but that's part of the priest's question to both of you – he'll ask you that before you make your vows in response."

They spent the next ten or fifteen minutes going through every bit of the service, including the readings. Helen appeared ecstatic when she saw the choices Saffy and Marco had made.

"We had 1 Corinthians 13 for our wedding, didn't we, Richard?" she beamed, looking fondly at her husband. "And what a romantic bit from the Song of Songs!"

Personally, Saffy thought the latter reading was a little over the top - Marco may as well have stuck a sign on her saying "Keep off the Bride!" – but she smiled sweetly and agreed that yes, it was lovely for her fiancé to have such powerful feelings for her.

*

The rest of the evening passed in much the same way. When they had finally reached the last page of the course booklet, Helen turned to them both with tears in her eyes. "It's been such a privilege to be part of your journey. I only hope the two of you are as happy together as Richard and I."

She turned and impulsively hugged first Saffy, then Marco. "Thank you *so* much. Spending time with you has reminded me of why *we* fell in love ourselves."

Saffy could not prevent a guilty blush from suffusing her cheeks.

"We've enjoyed every minute with you too," Marco lied glibly. He had especially hated tonight's session and all the talk of fidelity and trust. How on earth had Saffy managed to look so serious when they were discussing concepts she obviously didn't believe in?

The goodbyes were over and done. This time, Marco made no attempt to leave with Helen and Richard, or to pretend that he was catching them up in a few minutes. "We need to talk," he said abruptly as the front door closed behind the older couple.

Saffy quailed. That phrase never signified good news.

"Tonight's session has made me think," Marco said slowly. "These vows we are making, Saffy, they are not just for us and our families: we are making them in the sight of God – that means they are promises we must keep."

"I didn't think you were the religious sort, Marco," Saffy jeered defiantly.

"I'm not," he said simply, "but the Catholic Church is part of my heritage. I cannot stand in Church next week and lie."

"So, what are you saying? That we shouldn't get married after all?"

"No, Saffy – you don't get rid of me that easily." He was dangerously close to her now, the aroma of his aftershave almost masked by the scent of his anger. Helplessly, she let him pull her roughly towards himself as he began to kiss her with fierce desperation. When she was almost dizzy with desire, he released her. "You still want me, then?" He sounded surprised.

"Yes." The word dragged unwillingly from her lips. "I haven't stopped wanting you since the first time you kissed me," she told him raggedly, knowing it wasn't wise to admit to this, but past caring by now.

Marco let out a groan of frustration. There was only one thing preventing him from scooping Saffy up in his arms and carrying her into the bedroom, and that was the foetus inside her. No matter how much he longed for her, the thought of that unwelcome intruder permeated his mind, making it impossible for him to rise to the occasion. Part of someone else was growing in her womb: he found the idea utterly repellent.

"Good night, Saffy." He pushed her away, his inner turmoil too strong to let him do anything else.

Hastily pushing his feet into his shoes, he grabbed his jacket and was gone before she had time to protest.

Chapter Thirty-Eight

Saffy had never felt lower than she did after Marco left. He had wanted her, she was sure of it – and then he had suddenly pushed her aside like an undesirable beggar on the street. Was his jealousy really so overwhelming that he couldn't even kiss her now?

Twenty minutes later, her phone pinged with a text. Was it Marco? To her disappointment, it was only Eleanor. "You still haven't finalised the hen night."

She would have to ring Eleanor back, Saffy thought crossly. Her step-mother could send texts but not access them: somehow, she always managed to delete messages before she'd read them.

"Is there really much point going out?" she asked Eleanor wearily, as the older woman answered. "It's just you, me and Sophie really." Although she'd joked with James about inviting him and Connor, she knew that Marco wouldn't appreciate it if she did.

"And Marco's mother and sister-in-law," Eleanor corrected her. "They fly in on the Friday – I thought we could all go out in the evening."

"What about the little girls?" Saffy reminded her. Marco had said they were six and four. "Won't someone need to stay in and look after them?"

But it seemed Eleanor had thought of everything. "Your father and Lucas have agreed to baby-sit," Eleanor told her. "They're going to sit and drink wine – well, Lucas will drink wine; your father isn't allowed any alcohol for the next few months – and catch up on old times. Besides, it will be good for you to get to know your future mother-in-law, and Ricardo's wife is a similar age to you so you should have plenty to talk about."

*

Before she knew what was happening, Saffy's whole hen night had been organised for her. The five Vendrini and Benedetti women would go out for a meal – Eleanor had suggested *Zizzi's* but Saffy gave a firm no to that one, reminding her that taking two Italian women to an English-run Italian restaurant probably wasn't a good idea. She was tempted to suggest the *Village Mangal* instead, but the memory of her night there with Marco was too fresh in her mind.

In the end, they compromised on *Antonio's* - a small family restaurant which Eleanor often frequented with her friends at lunchtime. The menu offered 'European-Asian fusion', whatever that meant, and Eleanor said the sea bass was heavenly.

The weekend whirled by in a flurry of last-minute details: orders for buttonholes were confirmed and paid for; the cake was collected and stored in one of the spare bedrooms that wasn't going to be used by visiting Benedettis; and Saffy had an email from Bianca, her soon to be sister-in-law, whose English was fortunately very good. Bianca wrote that Giulia and Giorgia were both very excited about being flower girls at the wedding and equally so about having new clothes. She attached a photo of the latter and Saffy was gratified to see that the pretty blue satin dresses perfectly complemented Sophie's grown up one.

*

"How are you having your hair?" James asked her suddenly on the Monday morning.

Saffy shrugged. "Up, I suppose. It's more formal that way."

"Forget formal, Darling – it's your wedding!" James scolded her. "If there's one day when you're supposed to look sexy, Saff, this is it!"

Saffy studied her nails, wondering if sexy-looking hair would make any difference where Marco was concerned. He had made it very plain on Friday that he no longer wanted to make love to her. Uneasily she thought about Siân, picturing the scantily clad redhead knocking on Marco's door with a bottle of wine. How many times had the other girl kept him company recently? She would be willing to bet that Marco wouldn't have pushed *Siân* away if she was offering sex.

At James's insistence, Saffy took herself off to the local salon at lunchtime and asked her usual hairdresser for advice. When asked for details about the dress, she flipped through the photos on her phone until she found the one she'd saved from the website.

"Hmmmm." Claire sounded thoughtful. "Normally I'd say, 'Go for an updo,' but with a style like that, long and flowing might be better, otherwise you'll be all neck and shoulders." She gathered Saffy's hair in one hand and started to experiment. "Maybe partly up and partly down … We haven't got any clients for the next twenty minutes – shall we have a bit of a play around now?"

By the time Saffy left the salon half an hour later, Claire had tried five different styles and Saffy still couldn't decide. She had, however, booked hair appointments for herself and Sophie for the Saturday morning – more to give them something to do than anything else. Claire had asked one of the other stylists to take photos of each of the five possibilities, using Saffy's phone; she would ask Sophie to come over this evening and help her decide.

No, she wouldn't. She had forgotten that Sophie still had two exams left – she wouldn't be free until Wednesday and then she would be out most of the night at her Leavers' Ball.

Swearing under her breath, Saffy entered the shop and thumped her bag down on the counter. James watched her with amusement.

"What's wrong, Saff? Did the hairdresser say I was right after all?"

"I've got five possible choices," Saffy said shortly, "and I can't decide between any of them."

"Pictures?" James demanded. He scanned through quickly. "Not that one – that's far too old for you: makes you look at least thirty. Not that one either. Hang on – this one's all right."

The style he'd chosen was a combination of sexy and elegant: Claire had pulled Saffy's hair up, away from her face, and then fastened it with a sparkly barrette so that the rest of it tumbled in loose waves down her back. A few wispy strands framed her face, softening the look. James whistled softly. "It's enough to make *me* fancy you – and you know I'm not wired that way!"

"Do you think Marco will like it though?" Saffy asked anxiously.

"Who cares?" James looked his business partner in the eye. "If he doesn't want to marry you with hair like that, I'll do it myself!"

Maybe, Saffy thought sadly, as she lay alone once more that night, there was nothing she could do to change Marco's mind. She was also worried how he would react when she told him that it was Sophie who was pregnant and not her. *But you never told him you were pregnant in the first place!* her mind argued. *He just found the test and made assumptions.*

That was the part that really hurt: she had thought they were getting on so well, had been on the brink of sleeping with him for the first time, and then Marco had ruined it all by putting two and two together and making forty-six.

What would he think when he found out that she had never been pregnant in the first place? Would he apologise for maligning her; or would he be angry that she hadn't corrected his mistake sooner?

She tossed and turned fretfully, unable to think of anything else but the potential disaster of her wedding night.

*

Marco, meanwhile, was also struggling to sleep. He wanted Saffy so much that he was finding it hard to think about anything else – this was not a helpful situation at work when he, his father and Antonio were in the midst of finalising the details for the merger. Yet, at the same time, he still couldn't bring himself to touch her body; and his revulsion would only get worse as she grew bigger. Not that he had any aversion to pregnant women normally, he corrected himself. Bianca had glowed when carrying both her girls; and if Saffy had been pregnant with *his* child, it would have been a different matter entirely. No, what sickened him was the thought of another man's baby stretching Saffy's body out of shape, feeding off her like a parasite and making her sick, then tearing her flesh as it made its entrance into the world. She would have to suffer like that to have someone else's bastard when it should have been *his* rightful heir. And then the child would claim all her attention whilst she fed it and rocked it and lavished her love upon it. There would be no room for him in the marriage once this baby was born, he was sure of it.

You're jealous, he told himself bluntly. *Jealous of a child that isn't even born.*

Could he maybe find a nanny for the baby, so it didn't take up too much of Saffy's time? But then, if he did that, she might go back to work straight away and then he would be back to square one with her spending all her time with that licentious boss of hers. He didn't believe the story about James being gay: you only had to look at him and the way he flirted with Saffy to know that there was definitely something going on.

Maybe it was better to keep her at home, then. At least whilst she was breastfeeding, she couldn't go gallivanting about with one of her former lovers. But it wouldn't hurt to buy a baby monitor and leave it accidentally switched on so he could overhear Saffy's phone conversations – or, better still, one of those 'nanny-cam' things that Ricardo and Bianca had: a video camera hidden inside a teddy bear that would record everything Saffy said and did within a twenty-four-hour period.

Suddenly he came to his senses – what was he doing, planning to spy on his wife? This wasn't like him at all: it must be a side effect of not sleeping properly. He still hadn't recovered from last Friday's trip.

Saffy had claimed she hadn't been unfaithful, and he wanted to believe her; but the memory of Nadia, smiling up at him, promising forever, danced across his mind. Perhaps all women were like that and even Bianca – who seemed devoted to Ric – was leading a double life.

Trembling slightly, he reached for the bottle of wine by his bedside, hoping it would soon carry him into oblivion.

*

Marco overslept the following morning, which wasn't surprising given the amount of alcohol he'd consumed in a bid to help him sleep. He awoke with a raging hangover, his headache only exacerbated by the strident ringing of his doorbell.

Stumbling out of bed, he pulled on his bathrobe and swore his way to the door. His mouth felt like the bottom of a birdcage and he could only imagine what he looked like. He was supposed to be meeting a client at ten, but he would have to delay everything by at least half an hour if he were to have any chance of appearing human.

The ringing had been caused by a bored looking postal worker who had already turned to leave by the time Marco pushed the door open. Thrusting a large manila envelope into Marco's hands, he instructed him to sign for it on one of those ridiculous handheld contraptions that demanded a signature written with one's finger. Surely by now the Post Office should have invested in something more user-friendly? Maybe that was something to suggest to the directors? If they could get a contract to supply a national organisation with up to date technology …

Marco came to with a start, realising that his finger was still poised over the screen in front of him. "*Scusi*," he muttered, scribbling quickly. Walking back to his bedroom, he perused the back of the envelope. A printed stamp bore the legend 'SmartLoving' – this must be the certificate from the course, then: he remembered giving Richard his own address on Friday.

The certificate would have to wait: he had other, more pressing matters at hand. It was almost eight thirty and the train to London took up to forty-six minutes. Grabbing his mobile, he fired off a quick email: *"Running late. Reschedule Alan Jones for ten thirty. If he still arrives at ten, demonstrate some of the new specs."*

Walking into the bathroom, he caught sight of himself in the mirror and winced. Bloodshot eyes peered back at him and his unkempt hair resembled some sort of bird's nest. Forgetting his headache, he stood under a steaming shower until he was fully awake, then scrubbed his hair furiously with Paul Mitchell's tea tree lemon sage shampoo.

That was better: now he felt human again. He checked the time and realised he could manage an espresso before he left for the station. Flicking the requisite switches, he let the machine get on with it whilst he shaved and dressed. There would be several trains leaving High Wycombe within the next thirty minutes, but one of the faster ones would be better: if he found a quiet seat, he could read through Alan Jones's profile on the train. He checked his tie, grabbed his keys and mobile, and headed for the door.

*

"I hear you're getting married on Saturday?"

Marco felt like swearing. Phil, or one of his other colleagues, must have been gossiping to Jones, who had arrived at ten after all.

"Yes," he said shortly. "Saffy's father owns *Vendrini's*, part of our corporation."

"So, you won't be around next week, then? Where's the honeymoon?"

Marco hesitated. He and Saffy were booked into the reception hotel for three nights and should then be flying out to Venice for a week; but he was now wondering whether this was a good idea. What was the point of being on honeymoon if he couldn't bear the thought of touching his wife?

"Keeping it secret, eh?" Alan laughed. "Just make sure you switch your email off so no one from here can track you down and ask your advice about orders. It was the biggest mistake of my life booking into a hotel with internet access when I was on *my* honeymoon."

*

After the meeting was over, Marco contemplated his honeymoon once more. Maybe if he drank enough, he could get over his inhibitions and do the job properly? But then, if he drank too much, he might not be able to perform at all.

Angrily, he crashed his fist down onto the table. This was all wrong. He should be desperate to make love to his wife, not dreading it happening.

Sighing, he reached for his mobile, clicking onto the photo he'd taken of Saffy when they were in the park. She'd been unaware of the camera, her face animated, her eyes sparkling, looking at him as if she really loved him. At the time, he'd thought she did.

Would she ever look at him like that again? he wondered, or had it all been pretence? On Friday, she'd kissed him passionately, but maybe she was just a very good actress.

Opening his desk drawer, he removed the bottle of whisky and took a long, slow swig.

*

Wednesday. The day of Sophie's last exam and the Leavers' Ball. Saffy hoped her little sister would be sensible and remember that drinking was bad for the baby.

A text pinged through from Sophie just after half six: a photo of her ready to leave for the ball, resplendent in a green satin ballgown that showed far too much cleavage. Apart from her enhanced bosom, she wasn't showing yet – although the huge skirt on her dress could have easily hidden a nine months' bump, Saffy thought as she gazed at the picture.

James and Connor had invited her over for a "last night of freedom", but she'd turned them down. Much as she enjoyed their company, she knew she wouldn't be able to keep on seeing them once she and Marco were married. He seemed incapable of believing that men and women could be friends without something more happening.

She still wasn't entirely sure how things would change once the wedding had taken place. She and Marco still hadn't reached an agreement over where they would live, but perhaps that would change once he knew they didn't need room for a baby?

Feeling at a loose end, she decided to tidy her flat. Her booklet from the marriage course was still on the dining table – she'd eaten all her meals from a tray in front of the TV so far this week. Idly flicking through the pages, various snippets caught her eye: *"Never go to bed angry with each other … Always be prepared to apologise …"* Finally, as she turned to the last page, the final piece of advice jumped out at her: *"Ten words to save a marriage: It's my fault – I'm sorry – Forgive me – I love you."* A tear rolled down her cheek as she thought of how hard she'd tried to convince Marco that she hadn't cheated, that she loved him. How could it be her fault when she'd tried so hard?

No, marriage was a two-way street – that was one of the sayings from the course too – and if Marco wasn't prepared to meet her half-way, then she would stop moving towards him.

Picking up the booklet, she placed it carefully in the recycling pile, along with the other unwanted paper.

Chapter Thirty-Nine

Eleanor rang Saffy the following morning, full of alarm. "Sophie's got some sort of bug – she was throwing up this morning."

"She probably just drank too much last night," Saffy told her. "You know what these sixth form things are like."

Secretly, she hoped it was morning sickness and not a post-party hangover.

"I hope she's well enough for Saturday," Eleanor continued. "You can't get married without your sister, and everyone's expecting to hear her sing too."

"She'll probably be fine," Saffy said absently, her mind already on other things. Several weeks previously – before things had taken such a nasty turn with Marco – she had started making their wedding bands. This should have been a simple task – she had made plenty before – but Marco had specified that each one should be engraved inside with the date of the wedding and she had deliberately left this fiddly task until the last minute. Now, with only two days to go, she realised she couldn't put it off any longer. She'd only hesitated in the first place because a part of her had been half-expecting Marco to cancel the whole thing.

Getting rid of Eleanor as soon as she could, Saffy ran down the stairs, out of her front door and into the shop. James was in the middle of a telephone conversation. "Okay," he was saying, "email it across and I'll see what I can do."

Seeing Saffy, he terminated the call abruptly. "What was all that about?" she asked curiously.

"Nothing." James shrugged nonchalantly, but Saffy thought she detected a gleam in his eye.

"I'll be in the back of the shop if you need me," she told him, hurt that he was keeping secrets from her. "I've got some engraving to do."

"Okay, Sweetie." He was already engrossed in his computer screen, hardly aware of her at all. "Clever boy!" Saffy heard him mutter under his breath. She would have liked to know more, but he turned slightly, blocking out whatever he was doing. Deflated, she left him to it and entered the back of the shop.

It was an hour later before Saffy was satisfied with the design she was going to engrave. She'd originally thought of using their initials beside their date, but 'M&S' had connotations of 'Marks and Spencer', and 'S&M' was also no good – for obvious reasons. In the end she'd settled on a pair of tiny love hearts, one on either side of the wedding date. Hopefully the hearts were a good omen, she thought as she carefully etched the inside of each ring.

The shop was empty when she finally returned, but the printer was in full swing, churning out sheet after sheet.

"What's this?" She made to grab one, but James snatched it out of her hand.

"Just reprinting your Order of Service. I realised I'd made a mistake with the first batch."

"What mistake?" Saffy asked suspiciously. She hadn't noticed anything wrong with the one she'd shown Helen and Richard.

"Oh, just some spelling mistakes in the first reading," James said glibly. "I've fixed it now. By the way," he continued, changing the subject without a pause, "who's doing the readings? You didn't say when I typed everything up, so I've just left that part blank."

Saffy looked horrified. "I hadn't even thought of that. I'd just assumed the priest would do it."

"Don't you and Marco have a run-through tonight?" James wanted to know. "You could both check with him then."

"Yes, but …" Saffy stopped abruptly. "I didn't tell you about that," she accused.

"Didn't you?" James sounded innocent. "I must be thinking of that Kate Hudson Rom-Com, then – engaged couples in films always practise the marriage service the night before the wedding."

"Except the wedding's on Saturday," Saffy reminded him pointedly.

James shrugged. "I must be psychic, then. Who knew?"

Saffy wasn't convinced but there was no point arguing. She spent the rest of the day trying to work out who would be able to do the readings at short notice.

*

She received a text from Marco at just gone six. "On my way to the church. Do you want a lift?"

"Booked a taxi, thanks," she typed back, hoping that an Uber would now be available. She knew she was being childish, but she felt too emotionally fragile to spend any more time with Marco than she absolutely had to.

Arriving at St Aiden's with a few minutes to spare, Saffy noticed that Marco's Jag was already parked outside. Would the priest think it odd that they hadn't arrived together?

Father Nick greeted her warmly when she entered. "Good to see you, Sapphire. Feeling nervous about Saturday?"

"A little," she confessed, deliberately not looking at Marco. If truth be told, it wasn't the service she was worried about but the wedding night – if it happened at all, that was.

"Now, when you arrive at the Church, you, Marco, will come straight in with your best man -" Father Nick looked round expectantly. "Is he not here tonight?"

"My brother's still in Italy," Marco broke in. "He's arriving tomorrow."

"Ah, splendid. Well, you and the best man will be sitting at the front of the church here -" he indicated "and then when the bride arrives, you'll both stand up and Sapphire and her bridesmaids will come and join you. I will then give the welcome and ask if there is anyone present who knows of any reason why the two of you should not be lawfully wed, and then all of you will sit down for the first reading. Marco, you've just told me you're going to do that. Shall we have a try now?"

Saffy gazed at Marco in amazement. *He* was doing the Old Testament reading? Did that mean she would have to read the other piece herself? She began to feel nervous.

Rising to his feet, Marco turned to face the invisible congregation and began to read. With a shock, Saffy noticed that the words were not the ones from the Song of Solomon but something entirely different.

"Entreat me not to leave you," Marco intoned in his heavily accented English, "or to turn back from following after you; for wherever you go, I will go; and wherever you lodge, I will lodge; your people shall be my people, and your God, my God. Where you die, I will die, and there will I be buried. The LORD do so to me, and more also, if anything but death parts you and me."

Saffy listened, mesmerised, thinking that it was one of the most perfect things she had ever heard at a wedding. She tried to catch Marco's eye as he looked up from the reading, but he pretended not to see her.

"Splendid," Father Nick repeated. "Thank you, Marco. That was very clear. And now the New Testament reading, Sapphire."

"I'm not reading," Saffy confessed, still shaken by what she'd heard. Inspiration suddenly struck her: Sophie could do the reading. As a Drama student, she was used to performing in public.

"My sister's going to read for us," she said quickly. Marco shot her a quick look.

"Ah, I see. Well, it's a pity she isn't here now, but that can't be helped." Father Nick pressed on. "So, after the readings from scripture, which speak of marriage and God's love for us, the liturgy of marriage follows. I will ask you a series of questions about your understanding of marriage and your freedom to marry, and then you will exchange your consent." He paused. "You will be repeating the words after I say them, so we don't necessarily have to try that bit now."

Was he trying to get rid of them? Saffy thought suspiciously.

"The rings are then blessed and exchanged," Father Nick continued, "followed by the nuptial blessing where you, as a newly married couple, are prayed for and your future life together blessed." He regarded them both. "And then I say, 'You may now kiss the bride.' And that's it."

It all seemed as if it would be over very quickly.

"And the signing of the register?" Marco asked.

"Ah, yes. My apologies: I always forget to mention that bit. You and Sapphire will leave the congregation and come with me to the vestry at the back of the church to sign the civil registers. Your two witnesses will join us too. I understand Sapphire's sister is going to sing at this point?"

"No!" Saffy exclaimed. "I want to hear Sophie! I thought that was going to be part of the service – can't you put it in after the prayers?"

Father Nick consulted his Order of Service. "You'll have to change this," he commented. "It most distinctly says that 'There's A Place For Us' will be sung during the signing of the register."

James would have to retype it again, Saffy thought, realising now what her friend had been doing earlier.

"Was that you on the phone to James this morning?" she asked Marco accusingly. "Why didn't you tell me you'd changed the reading?"

"I wanted it to be a surprise." Marco couldn't tell her the real reason, that he'd wanted to watch her reaction as she heard the words for the first time. It was as close as he could get to telling her how much he loved her – even if the bit about his people becoming her people had made him think momentarily of the merger.

"I'm glad you changed it," she said softly now. "This one's much more suitable for a wedding."

"If that's everything," Father Nick glanced at his watch, "then I must be going."

He *was* trying to get rid of them, Saffy thought in triumph.

Marco looked at Saffy. "Can I offer you a lift home?"

"All right," she heard herself saying. "It'll give us the chance to talk."

For a few moments, awkward silence reigned in Marco's car. Then, as he began to navigate the twists and turns in the road, Saffy spoke up.

"That reading you chose … Why did you change it?"

"As you mentioned yourself, it's more suitable for a wedding," Marco said carefully.

"Wherever you go, I will go," Saffy echoed. "Does that mean you'll come and live in my flat after all?" she asked mischievously.

"I …" Marco felt flummoxed. "I thought we agreed your flat wasn't big enough for three," he reminded her.

"No, Marco, *you* decided, not me." Saffy struggled to keep the irritation out of her voice. "And there are only two of us at the moment anyway."

"But not for much longer," Marco muttered, keeping his eyes on the road.

Saffy hesitated. Should she tell him the truth now? Sophie's exams were over and she would be breaking the news on Saturday anyway. Surely it couldn't hurt to set the record straight a day or two early?

But Marco had started speaking again. "This is not going to be an easy marriage, Saffy – you and I both know that; but, if we try hard, I think we can make it work."

"What do you mean?"

"I can't touch you at the moment." Marco felt he had to tell her the truth. "I want you, but I can't bring myself to make love to you while you're pregnant. That should be my baby in your belly, not someone else's."

"What if I wasn't pregnant?" she asked softly, getting ready to break the news.

He glanced across at her quickly. "But then you'll have a newborn baby to look after, and you might be so tired that you don't want *me* – that's common after giving birth." Bianca had gone off sex for three months after having the second one. Ricardo had described it as the most frustrating time of his life.

They had reached her flat. Marco pulled to a halt and kept the engine running. "It will be difficult, but not impossible," he told her. "I might not feel like this forever."

"Marco, the baby …"

He cut her off once more. "I don't want any details, Saffy. If you say you are no longer involved with the father, I will believe you. I will try not to feel so jealous. But I am only human – don't push me too hard."

"But …"

"Goodnight, Saffy. I'll see you at the church on Saturday."

He kissed her cheek lightly and waited for her to alight. Realising that there was no point in talking to him now, she did as he wanted.

Chapter Forty

Marco was up early the next morning. Mindful of the fact that his family's flight was expected around midday, he had decided to arrive at the office for eight so he could get several hours in before meeting them at London City Airport. Since it was more of a business hub than a proper airport, they would all take a cab (he'd pre-booked an eight-seater) back to Saffy's parents' place in Buckinghamshire, where the whole Benedetti clan would be staying overnight (Marco excepted) to make babysitting easier.

Although it was only a week or so since he'd seen his father and brother, Marco found himself unexpectedly moved by the family reunion at the airport. Bianca looked stunning in a scarlet dress with matching stilettos, whilst his two nieces sparkled in glittery pink Barbie tee-shirts and trainers.

"Their choice, not mine," Bianca told him, kissing his cheek. "I wish now we'd had boys instead – at least they'd wear different colours!" She looked round expectantly. "No Saffy?"

"She couldn't get time off work," Marco said hurriedly. He'd deliberately not invited Saffy to the airport, knowing that she didn't speak Italian and that his mother spoke no English. Besides, he'd missed them all while he'd been living in England and he wanted this afternoon to be quality time together without him having his blood pressure raised by Saffy's presence.

"She sent me a lovely email," Bianca said casually. "It sounded like she's looking forward to the wedding – even if it has been a bit rushed." She lowered her voice conspiratorially. "Is there a reason it's happening so quickly?"

Marco looked round desperately for Ricardo, but Ric was busy with his two daughters.

"Well?" Bianca pressed.

Marco hesitated. He and Bianca got on well – she was like the sister he'd never had – but he wasn't ready to mention Saffy's pregnancy yet. He couldn't bear the thought of the congratulations when the news finally got out

"Let me get the wedding out of the way first," he said with forced laughter. "There'll be plenty of time to start thinking about a cousin for Giulia and Giorgia once that's done."

Bianca said nothing, but she resolved to try to talk to Saffy privately that evening and ascertain what was going on.

*

"Just think," James said to Saffy as they sat down together with baguettes from the sandwich shop next door, "this is your last lunch as a single woman."

Saffy chewed her bacon and avocado thoughtfully. "I suppose you're right," she said at last. "The ceremony's at twelve, so the first thing I'll eat as a blushing bride will be the food at the reception. I'll be starving by then!"

"Tuck a packet of crisps into your bouquet," James advised. "You can sneak them out one at a time when no one's looking!"

"Idiot!" Saffy swatted him playfully, almost sending her sandwich flying as she did so. "If I'm going to eat in church, I'll need something a lot quieter than crisps!"

"I'll miss all this," James said suddenly.

"Miss what?" She didn't understand.

"All this … *camaraderie*. You're getting married tomorrow, you're off on honeymoon for two weeks, and then when you come back, you'll be too loved up with Marco to have any time for me." James sighed dramatically and took a bite out of his custard tart.

"I wouldn't be too sure of that," Saffy muttered cryptically.

James shot her a sympathetic look. "Still no joy on the nookie front?"

"It's not worth talking about." Saffy brushed the crumbs from her lap and stood up. "Why don't I make us both a drink?"

"You don't wriggle out of it that easily, young lady," James told her, grabbing her arm and making her sit down again. "I thought you said you'd told him that I bat for the other side."

"He didn't believe me." Saffy wasn't going to mention the imaginary baby – that would overcomplicate things. And if she told James Sophie was pregnant, he would be bound to mention it loudly in her father's hearing, before Sophie got the chance to do it herself. "It's because he thinks you're too goodlooking to be gay," she said, grinning.

"What, and he's not too goodlooking to be straight?" James countered. "If I looked like Marco, I'd be unstoppable: no one could resist eyes like his."

"I'll tell Connor," Saffy warned.

James smiled disarmingly. "Don't worry, Darling: I checked Marco out on the Gaydar the first time I saw him, and that boy of yours is one hundred percent straight – so why he hasn't ravished you yet is beyond me – unless there's anything else you're not telling me?"

"I'll put the kettle on." Saffy said hurriedly, disappearing into the tiny kitchenette at the back. Hopefully things would go all right on the wedding night, and then James would stop asking her so many probing questions.

*

She had expected her hen night to be a respite from invasions into her personal life, but Marco's sister-in-law seemed just as nosy as James, although less direct. At first, Saffy had been glad to see Bianca – especially when the young Italian woman had acted as interpreter between her own mother-in-law and the Vendrinis; but now that Eleanor and Maria were both occupied with their food, Bianca had turned her attention to Saffy and was bombarding her with endless queries about herself and Marco.

"Ric's been telling him to settle down for a while now," she said thoughtfully, ignoring the food on her plate, "but he was never interested until he met you."

Saffy felt her hearbeat quicken.

"I always thought I was lucky to meet Ricardo first," Bianca continued, "because I know I would have fallen for Marco and he would have broken my heart – he wasn't the marrying kind. I don't know what you did to change him, Saffy – I can call you Saffy, can't I? – but whatever it was, it worked."

Saffy sat with her fork halfway to her mouth, somewhat stunned by Bianca's words. "It's more of a business merger than anything else, really," she said at last.

"*Sciocchezze!*" was Bianca's dismissive reply. "Marco may come across as a hard-headed businessman, but nothing would induce him to get married unless he really wanted to. He loves you, Saffy – and you must love him too. Why else would you be marrying him tomorrow?"

"I'm not pregnant, if that's what you're thinking," Saffy said hurriedly.

Bianca eyed her shrewdly. "No, but your sister is, isn't she? I can tell by her eyes."

"Sshhh!" Saffy hissed at her. "No one else knows yet, not even Eleanor."

"How far along is she?" Bianca asked next, more quietly this time.

Saffy counted rapidly. "Almost three months."

"So, she will announce it once she is sure the baby is safe." Bianca's eyes gleamed. "My little girls will have a new English cousin, then."

"Please don't say anything," Saffy begged her. "She's going to tell my dad and Eleanor tomorrow – she thought the news might go down better then."

"Yours is a strange family, Saffy." Bianca managed to sound amused and intrigued at the same time. "I will keep your secret, but I look forward to being able to tell my girls about their Auntie Sophie's *bambino*."

*

Meanwhile, a little less than seven miles away, Marco was celebrating his own stag night with Ricardo, Phil and a number of other people who worked for the London branch of *Benedetti's*. Mindful of the fact that he would be dressing at his own apartment the following morning, he had told Phil to keep it local, rather than arranging for them to paint the town red in London; he thought the other man seemed disappointed to be sitting in *Club Havana* rather than hanging out at *Tramp* or *Cirque le Soir*. So far, it seemed like a pretty tame evening and Marco felt relieved: the last thing he wanted was some clichéd, raucous strip club – which had been Phil's first suggestion.

One of his other colleagues – Andy, or was it Rob? – leaned over to him. "Is this it?"

"Nope," Phil told him, overhearing. "We're going on to *Signature* next, and then I've got something special lined up." He winked as he said it and Marco was hit by a sudden sense of foreboding. One of the other men chuckled knowingly, and Ricardo shot his brother a questioning look. Marco shrugged helplessly, wishing now that he had vetoed the idea of a stag night after all.

*

But it transpired he needn't have worried. The *Signature* nightclub was surprisingly empty for a Friday evening and so far no strippers had appeared – although the glamorous 'hostesses' were rather scantily clad. He began to relax, enjoying his wine for once, rather than using it to drown his sorrows.

As it approached eleven o'clock, Ricardo turned to his brother apologetically. "I must be going. I don't want Bianca to worry."

"I understand. It looks as though we're about to leave too." The others were already grabbing jackets and downing the last remnants of their drinks.

Ricardo gave Marco a brotherly hug. "The next time I see you, you will be in your wedding clothes!"

"So will you," Marco retorted. "Give Bianca my love. And I'll see you at eleven tomorrow."

As Ricardo began to make his way outside to look for the taxi he'd ordered, Phil gave the rest of the group a sidelong look. "All right, Marco," he declared. "Now your brother's gone, we can get started with the good stuff."

"What do you mean?" Marco said in alarm.

Phil's eyes gleamed once more. "There's a private club down the road. A friend of mine told me about it."

"What sort of club?" Marco asked suspiciously.

Phil didn't answer. Instead he and the others began ushering Marco outside. Marco looked around for Ricardo, but there was no sign of him. His brother's cab must have already arrived.

The building Phil led them to was rather dismal and seedy-looking in a less salubrious part of the town. Remnants of tattered posters fluttered from the outside walls; Marco thought he could decipher 'Lap Danc', but he wasn't sure.

Knocking on a battered door that looked as if it hadn't been opened in decades, Phil waited in silence. Moments later, an ugly brute of a bouncer opened the door and peered out at him. "Yeah? Whaddya want?"

"Party of six for the live floor show," Phil told him. "I've paid a deposit up front."

The man grunted. "Pay the rest of the money at the desk," he advised as he let them pass through the grubby entrance.

The décor inside was even worse than Marco had expected. Faded, peeling wallpaper in a garish velvet flock vied for attention with harsh, shadeless bulbs hanging sadly from the ceiling and a nasty plastic runner underfoot. Everything gave off a distinctly sad air, as if the venue itself were ashamed of how disreputable it had become. Through a slightly ajar door, pulsating music struggled to be heard against a backdrop of hooting and cheering. This wasn't what he wanted at all.

But apparently this was what everyone else wanted. Marco knew that most of his colleagues were married, some with children, and felt vaguely sick. What would their wives say if they knew? he wondered.

Phil was taking out his credit card, arguing about something with the girl on the desk. She was gesturing at a handwritten sign that proclaimed, 'Cash only'.

"Marco! How much dosh have you got on you?" Phil called to him.

Marco didn't see why he should have to pay for something he didn't want to do, but the others were already taking out wallets and peeling off twenties. With a sigh, he withdrew fifty pounds and handed it to Phil, telling himself that he didn't have to look at the stage. If Saffy asked him what he'd been up to on his stag night, he wanted to tell her truthfully that he hadn't seen any strippers.

It was so dark when they pushed their way inside the crowded space that Marco could hardly see anything anyway. Then, as his eyes adjusted to the gloom, he began to make out a pole on a podium in the centre of the room and a shadowy shape crouched beside it.

A harsh overhead light suddenly flicked on, focusing on the girl, who now straightened up and began to dance erotically beside the pole, wrapping her body around it suggestively. Marco felt his body begin to respond to the sheer sexuality of the dance. The girl's sinuous movements were strangely hypnotic, and there was something oddly familiar about her too … She turned to face him, and he realised why: it was Siân.

*

For a moment, his brain was unable to process the information. It couldn't be his neighbor: it looked like her, that was all. But no, it was definitely Siân – and wearing only marginally less clothing than she usually did.

Marco stared at Siân in horror, unable to comprehend why the girl from across the hall was cavorting round a pole in an extremely dodgy nightclub. Did that mean she was a stripper, then? Or, worse still, a prostitiute?

Beside him, Phil let out a low chuckle. "She's got her eye on you, mate – you lucky sod!"

Marco could understand why Phil was impressed. Siân was wearing a tiny crop top that barely covered her breasts and a skimpy G-string that left little to the imagination. But she wasn't Saffy. As the girl in front of him continued to twist and pose, he wondered briefly if all women led double lives, if Saffy had ever danced like this for any of her boyfriends whilst maintaining her demure exterior in public. The room was full of admiring whistles, but he could only think of his fiancée, desperate all of a sudden to hold her once more, to feel her body come alive to his touch.

What was he doing here? He started to stand up, intending to leave, but Phil dragged him back down. "Go to the Gents later - she's coming over."

As Siân approached, Marco formed his face into a disinterested look. He didn't want to encourage the redhead.

"Hello boys!" Her tone was mischievous, coquettish even.

"You got a lap dance for my friend here?" Phil asked her. "It's his stag night – he's getting married tomorrow."

Siân raised an eyebrow. "Well, if it's his stag night, he can have a lap dance for free."

She moved towards him, but Marco pushed her away. "Not tonight, Siân." Not ever.

Phil and Andy exchanged puzzled glances; Rob nearly choked. "You know her?"

"Marco's an old friend," Siân lied carelessly. "We've got … history."

Marco wanted to protest, to explain that he had kissed the girl once, that nothing else had happened, but the rest of his group were looking at him with a mixture of awe and respect, obviously imagining a much more exciting version of events. It seemed like too much effort to correct them, so he didn't.

If Siân felt aggrieved by his rejection of her, she didn't show it, moving from one of his colleagues to the next, smiling, laughing, flirting – was she trying to make him jealous?

*

Feeling more uncomfortable than ever, Marco stood up. "I'm going," he said shortly. "I need a clear head for tomorrow morning."

Weaving his way through the tightly packed tables and chairs, he found he couldn't wait to get out of this place. Even before Saffy, he'd never gone in for this sort of sleaze. He'd always been perfectly capable of getting a woman without having to pay for her.

He reached the exit with a sense of relief; then, pausing to check he hadn't inadvertently left his phone or his wallet on the table, he became aware of Siân. She must have followed him, he thought distractedly, but why?

"It's not going to happen, Siân," he told her bluntly, watching her expression.

Her face didn't register any emotion. "I'm finished for the night. I thought we could share a taxi home."

Marco hesitated. It sounded legitimate, but what if this were another of Siân's seduction techniques? He was suddenly too tired to care.

"Okay," he told her brusquely, "but keep your hands to yourself."

He reached for his phone to dial a cab, but she shook her head. "There's one on the way."

As the car arrived and Siân climbed in, followed by Marco, neither of them noticed Phil standing in the doorway, his phone filming the entire scene.

Chapter Forty-One

For several minutes, silence reigned in the cab. Marco felt too awkward to say anything – particularly when Siân was sitting so close to him.

"Aren't you cold?" he asked abruptly. She was only wearing the clothes she'd had on in the club.

"I'm fine."

But he took off his jacket and placed it around her shoulders – more to cover her up than anything else.

"So, you're really going through with it then?" she challenged, looking up at him with predatory eyes. "You're not the marrying kind, Marco – don't kid yourself."

He returned her gaze coolly. "Everyone has to settle down sometime."

"Not me!" Siân declared with conviction. He thought she was probably right.

"How long have you been dancing in clubs?" he asked her next, curious about this secret side to his neighbour.

Siân yawned. "About six months. I'm an accountant, actually," – Marco tried to reconcile the scantily clad siren next to him with the the smartly suited professionals who audited *Benedetti's* books - "but an old school friend told me about this place and how it's cash in hand – I can make pretty good money with all the tips I get for 'extras'."

Embarrassed, he looked away.

"I'm not a prostitute, if that's what you're thinking," she said sharply. "I don't mind giving the odd lap-dance, but that's as far as it goes. And I don't see anything wrong with what I'm doing either – men have been exploiting women for centuries: it's time we got our own back. Besides," she grinned suddenly, "pole dancing's good exercise!"

Marco began to relax. Perhaps this shared taxi wasn't going to be so bad after all. But then a moment later, he distinctly felt Siân's hand somewhere it had no business to be. Without saying anything, he removed it firmly, trying to ignore the reaction she had caused. They sat in silence for the next five minutes.

When the taxi pulled up to the security gates outside their building, Marco breathed a sigh of relief. He had felt uneasy being in such close proximity to someone wearing so few clothes.

It was obvious the cab driver thought Marco had picked Siân up. *It's not what you think,* Marco wanted to protest as he gave the man his credit card. Luckily, Joe, the security guard in reception this evening, knew them both and didn't make any comments.

As they reached the lift, Marco hesitated. Did he really want Siân to make another pass at him when they were once more in an enclosed space? It was so long since he'd taken a woman to his bed that he wasn't sure he'd make a very good job of fighting her off – particularly when she was already almost naked.

"Thanks for letting me share your cab," he said tersely, removing his jacket from her shoulders.

The doors opened and Siân shot him a look. "Coming with me for the ride?"

Marco shook his head. "I'll wait." He didn't want to cheat on Saffy the night before the wedding; and if he went up to his apartment at the same time as Siân, he couldn't guarantee he'd resist her again.

"It's your loss." She sounded like she couldn't care less.

He watched her enter the lift without him, feeling a small sense of triumph.

*

When he awoke the next morning, alone in a bed he now found ridiculously large, Marco thought fleetingly of Siân. Only a few months ago, he wouldn't have turned down her offer; but in a matter of hours he would be standing before his family – and God – and promising to be faithful to Saffy for the rest of his life. He couldn't do that with a clear conscience if he'd just spent the night with someone else.

And then his eyes clouded as he remembered that Saffy would also be making those promises and that he had no way of knowing whether she'd keep them.

*

Ricardo was in the shower when his phone pinged to alert him that something had just arrived. Bianca turned from the suitcase, where she was unpacking the girls' clothes from the day, to glance at the screen, then snatched the phone up hurriedly. A photograph of an almost naked girl looked up at her, accompanied by the caption, "See what you missed by going home early!" Seconds later, another image appeared, this time a ten second video of Marco, climbing into a cab with the *puttana* from the first picture. Bianca's lips tightened in anger.

When Ric re-entered the room, towelling his hair, she thrust the phone at him furiously. "I thought you said you went to a nightclub, not a *bordello*!"

Ricardo stared at his phone aghast. What had Marco got up to?

"Bianca, *carissima*, you know I wasn't part of any of that." He clicked on the photos and showed her the details. "See – both of these were taken after I left. I don't know where they were for the end of the evening, but I can promise you that there was nothing like that in the places we went to."

Inwardly he cursed Phil. He couldn't even remember now why he'd given the other man his mobile number.

"How could he do that to Saffy?" Bianca asked next, refocusing her ire on her brother-in-law.

Ricardo shrugged. "Lots of men have one last fling before they marry." Still, he couldn't help feeling disappointed with Marco.

*

Totally unaware of the drama that was unfolding, Marco ground the beans for his first espresso. They would have to live here, no matter how much Saffy objected – he wasn't going anywhere without this marvellous machine.

He began sifting through his mental checklist: the wedding was at twelve, so he would leave at eleven to ensure he arrived in plenty of time. Ric was expected at ten: they would don their morning suits together and Marco would check that the best man's speech was in order. He smiled briefly, having heard plenty of horror stories about speeches that totally embarrassed the groom by listing all his previous sexual conquests. Ric was so strait-laced that he would never dream of doing something like that.

He checked his watch. It was only a little past eight – plenty of time for as many espressos as it took to give him the adrenaline he needed.

*

Saffy had awoken early, the butterfly house in her stomach a testament to how nervous she was feeling.she was anxious not only about the wedding service and reception but, more specifically, what would happen afterwards. Having had so many aborted attempts at consummating her relationship with Marco, she was now terrified of everything going wrong again. At least she would finally be able to tell Marco the truth about the baby, she reasoned. Hopefully he would understand that she'd been protecting Sophie and not be angry with her for deceiving him.

While she made toast and sipped tea, she pondered how her father and Eleanor would react to Sophie's news. For as long as she could remember, her little sister had been the typical 'baby' of the family, being indulged, pampered and cosseted by everyone else. If she had ever been in trouble in her childhood, all Sophie had needed to do was let her big blue eyes fill with tears and her lower lip quiver. The cherubic six-year-old had grown into an equally angelic-looking teenager; but Sophie's pretty, golden exterior masked any number of hidden transgressions. In fact, if truth be told, Saffy's sister was a bit of a minx.

Still, none of that mattered now. Saffy was coming to the end of that chapter of her story and entering into the unknown territory of married life. Although she'd shared a flat with James and Connor whilst at university and had left home properly when she'd moved into her little haven above the shop, she'd never lived with someone in the sense that she would be doing now. Uneasily, she wondered if Marco snored, or had any other unpleasant habits.

Well, she would find out soon enough. For a moment. she paused to reflect on how ridiculous this situation was: arranged marriages belonged to some other era, not the twenty-first century, and yet she and Marco had allowed themselves to be manoeuvred into something that almost resembled a Jane Austen novel. The physical attraction between the two of them had been obvious from the start, but she knew she wouldn't have rushed into marriage with someone she hardly knew had it not been for her father's most recent heart attack and his desire to see Marco take care of both her and the family business.

"I'm still an independent woman, though," she muttered to herself. No matter what Marco wanted, she wouldn't give up *Jo Bangles*: she loved designing and selling jewellery.

Thinking about jewellery made her remember the two ring boxes on her table. Marco's wedding ring was polished to perfection, a chunkier, more masculine version of her own platinum band. She'd better not forget them when she and Sophie left later on, after their hair appointments. And there were other things she had to remember too: she and her three bridesmaids would be leaving from the family home – a proper wedding car had been booked - so she needed to make sure that everything for her honeymoon was packed and ready to be taken to the reception venue. She wouldn't be entering this flat again for at least another few weeks.

*

Marco had showered and shaved by the time his brother arrived. Ric seemed troubled by something and wasted no time letting Marco know what was on his mind.

"She's gone already, has she?" he asked, peering round the empty rooms.

Marco was mystified.

"That hooker you took home last night," Ricardo elucidated.

Marco's blood ran cold. Someone must have seen him going home with Siân. "It's not what you think," he said at last.

Ric sighed. "You and I are very different people, Marco. I only dated a couple of women before Bianca, but you - I know you've played the field for most of your adult life. If you choose to cheat on Saffy, that's your business; but you have to be more discreet." He fished his mobile out of his pocket. "One of your colleagues sent me this. Bianca saw it."

Blood drained from Marco's face as he stared at the video. It certainly looked incriminating.

"I didn't sleep with her," he protested. "She lives across the hall, so we shared a taxi home, that's all. Nothing happened."

"Let's hope Bianca believes you, then," Ricardo told him, "because this morning she was all for telling Saffy what a love-rat you are."

*

At the end of the awkward, ten-minute-long conversation, Marco still wasn't sure if Bianca thought he was telling the truth. She'd promised not to say anything to Saffy but warned him that if any more pictures like that turned up, she would be forwarding them straight away to her new sister-in-law.

Marco knew he would have to come clean with Saffy, and that included telling her about his recent encounter with Siân. He would pre-empt any possible misunderstandings by mentioning that he'd seen Siân in the nightclub he went to on his stag night and that they'd travelled back to their building together. He knew his fiancée didn't trust his neighbour; but surely if he explained that he had kissed her once in the past – and only once – and then walked away from anything else she was offering, Saffy would stop being so jealous.

Would she be as honest with him, though? So far, she'd said nothing about her baby's father except to tell him that she wasn't in love with this faceless stranger. *At least she didn't try to pass it off as your own,* a voice said inside his head. He knew that lots of women in her position would have done that: they would have dragged him into bed as soon as they could and then claimed the condom must have split. Saffy had done the complete opposite, keeping him at arm's length despite his desperation for her so that there could be no doubt at all that he wasn't the father.

He was slowly coming to terms with the idea of the baby now. He didn't like the fact that it wasn't his own, but at least it would keep Saffy at home, making her too busy to get up to mischief with anyone else. And the marriage classes they had done together had reassured him somewhat when Saffy had argued passionately in favour of fidelity and loyalty. No one could be that good an actress, he decided. She'd obviously meant what she said.

"Well?" Ricardo came out of the dressing room, buttoning his shirt. "Has she forgiven you?"

"I think so." Marco handed his brother the embroidered waistcoat that matched his own. "Now, what about that speech?"

*

Eleanor looked at Saffy with tears in her eyes. "You look absolutely beautiful, Love."

Saffy surveyed her reflection in the full-length mirror, thinking absently that she really should invest in one this size for her flat.

Beside her, Sophie nodded enthusiastically. "Your dress is amazing, Saff. Marco'll be ripping it off you before you know it!"

"Soph!" Saffy's cheeks flamed but Eleanor smiled. "I think that's okay on their wedding night, Sophie."

Saffy twisted her head slightly, trying to catch the full effect of both dress and hairdo. Claire had worked wonders earlier that morning, creating an even better version of the style that had previously made James's eyes pop out of his head. Wispy tendrils framed her face and her hair was pulled high enough for her neck and shoulders to be clearly visible in the tight-fitting corset-style bodice, yet still managed to fall gracefully down her back in a riot of twirls and curls. The total effect was everything she'd dreamed of – and more. Surely Marco wouldn't be able to resist her now?

"How do I look?" Sophie demanded, once Eleanor had gone to sort out her own outfit, pouting in front of the mirror in her vibrant blue dress. Saffy knew that her sister wanted to know if her condition was obvious.

"You look gorgeous," she said truthfully, "and not the slightest bit pregnant."

"Only because I was so fat in the first place," Sophie said cheerfully. "If I'd been a stick insect like you, I would definitely be showing by now. I think my boobs are bigger – is it noticeable?"

Since Sophie had developed a splendid bosom at the age of thirteen, it was hard for Saffy to tell what was due to hormonal changes and what due to nature. There was definitely a lot of cleavage showing at the moment, but that tended to be one of Sophie's trademarks – she had always been much more flamboyant than her older sister.

"Do Dad and Eleanor know about Adam yet?" she asked, changing the subject.

Sophie grimaced. "They know I've got a 'friend' coming to help with my song and keep me company at the reception afterwards – I just haven't told them he's a male."

"But hasn't Eleanor made a seating plan for everyone?" Saffu interjected in surprise.

"Yes, but Adam's down as 'A. Clarke'," Sophie explained. "I told her it looked more formal if the name cards just had initials and surnames."

"You do realise they'll know he's a boy when they see him," Saffy remarked. No matter how much wine people consumed at the reception, there was no way her sister's boyfriend could ever be mistaken for anything other than a gangly young man.

Sophie tossed her head dismissively. "Everyone'll be too busy looking at the blushing bride to pay any attention to the guests. Anyway, when we go for food, you, Marco, his brother and sister-in-law and both sets of parents are all on one table together, and Adam and I are sitting with the little girls. I persuaded Eleanor that it was better that way because if they get bored with the speeches, I can take them out to the park for half an hour."

"You've thought of everything haven't you?" Saffy tried to keep the irritation from her voice. This was supposed to be *her* big day, but already Sophie was manipulating events to fit in with what she herself wanted.

"Not quite," Sophie confessed. "I still don't have a clue how I'm going to break the news about the baby."

"Perhaps if you'd told them about Adam in the first place, the rest of your announcement wouldn't come as such a shock now," Saffy commented drily. "It's a bit much to expect them to find out you've got a boyfriend in the same breath you tell them they're going to be grandparents."

"I know." Sophie's eyes were downcast. "But they'll be so happy for you, Saff – you could tell them anything on your wedding day and they wouldn't over-react -"

"The answer's no," Saffy said firmly. "It's been bad enough keeping your secret for you these last couple of months, *and* having to lie to Marco, without being the one who tells Dad something that could trigger another heart attack."

Sophie paled. "I hadn't thought of that. Do you think I shouldn't mention it, then?"

"You can't *not* say anything!" Saffy exclaimed in horror. "You can't hide a baby forever, Soph – and it would be much worse if you left it until you went into labour!"

"But if I just put it off for another week or two ..." Sophie began hopefully.

Saffy shook her head. "Sorry, Sophie – you're going to have to woman up and get on with it." She looked at her sister's pale face and relented a little. "But, if you like, I'll come with you for moral support when you tell them."

Chapter Forty-Two

Marco and Ricardo were ridiculously early, arriving at the church forty minutes before the ceremony was due to start. No one else had arrived yet, but one of the parishioners was busy arranging flowers on the altar at the front.

"Oh my!" she remarked upon seeing them. "Which one of you's getting married?"

Marco sheepishly raised a hand, thinking as he did so that none of this seemed real yet. It was no wonder that most people took a year or two to plan a wedding because rushing through all the arrangements so quickly had meant that it was all a blur in his mind. The business side of him had snapped into gear, effortlessly arranging the practicalities – it was what he was good at, after all – but emotionally he still hadn't registered that this was his wedding day – until now.

With shaking hands, he straightened the carnation in his buttonhole, wondering if Saffy felt as nervous as he did.

As time passed and the church began to fill with people – who were most of them? he puzzled – he spotted a face that seemed familiar: wasn't that the youth he had seen chatting to Saffy's sister at the party where the two of them had met?

Whoever he was, the young man certainly knew his way around a piano. Slipping onto the empty stool, he began to play, softly at first, then, as his confidence grew, gradually loud enough so that people stopped chatting and began listening instead. Marco listened, entranced, as de Senneville's *'Marriage d'Amour'* floated round the room, followed by a piece that the Order of Service identified as part of Beethoven's *'Silence Concerto'*. As the music drew to a close, there was a ripple of applause – was that allowed in church?

And then, the pianist slipped from his seat and pressed the button on a remote control. The sound of violins playing Pachelbel's *'Canon'* heralded the arrival of the bride. Marco drew in his breath.

Saffy had never looked more beautiful. Her ivory dress seemed moulded to her figure, but her neck and shoulders were bare and a sapphirehe pendant adorned her throat. She was wearing her hair in a different way – partly up and partly down – and the style suited her perfectly. Her eyes were large and luminous, her lips full and soft. As he gazed at her, Marco felt a definite stirring and knew that nothing would stop him celebrating his wedding night in the manner it deserved.

The service seemed to last no time at all. One minute, the priest was welcoming the congregation; the next, Marco was declaring his promise to love Saffy for better, for worse, for richer, for poorer, in sickness and health, until death parted them, and she was repeating it back to him.

"And now the giving and receiving of the rings," Father Nick announced. Ricardo handed a small platinum circle to his brother. "Repeat after me," Father Nick intoned, "Sapphire Lucia Vendrini, receive this ring as a sign of my love and fidelity. In the name of the Father, and of the Son, and of the Holy Spirit." Marco recited the words, pushing the ring onto Saffy's fourth finger as he did so.

"And the bride ..."

Wordlessly, Saffy took the larger ring that Ricardo held out to her. "Marco Giovanni Benedetti, receive this ring as a sign of my love and fidelity. In the name of the Father, and of the Son, and of the Holy Spirit." The words came out in a whisper and Marco realised that she was more nervous than he was. Looking into her eyes, he smiled reassuringly.

Placing both their hands over each other, the priest proclaimed, "I now pronounce you man and wife." *Wasn't he also supposed to say, 'You may now kiss the bride'?*

They were finally married.

*

Prayers were said, but Marco didn't take in much of them – something about their life together being blessed. He still wasn't paying attention when Saffy's sister walked to the front of the church; but then the pianist pressed the 'Play' button on the remote control once more and everyone fell silent as Sophie's pure contralto voice soared to the rafters. "There's a place for us – somewhere a place for us. Peace and quiet and open air wait for us somewhere …"

Saffy felt a pang as she listened to the words. She knew Sophie had chosen that song for Adam and herself, not for the bride and groom. Meanwhile, Marco was amazed that a plump teenager could sing like that. He felt moved to tears.

Then his heart hardened as he reflected on the irony of the lyrics: there would be no "peace and quiet" in his marriage to Saffy once someone else's bastard was waking him up at three in the morning in a few months' time. Subconsciously, his fist clenched.

Beside him, Saffy's eyes glistened. At once, Marco felt ashamed of his reaction. He had just promised to love Saffy 'for better, for worse'. He *did* love her, in spite of everything – had to if he had put a ring on her finger in front of everyone.

*

The signing of the register passed as quickly as everything else had done. Saffy signed her name underneath the entry "Sapphire Vendrini, Spinster of this Parish", below "Marco Benedetti, Bachelor of the Parish of High Wycombe". It had really happened: the legal document proved it. From now on, she would be Sapphire Benedetti, a married woman.

Glancing up from the register, she felt Marco's arm around her shoulder and realised that they were supposed to pose for a photograph. She'd been vaguely aware of cameras and phones clicking throughout the ceremony, but she hadn't really taken any notice. This was different, though: now that the formalities were over, they would have to spend at least half an hour letting people form them into suitable positions so that every aspect of their union could be recorded. They'd deliberately decided against a formal photographer, aware that most people would be taking their own snapshots anyway; besides, Bianca was an accomplished photographer herself, combining motherhood with her own business that specialised in children and family portraits, and she had already agreed to produce a wedding album for them.

For the next forty-five minutes, the new *Signor e Signora Benedetti* posed, postured and positioned themselves into every possible combination of photograph, beginning with the essential walk down the aisle as husband and wife and culminating in a panoramic shot of everyone present, including Father Nick as well as some of Antonio's business associates who had come to watch their friend's daughter get married but were not invited to the reception.

Finally scrambling into the wedding car that would take them to the reception venue, Marco turned to his wife. "How does it feel to be married?"

"A bit unreal," Saffy confessed. "Everything happened so quickly …"

"And the priest forgot one very important part of the service," Marco commented, leaning in towards her.

Saffy panicked momentarily. Did this mean they weren't really married after all?

"I was waiting for him to say, '*You may now kiss the bride*'," Marco continued, his face now only inches away from hers.

Saffy swallowed. "Kiss me now," she breathed, her whole body quivering with expectancy.

Marco's lips met hers in a kiss so unexpectedly tender and gentle that Saffy was taken by surprise. She was used to Marco's fierce desire, to his mouth plundering her own with an intensity that left her in no doubt about how much he wanted her. Had that changed now she was legitimately his?

Taking the initiative, she pressed her body closer to his, her hands pulling him fiercely towards her so that he would know how much she wanted him. The reception didn't matter: all she wanted was for Marco to finish what he had started several months ago and make her totally his.

"Saffy! Don't do this to me – not now." Marco's breath felt hot against her face; his pupils were huge with desire.

"Don't you want me?" But she already knew the answer to that question.

Slowly, Marco pulled away from her, his breathing ragged. "Saffy, I have wanted you since the moment I first saw you, you know that – but I am not making love to you in the back of a wedding car when we have a far more comfortable bed awaiting us in the honeymoon suite of our hotel." He paused. "It was not my plan to wait so long for you – but why ruin what will be a perfect wedding night by snatching a substandard sex-snack now?" As she continued to gaze at him, he added, "It would be like grabbing a handful of crisps or peanuts before going into a banquet: it would spoil your appetite."

At least he was planning on making love to her, then, Saffy thought, as she tidied her hair and reapplied her lipstick. And, with luck, they would be able to escape to their room as soon as the speeches were finished.

*

Arriving at the hotel, Saffy and Marco mingled with the other guests – a pitifully small number which comprised just the immediate Benedeti and Vendrini families, Adam, and James and Connor – whilst sipping champagne cocktails. Saffy was relieved to see that Sophie was sticking to orange juice; meanwhile, Marco was almost incandescent with rage to see that James was present.

"What is *he* doing here?" he hissed in Saffy's ear, grabbing her wrist and steering her aside from the general conversation.

"He's one of my oldest friends – I've told you that before." Saffy stared at her husband defiantly.

Marco's eyes narrowed. "I am not having your ex-lover at our wedding reception. I assume he *is* an ex?" he added nastily.

"No," Saffy explained through gritted teeth, "James isn't an ex – he's just a friend." Before Marco could reply, she gestured towards the gathering. He swivelled his gaze in time to see James lean over and kiss the blond man next to him in a manner that suggested the two of them were far more than acquaintances. "I told you he was gay," Saffy said offhandedly.

Marco stared in disbelief. "I thought you were making it up," he said eventually.

"Oh, for goodness' sake, Marco!" Saffy could no longer control her frustration. "It's obvious to anyone else but you! Look at his clothes, for one thing, and his hair! And every time he's seen you, he's flirted with you!"

"I thought that was just how English men behave," Marco muttered, his heart full of embarrassment.

"He and Connor have been a couple since university," Saffy explained. "He doesn't like girls, Marco – I've told you that over and over again."

"But you can understand why I was jealous," Marco broke in. "You are a beautiful woman, Saffy, and James is a good-looking man. Anyone else would have been suspicious – especially after seeing him kiss you."

"On the cheek, not on the lips," Saffy corrected him. "You should understand that – you're Italian!"

She would have said more, but Ricardo was tapping his fork on his champagne glass to signal to everyone to take their seats at the table. Because there were so few guests, there was just one long table for the ten grown ups and another, much smaller table, for Sophie, Adam, Giulia and Giorgia. Saffy and Marco were at the centre of their table, flanked by Ricardo on one side and Bianca on the other, in what should have been Sophie's seat, had the best man and bridesmaid been in their traditional positions.

On the other side of Ricardo, Eleanor leaned across to Saffy. "I think that young man who played the piano must be Sophie's boyfriend – look how well they're getting on together!"

Sophie hadn't said anything yet, then. Saffy felt unease growing inside her.

The meal passed fairly pleasantly. Saffy felt she could relax now that Marco knew James wasn't a threat; however, Marco was worrying more than ever, desperate to ascertain the identity of the man who had impregnated his wife. At least when he'd thought it was James, he could focus his attention on an individual he'd met; but now the uncertainty of not knowing his rival was almost more than he could bear. He and Saffy would have to have a serious discussion after all.

Glancing over at the smaller table, Saffy could see that Sophie and Adam were doing a good job of keeping the two little girls entertained – despite the fact that Giulia and Giorgia spoke hardly any English.

Just before the speeches started, Sophie nodded to Adam and the two of them got up from their table, each leading one of the children by the hand. For a moment Saffy wished she could go to the park too – it might be more fun than listening to Marco and his brother reeling off platitudes about the dresses and the flowers.

Antonio was the first to rise to his feet. His speech, delivered in a mixture of Italian and English so that Marco's mother would be able to understand some of it, reminisced about Saffy as a child and thanked Marco for being willing to take care of his daughter. "As you know," he continued, "my health has not been good this year, but I can now die a happy man, knowing that my little Sapphire is in good hands."

Everyone dutifully made their toast, and then Marco stood up. He thanked Antonio for the gift of his daughter – first in English and then said something in Italian which Saffy assumed was the translation of what he had just said. Switching back to English, he added, "Sapphire, your parents named you well – you are a beautiful jewel and I will treasure you always. When I was looking for our readings for the wedding service, I found some Bible verses that said a good wife is worth more than rubies – I would rewrite that to say, a good wife is a costly sapphire – but one you are not allowed to keep in a safe!" The English-speaking guests nodded in agreement. "Ladies and Gentlemen," Marco concluded, "my wife, Sapphire Benedetti."

Finally, it was Ricardo's turn. The best man's speech was entirely in Italian – Saffy wondered why Ric had chosen to do this when she, Eleanor, James and Connor didn't speak the language. There was a smattering of applause and laughter from the Benedettis and Antonio, and then Ricardo began again. "And now, the English version of my speech."

How clever, Saffy thought admiringly, forgetting to listen to the first sentence and then realising she'd missed a joke. She tuned back in again. "Everyone, including myself, has always thought that Marco was a confirmed bachelor," Ric was saying, "but then he met Saffy and his world was turned upside down. This is the first time I have seen my brother genuinely in love – and I hope it's the last time." Polite laughter. "But to be serious ..." Ricardo looked straight at Marco. "I only have one piece of advice for you on your wedding day, little brother: make your wife happy and she will not make you miserable. Ladies and Gentlemen, the Bride and Groom."

As the final glass was returned to the table, Marco whispered in his wife's ear. "Do you think we will be missed if we leave now?"

"We can't!" Saffy glanced at the grandfather clock in the corner of the room. "It's not even five o'clock. What will people think?"

"They will think that I am a very lucky man to have a wife so beautiful that I cannot keep my hands off her." Beneath the table, his hand grazed her thigh. Saffy felt her bones begin to melt.

"Let's sneak out while no one's looking then," she murmured, not wanting to draw attention to their hasty exit; but as she started to rise, Eleanor shot her a look.

"Don't forget the cake!"

Saffy's eyebrows telegraphed an apology to Marco. Perhaps they could leave the room once this final photo opportunity was over? Hand in hand, the two of them approached the small side table where their cake was waiting and dutifully posed with a knife. It all seemed very silly.

"Meet me in the foyer." Marco's breath was warm against her ear. He patted his pocket conspiratorially. "I have the key to our room." Without another word, he was gone, leaving her to escape on her own.

Saffy wove her way through the dining room and out into the corridor. She would have liked to use the bathroom, but she didn't want to damage her dress. The thought crossed her mind that Marco would probably be quite happy to help her out of it.

And there was Marco now, skulking in the shadows as if not wanting to be seen. His face lit up in a grin when he saw her. "At last, *carissima*. I was beginning to think your *matrigna* had found yet another task for you to perform."

"There's only one thing I want to do right now," she said softly.

Marco took her hand once more and together they made their way upstairs.

Chapter Forty-Three

Their room was huge. Oak panelled walls and what looked like original beams created the impression that Saffy and Marco had stepped back in time when they entered the Honeymoon Suite. The bed, a four-poster with curtains in green and gold brocade, seemed lost amidst the large, heavy, period furniture - it was probably all reproduction, Saffy thought, but it certainly looked the part.

Marco closed the door slowly. "So ..." he began.

Saffy swallowed nervously.

Her husband indicated the ice-bucket on a table near the window. "Champagne?" Before she could reply, he answered his own question. "But I was forgetting, you don't like champagne, do you? Shall I ring Room Service and order you something else?"

"Champagne'e fine, thanks." It *was* her wedding day. Besides, the alcohol might help her relax. Her heart was pounding already. She needed to slow down.

Marco popped the cork expertly, filling the two glasses provided, then handed one over. "To our life together," he said as he clinked his glass against hers.

Saffy took a long sip, inadvertently imbibing much more than she'd intended. Bubbles shot up her nose, making her splutter. Gently, Marco removed the glass from her hand. *This is it!* she thought desperately.

But instead of leading her to the bed, Marco indicated one of the gigantic easy chairs in the part of the room that served as a lounge area. "Before we do anything else, we need to talk."

He sounded so serious that Saffy instantly thought something was wrong. Had Marco slept with a stripper on his stag night?

"I need to be completely honest with you," he continued, "and I hope that you will be honest with me."

Saffy nodded.

"When I found your positive pregnancy test," Marco went on, "I was angry."

"But I'm not …"

Marco silenced her. "I did something I'm not proud of."

"You slept with Siân," she said in a small voice. She had always suspected it, hoped that she was wrong.

"No!" his tone was emphatic. "I wanted to – at first. Not because I'm attracted to her, but to get back at you."

"And …?"

"I couldn't do it." Marco was watching her closely. "Do you understand, Saffy? Even when I was so angry with you, I couldn't make myself be unfaithful. I went to her flat. We kissed - but then I walked away. I realised it wasn't what I wanted after all."

"Is that the only time you've kissed her?" Saffy's mouth was tight.

He nodded.

"And is that the only confession you need to make?"

Again, his eyes were downcast. Saffy prepared herself mentally for the sordid details of a brief encounter with a stripper or a prostitiute.

"Siân was at the last club we went to for the Stag Night," Marco said slowly. No need to tell her Siân had been part of the entertainment. "We shared a cab home at the end of the evening."

"And?"

"And that's it. She made it clear she was interested; I made it clear I wasn't."

Saffy felt an overwhelming sense of relief. "Why didn't you tell me this before?"

Marco was still staring at his feet.

"I didn't know if you'd believe me."

"Just like you didn't believe me when I told you about James," she said pointedly.

Marco sighed. "I was wrong about James – but you can understand why I was suspicious." He paused. "I have been honest with you, *mon tresor*, and now I would like you to do the same with me. I want us to start this marriage properly – anything we tell each other now is over before our life together started."

Saffy gazed at the glass in her hand, wondering why she felt so nervous when technically she had nothing to divulge.

"I'm not pregnant," she sid at last.

Marco stared at her. "You mean you have miscarried?"

"No." Why was this so difficult. "I was never pregnant in the first place, Marco. That was Sophie's positive test, not mine."

* * *

Marco's heart stopped beating temporarily. "You were never pregnant?" he repeated finally. Then, "Why didn't you correct my mistake?"

"I wanted to." Saffy was feeling increasingly more uncomfortable. "But I was worried you might say something to my dad or Eleanor – they don't know about the baby yet: Sophie's supposed to be telling them today."

"So, all this time, we could have been making love …" She couldn't gauge his mood: was he angry with her?

Marco stood up abruptly, moving over to the icebucket and pouring himself another glass of champagne. He needed something stronger for the shock, but this would have to do.

"Sapphire Vendrini …"

"Benedetti," she corrected him.

"Sapphire Benedetti, you are the most exasperating woman I know! You have made me wait – and wait – and wait for you."

"Better late than never," she muttered, trying to lighten the mood. "Anyway," she challenged him, "*I* never said I was pregnant: you just assumed I was."

"But you let me think it!" His words escaped in a sigh of frustration. "You should have trusted me with your sister's secret."

For a moment, they both stared at each other. Saffy wondered, miserably, if this meant the wedding night was cancelled. How ironic it would be if they didn't consummate their union after all.

Finally, Marco put his glass down. "Perhaps we should pretend that none of the past few months has happened," he suggested. "We will wind the clock back to our first meeting, when I saw you across a crowded room and knew you were the only person I wanted to leave with."

She knew it was a cliché; nevertheless, her heart sang at his words.

As Marco began to move slowly towards her. Saffy felt a tingle of expectancy.

"*Buon giorno*," he began. "I know I do not know who you are, but I just wanted to tell you that you are the most delectable creature I have ever seen." As an opening line, it was horrendously corny, but Saffy didn't care.

"I bet you say that to all the girls," she countered, batting her eyelids in a way that definitely encouraged him.

"Only the ones I want to sleep with …"

The hungry look in his eyes made her heartbeat quicken.

"Is that a proposition?" she asked flirtatiously.

"That depends …" - he took the glass from her hand and set it on the table – "… on whether or not you want it to be."

"I'm not doing anything else this evening …"

He was now close enough to brush a tendril of hair away from her face.

"Then perhaps we should move this conversation somewhere more comfortable." He took her hand. "I happen to have a room not too far from here – perhaps you would like to see it?"

"I don't normally go home with men I don't know," she told him, enjoying the rôle-play – "unless they're very good kissers."

Marco's lips met hers almost before she'd finished the sentence. His kiss in the car had been soft and tender, but this one crackled with desire.

"Let's go to your room," she whispered.

In a gloriously melodramatic gesture, Marco scooped her up, still in her wedding dress, and carried her over to the bed. Pushing her back against the soft, white pillows, he began to kiss her again, plunging his tongue into her mouth, exploring, probing. She kissed him back with an intensity she hadn't known she possessed, moaning a little with her frantic need of him.

Marco's hands slid down her body, stroking the curve of her hip. Then, sliding his fingers underneath her, she felt him struggling with the multitudinous hooks and eyes as he tried to unfasten her corset top.

"*Che cavolo!*" He swore softly as he realised his task was impossible. "Your dress is very sexy, *bella*, but it is also very restrictive."

Scrambling off the bed, Saffy looked at him. "Undress me!" she demanded. As his eyebrows shot up, she added, "I can't get out of this thing myself, Marco: it took Sophie twenty minutes to get me into it!"

Not needing a second bidding, Marco positioned himself behind her, his fingers expertly popping open every one of the fasteners. He began kissing the back of her neck, then started moving down, bit by bit, until every inch of exposed skin had been covered.

Saffy stood still, enjoying the sensation of his mouth on her skin as it travelled slowly downwards. Then, moving his hands round to the front of her, he slowly slipped her dress from her body, cupping her naked breasts as he did so. "Have you any idea how much I want you right now?" he breathed in her ear.

Feeling slightly embarrassed, Saffy let him feast his eyes on her. She needn't have worried: she was everything Marco had imagined – and more. The sight of her, clad in only a lacy wisp of a G-string, made him almost lose control.

Almost. This first time had to be perfect: he needed to take her to unimaginable heights, to eradicate the memories of any previous lovers.

Slowly, he began to unbutton his shirt – his jacket and waistcoat had been discarded as soon as he entered the room. Saffy, feeling more self-conscious than ever in her nearly naked state, found herself flooded with longing as she watched him toss the garment aside impatiently. Surprising herself, she stepped forward to help him with his trousers.

Marco grabbed her hand and let her feel his arousal. "See what you have done to me, *carissima*." His voice was a throaty whisper.

Saffy wrapped her arms around him and he pulled her into his chest, the feeling of skin on skin driving them both wild. As he kicked off his trousers, she felt the urgency of him pressing into her; then, before she knew what was happening, she was back on the bed and Marco was kissing her everywhere, his hands and his lips making her come alive in places she hadn't known existed.

"Saffy!" He was thrusting into her, far more desperately than he'd intended, wanting to hold back and pleasure her fully but unable to stop himself. She felt a sharp tug of pain as he penetrated her fully, then a few quick thrusts before Marco collapsed on top of her.

She stroked the top of his head, feeling a strange mixture of triumph and regret: it was as if there was something still missing.

For a few moments, Marco was still, his breathing fast and shallow, the weight of him beginning to feel uncomfortable. Saffy shifted slightly. Marco looked up and caught her eye. "Ready for Round Two?"

Still inside her, he began to move again, slowly at first, then gradually gathering speed. Saffy felt a rising crescendo of sensation until finally she was teetering on the edge of something so wonderful that she almost wept.

"Marco!" She cried out as she climaxed, her whole body exploding in a series of never-ending fireworks. Every part of her fizzed with satisfaction.

Later, as they lay dozing in each other's arms, Marco felt he had to ask the question. "Are your orgasms always so spectacular?"

For a moment, Saffy didn't respond; then, "It was my first time," she confessed.

He stared at her incredulously. "Your first orgasm?"

"No ..." She felt her cheeks burn. "*My first time.*"

He hadn't even noticed, so caught up in his own need of her. Instantly, he felt ashamed.

"Saffy, *mon tresor*, you have given me the most wonderful gift a bride could give her husband."

"You're sure you don't mind?" She was hesitant, not knowing whether he was merely being polite.

He kissed her forehead. "I am deeply honoured."

He would have said more, but a frantic knocking at the door made him curse instead.

"Ignore it." Saffy didn't want to move, enjoying the unfamiliar feeling of a naked male body in such close proximity to her own.

The knocking continued, followed by a call of "Saffy!" through the door. In a temper, Marco extricated himself from his wife's embrace and strode towards the door, trailing irritability behind him like a cloak. Opening it, he revealed a frightened-looking Adam. "Where's Saffy? Something's wrong with Sophie – I think she's losing the baby."

Chapter Forty-Four

The next ten minutes passed in a blur as Saffy shot out of bed, only remembering that she was naked as Adam turned away in embarrassment, and hastily ransacked her suitcase for anything she could throw on quickly.

"Where is she?" Saffy demanded, once she was decent.

Adam shuffled his feet. "I booked a room for the two of us ... So we could be alone together."

"You did what?" Saffy was scandalised.

"We just wanted somewhere private ..." He was avoiding her gaze, leaving Saffy in no doubt what the two of them had wanted privacy for.

"Go on."

"We ... erm, I ... I mean, we started to ... and then she told me to stop and said something wasn't right and she was bleeding," Adam finished in a rush.

Saffy turned to Marco, who was zipping up his trousers. "You need to find my dad and Eleanor. What's the room number, Adam?"

"Sixteen. But don't tell them – Sophie hasn't told them about me yet," Adam begged.

"No!" Saffy was emphatic. "The two of you have spent far too long sneaking around behind people's backs. You should have said something months ago – or I should have."

Kissing Marco on the cheek, she hurried out of the room, dragging a reluctant Adam behind her.

*

Sophie was lying on the bed when Saffy entered the room, her face as pale as the sheet that was covering her.

"Soph." Saffy spoke gently, too concerned to be angry.

Sophie turned frightened eyes towards her sister.

"I'm bleeding, Saff."

"I know. I've sent Marco to fetch Dad and Eleanor. I think we need to get you to hospital."

A tear trickled down Sophie's cheek. "I don't want to lose our baby." Adam stepped over to the bed and held her hand. He looked as lost as she did. "We were both shocked to begin with," Sophie continued, squeezing her boyfriend's fingers, "but you've been so excited recently, haven't you?" She and Adam exchanged a heartfelt glance. "I know how much you're looking forward to it and to us living together in Guildford." Then, as her sister's words registered fully, "Did you say Dad and Eleanor know?"

"They need to know about something like this." Saffy spoke calmly, trying to allay the fear she saw in Sophie's eyes.

"Dad'll kill Adam," Sophie said bleakly. Adam blanched.

Saffy didn't contradict her: part of her thought that might be true.

Moments later, Marco tapped on the door. "Saffy? Your parents are here. Can we come in?"

As Saffy stepped towards the door, Adam looked round frantically. Was he searching for somewhere to hide? she wondered.

But there was no time for any of that. Antonio rushed in, despite Eleanor's attempts to slow him down. "Toni! Remember your heart!"

"*Sophia! Bambina mia!*" He pushed Adam aside and grasped Sophie's hands.

Marco said something rapid in Italian. Antonio nodded vigorously. "*Si, si.*" *What had he said?*

Then Eleanor took over. "We've rung the hospital and we're taking you in now for a check up. They'll give you a scan and confirm whether the baby's still okay." She shook her head. "You silly girl! Why didn't you say anything sooner?"

"She was thinking of her papa," Antonio murmured. "My Sophia is a good girl: she did not want to worry me – or you, *carissima*."

Saffy looked at Marco: whatever he had said to her father had obviously done the trick. Instead of the fury she'd feared, her father was exuding nothing but concern for his younger daughter.

"Are you coming too, Saff?" came the plaintive request.

"We're both coming," Marco promised, placing an arm around his wife's shoulders. Whispering in her ear, he added, "We might find another cupboard …"

Saffy shot him a look. Gratifying though it was to know that her husband desired her so intensely, there was a time and place …

Eleanor was now speaking to Adam. "It seems a bit late for an introduction, but I'm Eleanor, Sophie's step-mother. The two of you and Sophie did a wonderful job today with the music – and the children."

The young man's cheeks were flaming. He looked incredibly uncomfortable. "I'm so sorry …" he began, but Eleanor cut him short.

"I kept my first boyfriend a secret too – although things didn't progress quite as fast as they seem to have done with the two of you."

Adam blushed again. Saffy found his *gaucherie* strangely endearing.

The two Italians exchanged another hurried conversation in their native tongue. Saffy tried to catch the meaning from their tone: she didn't recognise any of the words.

"Come." Antonio spoke decisively. "We men will wait outside while Saffy and Eleanor help Sophie get ready for the journey to the hospital."

He and Marco ushered Adam out of the room before the poor boy could protest. Saffy thought uneasily of 'The Godfather' and wondered if her father were about to make Adam an offer he couldn't refuse.

"First things first." Eleanor was brisk and comfortingly in charge. "The hospital asked if you were still bleeding, Sophie?"

"I don't know." Sophie's eyes welled once more with tears. "I've been too scared to look."

"Saffy, fetch one of the hand towels from the *en-suite*," Eleanor ordered. Noticing her step-daughter's face, she added, "We need something between her legs, and we can always reimburse the hotel for any damage."

By the time Saffy returned from the bathroom, bearing both the hand towels, Eleanor had helped Sophie into a tee-shirt which looked as if it could be Adam's so that she was at least half-dressed. The crumpled bridesmaid's outfit was still in a heap on the floor – presumably it had been easier to remove than Saffy's wedding dress.

"Okay, Sophie, I'm going to have a look," Eleanor told her, pulling back the rest of the sheet. "Saffy, hand me those tissues."

Saffy averted her gaze delicately, not wanting to embarrass Sophie any more than was strictly necessary.

"There's no bleeding now," Eleanor reported. "Are you in any pain, Sophie?"

"Not now." Sophie's voice faltered. "It was when we … I mean …"

Poor Soph, Saffy thought with compassion. At Sophie's age she would rather have died than admitted to her parents that she was sexually active. Not that she had been, of course; even so, just the idea of it made her shudder.

"If you're not bleeding, it's probably okay for you to put your underwear on and then we'll find you some sort of skirt," Eleanor decided. "Did you bring one with you?"

Sophie shook her head. "Just my jeans."

"Is there anything of Saffy's that you could wear?" Eleanor asked next. Since Sophie was at least two sizes larger than her sister, this clearly wasn't a possibility. Eleanor sighed. "You'll just have to wrap the sheet around you like a sari, then. Even though you've stopped bleeding, we still need to get you to hospital."

And so that was how they left the hotel. Marco offered to carry Sophie out to Antonio's car, but she declined, insisting that she felt much better now and could walk. Once she was safely in the back of the Lexus, Adam climbed in after her. Marco nudged his wife. "My Jag's over there – Ricardo drove it here for me."

It all seemed slightly unreal, to be spending their wedding night driving to the hospital in Wycombe. She should have known Sophie would manage to disrupt things somehow, Saffy thought with resignation – still, at least this time she'd waited until the consummation had taken place!

"What did you say to my father?" she asked suddenly.

Marco grinned whilst keeping his eye on the road. "I reminded him how he felt when he first saw your mother. My own father told me the story when he first mentioned you. I said that obviously Adam had fallen for Sophie the first time he saw her – just like your father did with your mother – and just like I did with you."

"And the baby?" She'd expected her father to inflict serious injuries on anyone who had dared to seduce his little girl when she was still at school.

"Oh ..." Marco shrugged nonchalantly, his hands on the wheel. "I said they had been overcome with passion once ..."

"They were at it like rabbits every time they got the chance!" Saffy broke in indignantly.

"Let me finish. The version I told your father – and I have advised Adam not to contradict it – is that it only happened once. They were going to tell your parents as soon as they realised Sophie was pregnant, but then he had his heart attack and they didn't want to worry him." Marco paused. "I also told Antonio that if Adam loves your sister even a tenth as much as I love you, he will make a fine husband for her. Both his girls will be taken care of, should anything untoward happen with his health."

They were pulling into the hospital car park now. As Marco smoothly brought the Jag to a halt, Saffy stared at him in wonder.

"I don't know what to say," she said at last. "My sister ruins our wedding night and you still calm things down for her with my dad."

"I did it for you," he said simply. "I could see how worried you were when Adam arrived and I wanted to stop you feeling like that. I love you, Saffy – everything else I've said to you tonight must make you realise that."

"So it's not a marriage in name only, then?" she challenged him, aware of the answer but wanting to hear him say it.

Undoing his seatbelt, Marco leaned across and kissed her as tenderly as he had in the wedding car.

"That was never an option," he told her, stroking the side of her cheek and gazing intently into her eyes. "Even when I thought you had cheated on me, even when I thought you were carrying someone else's baby, I still wanted you as my wife. You stole my heart the moment I laid eyes on you – despite me thinking I was incapable of falling in love."

"As soon as we know Sophie's okay," she told him, her hand tracing his stubbled jaw in a gesture of ownership, "let's go and finish what we started earlier."

Hand in hand, they left the car and went to find the others.

Chapter Forty-Five

Sophie had not lost the baby. As soon as Saffy appeared at the door of the private room Antonio had managed to wangle, her sister beckoned her over to the bed. "I'm okay," she told her in a low voice.

Saffy's relief was tangible.

"Apparently," Sophie was still whispering, "a bit of pain and intermittent bleeding is quite common when …" Her voice tailed off.

"When you're having sex," Saffy finished for her.

"Ssshhh!" Sophie nodded in her father's direction.

"Soph!" Saffy tried to keep the exasperation out of her voice. "You're pregnant – I think everyone's realised that you and Adam are way past the kissing stage by now!"

By the time Saffy and Marco left the hospital, it was past ten o'clock. Sophie was being kept in overnight – her blood pressure was a little high – and Adam had asked if he could have a lift back to the hotel.

"I've paid for my room," he explained to the newly-weds. "I may as well use it."

Driving back along the A40, Saffy wished that she and Marco were alone. Adam seemed to want to talk – perhaps it was a relief that his relationship with Sophie was finally out in the open. By the time they reached *The King's Arms*, Saffy knew far more than she wanted to about her little sister's love life.

"Goodnight, Adam," she said firmly as they entered the hotel. "We probably won't see you in the morning."

Now that she knew Sophie was okay, there was no reason for her and Marco to leave their room.

"So, Mrs Benedetti," Marco began, as they reached the honeymoon suite, "shall we begin again?"

Lifting her off her feet, he carried her over the threshold and into their room, where he deposited her once more on the bed. The next few hours passed in a very satisfactory fashion.

*

"Do you think they're going to be okay?" Saffy asked Marco sleepily, snuggling into his chest as they lay intertwined.

Marco reflected for a moment before making his reply.

"I think your sister has found someone who feels something similar to the way I feel about you."

Adam's words echoed in Saffy's mind: *"When I'm not with her, I want to be with her; when I'm with her, she's all I can think about."*

"I think about you all the time too," she said slowly. "I haven't stopped thinking about you – and about us – since our engagement party."

Marco's arms tightened around her. "Promise me one thing, *carissima* ..."

"What?"

"For the rest of our honeymoon, let us forget Sophie and Adam – your sister has interrupted our time together far too many times already."

"Okay, then," she agreed, feeling his hand begin to trail lazily over her thigh in a way that suggested they might not be going to sleep after all. "For the next two or three weeks, I promise not to think about anything else but us."

It seemed like a perfect arrangement.